Light of the World

A Dream Walker Novel

MICHELLE MILES

Book Cover by EHD Professionals

First Edition May 30, 2023
Second Edition February 2026

ISBN: 9798215549063 (ebook)
ISBN: 9781734306880 (paperback)

For my husband. I did it, baby!

Our greatest glory is not in never falling but in rising every time we fall.

Confucius

You may have to fight a battle more than once to win it.

Margaret Thatcher

You are the light of the world. A town built on a hill cannot be hidden.

Matthew 5:14 (NIV)

In the same way, let your light shine before others, that they may see your good deeds and glorify your Father in heaven.

Matthew 5:16 (NIV)

CHAPTER 1

BLOOD FROM THE CUT over my left eye dripped onto the gray workout mat as I stood on all fours, trying to regain my breath. My chest seesawed in and out. My heart drummed in my chest from exertion.

"Did that hurt?" Kincade asked with a hint of humor in his voice.

I took a deep breath and exhaled. "I wanted to work out, not get my ass kicked."

I lifted my head, closing my left eye and squinted, trying to give him my best angry glare. His eyes widened when he saw the blood oozing from my forehead.

"I didn't mean to do that."

"Sure."

"Come on." He stepped next to me and wrapped his hand around my upper arm. I shoved him off.

"I don't need your help." There was more anger in my voice than I intended.

"You say that a lot, and yet, here I am."

I frowned. "Because you won't ever fucking leave."

The ugly truth was I hated how much my chest loosened every time he proved it.

Kincade became my constant companion since that one incident with the high lord that nearly killed me. The high lord killed my betrothed, Ronan, instead.

"That's right. I won't."

There it was again—comfort disguised as a threat. The kind I couldn't afford to want.

I hobbled toward the door as he fell in step behind me. I swiped the back of my hand over the cut, smearing blood over my skin. A lot of good it did. I still bled and the throbbing wasn't going away. I should have known not to engage Kincade in a workout session.

Kincade wasn't like my uncle. He wasn't going to push me into going after the relic. He wasn't going to prod me into making travel plans. Instead, he was biding his time, living in the manor house, and eating my food while he waited for me to announce my next move.

"You should let me clean that," he said.

"I think you've done enough damage for one day."

I practically growled the words, not understanding why I was so annoyed and angry. I'd been annoyed and angry with everything lately, though. Everything and everyone. Perhaps because I finally decided, deep down, to embrace my true calling as Keeper of the Holy Relics. Perhaps because my life was never the same as it was before when I lived in Dallas. Before I was contacted by both a messenger angel and a fallen angel.

I hurried across the damp lawn, trying to lose him, but it was no use. His legs were longer than mine, and he kept up with ease. At the back kitchen door, I banged through it, startling Piers and Grace, who were cooking something for dinner later that evening. The kitchen smelled of a decadent pastry in the oven. A huge stockpot simmered on the stove. A stack of cookies was heaped on a platter at the end of the kitchen counter. I swiped one on my way past.

Grace gaped at me wide-eyed as I stomped through the kitchen, biting my lip to keep from saying something to Kincade I'd regret later.

"Lord have mercy, what happened?" She wiped her hands on a blue and white kitchen towel as she came around the island.

"I'm fine," I grumbled, then halted and turned toward Kincade. I punched him in the chest with all the force I was able to muster. He didn't even falter. "You stay here."

He looked so surprised, I almost laughed. I managed to contain it as I spun on the toe of my pink boot and left the kitchen, stuffing the cookie in my mouth. I hurried through the house and up the stairs to my room where I paused in the hallway. I stole a glance down to the other end where Edward's bedroom—now mine—was undergoing a transformation. Contractors had been in the house for weeks.

Piers insisted I move out of my childhood bedroom and into the master suite since I was now the lady of the house. I was reluctant. He offered to have it renovated into something more my taste. I refused to pick a wall color or anything else and left it up to the old butler. He seemed content enough to handle the project himself.

Mild curiosity coursed through me. What did it look like behind that closed door?

I heard footsteps that sounded like Kincade and hurried toward my room where I slammed the door, leaning against it. My breath came in gasps, my hands shook. Cookie crumbs were stuck in the back of my throat and I wished I had something to wash it down.

For the last few weeks, I vibrated with unspent energy. I knew what my next destination was, but I was stalling to avoid the inevitable. There was something unsettling about facing what was to come and I wasn't ready to face it. Not yet. So, I asked Kincade to work out with me.

Sometimes Kincade didn't know his own strength. And he forgot I was a girl. Granted, I'm not a delicate flower, but I wasn't prepared for the punch I took to the head.

Honestly, I think he missed and hadn't intended to hit me. Which wasn't at all like Kincade. He was a man with purpose, who always knew what his next move was going to be. He always planned one step ahead.

I padded to the bathroom, trying to forget Kincade and everything else.

The cut over my eye wasn't all that bad, but it stung. I dabbed peroxide over it, cleaning it and wincing at the same time. Once I cleared away the blood, it looked like nothing more than a scratch.

I could live with that.

What I couldn't live with were the dark shadows deep under my eyes.

I still hadn't been sleeping.

And it wasn't because I forgot to put up my mental walls. No one visited me in my dreams of late and for that I was grateful.

No. Instead, my dreams were fire and brimstone. The world was ablaze with flaming chasms surrounding me. Lava poured out of a nearby volcano, spilling down the mountain. The intense heat seared my skin. Before me, the glowing gold Ark of the Covenant.

I walked through the flames, engulfed by them as Lucifer looked on, smiling that oily smile. Behind me were death screams. Everyone I had ever loved or cared about were tortured in the most horrific ways while I stood by, helpless at the control of Lucifer.

I didn't much care for these new nightmares.

I also hadn't shared them with anyone.

I didn't want to be psychoanalyzed by Kincade or Grace.

After I finished cleaning my wound, I covered it with antibiotic ointment and a small bandage. I leaned on the bathroom counter, peering at my face, the tired purple eyes, the hollow look residing there.

I didn't know who I was anymore. I had morphed into someone else from the person I used to be last summer in Dallas. Before Azriel had come to me with a demand to find the Holy Relics for Lucifer. Before Joachim, the messenger angel, paid me a visit with the same request to bring them to Michael and the Most High. Before I met Kincade.

Before Ben, my boyfriend, was brutally murdered before my eyes.

I was no longer that sad, lonely girl who used to be a phlebotomist. I was Keeper of the Holy Relics. The one who had tracked down four of the five. The Horn of Gabriel, the Spear of Destiny, the Staff of Moses, the Holy Grail all resided deep in the vault in the library.

The Ark of the Covenant was the final relic.

I still didn't understand what I was supposed to do with all these relics or how I was supposed to use them. I assumed that would come to me at some point.

A knock sounded on my bedroom door. I sighed. It seemed I never had a moment's peace. Someone always wanted my attention for some reason.

I trudged to the bedroom door and swung it open. To my surprise, Piers stood on the other side.

"Apologies for the intrusion, my lady, however, you have visitors."

I still twitched when he called me *my lady*, but he refused to stop doing it. When my uncle died, his baron title and the Walker estate passed to me.

Gah. Why did I always have visitors? The last ones who darkened my doorstep came with unwanted information—that I was betrothed and expected to marry Ronan Harred. I wasn't sure I was up for more visitors.

"Who is it, Piers?"

"They claim to be your cousins."

This took me aback. I stared at him as though he'd grown a second head. I didn't particularly want to get all chummy with cousins. Lexi had been a cousin, and she had betrayed me by stealing the Horn of Gabriel, giving it to Aziel, and leaving me to die on a rooftop in Hong Kong. Isobel Marques was a cousin who hated my guts, blaming me for the death of her husband.

Both were now dead. Both at the hands of Azriel.

I glanced down at my attire and realized I was still in workout clothes. "I'll change and be right down."

"Shall I bring tea?"

"Yes. And lemon cakes."

"Of course, my lady. They're waiting for you in the parlor."

I closed the door and headed to the wardrobe, not at all interested in meeting more cousins. I peeled out of my sweaty clothes and into something a little more respectable—my usual uniform of black cargo pants, pink combat boots, and Henley.

I half expected to see Kincade lurking in the hallway when I left my room, but he was nowhere to be found. Not even at the bottom of the stairs or hovering around the parlor. Fine by me. I'd had enough of his clingy presence.

As I entered the parlor, I steeled my nerves, took a deep breath, and sized up the two people waiting for my arrival. One was a man with striking good looks. His face looked as though it had been chiseled from marble with perfect angles. High cheekbones, a pointy dimpled smooth chin, jade green eyes, and a full head of wavy ash blond hair. He was dressed in a polo shirt, slacks, and nice shoes and looked as though he just walked out of the country club.

The woman gave me a good once over as I stood in the doorway, her long blonde hair cascading in waves over her shoulders almost to her waist. She had thick, pouty lips and the same high cheekbones and pointy chin as the man. The resemblance between the two of them was striking. They were clearly brother and sister. She wore a couture pantsuit in a lovely shade of pale pink with matching kitten heels and handbag with a gold chain over one shoulder. Perfectly manicured nails the same color as her pantsuit.

When I entered, the man stood and plastered on his best fake smile.

"You must be Anna," he said.

"I must be." I gave him a leery once over. "And you are?"

"William Bennett. This is my sister, Victoria." He extended his hand for a shake. "My friends and family call me Will."

I wasn't so certain I wanted to shake his hand, but I did anyway. "Okay."

He didn't seem to care for my response. I didn't seem to care for his presence.

"We're cousins, you know," he said. "My mother is Edward's sister, Josephina."

"Piers said as much." I waved him to a chair.

I was aware of who they were and how we were related now that I heard their names. Edward, my uncle, was the eldest and had three younger sisters. Matilda, or Tilde, as he affectionately called her, had a daughter, Isobel, and a son, Alaric.

Josephina was Lexi's mother and had two other children, William and Victoria, who now graced my parlor. Annabelle, the youngest and my namesake, was my mother.

William sat. Victoria sat. I sat. As though we were all chummy pals ready to catch up.

Piers wheeled in the tea cart then, breaking the awkward silence. He always had impeccable timing.

"Tea?" I asked and waved to the cart.

"Please and thank you," William said.

He took the offered cup and added a cube of sugar. Victoria waved away the offering as did I. Piers left the cart and retreated, closing the parlor doors behind him.

"Are you going to tell me why you're here or do I have to guess?" I finally asked.

William stole a glance at Victoria whose face was lined with what appeared to be annoyance and anger. Question lined his face. She motioned to him to get on with it.

"Ask her, Will," she said, her voice hard and unforgiving.

William turned his attention back to me. "We've come to ask you if you know the whereabouts of our sister, Lexi. We think she came to see you a few months ago."

I stared in stunned silence at the two of them. They really had no idea what she'd done to me?

"We haven't heard from her in quite some time, so we hoped you had some information about her," he continued.

"She did come to me a few months ago. She tracked me down and offered to help me find the Horn of Gabriel," I said.

Will scooted to the edge of his chair, eager for more information.

I didn't know how to tell him the truth about his sister. How she'd given herself to the darkness and allowed Azriel to use her. How he had given her to the lesser demons for their own pleasure. Remembering that sickened me.

"Did she help you?" he asked.

"Oh, she helped me all right. By betraying me and stealing the horn from me. She gave it to a high lord named Azriel. They were lovers."

"You lie," Victoria spat, the venom of her words hissing through her teeth. "Lexi would never do such a thing."

"But she did." I pinned her with my best glare, annoyed she challenged me. "We were attacked by demons in a building in Hong Kong. We barely made it out alive, but she had other plans. She left me to die of demon poison on that rooftop."

"Where is the horn now?" William asked, ignoring his sister's heated glare.

"I had to travel to Hell to steal it back. It's safe."

"Here?" he asked, looking eager.

"With all due respect, I don't think that's any of your damn business."

"I told you she wouldn't tell you anything," Victoria sneered. "I bet she doesn't even have it."

"Tori, please." Will placed his cup on the saucer and gave her an imploring look. "We came here to find out where Lexi is, not fling accusations."

I wanted to interject but bit my lip instead and remained silent. William turned back to me, a hopeful look on his face.

"Where is she now?"

I took a deep breath and steeled my nerves. "She's dead."

They both stared at me in shocked silence.

"I tried to save her from the depths of Hell," I continued. "But she didn't want to be saved. I dream walked her, but she didn't want to return. She stayed. Azriel tried to use her dream walking skills to find the remaining Holy Relics. She failed him and when she did, he gave her to his lesser demons."

"Stop lying!" Victoria shouted. "Come, William. There is no reason to continue to sit here and listen to this tripe."

"It's not tripe," I said, my voice astoundingly calm. "It's the truth." Suddenly, the ire rose in me. I slowly pushed to my feet. "And you're right. You don't need to continue to sit here and listen to me tell you the truth. Get out of my house."

"*Your* house?" She snorted derision as she looked me up and down, the hatred clear on her snooty face.

"Yes, my house."

"This estate belongs to *Edward*," she happily pointed out.

"Yeah, well, Edward died and left me his title *and* his estate. Seems I was his favorite niece." I couldn't resist the barb.

Color rose high in her cheeks. William placed the teacup and saucer on the nearby table and stood.

"Tori, I warned you before to keep your temper in check."

"I bet she killed Edward just to get her hands on the estate." Victoria seethed. Her hands balled into fists. "She was nothing but a grubby little thing when he brought her here in the first place."

I clenched my jaw, trying to keep my own temper in check. I readied a retort when the parlor door opened and Kincade strolled in. His massive, hulking form seemed to take up the entire doorway as he stood there, gazing at the two visitors with his best critical eye. He folded his arms over his chest and looked dark and dangerous.

I'd never been so happy to see him.

"Is there a problem here, Miss Walker?" He eyed the two of them with unabashed displeasure.

"No problem. They were just leaving. Weren't you?" I waved toward the door.

Victoria stomped toward Kincade who stepped aside as she went past, leaving behind a trail of expensive perfume in her wake. William didn't bother to hide his embarrassment. He raked a hand through his hair as he approached me.

"I hope you don't let Tori's behavior think ill of us. We merely wanted answers about our sister."

"I gave you all the answers I have. If there's nothing else...?" I let the sentiment linger between us.

He pressed his lips together. "Anna—"

"There's nothing else to say." I didn't want to hear any more excuses or lies or pleas or anything. "Unless you're here to pledge your help in the fight against Lucifer, this is goodbye."

He stared at me, remaining perfectly still. "The only way you'd fight Lucifer is if you have the Holy Relics in your possession."

I folded my arms. "Again, none of your business."

"You have them, don't you?"

"I believe Miss Walker specifically asked you to leave," Kincade said.

William gave him a curious glance with a smirk. "Who are you? Her bodyguard?"

"No," Kincade said, drawing the word out slowly, quietly. "Her guardian."

The word hit like a claim. Not loud. Not public. Just...true.

I glanced at him, trying to ignore my fluttering heart. William said nothing for a long moment before following his sister out the door. After they were both gone, I blew out a breath.

"What is it with you and cousins?" he asked.

I shrugged. "None of them appear to like me."

"That's because they're jealous."

"Of me?"

"Yes. You're the Keeper. The chosen one. Edward's heir."

He reached for me and ran the pad of his thumb over the bandage. It sent a jolt of heat through me.

Not lust—worse. Relief. The kind that made me want to lean in and pretend I didn't need anything.

"Head okay?"

"My head is fine, thanks."

He gave me *that look*. The one with which I was becoming all too familiar. The one that said he wanted to kiss me like he did back in the Fae forest before Lucifer burned it to the ground.

"I, ah, think I'll go see how things are going with Killian and Astrid."

I scurried out of the parlor leaving him behind.

CHAPTER 2

I STEPPED OUT INTO the damp early afternoon air trying to ward off a shiver. Despite my long months in England, I still wasn't used to the weather. It was mostly cloudy, rainy, chilly during the early months of the year. Did I miss blistering Texas summers? Not really. But it would be nice to have some decent warm weather for a change.

On the front lawn of Walker Manor estate, there was a sea of tents where what was left of the Fae resided. Lucifer had stolen the four Fae Treasures and destroyed their realm, which pushed them into hiding in the first place. When Lucifer burned down their hidden forest, I invited them to stay here. Well, more specifically in the trees surrounding Walker Manor, but a Fae forest wasn't built in a day despite the best efforts of Astrid, who had unimaginable powers.

She was Azriel's half-sister and a time warper. That meant she had the ability to bend the very fabric of time to her will. And create things out of thin air. She coerced me into freeing her from

Azriel's clutches by blowing up his underground crypt in a Dallas cemetery.

I wended my way through the tent village, listening to the sounds of the Fae at work. Deep in the forest, men's voices echoed back while within the tents, women were hard at work cooking and baking. They made themselves at home and seemed perfectly content on the lawn of the estate.

A few greeted me with smiles and a nod as I passed by looking for Astrid and Killian. I'd offered them a room inside the manor house, but they eventually moved to the lawn to be with the rest of Killian's people. He was, after all, the last Fae king.

One large tent stood out among the others. Voices wafted on the wind toward me. I headed there and paused at the edge of the tent to peer inside. Killian stood at the head of a long table, leaning over what appeared to be a map of the estate forest. A man stood to his right, sketching as the Fae king gave instructions. Astrid sat opposite them and watched them work. When she noticed me, she smiled and got to her feet. Killian and the other man never looked up from their work.

"Hi, Anna. What brings you here?"

"I came to see how things were going." I glanced around the little village, admiring how everyone seemed to be content.

"Killian won't let me use my powers to create the village. He says it's too much."

"I don't think he's wrong." I gave her a warm smile.

After Azriel captured and took her to Hell, he tortured and controlled her. She didn't talk about the ordeal, but it drained her power. And then, arriving here, she used what she had left to start creating the tent village. It took her days to fully recover.

"How are things going?" I asked, nodding toward the line of trees.

"Progressing. Much slower than I think he would like." She cut a glance at Killian, who was still deep in conversation with the other man. Then she hooked her arm in mine and started to walk away. "I have something to ask you."

"Okay."

"About Ophelia's sword," she added.

A chilly sensation crawled up the back of my neck. "What about it?"

"Killian thinks it's the lost Sword of Light. One of the Fae treasures."

She didn't have to ask me anything. I knew exactly where this was going. Ophelia and I met in Istanbul when she was wielding that shimmering broadsword decapitating high lords while I killed demons with my jade-handled dagger.

"That sword is her pride and joy. She loves killing Fallen high lords with it. I don't think it's a missing Fae treasure."

"Why is that?" Astrid asked, her query a careful question.

"Because I've seen the ivory handle. An alpha and omega symbol is carved into it like this one." I pulled the dagger from the holder at my waist and showed her.

The carving was unmistakable on the handle. Ophelia's sword had similar symbols in her handle. She had showed them to me when we first met.

She glanced down at it as we continued to walk. "Would you at least allow Killian to inspect it?"

"It's not me you have to ask." I wasn't sure how Ophelia would react to the thought her favorite sword was part of the Fae treasure.

"What I'm asking is if you will speak to Ophelia about it. She listens to you. Respects you. If you ask her to allow Killian to examine it, she will," Astrid said, clearly making her case for the king.

I hated being put in this position but nodded anyway. "I'll talk to her."

"Thanks."

"And if the sword is the Sword of Light? Then what?" I asked.

She dragged her lower lip through her teeth. "Killian will want it returned to him."

I took a deep breath, held it. "Of course. I'll talk to her but don't get your hopes up. That shimmering sword is a heavenly weapon. I'm sure of it."

"I appreciate you asking her for me." She paused, her gaze fixed on something in the distance. "Is that Piers?"

I looked in the direction of her gaze. Sure enough, Piers walked at a brisk pace across the lawn right for us. I didn't recall ever seeing Piers move that fast before. He waved, trying to get my attention.

"I suppose that means he's in need of me." I heaved a sigh. "I'll let you know what Ophelia says."

Astrid released my arm. I broke into a trot toward Piers. He had a pinched expression on his aged face as he approached, like something was terribly wrong. I braced myself for bad news.

"What is it, Piers?"

"There is someone here to see you."

I came to a halt in front of him and propped my hands on my hips. "Who now? And don't these people know how to use a phone?"

"He wouldn't give me his name, but your friend, Kincade, appears to know him."

I gave him a blank stare. Who would Kincade know, and why would this person come here? The only person I could think of was Kincade's brother. "Is it Decker?"

"I don't believe so, my lady."

Great. Another mysterious guest. "All right then. I guess I better make an appearance." I started for the front door once again.

"Very well. Shall I bring a fresh pot of tea?"

"Does the sun rise in the east?" I said over my shoulder.

Piers, ever the stoic one, made no reply or response. He didn't even crack a smile. He merely hurried to get in front of me and open the door for me. After I entered, he was off to the kitchen to see to tea.

Kincade stood in the doorway of the parlor, waiting for me. He stepped out and blocked my path before I entered. He had a stricken look on his face I'd never seen before. Alarm bells rang through my head.

"Who's in there?" I tried to keep my voice low. "Decker?"

He shook his head slowly. "Sebastian."

Sebastian Crane was the commander of the Brotherhood of Watchers and once Kincade's boss. I only had one interaction with him. When Azriel kidnapped Kincade, I had been taken to visit with Sebastian. He grilled me on where and what had happened to Kincade. What I remembered of Sebastian was that he was a cold, heartless son of a bitch who refused to help me save my guardian from the depths of Hell.

"What does he want?" The words came out on a breathless whisper.

Kincade clenched his jaw. He didn't answer as he stepped aside. I had no idea what I was about to walk into and I wasn't sure I wanted to find out. My gut churned acid as I entered the room and there was Sebastian.

The man was still drool-worthy. Nary a strand of wavy black hair was out of place on his head. His eyes were the brightest, most piercing green I had ever seen. Like a couple of mirthless peridots staring out at me. He wore similar clothing to Kincade—long-sleeved three-button Henley in a soft heather gray, black cargo pants, black boots. He stood at the fireplace, awaiting my arrival.

"We meet again, Miss Walker." Despite his warm greeting, no smile graced his handsome features.

I took a glance back at Kincade who stood behind me, but his green-gold gaze was fixed firmly on Sebastian. I returned my gaze to him, my stomach nothing but a ball of nerves. My palms broke into a hot sweat.

"What can I do for you, Sebastian?"

His gaze flickered from me to Kincade and back again. Imperceptible, but unmistakable. And my gut clenched even harder.

"Kincade, perhaps you should be the one to tell her." He sat on the sofa and leaned back as if he owned the joint.

Arrogant fuck.

"I don't think so." Kincade's voice was gruff.

Hot tingles danced up my spine and prickled the base of my skull. "Tell me what?"

"Kincade left the Brotherhood," Sebastian said, then paused for dramatic effect. He pinpointed me with those lethal eyes. "For you."

That wasn't news to me. I forced Kincade to tell me he left to protect me because I needed someone to trust, someone who always had my back, someone who was my self-appointed guardian. He was a general in the Brotherhood. A general who led a task force with which Ophelia fought with to hunt down and destroy Fallen high lords who were killing guardian angels and then stealing their humans' souls. All in an effort to build Lucifer's army.

I lifted a brow as I peered down at the man. "And?"

"And because he left, he broke certain rules." Again, the man's gaze flickered to Kincade.

I huffed out an exasperated breath. "Any idea when you'll be getting to the fucking point?"

Behind me, Kincade sucked in a breath but it was so quiet I might have missed it if my senses hadn't been on high alert.

"There are consequences for his actions, Miss Walker. He must return with me to the Brotherhood and face those consequences."

My heart dropped into my shoes. My head snapped around to look at Kincade, but he stood unmoving as though carved from stone. His face had zero expression but I noticed his clenched jaw and the muscles flexing there. It was his reaction to me when I was being particularly difficult.

I looked back to Sebastian. "He can't return with you."

"He can and he will. He must."

"No." My voice wavered only a little.

"I'm afraid this isn't up to you, Miss Walker. As the commander of the Brotherhood, it is my sworn duty to bring him back before the Warden of Nine."

"What the fuck is the Warden of Nine?" I demanded. My hands clenched into tight fists. My blood beat at a furious rate inside my head.

"The governing body of the Brotherhood of Watchers," Kincade replied.

And the terrible tone in his voice nearly sent me to my knees. He sounded unhappy and even a little disgruntled.

"They will be the ones to decide his fate," Sebastian said as though discussing the weather or the latest cricket match.

"What fate?"

"He will either be cast out from the Watchers for all eternity..." Again, the man paused. Such a drama queen.

"Or?" I asked.

"I'll be executed for treason."

CHAPTER 3

I GASPED AS I spun to face Kincade. It took everything in my power not to fling myself into his arms. I didn't want to show my emotions because then Sebastian would think I was weak.

"Executed?"

Kincade's gaze flickered away from Sebastian to me. His gaze softened. His hand twitched, as though he wanted to reach for me. I clutched my elbows to keep myself from falling into him. And there we were. Both of us denying our innermost emotions for each other.

"It's the most extreme of the consequences," he said. As if that would make me feel better.

"Has that ever happened before?"

"Yes." Sebastian sounded far too happy about that. He rose and walked toward us, pausing behind me. "But the Warden of Nine will be the ones to determine his fate."

I flung back around to Sebastian. "You can't take him with you. He has important work to finish here. With me."

"I'm afraid that's not possible. The Wardens are waiting for him. Come, Kincade."

Sebastian stepped around me as though I were nothing but a stone in the road. The thought of losing Kincade now, when I needed him the most, nearly made me unravel at the seams. I spun back to him, reached for him, and grabbed his hand. He halted before walking away with Sebastian, his gaze lingering on mine.

I had no words. I didn't know what to say or how to say it. I thought of the day I stood in the hallway, gazing at my mother's portrait days after saving his soul from Azriel, and how he stood there, telling me how much I favored her while wearing nothing but blue pajama pants and a blanket around his naked torso. I thought of all the torrid feelings I'd written about him in my journal. The one I wanted to rip the pages from. The one I refused to rip the pages from. I thought of all the things we'd been through together and would still face. I thought of kissing him while in the Fae's sacred forest before it burned to the ground. I thought of how he told me he wanted to kiss me when I asked him why he did it.

And yet, I had no words except for one.

"Kincade..."

He squeezed my hand. "I'll come back."

My breath came in short, raspy breaths. "You better." My throat closed. Because I believed him. And trusting anyone was the most dangerous thing I did lately. "I can't do this without you."

Not the relics. Not the war. Not the part where I had to keep choosing the light when the dark kept offering me easier answers.

I held on to his hand for as long as possible as he turned and walked toward the parlor door. And then he was gone, leaving me bereft in a lonely sea of emotions I didn't know how to handle. For months, Kincade had been my rock. The one I trusted and counted on the most. The one who refused to leave my side after my near fatal encounter with a high lord out for blood.

Sebastian, that bastard. I would never forgive him for this.

Frustration edged through me. My fingers twitched, and a moment later, lightning formed between them. A parting gift from Ronan, my betrothed, before he died. I took a deep, cleansing breath, closed my eyes, and released it. The crackle of the fire between my fingers was still present. Because I was angry and terrified.

"Everything will be all right, you know."

I recognized that voice. My eyes blinked open, and there was Sariel. He visited me a lot lately. He seemed to have a vested interest in me finding the Holy Relics. He was also the one gifting me the postcards with clues to the locations of them. He helped me since I was first tasked with finding them all. He'd sent me to Hong Kong to find the Horn of Gabriel.

"Where is Sebastian taking him? Do you know?"

He shook his head. "Unfortunately, the location of the Warden of Nine is secret. Only a few and the Most High knows where they meet."

I started to pace, my hands flexing into and out of fists. An idea formed. I wasn't going to allow Sebastian to win that easily.

"I need to know where it is. Somehow, I need to find out where Sebastian is taking him. Follow him. Plead his case. Something. *Anything*."

"Anna, my dear, you're upset—"

"You're damn right I'm upset," I interrupted, unwilling to hear him out. "Sebastian can't just take him like that."

"Yes, he can. Kincade is governed by a higher power than even you."

I halted and peered at Sariel, sizing him up. "But you know things. You sent me on these quests. You can find out."

He took a deep breath and exhaled it as he approached me. He placed his hands on my shoulders and gave a gentle squeeze. "Anna, darling, it's not that simple."

I shrugged away from him and paced again. "Yes, it is."

He pressed his lips together. "Execution is the most extreme punishment. It seems rather radical."

"Well, I can't let them execute him."

"Because you're in love with him."

That stopped me. I halted, not looking at him for fear my emotions would give me away. I never had a poker face. I never hid my emotions. They were written all over my face for all to see.

"What makes you think that?" I asked, facing the fireplace gazing at my uncle's picture in the 8x10 frame.

"You deny your feelings for the man. Why?"

I moved to the fireplace and leaned on the mantle, my finger tracing the edge of the gold frame. "I don't."

"Anna..." He said my name in a way that reminded me much of my uncle. When he was completely and utterly exasperated with me.

I did that to people. Exasperated them.

"What do you want me to say, Sariel? That I'm madly in love with the man?" I turned to face him, my pulse pounding hard and fast in my throat. My blood pressure heated and throbbed through me. "Is that what you want to hear?"

His face remained impassive. "Is that the truth? Your truth?"

I raked a frustrated hand through my long black hair, my fingers tangling in the locks. "I don't know. Everyone I've cared about has been taken from me."

"Then you care about him."

"Oh, hell, Sariel. You know I do! I went after him when Azriel kidnapped him and tried to destroy his soul. I traded the Spear of Destiny for his life. And yes, I got the spear back later, but isn't it telling how I feel about the man? By my actions?"

The words came out in a rush. I didn't know what I was saying, really, or why I said it to him. I doubted Sariel was all that interested in my love life.

Which was nonexistent.

He said nothing for a long moment, and then a small smile spread on his face. "I've watched you these last few months. It has taken you many months to achieve what you have achieved. To become what you have become. You persevered. You progressed from faithless to regaining faith. From hopeless to hopeful. Faith, hope and love. But the greatest of these is love."

I moved to the nearby chair and sank into the soft cushions, my hand on my head. "He is my salvation. I need him, Sariel."

As I said the words, a verse floated through my head.

I have found the one whom my soul loves.

Kincade and I were perfect unity.

Footsteps sounded on the staircase in the hall. Sariel glanced over his shoulder, a panicked look flickering over his features.

"I must go."

And then poof he was gone.

I shook my head. That was the way of things with these angels. They poofed in and out of my life as though it were a common occurrence.

Natasha appeared in the doorway of the parlor. Confusion was etched on her face. She glanced around the room looking for something. I got to my feet.

"You all right?" I asked.

Natasha was really my biological mother, Annabelle Walker. She was kidnapped by the Knights of the Holy Lance, a neo-Nazi fanatical group, and taken to Antarctica where she underwent horrible experiments on her brain. They wanted to find out what made her a dream walker and eventually turned her into a super dream walker. They used her as the prototype, stealing her DNA to make others like her. Her mind hadn't been the same since then. She occasionally had moments of clarity but mostly she lived in a fog that clouded her memories of her true self.

"I sensed a presence a moment ago. Was someone here?"

I hadn't talked to her about all the divine visitors I had of late. I shook my head as I walked to her side. "No one was here."

For a moment, there was lucidity in her purple eyes that were exactly like mine. And then the fog returned. As though whatever clear thought in her mind disappeared. She blinked as she focused on me. Her brows drew together.

"I...I'm sorry. I don't know why I'm here."

"Here?" I cocked my head to one side trying to read between the lines. But often times, she was impossible to read especially when she didn't know who or what she was.

"I remember coming down the stairs and then...nothing. Did I disturb you?"

"Not at all." I hooked my arm in hers and started for the stairs once again. "Are you hungry? I think Piers and Grace were cooking up something yummy in the kitchen."

"Yes, I think I am."

"Then let's eat. I'm starving."

I tried my best to sound cheerful, while deep down, my soul was dying over the loss of Kincade. I had no idea how, but I was going to find him and get him back.

CHAPTER 4

WE ENTERED THE DINING room where Grace was setting the table and humming a happy little tune. Something about that immediately raked on my nerves. I suddenly wanted to punch something, hard. Instead, I released my arm from Natasha's and motioned her to a seat. Grace gave me a wide smile as she placed a bowl on top of the charger.

"Where's Kincade? I haven't seen him since this morning."

I flushed so hot it burned my cheeks and scalded my innards. "He's, uh, working out."

"Didn't he already do that this morning with you?"

An innocent question to be sure, but I wasn't up for chit chat about Kincade's whereabouts. I was still trying to process the fact Sebastian took him away.

"He did." My voice cracked a little. She gave me a look that said she suspected something was amiss. I managed to force a smile and gave a little laugh. "You know how he is. He likes to maintain his muscular physique. He's a bit fanatical about it."

"One of these days he's going to work out too much and hurt himself." She clucked her tongue in a typical motherly fashion.

Piers, thankfully, bustled in then with a giant steaming serving bowl. He placed it on the server, then hurried back to the kitchen. He returned a moment later with a heaping plate of fresh bread from the oven.

"Piers and I made beef stew and homemade rosemary bread. Please dig in." She beamed as she waved toward the server.

Natasha pushed her chair back, picked up her bowl, and helped herself to a steaming serving. I admitted it smelled divine, but I wasn't sure I wanted to eat. My gut still churned acid and I didn't know what to do or how to handle it.

Grace grabbed a bowl and filled it, too. She settled in the seat across from Natasha. It was odd, really, seeing the two of them in the same room together. My biological mother and my adopted mother. I glanced between the two of them. They had never been together much. For the first time, I noticed how different they were. I wondered what Natasha was like before her mind was mutilated?

"Anna?" Grace's voice broke me out of my thoughts. "You're not eating?"

"Oh." It came out a breath. "I guess I'm not that hungry."

I shoved back from the table and left the two of them in the dining room. I pounded up the stairs to my room where I closed the door. I leaned against it, closed my eyes and took a deep breath. My hands shook as I tried to figure out what my next move was going to be.

I knew Kincade well enough to know he wouldn't want me to come after him. He didn't even want me to come after him when he was trapped in Hell with Azriel. He didn't want me to trade the Spear of Destiny to save his soul. I, of course, ignored all of that and did what I was compelled to do anyway.

I needed to find him. I needed to get to him.

The scent of strawberries and chocolate filled my nose. My eyes flickered open and there was Joachim, the messenger angel, perched on the edge of the chair opposite my bed looking as though he belonged there. His ice blue eyes pierced me. He still had the same short black hair. His massive wings spread behind him.

Joachim was the one who started me on the quest for the Holy Relics. Well, after Azriel threatened my life if I didn't search for them for him. Joachim was his heavenly counterpart and had visited me numerous times in the past. It had been quite some time since I'd seen him. He hadn't changed a bit.

"Hello, Joachim."

"Hello, Anna." His voice was strong, even.

"To what do I owe the pleasure of your visit? It's been a while."

A faint smile graced his pale pink lips. "Indeed, it has. I sensed your distress."

"So, you decided to pay me a visit. How kind of you." I sat on the edge of the bed, a ball of nervous energy. "I have a lot things to decide so if you don't mind, I'd like to be alone."

The thing about these angels was they always showed up at the most inopportune moments.

He steepled his fingers as he sat there, looking at me with a pondering expression. As though he were trying to decide what to do with me or what to say to me. I huffed out a breath.

"What do you want, Joachim?"

"I wanted to inquire how the quest for the Holy Relics is going."

There was something about the way he said it that sent suspicion skipping through me. Likely he was here on an errand for Michael, the archangel. "Don't you know? All you angels like to keep tabs on me."

"Humor me." He flexed his fingers then steepled them again.

"I have four relics with one more to go."

He lifted a dark brow. "The Ark."

"Yes."

"Good."

A pause. I narrowed my gaze at him. "And?"

"I sense your hesitation," he said.

I spread my hands as if in surrender. "What do you want from me?"

"When do you plan to search for the Ark?"

Anger pierced me. I took a deep, cleansing breath. Something I did a lot lately to control my temper. "I have no idea."

"You're worried because you lost your guardian."

He knew. My accusing gaze turned on him. "What do you know about that?"

"I know where Sebastian is taking him. I know where the Warden of Nine are."

I stiffened, my back going ramrod straight. "And is this a piece of information you intend to share with me?"

He granted a small smile. "For a price."

My shoulders slumped as I rolled my eyes. "Of course, there's a price. What is it?"

"Do you still have the Horn of Gabriel?"

"You know I do."

"Good. Would you be so kind as to retrieve it for me?"

"No," I said, my voice flat. "I'm keeping it along with the others."

He ran a tongue over his bottom lip trying to contain his own temper. "Anna, do you remember when I first came to you?"

"How could I forget?"

"I told you when you found the relics you were to hand them over to me. I must have the Horn of Gabriel."

I cocked my head to the side. "Why?"

"Does it matter?"

"Yes."

Annoyance flickered through those cold blue eyes. "Gabriel has asked for it to be returned to him."

An icy flicker of dread skittered up my spine. "May I ask why?"

"I think you know the answer to that."

When I was in Spain, I saw the first of the Four Horseman, Conquest. Across the world since then, there had been reports of famine, unrest, disease, natural disasters. I understood, unlike most humans, this was a sign.

"Judgement Day?" My voice was weak.

"That day approaches, Anna. It cannot be stopped."

"I thought that's what I was doing. Trying to stop it. Isn't that why I've been trotting all over the globe collecting these relics in the first place?"

He dropped his hands in his lap, defeat slipping over his face. "Yes, and you tried. However, there are powerful forces at play. More powerful than Michael or Gabriel or even the Most High expected. You are strong, Anna. But even you cannot hold back what is to come."

I had been told more than once the fate of mankind resided with me. Now Joachim tells me even I cannot stop the coming war. And that made me feel like all of this was for naught. Why even search for the Ark if that was the case?

"Then why should I continue if all of this is for nothing?"

A glint of regret flickered through his eyes as he realized his mistake. He took a deep breath as he rose from the chair. "It's not for nothing. There will come a day when you face the ultimate evil. When you face your fate."

"And?" I prompted when he didn't continue.

"And you still have a role to play in what is to come."

That wasn't very reassuring, but I accepted his answer.

"I'll give you the Horn of Gabriel," I said at last. He started to reply, but I cut him off. "If you tell me where I can find Kincade first."

"The Brotherhood of Watchers reside deep in the underground of London. Sebastian will take him there first while they await his trial with the Warden of Nine," Joachim said. "Even you won't be able to find their hidden lair without help."

London! Of course. Decker, Kincade's brother, took me to meet Sebastian in London at their headquarters after Kincade was taken by Azriel. I remembered that day as though it was yesterday. Which meant there was only one person who could help me and that was Decker. I hadn't seen him in weeks. I had no idea where he'd gone.

"And the Warden of Nine?" I asked.

"They oversee the Brotherhood and have taken to residing in Bagras Castle, one of the old Templar fortresses in what once was Antioch."

Antioch was now present day Hatay, Turkey. My brows drew together. "There are only ruins of a Templar castle there."

"That's what they want you to think. They have managed to restore most of the interior of the castle and taken to living underground there. This is where Kincade's trial will be held."

"Then that's where I'll go. Anything else?"

Travel was going to be a challenge since a pandemic was currently spreading across the globe. I tried to avoid the news, but even I wasn't immune to the gossip spreading government shutdowns were imminent. Which meant no more domestic or international travel.

He shook his head. "This is all the information I have."

"Thank you, Joachim. If you'll come with me, I'll get the horn for you. You might want to hide those." I waved at his massive wings.

Angels had the ability to hide their wings at will. Like the Fae used a glamour so they would appear human. He followed me out of my room, down the hall to the library where I kept all the relics I'd collected to date in the vault.

Once in the library, I closed the door behind us and went to the bookshelf behind the desk. There, I slipped one of the books out of its spot. The shelf hissed and clicked and then slid open. I pulled the shelf aside and stepped into the vault. Joachim remained in the center of the room, not moving as I used the dial to enter the numbers to the safe. Then I spun the dial and pulled open the heavy vault door.

Inside, the room was dust-free with a conference table and chairs in the center. On one side were ancient artifacts my uncle collected throughout the years including oil paintings, sculptures, first edition books. Nails from the Holy Cross. A box labeled the Shroud of Turin. Another box was identified as the Crown of Thorns. A sword leaning against the wall, forgotten.

On the other, the shelf where the four Holy Relics resided. The Horn of Gabriel was in a custom-made wooden box with a latch. It was lined with the softest red velvet. I flipped the latch and opened the lid. I hadn't seen the horn in a while. Admittedly, it was a relief to see it was still where I'd left it. The silver Horn of Gabriel was beautiful. Shiny and perfect, the horn was long and straight with a flared bell at the end. It had no keys or holes. No etchings, no fingerprints, no nothing.

I turned to show the horn to Joachim. He gazed upon it for a long, quiet moment. A look of reverence was on his face.

"It is more beautiful than I imagined," he said.

"Yes," I agreed.

When I blew the horn in Hong Kong, it summoned Darius, the warrior angel. When Gabriel blew the horn, it would signal the End of Days.

The last thing I wanted was for Gabriel to blow the horn.

"You should know there are some vampires hunting for the horn. They want it back."

He lifted a brow which seemed rather uncharacteristic of him. "Vampires?"

"They call themselves Partners for the Sanctified. They worked for Chen. I stole the horn from him."

"Ah, I see." He nodded as though he understood, but his tone of voice indicated he didn't.

"Maybe it's just as well you take it back to Gabriel."

I snapped the box closed and flipped the latch once again. If the vampires came after me again for the horn, I'd tell them the truth—I no longer had it. Of course, it would be hard to prove that to them since they were bloodthirsty undead creatures. I'd worry about that later.

I handed it to him. He slipped it from my hands and cradled it against his chest.

"Thank you, Anna. Until we meet again."

That meeting, I knew all too well, would likely not be a pleasant one. I nodded farewell and then he was gone.

CHAPTER 5

I REMAINED ALONE IN the library vault, gazing at the artifacts. A white tube leaned against an empty ornate gold frame. I wondered if the painting I'd tried to steal was still in the tube. Curious, I walked over to it, popped off the top. The white canvas material was still rolled up. I pulled it out and let it unfurl.

The oil painting was of a ship in the middle of the sea during a storm. It was a depiction of Christ's disciples fighting against a heavy storm to regain control of their boat. Several of them tried to maintain control of the sail. One vomited over the side. And one, in the center, was the only one who looked calm—Christ Himself.

The name of the painting was *The Storm on the Sea of Galilee*. A Rembrandt. Priceless. And also stolen from the Gardner Museum in Boston, missing since 1990. Not for the first time I wondered how my uncle came into possession of the pilfered painting.

I'd tried to steal it from my uncle to sell for a ridiculous amount of money. My intent was to use the cash to destroy Azriel, but my plan had gone awry when Abaddon, the destroyer angel, attacked and paralyzed me. I'd lost the tube in the escape tunnel under the garage. My uncle retrieved it and returned it to the vault.

There were numerous first edition books, some so old and so rare they looked as though they might crumble if picked up. I feared touching them. There were small sculpted busts of what appeared to be Roman Emperors, old pottery, a weird tablet of some sort, an old chess set that looked as though it belonged in the Middle Ages, an ancient sword in an even more ancient scabbard. More oil paintings and ancient artifacts. My uncle was a collector of antiquities. He loved old things. A lot of it looked like junk to me, but I suspected some held some sort of value or it wouldn't be locked in the vault.

I glanced around wondering what, if anything, I could use as leverage to get Kincade back. I wasn't willing to part with any of the other Holy Relics. Nothing else jumped out at me. I doubted the Warden of Nine would be interested anyway. I ran a hand over my chin in contemplation.

And then it hit me.

I didn't know where Decker was, but I had a way to find him. I could dream walk him.

I pulled one of the chairs out from the small conference table in the center of the room, sat down, laced my fingers on the shiny tabletop, and closed my eyes.

I concentrated on Decker, what he looked like and how he sounded. He had sharp, assessing eyes the color of coal. He stood a head taller than me with broad shoulders and upper arms the same circumference as my head. At one time, he had the ability to teleport and turn invisible. He'd lost those powers at the hands of the leader of the Knights of the Holy Lance—the man branded the bottom of his foot, which suppressed his abilities.

I hadn't seen him since my uncle's funeral. He disappeared shortly after that and hadn't returned.

I sensed his presence in my mind. He stepped out of the shadows looking angry and fierce.

"What are you doing here?" He practically snarled the words at me.

"I need your help."

"You always need someone's help. What is it this time, Anna? The fate of the world again?" He smirked, clearly unconcerned with my plight.

"Kincade," I said.

The smirk fell away. "What about him?"

"Sebastian plans to put him on trial in front of the Warden of Nine," I said. "I need to get to him."

A dark look flickered over his face. Something like anger followed by regret. "There's nothing you can do."

"There has to be something—"

"No, Anna. Nothing."

"But—"

"The Warden of Nine do not care about you or your Holy Relics or your fight with Lucifer. They only care about the fact that Kincade, a general, deserted them and they want him to pay for his actions. They want him to explain why he left in the first place and if his explanation doesn't suit them, then he will be punished. There is *nothing* you can say or do to stop that. Do you understand that?" Irritated undertones flickered through his voice, as though he were explaining it to a child.

"I do, but, Decker—"

"I will not help you."

Frustration edged through me. "Would you at least let me finish a fucking sentence?"

His jaw clenched, much like Kincade. And much like Kincade, the muscles flexed there. He remained silent for a long moment.

"You came to me once when Kincade was captured by Azriel and Sebastian refused to do anything to help. You asked for my help. I willingly gave it because I wanted him back, too. Because I couldn't allow Azriel to steal his soul and turn him into some mindless high lord who did evil's bidding. Why, now, do you refuse to help me?"

"It's not the same thing." His voice was low and gruff.

"It's exactly the same thing."

"No, it's not." He approached me, grabbed my shoulders and gave me a swift jerk. "You don't understand *anything* about the Brotherhood of Watchers. Once we're in, we're in for life. We are bound by our oath and duty to the Brotherhood and no one else. No one gets out. Not me. Not even Kincade."

I stared up into those harsh eyes of his, trying to peer into his soul, to find some weakness, but Decker was tough and not one to back down.

"I can't do this without him," I said at last.

He dropped his hands and stepped back. "You're going to have to."

"You never liked he gave up his position for me." It was impossible for me to keep the note of accusation out my voice even though I tried.

"No, I didn't because I realized what the consequences were for him. He has to face those consequences now and nothing you say or do will stop them from happening. Now get out of my head and leave me alone."

"I know where the Warden of Nine hide," I blurted. "I'm going there."

"Do what you must, but leave me out of it. And never dream walk me again."

And with that, he pushed me out of his mind as though he flicked off a light switch. The connection was broken. I blinked my eyes open. Despair filled me.

If Decker refused to help me, then what was I going to do?

Perhaps I needed to recruit someone else and do something drastic.

I closed and locked the vault, left the library, and headed to talk to the one person who could take me where I needed to go. Darius had the ability to flash from place to place. Granted, it made me sick to my stomach, but it was the price I was willing to pay to get to Kincade quicker than a commercial airliner or private jet. At Ophelia's room, I knocked and waited. After a long moment of silence, she finally opened the door.

Her face was drained of all color, her eyes red-rimmed and damp as though she'd been crying. Her blonde hair looked as though it needed a good brushing. Alarm shifted through me.

"Ophelia, what is it?"

"Darius...he...he's gone." Her bottom lip quivered.

"What do you mean gone?" My heart stuttered in my chest.

She turned away and shuffled to the bed, plopping down on it. She gripped one of the pillows to her chest and buried her face in it, inhaling deeply. I understood. She still smelled him there. I gave her a minute to collect her thoughts. Finally, she met my gaze.

"He said he had been called to return."

"Return?"

"To his life." She pointed upward to the ceiling.

Darius was a warrior angel, so perhaps he had been called by the Most High to return to his duties. Whatever those were. Ophelia had formed an attachment to him and who could blame her? He was super sexy and it was clear he had eyes for her. They had become inseparable since their first meeting and spent long days and nights tucked away in their bedroom. I didn't question it or give them hell about it. I understood what it was like to be wanted and needed by someone.

All my life I wanted that, too. And thinking about that now, about the loss of Kincade, made me understand her feelings all the more. I wanted Kincade back as much as she wanted Darius back.

"I'm sure he'll come back to you," I said.

She shook her head before I finished. "I don't know when I'll see him again. If ever."

"You will."

"How can you be sure?" Tears danced in her blue eyes.

I perched on the side of the bed next to her, my hands clasped in my lap. "Because I see the way he looks at you."

She clutched the pillow tighter to her chest trying hard to keep the silent sob at bay.

"Whatever it is he had to do," I continued, "I'm sure he didn't want to leave you, either."

Her response was to plop her head on my shoulder and openly weep. I wrapped an arm around her shoulders and let her have her cry. When she finally got it under control, she sniffed and lifted her head.

"I'm sorry, Anna. I haven't been much help to you lately." She hiccupped a gasp of breath.

"You've been a great help to me." I gave her a small smile. "I certainly couldn't have attended the gala in Spain without you."

A smile flickered over her face. "You did look amazing in that dress. Too bad it burned up in the Fae fire."

I nodded. It was definitely unfortunate, especially since the gown, which was covered in Swarovski crystals, cost a small fortune.

"I'm sure you didn't come to hear about my broken heart," she said. "Why did you come?"

I intended to ask Darius to take me to Turkey by flashing me there. "Oh...it doesn't matter anymore." I flashed a small smile, stood, and started for the door.

"Anna, what's your next move?"

I gave her a questioning look over my shoulder. "My next move?"

"You have another relic to find, don't you?"

I nodded, understanding where this was going. Ophelia, who suddenly had extra time on her hands, was about to ask to go with me rather than sit around and pine for Darius.

"Then when do we leave?"

I took a deep breath. I didn't want to tell her about Kincade. I wasn't ready to tell anyone. But then, I had to tell someone and who better than Ophelia. She'd been on his task force and worked for him killing high lords with her shimmering sword. The very one Killian suspected was his missing Sword of Light, which I rejected.

"I don't know yet. I have another task to complete first."

She cocked her head to the side. "You do?"

I clenched one hand into a fist, my nails digging into the palm of my hand. I took a deep breath, expelled it. "Something happened."

She tossed the pillow aside, her grief forgotten, as she jumped to her feet. "What happened?"

"Do you know who Sebastian is?"

"Leader of the Brotherhood of Watchers."

"He showed up here this morning and ordered Kincade to return with him to face a trial for leaving the Brotherhood." There. I said it and couldn't take the words back now.

Her face blanched, draining her red cheeks of all color. "Oh, shit."

"Apparently, they're governed by the Warden of Nine who will be the ones to decide his sentence. I understand his punishment could be extreme as..." I paused, a sudden lump in my throat. I swallowed it back. "Execution."

She sank to the edge of the bed, pressing her fingers against her lips and shaking her head. "We have to do something."

"Yes, we do," I agreed. "However, with the way things are in the world at the moment, it's going to be damned difficult to get to the Warden's hideout."

"Where is it?"

"In an old Templar fortress in Antioch, what is now the Province of Hatay in Turkey. Bagras Castle."

Understanding flickered over her face. "And you came to ask Darius to take you there."

I bit my lip, nodded.

"So, you could...do what exactly?"

"I can't let them execute him," I said. "I need him. I mean, I need his help to finish what we've started."

Too late, I realized my word choice. As soon as I said I needed him, a knowing smirk crossed her pretty face. I pointed at her.

"Not one word."

"Whatever do you mean?" Her eyes widened with her innocence, but I knew better. Then she waved away my chagrin. "I told you this before. Anyone with two eyes can see how you look at each other. It was apparent from the moment I saw you two together in that prison in Hell."

That was the prison I tried to break Kincade out of when Azriel arrived, used his dark demon magic on me, and invaded my mind. That same dark magic that shoved away the cobwebs in my mind and revealed the truth about his identity—that the fallen angel masqueraded as a human, pretended to love me, and tried to take my innocence. When he imprinted me with his tracking tattoo. The same one Kincade tattooed over with his own light magic to erase that from my skin. He'd turned the blue butterfly into magnificent angel wings. Thinking of it now made me reach up and scratch my left shoulder.

"What are you going to do?" she asked.

"I have no idea yet. But I'm not leaving his fate in the hands of the Warden of Nine, whoever the hell they are."

"I'm coming with you."

I shook my head before she even finished her sentence. "I'm going alone."

"No, you're not."

She folded her arms across her chest. I got the distinct feeling she wasn't going to take no for an answer.

"Fine, you can come," I consented. "But I have to figure out a plan first. Let me think about it some more."

"Don't think too long. Kincade may not have that much time."

I was afraid she was right about that.

CHAPTER 6

I LEFT OPHELIA'S ROOM, closing the door behind me. I stood in the hallway, thinking of everything that I'd been through. That we had been through. Her, me, Kincade. The others.

But mostly me and Kincade. He'd been with me almost every step of the way since Hong Kong. I'd faced this dilemma of losing him before. This time, though, seemed more dire. I had nothing to trade for his life. When Azriel took him, I at least had the option of handing over the Spear of Destiny to save him.

What I really needed to know was who were the Warden of Nine? What was their weakness? And how was I going to exploit it?

I glanced down the hall at what was once my uncle's room. Now closed off with giant sheets of plastic as the contractors renovated it. I wished he was here to help me.

"I'm always with you, you know."

His voice startled me. My heart leapt. I pressed a hand against my chest to slow it as I looked to my left. Cashiel was Edward's angelic name. After his death, he became a Seraphim. I hadn't seen him in a while.

His snowy white wings threaded with gold spanned behind him giving him that ethereal look.

"You scared me."

"Sorry, dearie." He gave me a small smile, his blue eyes crinkling with a touch of mirth.

"You angels like to appear out of nowhere to make sure my heart is still pumping, don't you?"

"I suppose some do. As for me, I'm not as adept at appearances as the others. You're in distress," he said.

Even when he was alive, Edward always sensed when my emotions ran high. That hadn't changed in his angelic form. I glanced up and down the hall. Though no one was about, I still motioned for him to follow me to the library. Once inside, I closed the door and immediately went to the beverage cart where there was a selection of decanters filled with luscious glittering brews. I picked my favorite—a rare 40-year-old whiskey. I poured the amber liquid into a highball glass. Two fingers, neat.

As I downed it, I thought of Kincade once again. How he'd plied me with whiskey when Ben died and then again when I lost my uncle. How we made a pact we'd drink whiskey together when I had a crisis. Except this time, he wasn't around to keep my glass filled.

"Kincade is gone," I said at last.

"What do you mean, gone?"

"I'm sure you'll recall he left his position as a general in the Brotherhood of Watchers." I peered at him over my shoulder. He nodded. "Sebastian took him to stand trial before the Warden of Nine for his desertion."

If he had a reaction, he hid it well. His face was impassive as he contemplated my words. Finally, he said, "An unfortunate turn of events. I was hoping that would be avoided."

Shock rolled through me as I spun to face him. "You knew?" Then anger punched through the shock. "Of course, you did. You never shared any pertinent information with me until it was too late."

"Kincade made his own choice, Anna. I did nothing to influence him."

"But you wanted him to give up his place in the Brotherhood for me, didn't you?"

"I didn't. In fact, when he came to me to discuss it, I encouraged him not to."

I stared hard at him, my hand tightening on the empty glass until my muscles cramped. I refilled it, downed it, refilled it again. The liquid burned down my throat and churned hot in the pit of my stomach.

"What do you mean when he came to discuss it with you?"

"After you arrived from Hong Kong, he came looking for you. He told me he intended to leave the Brotherhood to help you with your quest. While I found that to be valiant, I realized the consequences. We discussed the Warden of Nine, then, and he understood those consequences as well."

He allowed the implication of those actions to remain unspoken. We were both aware Kincade left the Brotherhood for me and why. Kincade said he came here looking for me because there had been more murders, more people ending up in the hospital in a catatonic state. We later learned that was because the Fallen high lords were killing humans' guardian angels and stealing their souls to build Lucifer's dark army. I took a seat in one of the wing-backed chairs, my head suddenly throbbing.

"Who or what is the Warden of Nine?" I asked.

"They govern the actions of the Brotherhood of Watchers. They are ever vigilant in their observance of the band of warriors to make sure they do not interfere with the realm of humans. When the

Templars were rounded up and arrested in 1312, even then they did not interfere."

"But Sebastian was the one to take Kincade away. Essentially his boss. To me, that's a betrayal," I said.

Cashiel shook his head. "It's not. It's what Sebastian, as a leader of one of the Brotherhood contingents, was tasked to do should one of his warriors decide to defect."

This was all news to me. "Brotherhood contingent?"

"Yes." Cashiel perched on the edge of the chair opposite me to make room for his massive wings. "The Brotherhood is divided into several contingents dispersed across the world. Some have specific duties to perform. Others are merely nothing more than guards intended to keep humans' guardian angels safe. Kincade, though, was special. As a general, he led a task force to hunt down high lords killing the guardian angels. When he discovered Azriel had chosen you as one of his targets, he decided he was better served leaving the Brotherhood to protect you."

I had no words for how much I was touched by this. Azriel was the mortal enemy for both of us. He wanted him dead as much as I did. The fact he decided to relinquish his general title and his task force to become my guardian meant a lot to me.

"The Warden of Nine," my uncle continued, "do not like defectors. They see that as a disloyalty to everything the Brotherhood of Watchers stands for. No matter the reason for their defection. However, they especially do not like when Watchers such as Kincade develop affectionate feelings for a human. It goes against all they stand for because they must remain celibate."

I stared at him as though he'd lost his mind. "Kincade and I are friends. Nothing more."

Because if I said the real thing out loud—what he'd become to me—I'd have to admit how much power the Brotherhood already had over my heart.

If that wasn't the biggest lie I told all day, I didn't know what was. And I hated myself a little for making it sound small. Thankfully, my uncle/Cashiel didn't have the internal lie detector Kincade did. There was no denying those affectionate feelings I had for Kincade even though I wanted to push them away. The kiss we shared in the forest flooded my traitorous mind no matter how much I wanted to forget it.

However, my uncle's expression said it all.

"I mean it," I said, more emphatically. "There's nothing between us."

He cleared his throat. "Even if that's true," and then paused, one dark brow lifting in suspicion, "the Warden of Nine will not see it that way."

A cold, dark fear skittered up the back of my spine. "Are you telling me they will punish Kincade because of me?"

A somber look flickered over his face as he nodded.

My shoulders slumped as my heart kicked into a wild beat. "I have to go to the Warden of Nine and plead his case."

"Do you think that's wise, Anna? They already have an opinion of you."

My gut clenched. "I have to try, dammit." I met his gaze, then. "When you were alive, uncle, you did everything in your power to push us together. Now, you want me to abandon him?"

"Getting to him will be difficult. These men are, shall we say, old school. They do not take kindly to women in positions of power. To them, you are a woman in a position of power."

I almost snorted but managed to keep it contained. "I'm not."

"You *are*. You are the Keeper of the Holy Relics. The one chosen by a higher power than them to bring light back into the darkness," he insisted.

I placed the highball glass on the coffee table in front of me. "Then I have to go."

A beat of silence passed between us as a small smile spread over his lips. "Yes, you do." He got to his feet then. "And I'm going to take you."

My brows drew together. "How do you propose to do that, uncle?"

"Cashiel," he corrected.

I waved that away. "I know your angel name, but as I told you before, you are still my uncle. Angel or not."

"I can't take you to the castle, but I can get you into the province of Hatay at least. I think."

"You think?" I lifted an eyebrow in question.

"I'm rather new at this." He gave me a ghost of a smile.

Did I trust him? How could I not? He was my uncle, after all. My only blood family for the longest time. "All right. And then what?"

"And then you'll be on your own. I cannot come with you."

"Ophelia wanted to come with me. She and Kincade worked together. She'll be displeased if I leave without her."

"She'll get over it."

I almost laughed at his uncharacteristic retort. "She will, eh? All right then. What's your plan?"

He waved me toward him. "Remember how Darius traveled with you? By flashing?"

I frowned. "Yes, and it made me want to puke."

"It's the only way, dearie."

I took a step toward him, then. "Great. Just don't get upset if I hurl on you."

His arm wrapped around my waist. My heart clawed its way to my throat as I hugged him close. And then the world disappeared beneath my feet.

CHAPTER 7

WE LANDED WITH LESS grace than I was used to. Darius was excellent at landing exactly where he intended. My uncle, however, not so much. In fact, we hit pavement. My knees buckled and down I went, crumpling on the concrete. Cashiel grunted as he released me, stumbled a few steps, but managed to keep his footing.

"Are you all right?"

He stood next to me, concern in his voice. I groaned as the nausea overtook me. My stomach cramped and seconds later I dry heaved.

"Anna?"

"One...minute..." I gasped the words as I tried to force back the illness.

There was something about surging through the air with an angel that made me sick to my stomach. I didn't have an explanation for it. Since I was huddled against a sidewalk, I guessed we hadn't made it to the ruins of the castle in Hatay, Turkey.

"Where are we?" I croaked.

"By the looks of the things...Hong Kong."

My head snapped up. Sure enough, I recognized the lights of the city as the sun set in the west. I shoved up to my feet despite the urge to vomit, clamping my lips together. I glanced at my uncle, whose snowy white wings threaded with gold spanned behind him for all to see. Passersby on the street gave him odd sideway glances.

"Uh, uncle, your wings are showing."

He craned his neck to peer over his shoulder to see if I was telling the truth. As he did so, I caught sight of pedestrians staring as they walked by. Gaping at his very large wings, looking him up and down. One person stopped to snap a photo with her cell phone.

"You're drawing attention. Maybe you should hide those things."

"I don't quite know how to do that yet."

He sounded sheepish which somewhat amused me. To me, my uncle was perfection. He always had a plan, how to complete that plan with flawless execution while never blinking an eyelash or ruining his suit in the process.

"Then we need to get off the street."

I reached for his arm and pulled him along behind me. I knew exactly where to go. When I was first in Hong Kong, my uncle had set up an apartment for me near Victoria Habour. It took several minutes to figure out where I was in the city and, I realized with some relief, we weren't far from the apartment. I dragged him along behind me, my mind quickly working how to get into that apartment since I had no keys with me.

But the longer we were on the street, the more attention we garnered. People paused and gawked at him. A couple passed us, openly staring. I flashed her a bright smile.

"Cosplay," I said and thumbed over my shoulder. "He's good, huh? He's award winning!"

The woman laughed and nodded.

"Anna, what are you doing?" Cashiel said as I pulled him along.

"Just be quiet and play along. Pretend you're in costume."

"But—"

"Do as I say, okay?"

He didn't argue further. Instead, he pulled at the collar of his button-down shirt. "I can't wait to get out of this costume."

He said it loud enough for those on the street staring and snapping photos to hear. I nodded and flashed them all a bright smile.

But as I looked around the crowd, I noticed something disturbing. When I was last in Hong Kong, humans had their guardian angels following along closely. Now, not so much. There weren't as many as there had been before and that was somewhat worrisome.

I hadn't been back since Kincade was in the hospital here when the bomb exploded next to him. Since Azriel tried to kill us both when I was searching for the Horn of Gabriel. I did wonder, though, how we ended up here instead of Turkey but I'd question Cashiel about that later.

I tried to ignore the stares as my uncle and I hurried down the street. Some people openly pointed at Cashiel and his giant, perfect wings. I pretended I didn't notice as I pulled him along to the high-rise. Inside the lobby, more stares. One kid's eyes were as wide as saucers. I wanted to stop and explain but instead, I pulled Cashiel along to the elevators and punched the up button with more force than necessary.

Finally, it dinged and the doors swooshed open. A couple and a young girl stepped out. All three of them gave me a cursory glance but then stared hard at my uncle. I flashed a bright smile and tugged him into the elevator, jabbing the number twenty-one button over and over until the doors finally slid closed.

I leaned against the wall and exhaled a heated breath.

"You really need to figure out how to hide those things behind a glamor or something."

"I am aware of the stares, you know."

I said nothing more as the doors opened on the twenty-first floor. We hurried down the hall to apartment number 2124 before anyone decided to make an appearance.

I paused at the door, staring at it as if willing it to open.

"You don't have keys?" he asked.

I cast him an annoyed glance. He rolled his eyes—something I had never seen in my life. I was momentarily taken aback by that as I gaped at him. He disappeared in a puff. A second later, the lock clicked and he pulled open the door. He stepped aside to allow my entrance.

It was exactly how I recalled. Sleek, ultra-modern, very European with marble floors, a small but functional kitchen opening into a large living room with floor to cciling windows and a view of Victoria Harbour. The lights from the port and surrounding city flooded through the windows illuminating the place in an eerie bluish glow. Just as I remembered.

I moved to the edge of the room and picked up the remote to the electronic shades, pushing the button to close them. We didn't need any more attention than we already had. Behind me, Cashiel flicked on a lamp, flooding the room with a pale-yellow glow. I stood a moment, staring through the opaque shades at the flickering lights of the harbor. In the distance, I made out a boat crossing the water.

"Why are we in Hong Kong?" I asked.

"I cannot answer that."

I spun to face him. "Maybe you figure that out. We're supposed to be in Turkey."

He spread his hands as if in surrender. "I realize that. However, my powers of... movement...aren't as advanced as Darius'."

I turned back to the window watching the watery shapes and the flickering lights. "I never thought I would be back here. Isobel came here to warn me about the Spear of Destiny. I slammed the door in her face."

Remembering that sent a flicker of guilt and regret through me. At the time, I didn't know she was my cousin, nor did I realize her husband—a dream walker like me—was searching for the Spear of Destiny and was killed by Azriel.

"She didn't tell me she was my cousin," I continued.

"I sense your guilt. There is no need for that," Cashiel said. "You were wary of her, which is understandable under the circumstances you were in."

I'd been through a lot then. Kincade was in the hospital after a car bomb exploded on the street near him. At the time, I was trying to understand my feelings for him which were far from warm and fuzzy. He'd followed me from Dallas to England to Hong Kong, hot on my trail. I did everything in my power to push him away.

And now, as I stood there looking at the pale lights thinking of him, my gut twisted at the thought of something terrible happening to him. Because of me.

"I need to figure out how to get to Turkey," I said.

"Not tonight. Tonight, you rest."

"But, Kincade—"

"He will be fine." I started to object again when he said, "You need rest, Anna."

I clenched my jaw and stole a glance to the one bedroom. "Are you going to hang out here while I sleep?"

"I will do what is necessary to help you find your way to the Warden of Nine."

That sounded ominous. I started to ask him how he intended to do that but he put a hand up to stop me. "Go sleep, Anna."

When he said that, I had a hard time stopping the yawn that wanted to split my head in two. I nodded, turned and padded off to the bedroom. It was small. The king size bed dominated the entire room. A bedside table was on one side with a digital clock glowing the time in green numbers and a lamp. A bureau was across from the bed. I kicked off my shoes, shoved back the coverlet and slipped between the sheets, still fully dressed. I curled around the pillow and instantly fell asleep.

* * *

I was so exhausted, I failed to put up my mental walls before falling asleep. I was instantly in the dream, walking through a world I didn't understand. There was darkness on one side. Light on the other.

In the darkness, shadows fluttered about bouncing against the light as if trying to find their way out. Negative emotions permeated the air coming from that side as though it had a life of its own. Fear, anguish, and despair.

The light was nothing more than bright white beams streaming down as though through big puffy clouds. I saw nothing and no one in the light but I sensed movement. In direct contrast from the dark, there was a sense of love, peace, and serenity.

And here I was stuck in the middle between them.

The light shines in the darkness, and the darkness does not comprehend it.

It was a calm voice that said the words in my head. A voice I sensed coming from the light.

"Who are you?"

Do you not understand? I am who I Am.

My heart rammed hard against my chest as I stood there, my hands balled into fists. I glanced from dark to light. I thought I understood who the voice was in my head, but deep down I was in denial.

You know who I am, Annabelle.

Gooseflesh rose on my arms at the sound of my given name. A name I had only been called by very few in my life. A name that was also my mother's.

Something caught my attention in the darkness. Shadowy movement beckoning me. I took a step toward it, sensing an amalgam of hate and anger. Sensing those who were, perhaps, trapped in Lucifer's web. Those who wanted to draw me in with them.

You cannot save them all. There are those who will turn away from the light. From you.

I turned away from the gloom and focused instead on the beams of light, peering into them as I tried to understand the message I was given.

"Where are you?"

I am everywhere and everything.

In the distance, I heard a voice calling me, muffled and almost incomprehensible.

"Anna, wake up!"

My uncle's voice was louder this time as someone shook me. I peeled my eyes open to see him, or rather Cashiel, standing over me with panic written all over his face. His white wings spanned out behind him.

"We have to go. Now."

My foggy mind had trouble comprehending. "What's going on?"

"We're under attack." He ripped the blankets away from me.

I leaped into action, the dream forgotten, disoriented as I tried to figure out where the hell my shoes were. A pounding sounded on the door of the apartment. In one fluid motion, I wielded both the flaming sword and my dagger. Without missing a beat, I handed off the flaming sword to Cashiel, which seemed the most natural thing to do.

He took it, grasped it between both hands and planted his feet shoulder width apart as though he really were still Edward and nothing was amiss.

And suddenly a sharp pang of sadness hit me right in the breastbone. It was as if nothing had ever changed and he was still Edward.

But he wasn't. My rational mind realized this. Especially with the span of his giant snowy wings threaded with gold.

"Here they come."

"Who?" I whispered, trying to ignore the fear shifting through me.

Just then, the door cracked open, splintering the wood as it split and then I sensed them. One, two. No, three. Three of them emerging into the apartment and heading straight for us. Cashiel held his sword aloft. I clutched the dagger in my sweaty palm, waiting, holding my breath.

The woman stepped into the doorway of the bedroom, her long dark hair flowing over her shoulders and her eyes glowing with a strange light I didn't understand. She smiled at me and lifted one hand toward me as though reaching for me.

The punch hit me with such a force I cried out. My knees buckled and then I was on the ground as everything turned black. The dagger clattered to the floor somewhere to my right but I was in too much pain to reach for it. I curled into a ball as I understood what was happening to me. Because it had happened before with my biological mother when she was in Antarctica and under control of the Knights of the Holy Lance.

This woman was like my mother—a super dream walker. A woman who had the ability to kill with her mind. And she was there, in my mind, whispering her death threat.

You will die now.

My gut twisted as the pain overwhelmed me.

I sensed movement in front of me, the flickering of the light.

"Get away from her, *you bitch*."

That voice...was my uncle?

I lifted my head but only saw a blur of images as blood clouded my vision. The light from his sword as he waved it back and forth. And then she released me. I curled in on myself, drawing my knees to my chest. In my haze, there was a commotion I didn't understand. The shuffle of feet. Glass breaking. Wood splintering. Voices grunting and crying out. And then silence followed by footsteps.

"Anna, are you all right?"

My uncle pulled me into his arms and pushed my hair away from my face. I blinked my eyes, trying to clear them. He swiped his thumb under one eye and then the next.

"What happened?" I croaked.

"You were attacked. We have to leave here as soon as possible."

I groaned. "By...who?"

"The Holy Lance super dream walkers. Can you move at all?"

I closed my eyes again, the pain pounding in my skull. These super dream walkers were created by that fucking crazy scientist in Antarctica used my who mother's DNA as a prototype to create these women. He also used nanites implanted in their brains to control them and make them into his own super army of death. It was unnatural. I understood that as much as I understood my mother should have been the only one of her kind.

"We...have to find them. And destroy them."

"Now isn't the time for that, Anna."

Cashiel put his hands under my arms and tried to lift me to my feet but I refused. I went limp, releasing all my weight. My vision was still cloudy from the blood that had leaked from the corners. I swiped my hand over them to clear my sight.

My angelic uncle looked down at me with those familiar blue eyes and that look of pure disdain and disappointment that oddly gave me comfort.

"We have to, uncle."

"Anna..."

He said my name in that breathy, annoyed way of his that was so much like Edward hot tears sprang to my eyes.

"They must be destroyed."

He patted my shoulder. "And they will be but you and I have other priorities."

I thought of Kincade, nodded, and shoved upward to a sitting position. Everything hurt from the top of my head to the bottom of my feet. My teeth ached. "Kincade."

He helped me to my feet. I wobbled, trying to keep my balance. He handed me my pink combat boots that were as much a part of my demon killing uniform as my dagger.

"This place is no longer safe. They know we're here. My guess is they will come after us again."

I perched on the edge of the bed as I stuck my feet in my boots. "How did they find us in the first place?"

He remained silent as I tied my boots. I glanced up at him and saw the remorse flicker over his face.

"I think it was my fault." He spread his hands as if in surrender.

I straightened despite the pain lancing through my beat-up body. "Yours?"

His wings fluttered with his agitated embarrassment. "I somehow got their attention when we fell through time and space."

I lifted an eyebrow. "How did you manage that?"

"As I said, my skills are not as advanced as others. I should not have attempted to bring you here."

"Yet here we are." I folded my arms across my chest.

"In our flight here, I saw flashes of things. Places we've been. People we've seen. These women...these dream walkers...have been looking for you and your mother since she deserted them in Istanbul."

I pressed my lips together, my jaw clenched. "What do they want?"

"You. Her. The Spear of Destiny. It's unclear. But what *is* clear is that we have to go now."

I sighed. "Where? How? We can't exactly board a commercial flight with you..." I paused, waved my hands at the span of his wings. "At least until you figure out how to hide those wings."

"I do understand that. Therefore, I have called in reinforce-ments. But you have to come with me now, Anna."

I reached down and picked up my discarded dagger from the floor, then hid it once again in the cloud. I waved him toward the door.

"I'm following you."

And so, we left behind the apartment in Hong Kong.

CHAPTER 8

I STUMBLED ALONG BEHIND Cashiel. My eyesight finally cleared. It was then I saw the destruction of the apartment. Windows shattered. The front door splintered and the pieces littering the floor. Furniture was overturned and broken. My feet crunched on the debris as we headed out of the door into the hallway.

A few people stood outside their own apartments, staring down toward mine. And when they saw my uncle and his glorious wings, they stared even harder. One woman wept and fell to her knees. A man openly gaped. A little boy, sucking his thumb, peered up at my uncle as he passed by, his eyes wide and full of wonder.

I was going to have to do some damage control.

"Nothing to see here. Back to your apartments."

I waved my hands to shoo them back inside. A few obeyed. Others, though, continued to stand in the hallway and gawk.

The elevator dinged at the other end of the hall. We both halted and watched as the doors slid open and two women emerged. Both wearing the black catsuit I had come to associate with the super dream walker killer bitches.

Fuck all.

Cashiel drew down the flaming sword and halted in the middle of the hall in attack mode.

"Get behind me," he demanded.

"Screw that." I pulled down the dagger, ready to do battle.

"Now is not the time for bravery."

I didn't have a chance to respond when they both targeted me with their minds. I cried out with the sharp pain and stumbled backward doing my best to clutch the jade handle of the dagger in my sweating palm. I heard a gasp somewhere nearby. Then a door slammed.

I hoped that meant the onlookers returned to their homes in a hurry. My eyes filled once again with bloody tears. My gut clenched as my knees gave out and I crumbled to the floor, dropping the dagger once again. It thumped against the carpet as I groaned, feeling around trying to find it. The pain, though, was all consuming as I crumpled to my side.

Then I smelled the demons. The swish of fire fluttered through the air and moments later I whiffed the acrid scent of death.

Well, well. Look who we have here.

The voice floated through my nearly destroyed mind. I was powerless to resist her. A hand slipped around the base of my skull and turned my face up toward hers. She was a devasting beauty with the most angelic face I'd ever seen. Her hair tumbled in auburn waves over her shoulders as she peered down at me with luminous blue eyes, I was sure had the sparkle of starlight in them.

We've been looking for you, Anna.

Someone I couldn't see hoisted me to my feet and dragged me away, my legs useless. The heels of my boots slid across the carpet with a scraping sound. Blood still caked my eyes. I blinked furiously, trying to clear them since I seemed to be paralyzed and controlled by whoever had me.

In my haze, Cashiel spun to face us as we headed down the hallway toward the stairwell. He still held the flaming sword. Somewhere behind him were dead demons that were likely used as a distraction for these bitches to incapacitate and kidnap me. It was going to be a long way with them dragging me and I wasn't sure how that was going to go down.

"Let her go," Cashiel ordered in a booming voice I had no idea he possessed.

Gooseflesh bloomed on my arms.

"Not a chance," one of the women said.

"Stand aside, angel."

"Never," he replied.

Somewhere to my left, the crashing sound of a door and then a high-pitched scream.

"Take care of him!" the one dragging me ordered. Then she said to someone else, "Help me, you imbecile."

Perhaps she was the one in charge. Which meant there had to be at least three more super dream walkers. Another person picked up my legs, taking up the rest of my weight. My head lolled to one side. We were in an apartment and headed for...the balcony?

"Open the door," the head bitch said. "Now!"

Whoever she spoke to complied and then we were on the balcony. I heard a distinctive *whomp whomp* of helicopter blades. My heart immediately clawed its way to my throat. I'd lost sight of Cashiel. I'd lost my jade-handled dagger. And, in a minute, we were going to somehow board that chopper hovering outside the balcony.

"Take her," head bitch said.

The one holding my legs dropped them and then I was on the floor of a plushy carpet that smelled as though it was brand new. My hand fisted in the thick shag fibers and I wondered, in my foggy irrational mind, who the hell still had shag carpet?

Strong arms hoisted me up, cradling me against a thick chest. I turned my head to look up into the face of a man who grinned down at me with a ferocious smile. Every nerve ending stood on end and my senses went on high alert. He reminded me of Abaddon, the destroy angel who had tried to kidnap me and bring me into the dark on more than one occasion. My entire body was paralyzed from the neck down. I was powerless to resist him or fight back. He carried me to the edge of the balcony.

Out of the periphery of my vision, I saw the rope ladder and wondered how the hell he was going to scamper up it carrying me. I didn't have to wait long for an answer because he didn't use the rope ladder. Instead, he used his powerful legs to push off the balcony and literally jump up to the edge of the helicopter.

He placed me into one of the seats as gently as he could and then buckled me in. A moment later, the super dream walker women followed up the rope ladder. The last one in pulled it up and away we went.

The one with auburn waves leaned over me, a wicked smile on her beautiful face.

"This won't hurt a bit."

A jab in my upper arm. Something cold flushed through my veins and a moment later, I was out.

CHAPTER 9

SEBASTIAN LED KINCADE, HANDS bound with zip ties, deep in the province of Hatay, Turkey, under the ruins of Bagras Castle. Once, long ago, the castle was a formidable fortress. Today, it was nothing but a ramshackle castle tourists flocked to see the remnants of the Knights Templar.

Kincade, though, recalled a time when the castle had walls that were intact and was inhabited by knights. When the world was a much different place. When they tried to spread Christianity across the land and convert the Moors. He was alive for all of it. He witnessed the First Crusade. He remembered Hugh de Payens as a man of great conviction. A man who did everything in his power to make sure the pilgrims from England had safe passage across the Holy Land.

He didn't know why those thoughts had come to the forefront of his mind now when it didn't seem to matter. Now when Sebastian led him to certain doom.

They hadn't spoken since he came to England and removed him from Walker Manor. The way Anna held his hand so tight as though she refused to let him go still burned in his memory, hot and bright.

He tried to forget the way her fingers had locked around his. The look in her eyes. The promise he'd made.

He failed.

And her last words haunted him.

I can't do this without you.

Part of him wanted to deny she meant that. But the other part of him...the part that warred inside him at the thought of losing her forever...it wanted to remind him why he did what he did in the first place.

Why he gave up his place in the Watchers.

It was for her.

Always for her.

His decision to leave the Watchers was almost immediate from the first moment he met her in Dallas at that hospital. From the first moment when he realized who and what she was. That moment when he understood she wasn't a killer, but she was the one...one of the Most High's chosen. The one who would lead all of them out of darkness.

And he realized at the moment, when he saw her exiting the hospital wearing scrubs and a weary look on her pretty face, he had to help her. He had to leave the Brotherhood to become her guardian. He had to be the one to help her lead them out of darkness.

It was a conscious decision.

He didn't regret it. Not one bit.

His mistake was refusing to tell Sebastian or anyone his decision. He merely left the Brotherhood without a word to anyone. He refused to report back. He refused to allow them to control his days one more minute.

Yet even though he never told anyone, Edward Walker somehow knew and understood. Edward Walker silently encouraged him to stick close to Anna. Everything cemented into place when she insisted on saving his life, his very soul, from Azriel. From saving him from becoming a Fallen High Lord.

Of course, the outcome with the Brotherhood would not have been any different. He would still face a trial by the Warden of Nine. He would have preferred it to be on his own terms, though.

Marcus, now Azriel, did not face the Warden of Nine since he willingly fell from grace.

Now, as they walked down into the belly of the castle, into the underground, he realized Sebastian's silence was anger, resentment, jealousy and perhaps a little fear.

Was Sebastian afraid of Anna and her power? That she finally fully embraced who and what she was?

He looked over the man who had once been his superior, his mentor, his most trusted advisor, and suppressed the urge to scoff.

Kincade believed Sebastian removed him from Walker Manor, from Anna's life, from his duty as her guardian *because* he feared her.

He understood so much more now.

"You fear her." His voice boomed in the silence of the underground castle.

Sebastian halted, his footsteps scraping along the path and turned to face him. Firelight from the torches lining the wall flickered over his face as he peered at him with a frown.

"Fear isn't the problem."

Kincade suppressed a laugh. "So, what, you hold her in high esteem?"

"I do."

He was no longer able to hold back the laugh. "Lie."

It was one of his favorite powers—knowing when others lied. Some were harder to read than others. Sebastian, for one. He was a master at masking his emotions and thoughts. Anna, on the other hand, was an open book. She wasn't one to hide her facial expressions and often wore her heart on her sleeve, something she would never admit. She was probably the most expressive woman he'd ever met.

Sebastian's jaw clenched as he pressed his lips together. "Do not use your lie detector on me."

"Too late." He smirked.

"She is nothing!" Sebastian slashed his hand through the air, as though slashing through something or someone in his imagination.

"She's the One Who Was Promised. Even you cannot deny that."

The man faced him and stepped a little closer. So close, Kincade saw the ire flickering through the depths of his eyes. He understood, then, the fear and hatred he had for Anna ran deep. He also understood his former superior would do everything within his power to keep them apart. And for the first time in a very long time, a flicker of fear skittered through him.

What was Sebastian willing to do to keep them apart? What was he willing to sacrifice? And why did he fear her so much?

"She is a destabilizing force. And destabilization is how orders fall."

His brows drew together. "The Brotherhood of Watchers has no jurisdiction over her. She's the Keeper of Holy Relics. She's been chosen—"

"I know who she is. I don't need to be reminded."

"She was *born* to be the Keeper," Kincade continued. "We both know who her parents are. We both know her father—"

"Enough." Fire flashed in his eyes as he stared Kincade down. "Her father must face his own consequences."

"You cannot control her. Or him," Kincade said.

"No. But I can make you useful."

Sebastian wrapped his hand around his bound wrists and dragged him through the tunnel, heading for the underground prison. Kincade recognized the long, dark, dank hallway lined with torches. He would be thrown in a cell until the Warden of Nine were ready to interrogate him.

Fine. He'd been in worst predicaments. He'd face this with all the grace within him.

And he would survive.

Because he had to.

He had to get back to Anna.

They paused at the first cell. Even today, it resembled a medieval prison with iron bars. Sebastian opened the door and shoved him inside. Kincade turned to him, holding out his bound wrists. Sebastian slammed the door in response.

"So that's it? You're going to leave me here with bound wrists?" Kincade asked.

"I'm going to leave you here until *they* decide what example you'll serve."

He said nothing else as he walked away. The only sound was that of his receding footsteps.

And Kincade was left alone with plastic zip ties cutting into his skin.

It didn't matter what Sebastian and the Warden of Nine did to him. He would find his way back to Anna. Together, they would search for the Ark of the Covenant.

And then the real battle would begin—one the Brotherhood would not survive intact.

"Hello, brother."

Kincade's head snapped up as he peered through the shadows. Across from him was another cell and deep in the gloom was a face he hadn't seen in quite some time. Obsidian eyes stared back at him as he sat against the wall with one knee up, his forearm casually resting there. Kincade moved to stand in front of the bars.

"Decker." He was the last person he expected to see in this horrible place.

"Sebastian got to you, too, eh?"

"Where have you been?"

"Causing trouble." He gave a cocked grin.

Decker hadn't been the same since Istanbul. Anna told him what happened to him—that the Knights of the Holy Lance had captured him, branded the bottom of his foot. The brand eradicated his abilities—invisibility and teleportation. Most of his brethren in the Brotherhood had powers. In addition to his lie detector, Kincade's was dream walking and the ability to move with a quick speed without his enemy knowing it.

"Sebastian captured me in Croatia," Decker said. "Things aren't looking too good for us, brother."

"Why do you say that?" Kincade asked.

"Because Sebastian has called in the Warden of Nine to prosecute us for all our wrong-doings."

"You left the Brotherhood, too, then?"

"Did I have a choice?" Bitterness laced his words.

He and Kincade hadn't talked about what had happened to him. They didn't have to. But Kincade understood. Having that part of himself taken away must have been difficult to accept.

"I wasn't any good to them anymore," Decker said.

"I have to get back to Anna," Kincade said.

"He's not going to let you go so easily, you know."

"I *will* get out of here. We both will."

Decker snorted derision. "I don't think so."

"You can help us—"

"No," Decker snapped. Even from the distance, Kincade felt the heat from that one word.

"My time is over. *Our* time is over, Kincade. The Brotherhood isn't one thing anymore. It's factions. Old vows versus new rules. And Sebastian's winning—because he's not pretending this is about justice."

His brows knit. "What do you mean?"

"You've been preoccupied with that woman—"

"She's the Keeper of the Holy Relics and—"

"It doesn't matter to me who she is," Decker interrupted. "While you've been globetrotting with her, the Brotherhood is falling apart. Sebastian leads the charge and the Warden of Nine are quite happy to punish those they feel have betrayed them. That's why I stayed away. Why I left. Maybe you were smart to get out while you could."

"Yet here we are."

He huffed a laugh. "Yeah. Here we are."

"What are they planning to do?" Kincade asked.

Decker shrugged a shoulder. "Question us. Torture us. Execute us. Their choice."

The Warden of Nine had a cruel streak. They would stop at nothing to punish those who left the Brotherhood and branding them traitors. Kincade never thought he'd end up facing them, though. Even though he broke their oaths. Once in the Brotherhood, it was for life. And they meant it.

"Are you sure?" he asked.

"You doubt me?" Decker retorted. "Why else would we be here?" He waved his hand to encompass the cell.

He had a point. But even so, Kincade had doubts.

They spoke no more. He had to find Anna, to see where she was. If he knew her, and he did, she would get some hair-brained idea to come after him. He didn't want her here. It was too dangerous.

He slid down the wall and leaned against the cold stone, closing his eyes. He whispered her name as he formed the image of her face in his mind. The way her hair smelled after a shower. How tight she held onto his hand when Sebastian came to take him back to the Warden of Nine. Her expressive, beautiful face. Those big, bright purple eyes that mesmerized him. How she drove him so crazy he didn't know if he wanted to punch her or kiss her.

Sometimes both.

He searched for her there in his lucid dream, hoping to find her. Moments later, he did.

CHAPTER 10

I HATED BEING UNCONSCIOUS. I hated more waking up from being unconscious. Especially with a raging headache. I laid on a soft bed but my wrists and ankles were restrained against the bed. I twisted my hand to see how tight the bindings were and discovered I had no range of movement. Even worse, I had an IV stuck in one arm and realized with some dismay I was no longer in my own clothes but a cloth hospital gown.

Son of a bitch shit fuck.

I kept my eyes closed as I listened to the sounds around me trying to discern where I was. The only sound was a buzzing overhead which I assumed was fluorescent lights and the hum of some type of machinery. Perhaps an HVAC system.

I had a really bad feeling about this.

A swish of a door opened and then closed. Footsteps neared the bed.

"Wake her," a man said.

Before anyone injected anything into me again, my eyes popped open. A man stood to my left. A woman to my right. The same woman with the wavy auburn hair who abducted me.

The man was tall with dark eyes, black hair and a smooth olive complexion. A smile that didn't reach his eyes creased his mouth. He wore a white lab coat over a button-down shirt. The name Mueller was embroidered in blue over the left breast pocket. A stethoscope was around his neck, the earpieces on one side, the chest piece on the other.

Yep. A really bad feeling for sure.

"Hello, Anna."

"Who the fuck are you?" I was never one to mince words.

The woman wrapped a blood pressure cuff around my upper arm and began pumping it. He continued to smile as he took the stethoscope from around his neck and placed the diaphragm against my arm to listen as the women released the pressure allowing my pulse to pound against it.

"One-twenty over eighty. Perfect." He removed the earpieces and slung the stethoscope over his neck once again as the woman removed the cuff.

It was good to know my stressful situation had no effect on my blood pressure.

"What do you want?" I asked.

"I think you know."

The woman wrapped a tourniquet around my upper arm—the one without the IV. The doctor used two of his fingers to press against the bend of my elbow looking for my veins. I understood with a distinct and terrible horror what came next. I'd done enough blood draws as a phlebotomist to realize what was happening.

A prick of the needle followed by the release of the tourniquet. And then I watched in sickening dread as they took four vials of my blood. Neither of them said another word as they took the vials and left the room, leaving me alone once again.

"Fuck," I whispered under my breath.

My mind raced as I thought of ways to escape this horrible imprisonment. I twisted against the bindings on my wrists, but they held firm. Likewise the ones on my ankles. My gut cramped as I thought of all the horrible things they'd do with those vials of my blood.

And I thought again of the vials of blood labeled WALKER I found in the lab in Antarctica. The ones I was sure were my mother's DNA. The ones I was also sure were used to create the super dream walkers who managed to capture me.

Double fuck.

I was so screwed.

There was no doubt in my mind this Mueller guy was going to use my blood, my DNA, to make more super dream walkers. That they would be able to enter minds like my mother and use their powers to control and to kill.

I had to stop him.

But how?

I was currently trapped with no way out.

Or was I?

I paused to think through how to use the lightning fingers. I closed my eyes and thought of it encircling my fingers. I closed my hand into a fist feeling the first tingle of sparks fluttering against my palm. I opened my fingers one by one on my right hand and watched the bolt of light soar toward the ceiling. Elation punched through me.

A moment later, the door burst open and the next thing I knew the auburn-haired woman was at the IV bag. I jerked to one side, the bolts of light cascading in a violent arc around the room. She pumped something into the IV. A coldness spread throughout my body and then I was out.

* * *

Darkness. Shadows. Destruction. A black ring of death. Fire in the air. Blood soaking the ground red and black. Dead men, women, angels, Fallen, demons. Across the gloomy plain, a lone figure stood.

Tall, broad-shouldered with a stance I recognized and admired. My breath caught in my throat.

I bolted into a run. He did, too. We both dodged dead bodies as we headed toward each other. I fell against him. He caught me in his strong arms. And there we stood amidst the carnage holding onto each other as though we were each other's anchor in the dream.

"How did you find me?" My words came out a roughened whisper.

"I'll always find you."

"Sebastian took you—"

"Yes. I'm all right."

I searched his green-gold eyes for something that told me otherwise but Kincade was good at masking his emotions.

"I'm coming after you," I said.

"No." He shook his head. "You can't. Don't." I started to protest but he added, "I mean that, Anna."

I huffed. "Remember when you told me not to come after you when Azriel took you?"

His jaw clenched. He remembered. "You don't listen."

"I listen very well, thanks. I *will* come for you. Besides, remember what happened the last time you told me not to come after you?"

"You traded the Spear of Destiny. The Warden of Nine aren't interested in Holy Relics, Anna." He clutched my arms tighter. "There's nothing you can do for me. My fate is sealed."

"Not if I have anything to say about it." Determination swelled through me even in the dream.

"You're in danger, aren't you?"

I stared at him long and hard choosing my words. How in the world did he know that? Did he sense it? "No, and don't change the subject."

"Lie. Now the truth."

I said nothing. How was it his lie detector worked in the dream? That was so not fair.

"Everything is fine." I did my best to sound reassuring.

"I don't believe you."

If there was anything I learned by now, it was that Kincade knew me better than I knew myself. Sometimes that was great. Other times, it really annoyed me. I huffed out a breath.

"I know you don't but you don't need to worry about me right now. I'll be fine."

He looked less than convinced. But I was certain I would be able to get myself out of my predicament. Perhaps my uncle would come to my aid once again, even if he was terrible at being an angel. He mentioned something about calling in reinforcements. I clung to that hope.

"I have to go."

He released me and disappeared with a suddenness that jarred me awake.

Darkness enveloped my mind as I returned to consciousness. There was nothing but dead silence and no more dreams. I peeled my eyes open and peered overhead at the round fluorescent light buzzing away. The only sound in the frigid room. My wrists were still bound but now with a cold biting metal. The IV was still in my arm.

"Awake again. Good." It was the man who stole my blood. Mueller. "I'm afraid we had to use iron shackles on your wrists to keep you from using your magic."

"Magic?" I blurted.

Did he think I was a witch? No, that was ridiculous.

Perhaps he thought I was Fae. Iron worked on suppressing the powers of the Fae, but not me. At least, I didn't think iron would suppress the lightning Ronan gave me. Or the Godlight residing deep inside me.

"Your DNA is remarkable," he said, ignoring my outburst. "I've never seen anything like it."

I heard movement then he appeared in my line of vision, blotting out the horrendous overhead light. He pulled up a chair and sat next to my bed. When he smiled, revulsion shifted through me.

"What do you want with my DNA?"

"The same thing I wanted with your mother's. Since we can't find her, you'll have to do."

A chill trickled through me. It was as I suspected. "Who are you?"

"I'm the scientist who figured out how to use your mother's DNA to create an army of super dream walkers." He paused. Smiled. "Just like her."

My gut clenched in terror. He was Schneider's scientist in Antarctica. When we were there, we found notes and a journal on all the experiments his scientist performed on the women to make them into someone as powerful as my mother. He figured out how to make the others like her by using the nanobots implanted in their neocortex to inject a drug derived from her blood into their brains.

I killed Schneider, leader of the Knights of the Holy Lance, in Istanbul. I hadn't considered the work his scientist was doing continued on even after his death.

I thought stealing the journal and the notes from Antarctica would stop them from creating more super dream walkers. I was naïve to think that would be the end of it. Dr. Mueller had copies of his notes. Maybe even had them stored electronically somewhere.

Somewhere like the lab in Antarctica.

And then something else struck me. Certainly, they hadn't brought me all the way back to the lab in Antarctica? And if they didn't, then where was I?

The last thing I remembered when they abducted me from the apartment building was boarding a helicopter.

Helicopters couldn't go that far. But then, I didn't know how long I was out. For all I knew, they took the helicopter to a local airport and loaded me onto a private jet.

"I see you have questions," he said. "Anything I can answer for you?"

I was beginning to hate that oily smile on his stupid face. "No."

"Pity. I was hoping to chat to get to know each other more."

"You can go fuck yourself."

Shock registered for a brief moment before he masked it with that disgusting smile again. The one I wanted to slap off his face.

"I don't need you to be pleasant to get what I want from you. Just compliant."

He rose, the chair legs scraping on the floor. He said nothing more as he walked away. A door swung shut, leaving me alone once again.

If he thought he was going to get away with stealing my DNA, making more super dream walkers and terrorizing the world, he was sadly mistaken. I had to find a way out.

I tried to twist my hands again in the shackles. All I got in return was burning pain and metal biting into my skin.

I closed my eyes, clenched my hands into fists, and envisioned the lightning Ronan gave me. The first flickers of it tickled my palms as it tried to come to life. I opened my left hand. Light shot out and immediately disappeared.

That didn't seem to work.

Then I recalled I had the ability to set Edward's sword aflame. And once I was able to light a fire in the fireplace back home with a ball of flames out of my hand.

Closing my eyes and hand once more, I imagined the ball of flame, the way it felt. The warmth of it. The flickering flames as they fluttered against my palms and yet didn't burn me.

I imaged the ball of fire in my hand as my fingers opened one by one. The heat of the flames danced in my palm. I opened my eyes to see the bright orange and yellow light there.

But it would have to be some serious heat to melt the iron shackles around my wrists. I wasn't certain the fire in my palm would do that without burning my wrists.

There had to be another way. Perhaps some way to combine the lightning with the flames with the Godlight. Kind of like a trifecta.

I closed my fingers around the ball of flame in one hand. In the other, the lightning came to life. Somewhere deep inside me was the glimmer of the Godlight as I tapped it and called it. Warmth spread across my breastbone as I thought of how the Godlight felt inside me when I used it to destroy demons and minions. It stirred deep in my breast, ready to explode.

I clutched my hands tight into fists to bring forth the most power possible in one shot.

And then the Godlight was ready to release. My back bowed as it pushed outward with such searing pain there was no way to stop the scream that erupted from my lungs. My hands flew open as lightning and flame collided with Godlight and suddenly a bright flash of orange, yellow, white, and blue flames filled the entire room with a furious eruption. It cascaded over me.

The scent of burning hair and charred skin and cotton filled the room. My wrists snapped free of their bindings and I bolted to a sitting position.

Sweat poured down my face, neck and back. My hands throbbed with horrible pain. My fingers and hands were bright red. My thin hospital gown smoked around the edges from being singed. Even though my bindings were free of the bed, the iron manacles were still firmly wrapped around my wrists.

I'd deal with that later.

My ankles were also freed but the iron shackles still circled them like my wrists.

I shoved off the edge of the bed. My bare feet landed on black and white linoleum. I jerked the IV out of my arm and then immediately regretted it as blood spurted and slipped down the crook of my arm. Several armed men burst into the room. The door banged against the wall with a loud thud. Dr. Mueller and the auburn-haired woman entered right behind them.

"You stupid girl!"

And then it was on.

CHAPTER 11

I HELD MY HANDS down, clenching my fingers into a fist. The lightning danced in my palm, the heat against my skin. The way it tickled reminded me of holding a baby lizard that squirmed, desperate to be released back into the wild. With a smile, I opened my hands and freed the bolts of light. Several of the armed guards went down, their chests smoking as they dropped the guns. The Godlight, too, swelled once again in my chest. A burning sensation was there in the middle of my breastbone.

More guards charged into the room. One crashed into me, tackling me against the bed. Two more were on me as I struggled against the first. They were bigger and stronger than me and manhandled me back into the bed. I wiggled against them but it was no use. Cloth restraints were back on my wrists and ankles in no time, tightening them to keep me immobile.

Sweat dampened the back of my neck as I struggled to get out of my bindings. Mueller appeared at the side of the bed. A crease formed between his brows as he looked down at me.

"Try that again and you will face dire consequences," he said.

"You aren't going to win. You—"

A jab in my arm. I'd forgotten about the bimbo and lost sight of her during the fray. Cold dread spread through me. Mueller leaned down close and lowered his voice to a whisper.

"I did not wish to keep you drugged, but it's clear I cannot trust you. This will keep your senses intact but paralyze you from the neck down."

Another jab in my other arm. The IV was back.

"And this..." Mueller pointed to the IV, "will keep you hydrated. We'll be back later."

He gave a nod to the guards in the room. They exited, leaving me alone once more.

* * *

I drifted in and out of consciousness. At times, I sensed the woman there drawing more blood, leaving me weak. I had no concept of time. Each time I drifted into sleep, I searched in the darkness for someone—my uncle, Kincade, anyone. But there was no one and nothing. I was adrift in a black shadowy sea of solitude.

Since I was paralyzed, I was unable to use the lightning in my hands. I was also unable to call up the Godlight. Whatever drug Mueller used rendered my body useless. I hadn't a clue as to how I was going to get out of this place without help. And I had no way to contact Cashiel. Now that he was an angel, he popped in and out at will. All angels seemed to be able to do that. They all showed up when I least expected it or needed them.

Why did they never appear when I needed them the most?

I was fairly good at self-preservation but not when I was restrained in a hospital bed.

The doors swung open then. Footsteps. Mueller appeared in my line of vision. I was still unable to move.

"We're going on a little field trip," he said and gave me that oily smile.

"Keep smiling, you bastard. I plan to punch you in the mouth as soon as I can."

He continued to grin but said nothing. He made a hand motion to someone behind him. Several orderlies came to the side of the bed. One grabbed the IV stand. They wheeled me out of the room. I saw nothing but the round fluorescent lights flashing by overhead. I hadn't a clue as to where they were taking me and, quite frankly, I was somewhat terrified of that.

I didn't want Mueller to know that, though. I tried hard to keep my facial expressions in check but I was as transparent as cellophane.

I heard the bang of double doors as they pushed them open and then wheeled me through. The medicinal smell of an operating room invaded my nose. I nearly gagged. I'd worked in a hospital for several years and I recognized the sterile smell. I hoped to never smell it again yet here I was.

I came to a halt. Mueller, still smiling, used the foot pedal to raise my bed to a sitting position. When he did, I got the lay of the land and realized I wasn't here to be operated on; I was here to watch.

There was a woman already being prepped for surgery. She was on the table, her body covered with a surgical gown. Her head was the only thing exposed.

"You see her here?" Mueller offered. "She volunteered for this. She trained for months to become stronger, faster than all the others. She went through several physical tests as well as mental ones to become part of the elite. And now, she will become like you. I wanted you to see and know for yourself how she came to be."

"She will never be like me, you monster." The words came out a raspy whisper.

He kept grinning. "We will see."

I watched in utter horror as they put her under and then proceeded with the surgery to her brain. Whatever drug Mueller injected me with continued to keep me immobilized. Every time I tried to close my eyes and refuse to see, Mueller would threaten me with ways to keep my eyes open.

So, I watched as my stomach churned acid while they cracked open her head and injected the blood-infused nanites—my blood. He used my DNA like he used my mother's to create this super dream walker. I prayed it wouldn't work, that somehow her body would reject the foreign objects. But she didn't. Hours later, when the surgery was complete and they closed her up, they wheeled her into recovery.

Meanwhile, I was left there alone with the medicinal scent, the blood, the sweat still permeating my nose.

I didn't know how much time passed when Mueller finally returned. He lowered the bed. Several orderlies pushed the bed out of the room along with the IV, taking me back down the hallway to my previous room.

"She's doing quite well," Mueller said as if making pleasant conversation. "I have no doubt she will make a fine soldier."

"I don't care," I said.

"You do care." He smirked.

"You know what? You're right. I do care. I care that you are playing with powers you cannot even begin to comprehend."

"I am creating a powerful force to lead the Knights of the Holy Lance back into the light," he said.

I almost snorted but managed to keep it at bay. "Without your leader?"

He tsked. "Schneider was a good leader. But there were others waiting to take his place. One has. You may have cut the head off the snake, but you didn't kill it."

We came to a halt inside my room.

"Then that was my mistake. I will destroy everything in this facility including you."

"You will never be able to destroy us."

He sounded confident about that as he left. He may think I wouldn't be able to destroy him, but he was wrong. He just issued me a challenge and I intended to take it on.

* * *

I drifted in and out of sleep. After some time, feeling came back in my extremities. I was no longer paralyzed from the neck down and relieved the drug had worn off. Now I had to convince the nurses coming to check on me I was still unable to move.

I held as still as possible when they came in to check my IV. My stomach growled with a fierce roar. I was aware they kept me hydrated and that was all. I hadn't been presented with any type of food since my arrival. I'd lost complete track of time and had no idea how long I'd been there. Days or weeks, I didn't know.

Where was Cashiel?

After the last nurse left, I wiggled my fingers. My wrists were still bound to the bed, but not with the metal shackles as before. Mueller must have decided I didn't pose much of a threat since I was drugged. Boy, was he wrong.

With movement in my fingers, I might have a chance to get out of my current hell. I needed to focus. Last time I tried it, I used all the power within me to release my bonds. But maybe I didn't need the Godlight, the lightning, and the fire within me.

I wiggled my fingers again, letting the lightning form and weave between my fingers. I craned my neck downward to get a look at my right hand to see the flicking of blue-white light. Since Ronan gifted me with his power, I hadn't really stopped to examine it. I knew what it did, but I hadn't examined the way it flickered against my skin.

Certainly, there was a way to control it and direct it to where I wanted it to go.

I cupped my fingers around the ball of light and lifted my palm upward toward the binding on my wrist. And then marveled at the way the light danced there. I *willed* it to dance up my arm and it did, flickering along my skin and skipping right over the material around my wrist.

I concentrated harder, turning my hand this way and that trying to control the flickering mini bolts of light. Trying to make it strike where I wanted it to strike. And then...a sizzle as one of the bolts struck the material around my wrist.

Progress!

But not enough progress. It didn't do much but singe the material, leaving a smoke trail behind and the stench of burned cotton.

When I failed to make further progress, I finally gave up on the lightning and relaxed my hand, my muscles aching from the exertion. I squeezed my palm shut, thinking about the flame to light my uncle's sword, and then let my fingers open one by one.

The flame snuffed out almost as quickly as it appeared in my palm.

That wasn't going to work either.

I sighed, angry and annoyed I was still trapped in this awful place.

In the distance of the building, there was a *rat-a-tat-tat* of gunfire. My heart immediately pounded against my chest, my senses on high alert. Someone was firing guns at someone else. And here I was nothing but a sitting duck. Damn it all.

The gunfire approached and got closer. My heart pounded harder. I wasn't going to sit here and be captured or—worse—killed. I closed my eyes and concentrated all of my power from within. I called up the Godlight, I closed my hands into fists and allowed the lightning to form in both palms. I pulled the power upward as much as I was able, letting it build and build and build.

And then released it.

I opened my hands, hoping the lightning would hit the bindings around my wrist. I released the Godlight into the room. It flashed bright and hot against my closed eyes.

I smelled the acrid scent of burned material.

When I opened my eyes, I had managed to weaken the material around my wrists. It was enough for me to give it a swift jerk and the bindings fell away. I sat up so fast, my head spun. Dark shadowy stars crossed my vision as dizziness swept through me. I groaned, putting a hand to my head but I didn't have time to waste. I shook my head to clear it, then reached down for the bindings on my ankles. They came free with simple Velcro attachments. How lame was that.

Moments later, I was free. I slid off the bed, my bare feet landing on the cold linoleum floor. I yanked the IV out of my arm once again. Blood seeped from the opening. The door burst open. Mueller and the auburn-haired woman with several guards entered, crowding the doorway.

"You trying to escape again? Oh, Anna," Mueller chastised.

Rage filled me and I charged. Without thinking, I punched him in the face as hard as I could. His head snapped back, his teeth clacking together as he stumbled backward a step or two. My hand exploded with pain but it was worth it. His nose spurted bright red blood. Everyone was so stunned by my actions, no one moved.

"I told you I'd punch you in the face, you rat bastard."

"Seize her! We have to move now!" he ordered.

Two guards shoved into the room. One grasped me with a vice-like grip around the upper arm. But I spun and punched him in the face, then spun again and kicked him in the chest with as much force as I could muster. Languishing in the hospital weakened me, not to mention the drugs they pumped into me.

I tapped into the Godlight deep inside my chest and released it as the second guard came at me. He turned into nothing more than a pile of ashes.

And that's when I realized they were not ordinary men. They were demons. I inhaled deeply to try to scent them and caught a faint whiff. The medicinal smell of the room masked their scent.

How very clever of Mueller. Too bad I didn't have my jade-handled dagger to do some real damage.

"Do not test me," I said to Mueller and his bimbo.

They were both wide-eyed as they gazed down at the pile of ash. But there were still two more guards pointing guns at me. I looked between them.

"Do you really want to meet the same fate?" I nodded toward the ashen remains. "Lower your weapons or I unleash more."

"More what?" Mueller asked. "What are you?" There was a quiver of fear in his voice.

"Something you could never comprehend." I gave him a bright smile. "You thought you were going to clone me, to make more super dream walkers like me. But the truth is, doc, there is no one else like me and there never will be."

It was in that moment, I truly grasped who and what I was. I had the power of two other dream walkers inside me—my uncle and Ronan. I had the dream walker power of my mother inside me. I had the Godlight power inside me which I assumed came from my father. Edward once told me my father was an angel. I believed him now more than ever.

I was unique and I was powerful.

In truth, I didn't want to kill Mueller. I merely wanted to destroy the lab and the contents of the lab, including my blood samples they'd stolen. My next target was going to be the lab in Antarctica.

Mueller squared his shoulders then, as if deciding he wasn't afraid of me. "Your uniqueness is exactly why I need you."

He snapped his head toward me indicating to the remaining guards to grab me. I instantly went into action. All those months of getting my ass kicked by first Gideon and Gilli and then Kincade paid off. I kicked, punched, and fought every single one of the guards who came at me. Sweat poured down the back of my neck as I fought them all barefoot in a hospital gown.

In the distance of the lab, there was more gunfire. The woman backed out of the room and stood in the hallway, peering down it with wide, terrified eyes.

"They're coming," she shouted.

When I dispatched the last guard, I turned to Mueller. My chest heaved from the exertion, the adrenaline rush pumped through me as my hands clenched, staring him down.

"You want to come at me next?"

"We are under attack," he said. "I came to take you with us."

"I'm not going anywhere with you."

I stood there, trying to come up with a plan, when a sudden explosion rocked the lab somewhere behind the doctor, the woman, and his guards. Mueller spun toward the hallway and shouted something in German. Footsteps pounded the hallway. Shouts and shots fired and screams of agony.

I backed away from the door until I ran into the bed on which I'd been imprisoned, my heart ramming hard. Mueller and his woman disappeared into the hallway. A moment later they backed into the room, hands in the air. The angel appeared in the doorway. His silvery white wings were so large he had to turn sideways to enter. He held a sword in one hand, pointing it at the two of them as they halted in the middle of the room. Two more angels entered behind him. One of them was Cashiel.

Relief sputtered through me at the sight of the three of them.

"Anna, are you all right?" Cashiel moved around the two angels to get a good look at me.

"I'm fine."

Cashiel turned to the angel holding the sword. "Zakiel, will you escort the doctor out of here? Ishim, take the woman."

Sword-wielding Zakiel ushered Mueller out of the room. Ishim took the auburn-haired woman by the arm and tugged her out behind him. Cashiel moved to stand in front me, looking me over from head to toe as if inspecting me for damage.

"How did you find me?" I asked. "And where the hell are we?"

"I told you I called for reinforcements, did I not?"

I thought back to the attack in Hong Kong and recalled that he did say something of the sort. I nodded.

"It took some time to find you, Anna."

"How long have I been here?" I demanded.

"Five days."

"Took you long enough."

He ignored my barb. "There are more warrior angels in the compound rounding up the guards."

"More warrior angels?" I repeated, dumbfounded. "Warrior angels like Darius?"

"Yes," he nodded. "Zakiel and Ishim led the charge here."

"What are they planning to do with the guards once they round them up?" I asked. "And you didn't answer my second question."

"We're in a warehouse in Taipei. They brought you here after kidnapping you in Hong Kong. I tracked them. I called for aid from Archangel Michael. He's the one who sent in the reinforcements."

I stared at my uncle as though he were a stranger. He may be a terrible angel with transporting from one place to the other, but he sure did have connections. Much like my uncle when he was alive.

Zakiel returned to the room.

"Where's Mueller?" I asked.

"Detained," Zakiel said in the deepest, most baritone voice I'd ever heard. It sent a thrilly little chill through me.

With him standing so close to me, I got a good look at him and was not disappointed. What was it about warrior angels? Was there a rule they had to be super-hot? He had the most dazzling eyes the color of nutmeg and auburn wavy hair. When the light caught it just right, red-gold strands shimmered in the light. Of course, like Darius, he had miles of muscles and magnificent wings.

Cashiel cleared his throat. "Anna, you're staring."

I hastily looked away and fixed my gaze on my uncle. "Was not."

"Come, we must make haste. We've imprisoned Mueller and the woman who calls herself Katrina. They will be dealt with later." Zakiel motioned for me to follow him.

"Not so fast," I said. "I have one more task to complete before I leave this place."

"Killing Mueller is not an option, Anna. I won't allow it," Cashiel snapped.

I huffed out a breath. "That's *not* what I was thinking. There's a lab here somewhere. I want to see it."

"There's no time for that. We must leave this place," Cashiel said.

"He is correct," Zakiel said. "I suspect that Mueller or one of his guards tripped an alarm. There will be others here soon."

"I don't care about that." I waved away their objections and met Cashiel's gaze. "Take me to the damn lab."

"Why?"

"You *know* why!" I snapped.

He was silent for a long moment and then understanding crossed his face. "They took your blood, didn't they?"

"Like they took my mother's—your sister's."

"And you plan to destroy it."

"Yes. And then I'm going to Antarctica to destroy that lab, too." I pushed him aside and exited the room.

It was a stark white hallway with harsh, bleak lighting. There were a few doors on either side. At the end, another hallway that either went left or right. I started down the hall for that dead end, intending to find my way to the lab since they didn't want to give up the location.

"Are you certain this is a good idea? The others are waiting out-side for us." Zakiel's concerned voice floated to me from behind.

"They can wait. Or go. I don't care. But I'm not leaving here until I stop this."

"Why must you?" the warrior angel asked, genuinely bewildered.

I halted, spun, and came nose to chest with him. I craned my neck to look up at him. "Because they stole my DNA. They stole my mother's DNA and they made an army of super dream walkers like her. They used my DNA for the same thing. And I'm not going to allow them to play God anymore."

Zakiel pulled his sword from the scabbard at his back. "Follow me."

I was starting to like this guy a lot. I fell in step behind Zakiel. Cashiel was behind me. He hurried down the corridor. At the dead end he went left. Another bleak hallway but I was too busy keeping my eyes on Zakiel in front of me and thinking about what I was going to do once I got to the lab. My heart pounded hard as we moved along at a rapid clip.

He paused at the last door on the left and turned to me. The door had a glass window in it. Through it, I saw the lab equipment much like the one in Antarctica. There were Bunsen burners, beakers full of fluid, a refrigerator with a glass door, a bank of computers along one wall.

I tried the knob but the door was locked. I cut a glance to Zakiel. He gave me a gentle nudge backward. I stepped back and watched as he lifted his foot and kicked in the door as though it were nothing. He didn't even flinch. The door swung open and banged against the wall, thudding and bouncing back toward me.

I hurried inside and then stood in the center of the sterile room staring at the refrigerator. They'd kept my mother's DNA in a similar place. I recalled throwing the vial with the name A WALKER on it to the ground, but it didn't break. Instead, I had to stomp on it to shatter it.

I approached the appliance and peered through the glass at the vials of blood. One had the name WALKER written in black marker in a careful hand. The others had names I didn't recognize written on them. I stared at them all, wondering how the hell he managed to get all this DNA. And did he still have my mother's?

I turned to the bank of computers along the far wall. One was on and ready. I hurried over to it and saw that someone had left the screen unlocked. I opened File Explorer, right-clicked on the hard drive and then clicked Format. My heart beat wildly as I then clicked OK and stepped back from the computer.

Satisfaction oozed through me as I watched the hard drive begin to format. Then I turned back to the vials of blood, deciding my next move. That's when the alarm in the lab started blaring.

"Anna, we must hurry," Cashiel urged.

I didn't have time to destroy them all. Instead, I turned to a Bunsen burner and turned it on. Then I glanced around at the colored liquid in all the test tubes and beakers. Surely something in the place was flammable?

I ripped a piece of material from the hem of my gown and approached the Bunsen burner. Then I tipped over a beaker full of blue-white liquid, letting it spill across the countertop. I soaked the material of my gown in it. It had an odd, oily smell to it. Maybe this would work.

I tossed the damp rag at the open flame and stepped back.

It landed right on top of the little flame and immediately snuffed out.

"Are you trying to burn down the lab?" Cashiel asked, incredulous.

"Yes," I replied, matter-of-factly. "It would be great if you could help me."

"I will do no such thing." He sniffed derision.

"But I will," Zakiel replied.

He swiped his hand over the blade of his sword and lit it on fire. He cut me a glance, a twinkle in those nutmeg eyes and cocked a grin.

"You might want to stand back," he warned.

I moved back a few steps as he swiped his sword through the liquid on the countertop. It immediately burst into flame. Why didn't I think of that?

"Let's go, Miss Anna."

In one swift move, he snuffed his sword, sheathed it, and then clamped a hand around my upper arm as he dragged me from the room. Cashiel was already out the door and running down the hall.

"What about the others? The prisoners?" I panted.

"They'll find a way out." Zakiel gave me a wicked smile and I shivered all the way to my toes.

The second we were outside, the lab behind us exploded in a fiery bomb. A tower of orange-yellow flame bubbled upward into the night sky, illuminating the entire warehouse district. We appeared to be in an alley behind the building. Shadows pressed around us as we watched the fire lighting up the night. There was no sign of any other warrior angels.

"You should not have done that, Zakiel," Cashiel scolded.

"Anna is right. This Mueller should not be playing God. As I see it, he got what was coming to him. If, in fact, he didn't escape before the explosion."

I swallowed hard, a sudden lump in my throat. I wasn't sure if I should thank him or not. Cashiel folded his arms over his chest. "Your services are no longer needed."

Zakiel started to nod but I put a hand on his chest and stopped him.

"Hold on a second." I turned to Cashiel. "There is still the matter of the lab in Antarctica. I intend to destroy that one, too."

"And Kincade?"

I bit my bottom lip. "I haven't forgotten about him."

"Who is Kincade?" Zakiel asked.

I removed my hand from his chest, trying not to dwell on how hard and angular it was. "A friend. He's in trouble with the Brotherhood of Watchers. I need to get to him."

He stared at me a long quiet moment. At least I thought he was staring at me. The flames from the burning lab behind him blotted out his face. I thought of the people left in the building—Mueller, Katrina, the guards, the women he experimented on—and wondered if any of them made it out alive.

Then I decided I didn't care.

"He's being held by the Warden of Nine," Cashiel added.

So not helpful.

"Then he is a lost cause," Zakiel said. "Cashiel, our duty here is complete. Farewell."

"Wait!" I wrapped my hand around his wrist before he could disappear. "What did you mean he's a lost cause?"

"If he's facing the Warden of Nine, then he's broken the laws of the Brotherhood. He will be punished by being removed from the group and branded a Fallen Watcher."

I removed my hand from his wrist and spun toward Cashiel, my heart in my throat. "Did you know about that?"

He slowly shook his head. "I did not."

"And," Zakiel added, "there is much turmoil within the Brotherhood."

This was a lot of information to take in. I had questions. What did it mean for Kincade to become a Fallen Watcher? What sort of turmoil was brewing inside the Brotherhood? I rubbed my forehead as I paced a small section of the alleyway.

"What sort of turmoil?" Cashiel asked.

"The kind that will break apart the Brotherhood itself. Fracture it from the very core."

I didn't like the sound of that. I stopped pacing and looked at them both. "Then it's imperative I get to Kincade sooner rather than later."

"And how do you intend to get there?" Cashiel asked.

Good question since he didn't seem to know how to transport himself from one place to another without getting lost. I eyed Zakiel, a smile creeping across my lips.

"He's going to take me."

Zakiel stared at me a long, quiet moment. His face was impassive and it was impossible to read his expression or his thoughts. I shifted from one foot to the other, waiting for a response. When one was not forthcoming, I put my hands on my hips.

"Well?" I demanded.

"You do not know what you ask of me, Keeper," he said at last.

"I do know. I need you to take me there because as much as I adore and love Cashiel, he sucks at transportation."

"Thank you very much for that, dearie." He said it in the flattest, most deadpan voice I'd ever heard.

I cut him a glance. "It's not a lie." Then back to Zakiel, I said, "Please. I need your help. I have to get to him before something happens to him."

He tilted his head to one side. "You care for this man."

"Of course." I huffed out an exasperated breath.

"But it goes beyond friendship."

Now I glared at him. "That's none of your concern. Are you going to help me or not?"

"It is forbidden for a Watcher of the Brotherhood to mate with a human," he continued as if I hadn't spoken. "There are consequences."

"We haven't mated!" I flopped my arms against my sides in utter frustration.

The only thing Kincade and I did was kiss and that was it. A kiss I was unable to forget. That had burned deep into my memories. Even now, as I thought about it, my lips tingled.

Fuck all.

"Listen, angel boy," I said in my most sarcastic tone, "I need to get to Kincade. If you're not going to take me, I'll find someone who will."

I shoved him aside and started down the dark alleyway, my bare feet pounding the pavement as I went.

"Anna, wait." Cashiel was hot on my heels but I ignored him.

"Who will take you, Keeper?" Zakiel called.

"I'll find *someone*," I flung over my shoulder.

Suddenly, Zakiel stood in front of me. I came to a shuddering halt, surprised by his sudden appearance. His wings ruffled with his agitation.

"If you insist on this suicide mission, then I will take you as far as I can. But then it is up to you to enter the fortress and find him. Alone."

"Anna, are you sure about this?" Cashiel asked.

I didn't even hesitate. "Yes. Let's go, angel boy."

"But first..." Zakiel looked me up and down. "Perhaps you would prefer some clothes?"

I glanced down at the hospital gown splattered with blood from my arm and the edge ripped. "You have a point. First clothes. Then Kincade."

CHAPTER 12

DAYS PASSED SINCE HE dream walked with Anna. He tried to re-establish a link but something was wrong. She wasn't responding which wasn't like her at all. Worry gnawed at him. Where was she? What was happening to her?

He had yet to meet with the Warden of Nine. He suspected Sebastian was already making his case for him and he would have to defend himself. He was likely doomed. Sebastian would no doubt damn him to his fate.

Footsteps echoed through the chamber. Sebastian arrived moments later. Kincade remained on the floor, peering through the shadows and the bars of his cell until the man's face came into view. He paused outside the cell door. The clink of the key in the lock indicated it was time for Kincade to face the Warden of Nine.

He'd been part of the Brotherhood of Watchers for centuries. He had served the Brotherhood for centuries and had never once stood before the Warden of Nine. He had never needed to. He knew, of course, they were the ones who oversaw the laws of the

Brotherhood, who made sure none of them defected. And if one did, they would be the ones to pass judgement.

As Sebastian swung open the door and two others entered, Kincade wondered, then, why Azriel—who had once been Marcus and a part of the Brotherhood like him—was never punished by the Warden of Nine. Was it as simple as Azriel had never been caught? Or was he ignored since he had turned to the dark side?

"On your feet," one of two said.

Reluctantly, Kincade pushed up the wall and stood. The one who spoke used a knife to slice the zip tie in half, releasing his wrists. When the plastic fell away, he saw the angry irritation it left behind.

Sebastian headed back down the hallway. He and the two guards fell in step behind him. The only sound was that of their footsteps as they made their way through the long corridor through the prison cells. When they left the prison area, they wound through more endless hallways lined with torches. It was as though these men had never left the Middle Ages. They still lived in a world with no running water, no electricity, no modern comforts.

They ended up at the great hall, where an enormous stone fireplace dominated one end of the room. A cheerful fire flickered inside, warming that end of the cavernous room. Multi-candle candelabras were scattered about the room, giving it what should have been an inviting glow. In the center of the room was a long wooden table with nine chairs. Several ewers were placed along the length of the table as well as nine pewter cups. A small silver bell rested on the table in front of the center chair which Kincade assumed was meant for the leader of the Warden of Nine.

They halted in the middle of the room in front of the table and waited for what seemed to be an eternity. Finally, the nine men of the Warden of Nine entered the room. Each wore the white mantle with the red cross down the center in the way of the Templars. Kincade eyed them as they took their seats in unison, like a well-choreographed dance. Each of the men were older, with graying beards and in various degrees. Each wore the same grim expression. Or maybe it was bored and annoyed they were disturbed from whatever they normally did to attend to such a trivial matter as Kincade's desertion from the Brotherhood.

The man in the center, the one with the longest white beard, reached for a small silver hammer and hit the bell three times.

"The Warden of Nine are now in session. Sebastian, Watcher of the London Realm, state your business here."

Sebastian stepped forward and bowed his head in reverence. "Master Philip, I bring to you and the other Wardens today a defector from the Brotherhood." He waved his hand toward Kincade. "Kincade de Burres, which is his true name, though he has used many an alias, including the name Kincade Harrison."

Master Philip turned his pale gaze to Kincade as he looked him up and down. "His only crime is that of defector?"

"No, master. The list of his crimes is lengthy. He was a general leading the charge to hunt and eradicate Fallen high lords. He gave that up for a human woman."

Philip's gaze flickered to Kincade. "Is this true, Kincade?"

Kincade clenched his jaw tight as he decided how to answer. "She is no normal human woman, master."

He lifted one gray brow. "Who is she?"

"She is—" Kincade began.

"Master, that makes no difference. Kincade, I believe, has fallen for her. Even has gone so far as to mate with her."

"That's a damn lie," Kincade said through clenched teeth.

Philip held up a hand to silence them both. He pinpointed his gaze on Sebastian. "With all due respect, Sebastian, I wish to hear Kincade's explanation." He turned his attention back to Kincade. "Pray continue. Who is this woman?"

"She is no ordinary woman. She is the Keeper of the Holy Relics, master. The one who was prophesied to balance the Dark and the Light. The One Who Was Promised."

A tittering of whispers broke out between the other men at the table. Philip, however, remained silent as he stared at Kincade. He held up a hand to quiet the others.

"The Keeper, you say?"

"She is every bit as powerful as was foretold. She has the God-light," Kincade continued.

"She is *nothing*," Sebastian interjected.

Kincade ignored him and kept talking. "She has four of the five Holy Relics, master."

"Do not listen him. He is—"

"Sebastian, remain silent until called upon," Philip said, clearly agitated with Sebastian's constant interruptions. "Continue, Kincade."

"She has recovered four of the five Holy Relics. I've been on several of these quests with her. She *is* the one who was promised to fight against the darkness."

Kincade glanced at Sebastian. The man remained rooted in place, his hands in tight fists. His lips were pressed so tight together, a ring of white surrounded them.

"And so..." Philip began, speaking slowly. "You left the Brotherhood to assist her in these quests."

"He was taken by Azriel," Sebastian blurted. "His soul was almost corrupted."

Kincade glared at the man before glancing back at Philip who had a look of disdain on his face.

"I told you to remain silent. If you cannot obey, then you must be removed." Philip turned his attention back to Kincade. "Is this true, brother?"

"It is," Kincade answered without hesitation. "If not for her, I would not be standing here. She saved my soul. She saved my life."

A huff from Sebastian but he remained silent.

"She sounds quite remarkable," Philip said. "However, our laws are clear. It is against the Brotherhood to leave to help a human. Just as it's against the Brotherhood to leave and mate with a human. You left your task force without a leader. Most of them scattered across the human realm. We have not been able to recover them. The others returned to the Brotherhood for reassignment. Therefore, there will be consequences for your actions."

Reassignment. Not justice. Not honor. Control.

His task force. Ophelia was part of it, hunting down Fallen high lords and killing them with her shimmering sword before they could take out more guardian angels. The guardian angels were the only ones protecting humans from high lords killing the humans and stealing the souls to build Lucifer's army. If he'd never met Anna, perhaps he'd still be leading that task force.

The men rose from the table, but Philip still had his gaze fixed on Sebastian. "You and I, Sebastian, will have a private discussion about your own actions later."

Sebastian stiffened—just for a fraction of a second. Long enough for Kincade to see it.

To that, his former boss stiffened. He gave him a curious glance, wondering what Sebastian did to warrant a private audience with the Grand Master.

"As for you, Kincade, you must be punished for your actions." He gestured to the guards in the back. "Take him to the courtyard. I will join you momentarily."

Two guards, one on each side, led Kincade out of the great hall and through a hallway to a set of stairs. They ascended and exited into the balmy night air. Torches lined the courtyard, flickering in a violent dance in the breeze. In the center of the courtyard was a platform hosting two large pillars on each side with ropes dangling down.

Kincade knew what came next.

He mentally prepared himself for that as they pushed him between the pillars. Each guard placed his hand in the loop of rope and tightened them against his already abraded wrists.

And then he waited. The Grand Master's voice came from behind him.

"For deserting the Brotherhood, I sentence Kincade to ten lashes. For leaving his task force, I sentence Kincade to ten lashes. For aiding a human woman *in defiance of the Brotherhood*, I sentence Kincade to ten lashes."

Thirty lashes.

Fine.

He could handle that. It was better than death.

The first lash came, pounding his back. The searing pain went through him hot and wild. He clenched his fists and his jaw, refusing to cry out. The Warden of Nine never did anything without an audience, and he suspected the nine of them stood behind him, watching and counting. Likely Sebastian, too.

The second lash came. Then the third. Then fourth. By the fifth, he had stopped counting. Instead, he concentrated on keeping the pain at bay, putting it to the back of his mind. Sweat rolled down the side of his face and the back of his neck.

In his haze, he thought he saw a flash of light in the night sky.

The lashes halted for a brief moment. There was confusion behind him, incoherent voices.

"Continue," Philip ordered, his voice hard and firm.

Another lash came.

"Stop." A woman's voice echoed through the courtyard. "Stop this madness."

He lifted his head and looked into the shadows to see the Keeper of the Holy Relics glowing bright like the full moon standing across from him. Her hands flickered with lightning as she clenched and unclenched her fists.

Silence descended on the courtyard—heavy, shocked, absolute. The only sound that of the flickering torches in the wind.

What the fuck are you doing here? I told you not to come.

Anna's purple gaze met his. She smiled and returned his mind speak. *Since when do I listen to you?*

She walked around the platform. Her footsteps halted behind him. But even so, the way she shined still lit up the courtyard with a blue-white luminosity. In that moment, he could not have loved her more.

CHAPTER 13

I REFUSED TO LOOK at Kincade's flayed back as I walked by for fear I'd be sick. I'd deal with that horror later. I stood before the Warden of Nine and a group of the Brotherhood watching the lightning flicker between my fingers and the Godlight light me up like a candle. It was a handy trick I managed to quickly learn before Zakiel dumped me outside the ruins of the castle.

I also managed to get some decent clothing, though I was missing my pink combat boots. Something I'd rectify later. My uncle returned my dagger and his flaming sword to me, both of which I stashed in the cloud.

"Women are not permitted here in the sanctity of the Brotherhood halls," Sebastian said.

I eyed Sebastian with every ounce of anger within me. I clenched my fists, snuffing out the lightning in my hands, then I allowed the Godlight to fade away. All of it was theatrics. Power was something else entirely. I pointed at the man who took Kincade away from me.

"You did this to him. And you'll pay," I said.

"You do not have power here," a man with a long white beard said as he stepped forward. He wore a white mantle with a red cross down the center reminding me of the Templars.

I regarded him with a cool stare as if I owned the place. "And who are you?"

He tilted his head up and looked down his nose. "I am the Grand Master, Philip. And you are?"

"Anna Walker. Keeper of the Holy Relics. You will release this man to me." I pointed to Kincade.

"I will do no such thing." Philip snorted derision.

"He must be punished for his crimes against the Brotherhood," Sebastian said.

"You shut up." I turned my glare back on Sebastian. "I didn't ask for you to speak."

Someone in the crowd snickered. Another gasped.

"Kincade said you were powerful, that you had the Godlight, and were the one who was prophesied."

Philip stepped toward me, his dark eyes roving over me. I shifted from one foot to the other. If he thought to intimidate me, he was wrong. I faced scarier foes. This guy was nothing compared to them.

"Sebastian is correct, though. You aren't permitted here. No woman is."

"Ask me if I care." My fingers twitched. Lightning would return with only a thought, but I kept it in check. "I'm not leaving without Kincade."

"I'm afraid that's not possible," Philip said, his voice even and calm. "Kincade has returned to us. He will not be permitted to leave us again."

"Sounds like a challenge. I accept."

Philip blinked confusion. "Not a challenge. And you must leave."

He snapped his fingers. Several guards emerged from the shadows toward me. I flickered my fingers and allowed the lightning to return. I was getting pretty good at that. I held up my hands.

"One more step and I fry them."

"Halt," Philip ordered.

They stopped, each of them eyed Philip for their next order. Philip, though, moved closer to me.

"I do not believe you pose a threat. This is merely some form of magic. And if you have magic, then you are nothing more than a demon wearing borrowed light."

"It's not magic, it's dream walker power. *My* power. And I *do* pose a threat. Though if you wish me to prove it..." I closed my hands into fists, then pushed them upward to the sky, and released the bolts of light. It lit up the night sky in blue-white streaks before sizzling and burning out.

Philip's gaze met mine and, without blinking or flinching, he said, "Continue with the punishment, Jacob."

I spun around in time to see Jacob, who held the whip, lash Kincade's back one more time.

"Stop!"

He didn't stop, though. He did it again.

Fury erupted inside me. I clenched my fist, then released the lightning toward the punisher. The bolt smacked into him so hard, he dropped the whip and stumbled off the platform, his shirt smoking. Several men hurried to his side to aid him.

I turned back to Philip. "I could have killed him, but I didn't. Now, you will release Kincade to me, and I will be on my way."

But Philip's face was unreadable. His impassive expression infuriated me.

"Why is it so important that he come with you?"

That was a loaded question and one I wasn't ready to fully answer. But if I didn't, then Philip would have me thrown out and I'd never get another chance at this. I took a deep breath.

"I need him to help me find the last remaining relic. The Ark of the Covenant. I can't do it without him."

He lifted one white brow. "Why?"

"Because he's the only person left on this planet I trust with my life."

There. I said it. And I didn't mean it like a strategy. I meant it like a vow I hadn't asked permission to make.

It was out there and Kincade heard every word. I couldn't look at him. If I did, I'd see it—the cost of what I'd handed him.

I wanted a black hole to appear beneath my feet and swallow me whole, but it didn't. I was still standing there staring down an aging Grand Master.

I expected Kincade to bark something in my head, but he remained silent. And that was even more terrifying than his bark.

"Very well. Then you will fight for his release," Philip said.

"Fight?" A twinge of fear went through me. I wasn't sure I had the energy to fight since I'd been laid up in a hospital bed for several days.

Anna, don't.

"Yes, fight. Whoever wins, wins Kincade's freedom."

Shit. I didn't like the sound of this at all. "And who will I be fighting?"

A slow smile spread on his lips. "Sebastian."

Surprise flickered over Sebastian's face. "I will not fight her."

"You will. No weapons. No magic tricks." Philip pointed to my hands. "Hand to hand combat. May the best...person win."

"Fine, I'll fight him. On one condition," I said.

"And that is?"

"Release Kincade from those bindings."

"So, he can watch me destroy you?" Sebastian said and nodded. "I agree."

Kick his ass, Anna. Put all that training to work, Kincade said in my head.

I cracked my knuckles as I stared down the man, despising him even more. "Bring it on, *punk*."

Either I was going to seriously regret this, or it was going to be a hell of a lot of fun. I had trained for this for months. And I was going to win.

Two guards released Kincade from his bindings and lowered him to the ground off to one side. The others made a semi-circle in the courtyard. Sebastian and I squared off, fists raised. We circled each other with slow, methodical steps, each one waiting for the other to make the first move. Adrenaline pumped a wild beat through me.

Sebastian took a swing, but I dodged with ease. Annoyance flickered over his face. We sidestepped another circle around each other as I planned my first move.

He's afraid of you, Kincade said in my head. *That will give you an edge.*

How do you know that?

Trust me. I know.

Kincade was never one to steer me wrong. I appreciated the intel. I swung my fist at Sebastian and connected with his jaw. His head snapped back. His eyes went wide with surprise. He didn't like I got in the first punch. He charged me, fists swinging. I tripped him. He crashed against the ground with an oof and a thud. All that did was piss him off more.

He shot to his feet and charged me. Something Kincade did during our numerous training exercises. He caught me mid-torso and shoved me backward. I stumbled, unable to maintain my footing and fell. I smacked the ground but managed to keep my head from hitting the dirt.

Cheers and jeers erupted from the crowd. I wasn't sure if it was for me hitting the ground or Sebastian ramming me.

I jabbed him in the ribs, then kneed him in the groin. He grunted and rolled off me. I sprang to my feet, ready to do more battle. He was slow to get up. I took the opportunity to upper cut his jaw. The punch took its toll on my hand—my knuckles burned.

Sebastian regained his composure, fury written all over his face. Instead of charging me, this time he swung a fist. I wasn't fast enough to dodge. He landed a punch on my cheekbone. Pain exploded across my face. I high kicked him in retaliation, my foot connecting with his chest.

He fell again. This time when he got up, he had a fist full of dirt which he threw in my face.

Cheater.

While I coughed and sputtered and blinked to get the dirt and grit out of my eyes, he made his next move. His fist connected with my face. My lower lip burst. Blood spilled into my mouth. As I was still reeling from that, he swung again. I ducked, but he managed to smack my head above the eyebrow. The skin split.

Stop letting him win, Kincade said in my head.

I stumbled backward to put some space between me and Sebastian to regain my composure. Blood seeped down into my eye, reminding me of that morning Kincade punched me in the same place.

I clenched my fists and went after Sebastian with all the fury I possessed. I spun in a half circle and high kicked him again. This time I managed to connect with the side of his head. He grunted. I didn't give him time to recover. I threw another punch and smacked him in the jaw. My hand reverberated with the force of it. My knuckles were red and raw already.

Sebastian retaliated with his own high kick, connecting with my gut. It knocked the wind out of me. I clutched my stomach, trying to catch my breath. More shouts and cheers from the crowd. They were getting into it.

I looked up at Sebastian to see his face bloodied. That gave me satisfaction and a burst of energy. I went back after him, both fists at the ready. I punched him numerous times until he backed away from me. My hands bled with both his and my blood. He had a cut on his cheek. His nose spurted blood.

He's on the defensive. Take him down and you'll win.

I charged while he was trying to recover. I smacked him in the jaw with my elbow, then kicked his knees. There was a loud crunch as he cried out in pain and crumpled to the ground. I stood over him, ready to do more damage. He held up his hand in surrender.

"No more," he breathed, then spit blood onto the ground in front of him.

Silence descended on the courtyard. A murmur rippled through the crowd—uneasy, uncertain.

My hands throbbed. My face throbbed. My gut clenched. I wiped the back of my hand across my nose. It came back smeared with blood.

Philip moved to stand between us, clapping his hands slowly.

"Impressive," he said.

My chest heaved with exertion as I tried to catch my breath. I waited for him to claim me as the victor. He didn't.

"Kincade and I will be leaving now," I said.

I turned toward him, elation spreading through my breast. Our eyes met. He gave me a small smile. And then his expression changed.

"Behind you."

He said it just as Sebastian crashed into me. His arms wrapped around my upper torso. We crashed to the ground in a violent face plant that stole my breath. His hand was on the back of my head, shoving my face into the dirt with a powerful force. He had managed to pin my body underneath his while he did so and proceeded to punch me over and over in the ribs.

The next thing I knew, Sebastian was yanked off me. I heard a loud thud and rolled to my back, coughing. Sebastian was in a heap on the other side of the courtyard. Kincade stood over me, his chest heaving and sweat pouring down the side of his face and beading his forehead. Anger creased his face as he glared at Sebastian, who remained immobile.

"She wins," Kincade said. "And we're leaving. Now."

He reached a hand down to me. I took it and allowed him to pull me to my feet. Together, we limped out of the courtyard. He knew the way and took us through a long tunnel and out of the ruins of the castle.

In the distance in the east, the first flicker of dawn lightened the sky with an orange hue. We paused there as we both tried to catch our breath. He eased down onto a large boulder, his legs taking his weight. A deep weariness edged across his face as he looked at me.

"You came after me when I told you not to."

"I came after you because I had to. I wish I'd gotten here sooner."

"I'll heal." He said nothing for a long, quiet moment. Then, "Where were you?"

"That's a long story. I'm going to destroy the lab in Antarctica."

He peered at me, his brows knit for a moment and then he gave a nod of his head. "Then that's where we go next." He stood, winced in pain, and then sat again.

"After you've healed. You need a doctor."

"I'll be fine."

"Stop trying to pretend you're not in pain. You are. I'm getting you to a doctor."

"And how do you propose to do that? It's not like we can call a taxi from here." He waved his hands to encompass the desolate area outside the ruined castle.

"Fear not, good sir. I have a plan." I flashed him a smile and then said, "Zakiel."

The warrior angel appeared in front of us. Kincade heaved an annoyed sigh.

"This is your plan? A warrior angel?"

"Yes, and don't be a grouch. Zakiel, take Kincade to Walker Manor."

The warrior angel said nothing as he nodded. He took Kincade by the arm and then they flashed away. A moment later, Cashiel appeared.

"You do understand, Anna, Kincade is forever banned from the Brotherhood of Watchers."

"I assumed. Somehow, I don't think he'll mind all that much."

He glanced toward the ruins, then back at me. "Your face is a wreck. And your hands…"

He paused, shook his head. I glanced down at my hands to see them bloodied. I flexed my fingers, the pain shooting through every digit and up my arm. I hadn't realized how much pain I was in until that moment. I'd punched Sebastian with everything I had, and it showed in every knuckle.

"What happened to you?" he asked.

"I gave as good as I got."

He sighed a long-suffering sigh. "Come then. Let's get you home."

He reached for me, but I stepped back. "Wait. Are you sure you can get me there? You aren't the best with your flashing skills."

He gave me a look of disdain that reminded me much of Edward. "Zakiel and I had lessons. I am sure I can get you there now without incident."

"All right, then. Let's go."

And with that, we flashed away together back to Walker Manor.

CHAPTER 14

We arrived back at Walker Manor in the foyer. At least he was able to get me home and not some other random place like before. As soon as we came to a halt, I sank to my knees and dry heaved. My stomach clenched into a knot, threatening to heave again. I groaned, huddled against the floor as Cashiel stood over me.

"Apologies," he said.

"I'm fine," I gasped, trying to get myself under control.

I pushed off the floor and sat there a long moment, heat flashing through me as sweat trickled down the side of my face and back. I took several long, deep breaths to ward off the sickness.

"Are you going to tell me what happened to your face and hands?" Cashiel asked.

"I fought for Kincade's freedom."

"By the way you look, I hope that means you won."

"Sort of."

I didn't want to mention Kincade came to my aid. If he hadn't, Sebastian would have likely killed me. My neck and face still pounded from where he shoved them into the dirt. There was something deadly about him. Some deadly anger that drove him to try to murder me. Kincade said he was afraid of me, though I didn't understand why.

"Your lip is bloody and you have a black eye, among other things."

"I'm sure I look terrible. Thanks for pointing that out."

He frowned as he held his hand down and helped me to my feet. "Where is Kincade?"

"Likely in his room by now. I asked for a healer to tend him."

I headed for the stairs, my legs shaking from the exertion. Fatigue hit me hard and fast as I climbed the stairs, slowly. I wondered where the other inhabitants of the manor were. I hadn't seen anyone else, yet. Cashiel was right behind me as if waiting to catch me if I fell. I headed for Kincade's room, limping along the way.

The door was open. Zakiel was gone but the healer Cashiel promised was busy cutting away his ripped shirt from his flayed back. Kincade laid face down on the bed. His skin looked angry like raw meat.

"He will be fine, you know," Cashiel said in my ear.

"I know." But I didn't need to see anymore. I turned away and headed to my own room.

"You need medical attention, too," Cashiel said, still following me.

"I need a shower and a bed," I replied. "I'll be fine."

"Anna..."

"I'm *fine.*"

And truthfully, I'd rather tend to my own wounds alone. In my room, I closed the door leaving Cashiel in the hallway. I kicked off the shoes I'd purchased in Taipei and headed to the bathroom. I got a good look at my face in the mirror and was horrified. Dirt and blood caked my face. My lip was split, my nose bloody, my eye black and blue. I had a cut on my forehead that still seeped blood. My ribs ached from where he'd punched me.

I started the shower, stripped, and got in. The hot water stung all my open wounds, but I figured it was better than letting them fester. At least they'd be clean. After toweling off, I cleaned them with antibacterial cream and covered the cut on my head with a bandage. My hands throbbed with a deep stinging ache.

And then I crawled into the bed to sleep.

* * *

I awoke later with every ache and pain still pounding through me. Everything about having my ass kicked by Sebastian sucked. I was even more disappointed in myself for not being able to finish the fight. I was so focused on winning and getting Kincade out of there, I let my guard down giving him the opportunity to attack.

I shoved off the bed clothes and slid to the edge. My bare feet hit the cold floor, sending a shiver up my spine. It took me a few minutes to gain the strength to stand, but I managed. I pulled on a pair of sweats and a sweatshirt, then headed off to see Kincade.

He was alone. The healer had done his job and was gone. Kincade still lay face down on the bed. His back had been treated and bandaged. I paused in the doorway, clutching my elbows and wishing I'd thought to put on socks. My feet were cold.

"Are you going to stand there all night or come in?" His voice was muffed against the pillow.

"Stand here all night." I wasn't sure what I was afraid of and why I was unable to force my feet to move forward.

"Suit yourself."

The lamp by the bed was on, bathing a small circle of light in a yellowish glow. As I stared at the old-fashioned lampshade with the pompoms, I wondered why I hadn't noticed it before. Had it always been in Kincade's room? Granted, I didn't spend a lot of time in there with him, but I still wondered. I also noticed, for the first time, the green and red plaid coverlet pulled up to his waist and tucked neatly around his thick frame.

"Really, Anna, come in. You standing there is starting to make me edgy."

"Sorry." Still clutching my elbows, I padded across the room and paused next to the bed.

"Sit." He pointed to the chair next to the bedside table.

I sat. The side of his head was flat against the pillow. He peered at me from his lateral position on the bed, one arm dangling off the edge of the mattress.

"You look like hell," he said at last.

"That's because Sebastian used my face as a punching bag." I frowned, tasting the bitterness of my own defeat at the back of my mouth.

"You held your own."

"I lost, Kincade."

"Is that what's bugging you?" He shifted slightly on the bed to tuck his arm under the pillow and lift his head to level it.

"He had me pinned to the ground, shoving my face into it, and punching me in the ribs. I have lots of bruises as his parting gift. He was going to suffocate me."

"But he didn't," he pointed out.

"Thanks to you."

"You're welcome."

I bristled, my back straightening and my shoulders squaring. I was ready to stomp out of the room.

"He attacked you from behind, Anna. In my book, that makes him a coward."

I hadn't really thought of it that way. I was too busy throwing myself a pity party for allowing him to nearly kill me. And not getting to Kincade in time before they massacred his back. I also hadn't considered how much it must have hurt him, physically, to shove Sebastian off me.

"What's going to happen to him now?" I asked. "Not that I care, really. I'm curious."

"The Warden of Nine will punish him most likely."

"Do you think they'll kill him?"

"Maybe. Who knows. My impression was that he'd fallen out of favor with them to begin with." He took a deep breath, expelled it. "Decker was there."

I stared at him as shock rolled through me. "Decker was there? At the castle?"

"Yes. Imprisoned like I was."

"Why didn't you tell me? I can go back to—"

"No."

He said it so sharply, I blinked. "No?"

"Things are...different between us." He shifted again on the bed and huffed out a breath. "I'm tired of laying like this."

"Try your side."

"I did. It hurts too much."

I frowned, thinking of the last conversation I had with Decker. He was unwilling to help me find Kincade, though I wasn't sure why. Perhaps he was upset with Kincade for leaving the Brotherhood to help me. He'd told me they were bound by their oath and duty and no one got out.

But Kincade did.

I sensed he wanted to tell me more about Decker, so I waited.

"He said the Brotherhood is shattered."

This was also something Zakiel told me, that there was much turmoil within the Brotherhood. I chewed on my bottom lip, wondering if I should mention it.

"What does a Fallen Watcher mean?" I asked.

"It's when a Watcher is sent to join Lucifer's army as a high lord. It's what happened to Azriel."

I nodded, recalling the story Kincade recounted to me about how Azriel—who was once Marcus—had betrayed him and became a high lord for Lucifer.

"What's going to happen to Decker?"

"He'll likely face a similar punishment as I did. Perhaps even end up a Fallen Watcher like Azriel."

It pained me to hear it. Despite the way he'd treated me before, when he told me to never dream walk him again, I still felt some sort of unexplainable allegiance to him. I sensed the same from Kincade.

"Then allow me to return with Cashiel or Zakiel and bring him back."

"No," he said again. "He won't want that. And he'll resent me even more if I send you. He already resents me enough for stepping down to help you. Even though it was the right thing to do."

I was touched and I understood so much more then. Decker didn't like me because Kincade wanted to help me. He also didn't like I'd exchanged the Spear of Destiny for Kincade's soul. Imagine what he'd think when he discovered I'd fought Sebastian for his freedom. I rubbed my forehead between thumb and forefinger.

"This rift between you is my fault, isn't it?"

"If it's anyone's, it's mine," he said, his voice muffled against the pillow again.

Even so, guilt swept through me. If we had never met, then things would have been much different for the two of us. Maybe I'd never become the Keeper. Or, at least, a very bad one. I was better with Kincade at my side. Stronger. Braver. More Resilient.

"Are you going to tell me where you were and why we need to blow up the lab in Antarctica?" he asked.

I shifted in my seat. "I told you it's a long story."

"I have all day." He rolled to his side, bunching up the pillow under his head with a wince.

"I thought you said it hurt to lay like that."

"It does but I'm sick of laying on my stomach. Now tell me."

"When I resolved to come after you, my uncle, who is now known as Cashiel, tried to help me get there. Only he missed and we ended up in Hong Kong. It somehow alerted the Knights of the Holy Lance. Their super dream walkers came after us. They captured me and took me to a lab in the warehouse district of Taipei. Their scientist, Dr. Mueller, stole my blood to continue the work he started with Schneider in Antarctica.

"I was there for days. I tried to escape but they were determined to keep me. Cashiel brought reinforcements in the form of warrior angels. They helped get me out. Zakiel helped me blow up that lab. I don't know if Mueller and his super dream walkers survived, though."

He remained silent for a long moment as he looked at me. "That's where you were while I was facing the Warden of Nine."

I nodded. "And why it took so long to get to you. I suspect Mueller and his Knights of the Holy Lance are continuing their work in Antarctica. He still has my mother's DNA and mine."

"Then we have to go there, don't we?"

He started to push to a sitting position. His face contorted in pain. I jumped to my feet and pushed him back down with a gentle nudge.

"Not until you've healed."

"I'm fine." He grunted, clearly in discomfort.

"You're not." I shook my head. "I'll let you rest. I shouldn't have bothered you." I started for the door.

"Anna..."

He grasped my hand. I turned back.

"I owe you one."

I cocked a half grin. "I'd say we're even by now."

* * *

Days passed. While Kincade healed, I plotted the demise of the Knights of the Holy Lance. If they'd moved operations to Taipei, what was to stop them from moving to other cities around the world? I had no way to know that, of course, but perhaps there was more information in Antarctica. Which meant I had to infiltrate the lab before destroying it.

Which also got me thinking about how I was going to destroy it. When I blew up Azriel's crypt, Astrid helped me. She used her powers to produce C4. I needed some way to take out that lab completely and not leave any trace of Walker DNA behind. To do that, I needed to find out if they were still operating out of there.

Before, I had Decker and my uncle to help me get inside the lab. I needed a way in. I needed someone to get me inside undetected.

"You look deep in thought."

Ophelia entered the dining room that morning without me noticing and I jumped at her sudden appearance. I realized I was holding a slice of bacon halfway to my mouth and dropped it back on the plate.

"Oh, you're talking to me now?" I asked.

When I returned with Kincade, she was furious I'd gone without her. I tried to explain to her it wasn't planned and just sort of happened, but she was having none of it. She hadn't spoke another word to me in days.

She shrugged a shoulder as she poured a cup of coffee from the server. "I guess I can't be mad at you forever."

"I'm sorry I went without you."

I deeply regretted leaving her behind when she was so adamant about going with me to find Kincade. She'd worked with him on his task force long before I came into the picture. She had a loyalty to him I hadn't realized ran so deep.

She sat in the chair across from me at the table, holding her steaming mug of coffee. "It's all right. I admit I was upset at first but I understand why you did it. And why it had to be you."

That was news to me. "You do?"

"Sure, I do. It's hard to separate you two anyway."

I flushed at her insinuation. "No idea what you're talking about."

She sighed. "Still in denial, I see. You both are. But eventually, you will realize it."

"Realize what?" I played dumb, even though I knew exactly what she was saying.

"Please, Anna." She rolled her eyes. "Anyway, I didn't come down here to badger you about Kincade. Piers says he's doing much better."

"Yes," I agreed. "The angel healer Cashiel brought helped him immensely." And then it occurred to me she could help me. "So, what are your thoughts about Antarctica?"

She sipped her coffee, a perplexed look on her face. "What an odd question. It's a damn cold place."

"It is. And it also has the lab of the Knights of the Holy Lance. The one I intend to destroy."

"The one that creates the super dream walkers like your mother?"

"The very one," I said with a nod. "As soon as Kincade is well enough to travel, we're going. I could use your help."

"Sounds like fun. I'm in."

"As am I," Natasha said from behind me.

Ophelia's gaze lifted to her as I turned. My mother stood in the doorway, a fierce look of clarity in her purple eyes. It had come and gone over the last few weeks.

"Are you sure?"

"He has my DNA, Anna," she said. "I want to see that lab burn as much as you do."

"Then I guess that's settled," I said. "The four of us will go."

"Five." Sariel appeared behind my mother.

My heart pumped hard and fast as I pushed the chair back and got to my feet. Natasha turned to face him, then. Their eyes met and something...some little spark...flickered between them. Something I didn't quite understand but made my knees weak and my hands shake. I gripped the back of the chair as I watched them gazing at each other as though there was a flicker of recognition there.

A strange sort of silence descended on the dining room. Natasha reached for him, placed her hand on his chest as she gazed up at him.

"I...know you."

He smiled, gripped her hand and, with a gentle push, removed it from his chest. He said nothing more to her as he turned his gaze back to me.

"When you are ready, I will be."

And then he disappeared.

Natasha faltered. The clouds returned to her eyes as she looked back to me, confusion knitting her brow.

"How did I get here?"

Ophelia's chair scraped backward as she stood. She rounded the table and paused next to my mother. She wrapped an arm around her shoulders.

"Come on. Let's get you back to your room."

As they walked away, Ophelia cut me a knowing glance as if to say she understood something I didn't. There was some reason why my mother would have clarity one minute and not the next. Eventually, I'd figure it out. Hopefully, before I left for the quest for the Ark.

CHAPTER 15

I WANTED TO FOLLOW Ophelia but didn't. I sat back in the chair and thought about what I'd just witnessed. There were a few times when my mother had that sense of clarity and then her eyes clouded again and she returned to who she was before.

I didn't understand it.

The bacon was left untouched on my plate as I shoved away from the table. I left the dining room. Ophelia descended the stairs.

"Is she all right?" I asked.

"She's fine."

"I don't understand what happened."

"I think I do. And I think it has something to do with Sariel's presence," she said.

"Sariel?"

"When he left, she lost all lucidity. Something about having him near helps clear her mind."

"I need to talk to him about it, then," I said.

"I think you should."

While I wanted to pursue that thread more, I had to start making plans for Antarctica. I headed off to the library to make those arrangements. I booked the private plane to get us across the globe to the frozen continent in one week's time. I made hotel reservations in Punta Arenas, Chile on the southernmost tip of South America. I assumed Sariel would do his appearing act once we arrived there. He was needed to get me into and out of the lab.

Kincade appeared in the doorway with a faint knock on the jamb.

"Should you be out of bed?" I asked.

He grunted in response as he moved deeper into the room. He walked slowly, still in pain from the healing lashes on his back. I hadn't visited him much over the last few days so he could rest and heal. He lowered his bulky frame into the chair opposite me and expelled a deep breath.

"What are you doing?" he asked, his gaze on the paper in front of me.

"Making a travel itinerary." I finished writing the hotel information and then started on the elaborate plan to destroy the lab.

"I understand Ophelia and your mother are joining us."

I kept my head down as I scrawled notes I didn't want to forget. "And Sariel," I said absently.

"Sariel?"

I paused writing and met his gaze. "We need him since Darius has been called home and is currently unavailable. He can get me into the lab."

"And how do you intend on destroying it?"

"I plan to talk to Astrid to see if she can help me out like she did with Azriel's crypt." I returned to my note making.

"Were you going to consult me on any of this?" He almost sounded offended.

I suppressed a sigh and put down my pen. "I was trying not to bother you."

"We're in this together, Anna. Until the end. Let me help you."

A warm tingling sensation went through me. Something akin to a feeling of fondness for Kincade. I tried to ignore it, but the more time we spent together, the more I felt it and the more I was starting to want the same from him.

"All right," I said slowly.

"I have a way to get charges and a detonator."

I lifted a brow. "You do?"

"I know a guy."

"You never mentioned this before."

"I can't tell you all my secrets, can I? Then I'm no use to you." He smiled and gave me a wicked wink. "My contact is in Dublin. I'll need to meet him in person for the exchange."

Oh, he was a lot of use to me. He just didn't realize it. I gave him a once over. He hadn't shaved in a while. His face and chin were covered in a scruff of beard. He had dark circles under his eyes. Exhaustion lined his face. The pain and recovery had taken a lot out of him.

"What sort of exchange?"

"Money for goods, Anna." He sounded bored and annoyed, like his old self.

"Then I'm coming with you."

"No, you aren't."

I pushed to my feet. "I am, too. You said it yourself. We're in this together until the end. And I have a private jet. It's the only way we'll be able to get there with all this pandemic stuff happening."

"You have a point. Fine, then. Make the arrangements. I need to be there by dawn tomorrow."

"Tomorrow? Isn't that short notice?" Then another thought crossed my mind. "Wait a second. Did you already contact this person?"

"Perhaps." He flashed a grin as he pushed from the chair.

"So, you made plans without consulting *me*?"

His reply was a wicked smile as he hobbled out of the library.

"I guess I'll pack a bag," I said to no one in particular.

I scrawled a few more notes about the mission in Antarctica, then picked up the phone and called the pilot, Harry Humphrey.

* * *

In the middle of the night, Kincade and I made our way from Walker Manor to the airport that housed the private jet. I hadn't been sleeping much anyway so it made no difference to me what time we left. Still, I boarded the plane with a giant yawn. I took a seat near the front. Kincade took the seat across the aisle from me. We expected this to be a day trip, so neither of us brought a carryon.

I was curious to know who we were meeting, where, and what he was getting from this guy. But Kincade was silent on the matter. He didn't want to share that information with me, but he was going to have to.

"I hired a driver. Where are we meeting this person when we land?"

"Outside Temple Bar."

"Strange place to meet at dawn." I stifled another yawn.

"Best place to meet."

I shifted uneasily in my seat. He noticed.

"Relax, will you? It will be fine."

"How do you know this person?"

"Former Brotherhood member. A defector. Like me." He flashed a grin, seeming to be pleased with his defector status.

A gnawing sense of dread came over me but I didn't question him anymore. I settled into my seat and closed my eyes as we took off. It was a short flight. I managed to nap a little, dreamless, before we landed.

The car waited for us outside the airport. I instructed the driver where to take us. He didn't seem bothered by the destination and drove off through the early morning streets of Dublin. We arrived at the front of Temple Bar where the only vehicle was that of the trash collector.

"Instruct the driver to come back in an hour," Kincade said when we got out.

I relayed the instructions and the man drove off, leaving us alone in the middle of the cobblestone road in the quiet morning. I glanced up and down the deserted street, but saw no one and nothing. The air was chilly and I shivered a bit, my hands shoved deep into the pockets of my coat.

Kincade's keen eyes kept watch down the darkened street between the buildings. The lumbering trash collector vehicle had long since disappeared around another corner. I heard the clanging of the trash cans as they hit the pavement once they were emptied. I shifted from one foot to the other, glancing up and down the road.

"Be still," he said. "You look suspicious."

"I'm cold," I complained. "And where is this guy?"

"There." He gave a nod of his head toward the darkened roadway.

I saw nothing but deep shadows. And then movement. The figure came out of the dense darkness, lumbering down the street with a heavy limp. He paused under a lamplight, the garish light bathing his hideous face in a yellow glow. He wore an eyepatch over his missing left eye. His left hand was mangled beyond use. The fingers were curled in on his palm, frozen in whatever injury had happened to him. He dressed in all black to blend in with the gloom.

"I told you to come alone," he said, his voice gravelly with the hint of a Scottish accent.

"This is Anna. You can trust her."

His one good eye was a silvery gray that seemed to pierce me to my soul. His mouth was drawn down into a permanent grimace.

"You give me your word?" he asked.

"On my soul, I do. Anna, this is Silas. We served together in the Brotherhood."

"Humph. Bloody Brotherhood. Heard you got out."

"I did, but not without cost."

Silas looked him over. "What'd they do to you?"

"Flayed my back." He said it matter-of-factly, as if it was the most normal thing in the world.

I understood then, as I looked at Silas. I suspected he lost the eye and had a mangled hand because of the Warden of Nine and the Brotherhood's punishment.

"But Sebastian suffered as well." Kincade cut me a glance with the hint of a smirk.

He snickered. "That old bastard deserves every misery he gets. What happened to him?"

I also understood there was no love for the leader of the Brotherhood Kincade once worked for.

"She kicked his ass." He nodded to me.

This time Silas laughed out loud as he moved toward us, closing the gap. He gave me a good once over, eyeing the cut on my forehead, the black eye, the broken nose.

"Hope ye gave him as good as ye got, lassie."

"I did," I said.

"Good on you." He chuckled again, then turned his attention back to Kincade. "Now on to business. I know what you want and what you came for. You'll have it. But I need more time. Meet me on the Ha'penny Bridge at noon. I'll have the package ready."

Kincade gave a nod. "We'll see you then."

Silas melted back into the shadows, his form blending in with the dark, and was gone.

"He seems nice," I said, not sure what else to say about Silas.

"The Brotherhood wasn't kind to him."

"His eye...?"

"They took it as punishment for his crimes."

"What'd he do?" I whispered.

"He fell in love with a human woman, married her, and had three children." He gave me a pointed look.

Interesting word choice he used—a human woman. But I understood what he meant. Those who were in the Brotherhood weren't exactly human or angel. They were somewhere in between. They were sent by the Most High to watch over humans but were forbidden to interfere in their affairs. Some, like Kincade and his brother, Decker, were sent to protect humans from dark forces, such as demons and the Fallen. Kincade was once a protector of the Knights Templar and was at their fall in Acre.

"And his hand?"

"When he discovered his wife and children were murdered in their flat in Seville, he tried to flee. He fell from a three-story building and broke it trying to escape the Warden of Nine. It never healed correctly. The limp was an old war injury."

Horror flickered through me. "They murdered his wife and children?"

"He never proved it, but he always suspected it."

I shivered in the wind, peering down the dark street Silas had disappeared. Poor guy. If it were true, how could the Brotherhood do such a thing? How could an organization that supposedly protected humans kill them in cold blood? I didn't understand.

The Brotherhood really did a number on him. I wondered what would have happened to Kincade had I not showed up to intervene.

"Are we supposed to hang around here until the driver returns?"

"No. Let's go find some breakfast. There's a place up the street."

I got the sense Kincade had been in Dublin more than once. He was familiar with the area. We started down the cobblestone street. Two figures stepped out into the middle before us. As we neared and their features came into focus, I realized who it was.

Lucifer and Azriel.

We both slowed our gait and came to a halt a few feet from the devil. I took a deep breath and smelled the demons behind us. A few more appeared behind Lucifer. I cut a glance at Kincade. He met my gaze as if to say bring it on.

"What do you want, Lucifer?" Kincade asked.

"Heard you were kicked out of the Brotherhood. Also heard your girlfriend came to your rescue. I must say I'm disappointed you were not able to join the ranks of Fallen," he said.

"Sorry to disappoint," Kincade replied.

Interesting he didn't deny my title of girlfriend. I gave him another sideways glance, but his green-gold eyes were fixed on the two in front of us.

"No matter. I've come to claim what belongs to me."

"And what is that?" I asked, my fingers twitching.

"Kincade." He smiled a devilish smile.

I stepped forward, putting myself between him and Kincade. There was no way I was letting him take him after all the shit I went through to get him back.

"Over my dead body."

Azriel snickered. "Don't worry, *chérie*, you will be joining him. And us."

"One last ditch effort to get me to come to the dark side, I see. I'm not handing over the four relics."

Lucifer waved that thought away. "The most important relic is the Ark and we must have it. You two are going to help us get it."

I snorted. "Sure, we are. That'll happen when Hell freezes over."

He gave me a long-suffering glare. "That phrase is as tiresome as you are, girl."

"Bite me," I snapped. "Do you honestly think your demon reinforcements are going to help you turn us to the darkness?"

"Oh, I assure you, there are more you cannot see," Lucifer said. "Now, will you both come quietly? I'd hoped to avoid a fuss."

I looked up at Kincade. He looked at me. The moment our eyes met I understood what he was thinking. Fight or die.

I drew down my dagger.

CHAPTER 16

I WASN'T SURE HOW this was going to go. Kincade's back hadn't completely healed. I still had cuts and bruises on my knuckles. Not to mention all the bruises and cuts on my face.

Lucifer smirked when he saw the dagger in my hand. "You plan to defeat us with merely a dagger?"

I scowled and handed it to Kincade, then drew down the flaming sword.

"How about now?" I asked.

He didn't react. I smelled the demons charging toward us from behind before I heard them. I spun and charged. Kincade did the same. We attacked in unison. This wasn't our first fight together and I doubted it would be the last. We killed several demons that attacked first, but another group was headed right for us. And more behind us.

Kincade took on the ones behind us while I continued to kill the ones coming at us using the sword. He did a fair amount of damage with my dagger.

In the distance, Lucifer laughed.

The demons in front of me parted. Lucifer walked through them toward me. I clutched the flaming sword with both hands, ready to do battle.

"You defeated my destroyer angel, the Prince of Greed and one of my very best high lords. But can you defeat me?"

His demon magic washed over me like a wave of oily hatred. It punched me in the gut so hard, I stumbled back a few steps. The sword in my hands faltered. My muscles were suddenly weakened, making it difficult to hold the weight of the weapon. He smacked me again with it. This time, the sword clattered to the ground and snuffed out as I fell to my knees.

"Anna!"

Kincade tried to help me, but he was battling his own demon horde. Then I heard Azriel's voice.

"Did you miss me, brother?"

Lucifer stood in front of me now. In my weakened state, I looked up at him. He smiled down at me.

"Weakening you is the first step. Then I will strip away your other powers one by one."

I shook my head. "You won't."

"Let's see, shall we?"

He reached for me. I watched as if in slow motion as his hand with the long pointed black nails was nearly upon me. Deep inside, the Godlight came alive, as if sensing the devil. As his hand landed on my shoulder, the light exploded within me and burst forth in a bright, white flame that sent him reeling backward. He crashed to the cobblestone street, slid a few feet, and finally came to rest. My power had taken out several demons as well.

Sadly, Azriel still stood.

Thankfully, Kincade did, too.

I picked up the sword, the blade scraping along the ground as I rose to my feet. The power drained all my energy. It took everything I had inside me to stand but I managed. My labored breathing made my chest rise and fall in quick succession.

Azriel stopped fighting Kincade to see about his master. Kincade turned to me, giving me a once over. His face was dotted with sweat. His clothes were splattered with black demon blood.

"I guess you answered his question about defeating him," Kincade said.

"But I didn't kill him," I said, dazed.

"No, but you stung him." He took me by the arm. "Come on. Let's get out of here while we can."

"Why didn't it kill him?" I mindlessly followed him back the way he'd come, still griping the sword in one hand.

"I don't know."

As we took another step, light exploded in front of us and suddenly Silas was there, materializing out of the flash of light. We both halted mid step. I gaped, surprised at his sudden appearance.

"I sensed trouble." He looked past us to see the dead demons littering the ground. "You must be something special to garner the attention of the dark lord and his cronies."

"Do you have somewhere safe we can hide?" Kincade asked.

"Yes."

He stepped closer, opened his arms, and wrapped them around both of us in an awkward three-person bear hug. An enveloping warmth came over me and then that bright flash of light and suddenly we were no longer in the street in front of Temple Bar. We stood in the middle of a living room with plush seating, a thick rug, and lamps on each side table lit in a warm yellow glow. Moving through time and space with Silas didn't make me ill like it did with the angels. I suspected his ability was much like the Fae, who could sift.

"There are wards here to keep the darkness out," Silas said as he stepped away from us. He waved to the nearby seating. "Make yourselves at home."

Exhausted, I dropped the sword on the floor with a muffled thud and sank into the nearest plush velvet chair. Kincade placed the dagger on the coffee table and took the chair next to me. We both sat in silence as we listened to Silas banging around in the kitchen.

"It's never going to end, is it?" I asked, more as a rhetorical question than anything. "I'm so tired, Kincade."

"I know. But you have to keep fighting."

"Aye, keep fighting, lassie."

Silas came out of the kitchen carrying a tray with a pot of tea, sugar bowl, creamer, and cups. He placed the tray on the coffee table, eyeing the dagger. He picked it up, gazing down at the jade handle with the engraved alpha and omega on it. Then he pinpointed me with his silvery eye.

"This dagger can only belong to one person. Who are ye, lassie?"

"Anna Walker," I said, matter-of-factly.

He shook his head. "No. Who *are* you?"

I blinked confusion, glancing at Kincade for clarification. He cleared his throat and leaned forward.

"She's the Keeper of the Holy Relics."

Recognition of the title flickered over his face. "The one who was prophesied."

"That's what people keep telling me." I sighed, as if it was the most boring thing ever.

He lowered the dagger to the table with a sort of reverence, as though it were a sacred object. "Does she not know of the prophecy?"

"I do," I answered before Kincade. "The one that was written in my family history book told of the coming of a Keeper of the Holy Relics to fight for all mankind."

He looked at Kincade. "Tell her."

"There's only one prophecy," I said, confused. "The one that was passed down through the Walker line to me. The one that says I will carry the Light inside me and will stop the evil."

Silas poured tea as if we were at a tea party. "That's not the one I mean, lassie."

Kincade shifted in his chair toward me. His gaze met mine. I saw there, deep in his eyes, something that seemed to weigh on him. Some bit of information he knew but didn't want to share with me. And that bothered me. Because that meant he had known about it since the day we met.

"There has long been a prophecy in the Brotherhood of Watchers that foretold of a Keeper of Holy Relics. Long before your great-grandfather penned it in the family history book."

My brows knit together as my tired mind tried to understand what he was telling me.

"Och, lad—"

"I'm telling her," Kincade snapped. "Your great-grandfather is the one who called you the Keeper of the Holy Relics. The Brotherhood knows you by a different name."

I stared at him, dumbfounded. "And what is that?"

"The One Who Was Promised," Silas said.

I looked from Silas to Kincade. "I don't get it."

"The One Who Was Promised was the one foretold to bring balance between the Darkness and the Light. The one who would defeat the evil," Kincade said. "The Brotherhood has known long before John of Yorkshire became the first true dream walker. The first demon-seer."

"Legend states John of Yorkshire found remnants of the True Cross in Portugal. Michael, the archangel, decreed for him to return to England, marry, and pass it down through his line of succession for safekeeping. He also named him John Edward Walker of Yorkshire." Silas handed me a cup of steaming tea.

It smelled like Earl Grey. I took it without thinking, holding the warmth between my hands, as Silas's words rang in my head. I thought of all the relics and artifacts back in Walker Manor hidden in the library vault. All the things my uncle—and apparently his predecessors—collected over the years. If what he said was true, then the remnants of the True Cross must be there.

"What does the True Cross look like?" I asked.

"It would have been in a jewel-encrusted box with a cross on the top resembling the cross of the Templars," Kincade said. "It's a tiny crucifix carved from the remnants of the True Cross."

A hot prickling sensation went through me. I was certain I had seen that box in the vault on a shelf. A tiny little box with a hinged top with a Templar cross on top. I had never opened it. But as soon as I returned home, I would.

"You know of it, don't you?" Kincade asked.

I nodded, the words frozen in my throat. I thought the first dream walker was Ezra, the one who had betrayed our family and the angels' trust. The one Kincade killed centuries ago in Acre for his betrayal.

"The Darkness—Lucifer's darkness—has been growing since the time of the Crucifixion," Silas continued. "For centuries, he's gained more power, more high lords, more souls to build his army. He's been waiting for the right time to strike."

"Now he has the numbers," Kincade said. "He has the army. He knows he can't win, though, if you're alive. That's why he's so determined to bring you into his fold. Why he wants you."

Silas walked to a bookshelf behind the blue velvet Chesterfield and picked up an ancient leatherbound tome. He cracked it open and flipped to the middle of the book, as though he knew exactly what he was looking for. He brought it to me and held it down to show me.

There was a colorful picture of a woman holding a flaming sword, her dark hair billowing out behind her. She wore an angelic robe and sandals. The name under the picture was The One Who Was Promised. Her face looked eerily familiar. Much like the one I saw when I looked into a mirror. I stared at the picture in silence, my heart beating hard and fast.

"Where do the relics fit into all of this?" I suspected I already had the answer, but I asked the question anyway.

"They are meant to be weapons against the Dark," Kincade said.

"Weapons how?" I asked.

"No one knows," Silas answered. "That's where you come in."

"I don't know how to use them as weapons," I admitted. "I only know I'm supposed to find them and keep them hidden. I had to give up the Horn of Gabriel."

Kincade stared at me. "To whom?"

"Joachim came to me and demanded I hand it over for Gabriel. I traded it for information about where Sebastian took you."

Kincade's lips thinned into a straight line, as though he were ready to chastise me.

"You realize what this means?" Silas asked.

"I do." I nodded again and sipped my tea. "Judgement Day is upon us."

There. I said it out loud. I'd already seen one Horseman. I suspected the other three were on the way or perhaps already unleashed. The world was facing a pandemic of epic proportions. Deep down, I understood that. There was no sense in fearing what was to come because, even with the Holy Relics, I couldn't stop it. It would be like trying to stop a tidal wave with my bare hands.

Silence descended between us. Kincade remained where he was, not moving. Silas paced the small confines of his flat.

"Why do you need the explosives?" he asked as he paced.

"Because I'm going to destroy a lab that's creating super dream walkers like me. They stole my DNA and my mother's DNA and I want them to pay for that."

Silas halted his pacing. "Who is they?"

"The Knights of the Holy Lance," Kincade said.

"They are conspiring with the Brotherhood," Silas said.

That got my attention and Kincade's. He sat up straighter and fixed Silas with his piercing gaze. "How?"

"It's unclear to me, but I understand they have had dealings with one another. You said the Knights stole your DNA to make a super dream walker?"

"Yes. An army of women who can kill with their mind," I said.

"Why would the Knights and the Brotherhood work together? It doesn't make sense," Kincade said.

"I agree, it doesn't. However, I believe the Brotherhood was helping them find women for their experiments. They targeted those of us who left the Brotherhood and married."

"You've never told me this," Kincade said.

"I've never told anyone." Silas started pacing again.

I held the cup so tight, my hands ached and my nail beds turned white. My breath pooled in my chest as I waited for him to continue.

"A man named Schneider came for my wife. When I refused to give her up, she was killed."

Schneider had been the leader of the Knights of the Holy Lance. My gut clenched at the thought of this disgusting arrangement between the two factions—one helping kidnap women to hand over for experiments on their brains.

"Then they both need to be destroyed," I said.

"I'm afraid it's not that easy, lassie. The corruption of the Brotherhood of Watchers and the Warder of Nine runs deep. I spent years searching for the answers after they stole my life. I believe their perfect façade is beginning to crack." He paused, stopped pacing once again and looked to me. "I will help you destroy that lab, lassie. I will give you whatever weapons you need to do it. Because they have to be stopped."

"As does the Brotherhood. We need to find out the truth," Kincade said.

"We will in time. I will continue my underground work. In the meantime, I'll meet my contact for the explosives you need." He glanced at me then. "You look exhausted, lass. You should rest."

Hearing those words made me fight back a yawn. "I'm not tired."

"You are," Kincade insisted. The softness in it pissed me off—because it worked. "Do you have someplace she can sleep?"

"Of course." He motioned toward a door off the living room. "My bedroom is small but it will do."

I *was* tired, but it irked me they were pushing me out of the room. As if I were a child in need of a nap. Kincade slipped the cup of tea out of my hands and placed it on the table. Then he took my arm and gently hauled me to my feet. He didn't ask if he could touch me. He just...took responsibility. And my body, traitor that it was, let him. He led me to the bedroom and opened the door.

"Get some sleep. You need all your energy."

We eyed each other a long moment and then I finally nodded. I entered the small room. He closed the door behind me. I stood there examining the sparse furnishings. Silas didn't have much. A queen size bed dominated one wall, a small bureau on the other. One nightstand and a sad looking lamp. I crawled into the bed on top of the comforter, my legs hanging over the side. I kicked off my shoes and allowed my body to sink into the softness of the mattress.

I didn't want to admit how good that felt.

Outside the room, Kincade and Silas continued to talk, their voices nothing but a low murmur. I made out a few words here and there.

Silas saying something about telling me something.

Kincade saying I wasn't ready in a muffled tone.

Tell me what?

In my haze, I thought I heard Silas say, "She's ready as she'll ever be. *Tell her*, Kincade. Tell her who her father is."

As I drifted off, I was both stunned and outraged. And then decided I had misheard whatever Silas said. I vowed to question Kincade with a relentless determination as soon as I woke up.

CHAPTER 17

KINCADE WOKE ME WITH a gentle shake of my shoulder what seemed like minutes later. In truth, it was two hours later.

"It's time," he said.

Groggy, I sat up and stretched. I stuck my feet back into my boots. "Did you get what we needed?"

"Yes."

I followed him out of the bedroom. Silas was nowhere to be found. I realized as I stumbled along behind him, I'd forgotten to call off the driver earlier that morning.

"The driver—"

"I rescheduled him. Silas is waiting for us on the bridge."

I should have known Kincade would have it covered. We left the apartment. He closed the door behind us. We were in a shadowed corridor. Kincade headed down it like he knew where he was going. I followed.

"Do you know who my father is?" I hadn't intended to blurt it out but there it was.

Kincade halted so suddenly I nearly ran into the back of him. He turned to look at me, his green-gold eyes unreadable.

"What made you ask that?"

"I thought I heard Silas say something about you telling me who he is and, well, the walls are thin."

His face masked his true emotion with whatever he was thinking. I tried to tap into his mind, but he closely guarded that, too. He was better at that than I was.

"You misheard." He started walking again.

I was unconvinced. And not ready to give up so easily. "I don't think I did, Kincade." I grasped him by the arm and pulled him to a stop. He turned to face me. "If you know, please tell me. My uncle kept information from me all the time and I hated it."

"He did it to protect you."

"I don't need protection from information."

"Sometimes the truth is hard to hear."

Was that an admission that he knew who my father was? And if he'd known all this time, why had he never shared that with me? Why was it such a secret?

"My uncle told me once he thought my father was an angel. Is that true?"

His poker face remained in place. "It is."

"And?" I prompted.

"It's not for me to say, Anna."

I dropped my hand from his arm and took a step backward, crushed and betrayed. "Then you do know and refuse to tell me."

Frustration flickered across his features. "As a member of the Brotherhood, I was sworn to secrecy."

"But you're not a member anymore," I pointed out.

He nodded. "You're right. I'm not. But some things you need to find out on your own, Anna."

Angry, I shoved by him. "Just like my uncle. If my mother was in her right mind, she would tell me."

In the stairwell, I didn't wait for him and pounded down the stairs in a fit of fury.

Kincade was right behind me. "Anna, wait."

I spun around to face him, my rage evident. "I'm tired of everyone trying to protect me from information. My uncle, you, Sariel."

Question flickered over his face. "Sariel?"

"He's the one who gave me the postcards. Until recently, I hadn't a clue. He told me when he handed me the card for Egypt. He admitted he did it to help me."

"Sariel gave you the postcards," he repeated as if he were shocked to hear it.

"Yes. Is that so unbelievable?"

"No," he said slowly. "What else did he tell you?"

"Nothing of note, though I'm sure he has secrets of his own he doesn't want to share."

I walked into the early afternoon. Despite the bright sunshine, there was a cold bite to the wind. I pulled my jacket closer as I headed down the street, unaware of where I was going. I hadn't a clue where the Ha'penny Bridge was.

Kincade pulled me to a stop and turned me to face him. He gripped my upper arms, holding me in place. "I made a promise I wouldn't tell you. That you would find out on your own."

I shrugged him off, a variety of emotions pounding through me while I tried to make sense of them all.

"All this time, I thought he was dead. I thought my mother was dead. Neither of them were. They *abandoned* me, Kincade. Do you understand how devastating that is to discover? They didn't want me." My breath hitched, a sob threatening.

Something in his expression softened. He stepped toward me and lowered his voice. "They did want you. Desperately. But their circumstances were as such they were unable to keep you with them."

More enlightening information. "You've known since we met, haven't you? Who they were, that they were alive, that they left me to be raised as an orphan. You probably even knew who I was and that's why you inserted yourself into my life."

There was no way to stop the spew of angry words.

"No, not since we met. I had no idea who you were until I met your uncle. When I was looking for you but you'd gone to Hong Kong. Even then I didn't realize the truth but as we spent time together, I put the pieces together. As you learned more about who you were and what you can do, I was certain you would figure it out on your own." He moved closer still, and took my arms again, pulling me toward him. "You are so close to discovering the truth yourself."

I said nothing as I stared at him, resenting him for keeping the truth from me. Feeling betrayed by the one person I trusted with my very existence. The one person I counted on to have my back at all times and never keep things from me.

"You're angry with me," he continued. "I understand and deserve that. But trust me when I say finding out on your own will be better than finding out from me."

I pushed him away again. "I disagree."

Our argument was forgotten the moment the shadowy veil came down around us. We both did a three-sixty to see where the threat came from. The rider on the red horse approached at a rapid gallop heading right for me. He brandished a golden sword in one hand, holding it aloft. Kincade grabbed my arm and dragged me out of the way as he rode past.

Neither one of us had to say out loud who the rider was. We both knew.

War.

He rode through the veil as though it wasn't there. He swiped his sword through a group of people, killing several. Screams rose up. And then the people in the street turned on each other. Fights broke out. Fists were flying.

I was frozen in place. "What do we do?"

Kincade took my hand. "We run like hell."

We took off at a dead run trying to avoid the crowds of angry, fighting people. Past Temple Bar where we'd met Silas just hours before. But our run had to slow to nothing more than a quick pace as he dodged people. An angry man confronted Kincade, taking a swing at him. Kincade was faster, though, and ducked.

Someone grabbed me from behind in a chokehold, punching me in my already sore ribs. I elbowed the assailant in the gut hard enough to elicit a grunt. It was enough to create slack around my neck. I stomped on the top of his foot, slamming my boot down. He cried out and released me. I turned and punched him, pain flaring into my already destroyed knuckles.

Kincade stepped between us when the man tried to attack me again. He took one look at Kincade's hulking form and took off. He fled through the crowd but it wasn't long before he was in another fight.

"Let's go. Stick close."

I wrapped my fingers in his and let him lead me out of the chaos. Or at least what we thought was the chaos. We turned left down a street. Kincade pushed and shoved his way through, throwing a punch here and there. At the corner, we took a right, passing the Ha'penny Bridge Inn and heading north toward the bridge. It was in the distance. Not far now. I tried to peer over his shoulder to see if Silas waited for us there, but it was hard to see over his hulking form.

Kincade swore under his breath.

"What is it?"

"There are demons ahead. Heading right for us."

I inhaled a deep breath. Yes. I scented their death and rot on the air. No doubt War had brought them with him.

"I need to draw down the weapons," I said.

He paused long enough for me to pull down first the dagger, then the sword. I handed the dagger off to Kincade, then lit the sword. We took our side-by-side stance and waited.

Behind us, the sound of galloping. We turned in unison to see War riding down the crowd, slashing with his golden sword, killing without a thought. He spotted us, standing still in a sea of motion, and pulled his red horse to a halt. He jumped down from the saddle in one fluid motion, his lethal gaze on me and my flaming sword.

"Anna—" My name a word of warning on Kincade's lips.

But I didn't have time to listen or react. War was upon me in an instant. Our swords clanged with a deafening roar, reverberating throughout the street. It caught the attention of several nearby brawlers who stopped fighting long enough to get out of our way.

War was tall, muscular, dressed in nothing but a tunic, pants, and boots. No armor. His flaming red hair was long, plaited on both sides. His eyes were bright blue, sharp, deadly. He slammed his sword against mine again without much effort while I held mine in both hands and tried to maintain my footing.

He was stronger than I was. And more powerful. And more skilled. I hadn't a clue what I was doing other than trying to stay alive and keep the sword in my hands. I swung for his head, but he blocked the blow. When my blade met his, it was so jarring my back teeth rattled.

I stumbled backward, tripping over a felled body that was likely dead. I refused to look. I managed to maintain my footing but War kept coming, swinging that golden sword trying to lop off my head.

I caught a glimpse of Kincade long enough to see he was locked in his own battle with the demons infiltrating the crowd. He was doing his best to hold his own, but he was losing and nearly overcome by them.

I had to do something. I had to get away from War as fast as possible. But he wasn't making it easy to do that. He thrust his sword toward me. I batted it away with a weak swing. My arm muscles burned with the exertion of it all. I wasn't sure how much longer I could keep it up.

An explosion rocked the entire world. It was so loud it left my ears ringing. Plus, it distracted War long enough for me to attack. I swung my sword toward him but he sensed it before I was able to follow through. My sword glanced off his upper arm and then immediately snuffed out.

Blood streamed down his arm. He pinned his bright blue glare on me. He said nothing as he turned and mounted his horse, galloping away toward the fireball billowing into the sky.

Another explosion, as if a grenade went off. Bodies went flying into the air near the bridge. Clutching the sword, I ran toward Kincade. Most of the demons joined War as he rode through the crowd toward the bridge.

"It's Silas!" Kincade shouted and took off at a dead run toward the bridge.

I followed, trying to keep pace with his long legs. And while I tried to see Silas on the bridge, I was unable to make out anything through the thick black acrid smoke. It stung my eyes and nose. I managed to keep my mouth closed but running without panting was taking a toll on my lungs.

Kincade killed demons along the way, each of them turning to ash in the middle of the street. A few tried to attack me, but I fended them off with the sword. Screams and shouts filled the air. People pushed and shoved to get away from the fire and the explosions and all the while Kincade and I headed for it.

And War still on horseback causing all kinds of death and destruction. I had to do something to stop him.

Kincade made it to the bridge. I saw Silas, then, standing in the middle of it. He hurled another grenade into the crowd. It bounced several times on the street, then rolled and came to a halt in the middle of a group of demons worshiping War. I ducked as the thing exploded, sending black blood and demon parts flying.

It missed War.

Too bad.

Kincade stabbed his way through the crowd and onto the bridge. Silas handed him an oversized duffel that must contain more explosives. He shouted something to Kincade who ushered him off the bridge and back onto solid ground. Meanwhile, War took off at another gallop and disappeared down Wellington Quay, leaving a path of destruction and screams in his wake.

Most of the crowd had dissipated by now. Sirens blared through the air, heading for the fiery chaos Silas created with his grenades. I finally caught up to them both, my chest heaving, my eyes watering from the smoke.

"You know how to make an entrance," I said.

He pinpointed me with his one good eye. "Only thing to do to save your hides, lassie." Then he looked to Kincade, "I can't stay in Dublin. It's too dangerous for me now. The Brotherhood is looking for me. I suspect that's why the demons attacked. And…" he paused and glanced the way War disappeared. "Who was that rider? Was it who I think?"

"Yes," I answered simply. I refused to say the name aloud. We'd already had a run-in with Conquest and I didn't want to invoke his presence. Not that saying the name would, but one could never be too cautious.

"Where will you go?" Kincade asked.

"Don't know yet."

"Come with us," I urged. "We can use your help."

"Not if your next stop is Antarctica." He gave me a lopsided grin, his one good eye crinkling with mirth. "I'm sure our paths will cross again, Keeper."

Then he gave Kincade a farewell nod. Before either of us had a chance to tell him goodbye, he bolted into the crowd and was gone.

CHAPTER 18

WE HAD TO FIGHT our way from the Liffey River. There was so much death and destruction. Dead demons and dead humans alike. It looked like a full-blown war zone. Kincade carried the duffel in one hand and stabbed with the dagger in the other. It was truly something to watch his skills at work.

I used the sword, which I'd relit, as we made our way through. We had to get to the airport and get back on the plane to home to pick up the others before our trip to Antarctica. I needed to stop long enough to contact the driver but with all the demons chasing us, it was damn near impossible.

Kincade turned down a street and then led us into an alley, out of the fray. Both of us stopped to catch our breath. My arm muscles burned with the pain of swinging the sword and trying to stay alive. I extinguished the sword and sagged against a brick wall, the weapon at my side. Kincade kept his eye on the exit to the alley, watching for more attackers.

I took the opportunity to call the driver. As it rang, I asked, "Where are we?"

"Off Aston Place between Aston Quay and Fleet Street," he said.

"He's not answering."

"We'll have to grab a taxi," he said.

I eyed the duffel with a dubious expression. "Are you sure?"

"We can't walk," he said. "It's a thirty-minute drive north to the airport. It's our only option."

"Maybe we have another?" I suggested, thinking of several winged friends with the ability to transport.

"Like what?"

"Like..." I chose my words slowly as I thought it through.

"No angels," he said, then, as if reading my mind.

"But—"

"The teleporting makes you sick," he pointed out.

"I know, but..." My words trailed off. He wasn't wrong but I was convinced it was the only way to get out of our current predicament.

"She's right. It's the only way."

Sariel made a sudden appearance standing at the exit of the alleyway. His alabaster and gold threaded wings were spread behind him in splendor. He eyed Kincade, the duffel, the dagger, and then me. Question etched his face as if he was trying to decide what to ask first.

"How did you know we were here?" I demanded, standing straight.

"I know lots of things. The streets are clogged with demons and high lords," the angel said.

"You saw them?" Kincade asked, as though he didn't believe him.

"Yes. I saw the high lords killing humans and stealing their souls. Many guardian angels died today."

"Because of War?" I asked.

"Yes." He waved me toward him. "Come. I will take you to the plane."

I didn't have to look out onto the street to confirm what he said. I believed him. I stole a glance at Kincade whose expression was less than happy about the idea. He clenched his jaw, the muscles ticking along the edge.

"I'll take her first," Sariel said. "Then come back for you."

"Here, take this." Kincade handed me the duffel.

"Why?" I demanded.

"In case anything happens."

He didn't finish the sentence, but I understood. In case anything happens between the time Sariel dropped me at the plane and then returned for him. The angel wrapped his arm around my waist. I held on tight and then we flashed away.

* * *

I needn't have worried. While I was trying to recover from my teleportation sickness—I decided that's what I'd call it from now on—he returned moments later with Kincade. I managed to stagger onto the plane and fall into one of the leather seats, curling my body as small as possible with my knees drawn up to my chest. I groaned as he boarded the plane moments later.

"I told you."

"Please," I breathed. "None of that."

I dropped my legs and slid down into the leather seat, clutching my stomach and waiting for the nausea to pass. Kincade, meanwhile, talked to the pilot and told them we were ready to depart. When he returned, he stashed the duffel of grenades and who-knew-what-else under a seat.

It occurred to me then it probably wasn't the best idea to carry that many explosives on a plane but there we were.

When we were airborne, and my illness was gone, I pushed to sit up straight into the seat. Kincade was across from me, his arms folded over his chest as he glared out the window.

"What's wrong?" I asked.

"Sariel. How did he know where you were?"

I shrugged. "He often pops up when I least expect it."

"Seems convenient."

I supposed he was right. When I was blinded in Rio de Janeiro, Sariel was the one who restored my eyesight. My uncle didn't much like him. He was the one responsible for giving me the postcards and leading me to the relics and also my mother.

My mother.

Why would he lead me to my mother?

I looked at Kincade who was still glaring out the window. Why was he so angry Sariel showed up to get us out of a jam? I wasn't the one who summoned him. Well, ok, I thought about it but I hadn't actually done it.

And then I recalled the tale Kincade shared with me about the death of my ancestor, Ezra. The one who betrayed the angels and sullied the dream walker name. The one who was determined to take over the world using three of the Holy Relics.

"Sariel was in Acre with you," I said. "He and Michael took the Holy Relics from Ezra after you killed him."

Kincade met my gaze. "Yes, but you know that already."

"You don't like him."

"Who says?" he countered.

"Because he helps me."

Kincade said nothing as he stared at me.

"He helps me find the relics and he helped me find my mother."

He lifted an eyebrow as if to encourage me to continue working out why Sariel would do that. A cold trickle of realization hit me. My jaw clenched.

"He *wanted* me to find my mother," I said.

"He led you to her with a note about Station 211," Kincade said.

"That's right. Why? Because he wanted me to see the lab?"

Again, Kincade said nothing. My thoughts whirled as I tried to understand. I glanced down at my hands, twisting the edge of my shirt as it struck me.

"Because...he..." My words faltered. "He's my father."

I lifted my gaze to Kincade's and though he said nothing, the truth was evident in his green-gold eyes. Sariel was my father and he knew that.

"Is he?" I demanded.

"You should ask him."

I growled with frustration. "I'm tired of these mind games. Just answer the fucking question!"

His brows rose in surprise at my outburst. There was a long beat of silence and then, he said, "He is."

Upon hearing the confirmation, I burst into tears. I put my face in my hands and let the sobs come. So many questions flickered through my mind.

Uncle Edward knew who Sariel was, too. He'd had dealings with him on more than one occasion. He'd hinted to me that an angel was my father, which meant he also knew the truth and yet didn't share it with me. He and Sariel had banished Azriel—who masqueraded as a stable boy named Marcus—from Walker Manor when I thought I was in love with the high lord. The angel put protection over the manor and then removed my memories of the man I thought I loved, the one who had deceived me. Azriel was determined to keep me from my ultimate destiny and used whatever tools he had to achieve that.

Edward, of course, would have known all that. He would have known Sariel was my father. Why all the mystery? Why keep it a secret?

And Kincade. The man I trusted with my life, with my very existence had known, too. And yet kept it from me.

But the biggest question I had was why did my parents abandon me? Why did I end up in the foster system being raised by a stranger—who I had grown to love as my own mother?

When I finished with my emotional outburst, I wiped my eyes and peered out the window, trying to make sense of it all. Trying to understand the whys and hows everything had come to be. If my parents kept me, would I have become the Keeper of the Holy Relics?

"You said their circumstances wouldn't allow them to keep me." My voice was thick with emotion, raw with tears. "Do you know what those were?"

He shook his head. "No."

I narrowed my gaze. "No, you don't know or no you won't tell me?"

"It was an assumption to put your mind at ease."

I pressed back into the leather seat, the material crinkling with my weight. "You lied."

"I was trying to help."

I bit back the words I wanted to spew, to tell him I didn't need his help. Instead, I pressed my chin into my hand and stared out the window. We said nothing more the remainder of the flight.

But I had decided the next time I saw Sariel he was going to get a piece of my mind.

* * *

The drive to Walker Manor from the airport was silent. I wasn't in a talking mood and neither was Kincade. Fine.

I also wanted to tell my uncle off, but there was no telling if he would show up as Cashiel any time soon. I thought about trying to summon him but then decided against it. I wanted to ask my mother, but her mind was so far gone there was no way she would understand what I was trying to ask her. I doubted she'd remember the truth anyway.

Kincade carried the duffel to his room without another word. I followed him, trudging up the stairs feeling utterly defeated. We'd gone to Dublin to get what we needed for the mission in Antarctica, sure. But I came home with a weight pressing on me that I wasn't going to be able to shake for a long time.

As I entered my room and shut the door, I leaned against the door thinking of everything that had happened over the last few months. I was utterly exhausted from it all. From searching for the Holy Relics to fighting the demons to fighting Azriel and even Lucifer. And sometimes fighting Kincade. It was hard not to feel as though he betrayed me.

As I stood there thinking about the lab in Antarctica, the one that stole my mother's DNA and created these super dream walkers, a terribly insane thought crossed my mind.

Go there, alone, and destroy the lab. Not tell anyone my plans lest they try to talk me out of it. Return home with no one being the wiser.

If I did it, alone, it was a risk. I realized this. And one I was more than willing to take. One that would keep those I cared about the most safe here in Walker Manor.

The biggest question was how was I going to do it? I didn't want to waste time to trek across the frozen tundra. I needed a way to Station 211 that was quick.

When I'd gone before with my uncle, we jumped from an airplane.

I did it once and was certain I could again. I needed to act fast, though. The others were expecting to leave in the next day or so. Instead of sleeping, I pushed away the urge and began to make my covert plans.

* * *

In the dead of night, I crept from my room closing the door with a soft snick behind me. I stood in the hallway, listening to the quiet of the house and the faint tick of the clock downstairs. I paused there, my heart hammering.

Kincade had the duffel with the explosives. I needed that duffel. I glanced down the hall to his room, peering at the closed door wondering if I could get in and out without him knowing I was there.

It was worth a shot.

I took long slow, quiet steps down the hall, then stopped outside his door. I leaned an ear on the door to listen. Nothing but the whoosh of air. I tried the knob, turning it with as much silence as possible. The door swung open with ease. Peering inside, I spied the duffel in the middle of the floor. His hulking form was in the bed, a soft snoring from him.

This was my chance.

I tiptoed into the room on silent feet, keeping an eye on the bed as I made my way to the duffel. When I was there, I picked it up. The material rustled. Something inside shifted. Kincade made a movement. I froze, waiting to see if he was awake.

When he emitted another snore, I headed back to the door, closing it behind me. I blew out a breath, relieved to have the duffel in hand and Kincade none the wiser.

But I wasn't out of the clear yet. I hurried down the corridor, the old wood planks of the floor creaking slightly with my weight and frowned. At the stairs, I hurried down them, intending to get to the bottom before anyone—Kincade—awoke to stop me.

As I took the final step, I sensed movement to my left. I halted at the bottom of the stairs, peering into the shadows with a squint as if that'd help. My mother emerged from the kitchen. She halted with a gasp when she saw me standing there in the darkness.

"Anna?"

"I didn't mean to scare you." I stayed rooted in place, trying to decide how to get by her and to the front door without a million questions.

She moved closer. Her eyes, the same purple as mine, paused on the duffel in my hand.

"What are you doing?" she asked.

"Please understand I have to go. I have to do this alone."

"Do what?" She sounded confused. Her gaze flickered back up to mine.

I took that moment to continue to the front door. "You'll understand soon enough."

"You cannot do this alone, Anna." It was Sariel's voice that stopped me from opening the door.

I looked over my shoulder at him. He stood in the parlor door, his alabaster wings spread behind him in an ethereal glow. I stole a glance at my mother, who had her wide-eyed gaze fixed on him. Recognition flickered over her features and then she pressed shaking fingers to her lips.

"Sariel?" His name came out a roughened whisper.

He turned to look at her with a sort of reverence I'd never seen before. His face softened when she took a step toward him. Her hands dropped to her sides. He closed the gap between them, reaching for her. And for a moment, they forgot I was there.

My breath pooled in my throat as I watched them reach for each other, falling into each other's arms as though they hadn't seen each other in years. And maybe they hadn't. My heart pounded so hard I thought it might burst from my chest.

There they were. The two people who were my parents. The ones who abandoned me as a baby and left me in the American foster system. So many emotions warred within me as I watched them embrace, then pull apart. Sariel held her at arm's length. He brushed a hand over her hair. Tears were in her eyes.

"I thought I'd never see you again," she whispered, her words shaking. She sounded more lucid than she ever had.

"And I thought you were forever lost to me," he replied.

"What happened to you?"

"A long story I will share with you one day."

I cleared my throat. They both turned to me. There was a light in my mother's eyes, one I had only seen once or twice. One that told me her mind was clear and she realized who she was.

"Anna." She said my name on a breath.

"I have to go." I turned back and reached for the door.

"Not alone," Sariel said.

"You aren't the boss of me," I snapped. "And you don't even know where I'm going anyway."

"To the lab at Station 211," he said. "To destroy it."

"You were supposed to take us with you," my mother added, as if she remembered the morning we all agreed to go together. "With the others."

"The situation has changed," I said, staring at the door. "I need to go alone."

Footsteps were behind me and then a hand on my shoulder. My mother.

"Don't, Anna. Let me go with you. Let me help you. No one knows that lab better than me."

"And I can take you both there," Sariel added.

My hand hovered over the doorknob as I hesitated. My mother, who called herself Natasha, made a valid point. And so did Sariel. I was wondering how to get to Antarctica with the explosives. It was a long journey but one I was willing to face alone. I had some desperate need to make sure it was done without anyone's help. Mostly because I was angry with Kincade for keeping the identity of my father from me. And angry with Cashiel and Sariel both for never telling me the truth.

"Those men took a piece of me," Natasha said.

I turned to face them both and nodded. "You're right. They did. And they created monsters from your DNA. You have every right to want to destroy them as much as I do. But I have a lot of questions. And you both have a lot of explaining to do."

I didn't miss the guilty expression on Sariel's face as he nodded. "You're right. All will be explained to you in time."

"All right then. Let's go."

CHAPTER 19

WE NEEDED COLD WEATHER gear. Well, maybe not Sariel but for sure me and Natasha. I conveyed this to Sariel before he flashed us both away across the world. We were in Punta Arenas in southern Chile, a town that catered to sightseeing trips to the frozen continent. I booked a hotel room for the three of us, left the duffel in Natasha's care, and went in search of coats, hats, and scarves for the two of us. Sariel declined.

It was odd, really, thinking about doing this mission with the two of them. My mother's mind had become very clear. She remembered things about her stay at Station 211. She remembered trying to kill me with her mind in Rio and ultimately blinding me. But she did not remember how or when she came to be in the company of the Knights of the Holy Lance. That seemed to be nothing but a black hole in her mind.

I returned a while later to the tiny hotel room with an armload of winter gear. Snow boots for both of us, thermal pants and shirts for the first layer, thick pants and sweaters, thick socks, coats, gloves, hats and scarves. We were ready.

"I'll take you first," Sariel said. "Then return with your mother."

"I need you to get us as close to the station as possible without being detected." He nodded, then I said to Natasha, "You know how to get us past the guards?"

"Yes," she said and didn't elaborate.

I didn't ask further questions. I picked up the duffel and gave a nod to Sariel I was ready. He wrapped his arm around my waist. I held my breath, preparing myself for the teleportation sickness I was soon to enjoy. He flashed away.

We landed in the middle of a cold whipping wind that stole my breath. I dropped the duffel and landed on all fours in the snow, taking deep, frigid cleansing breaths as the illness washed over me.

Sariel disappeared and a moment later returned with my mother. She dropped down next to me, her hand on my back.

"Are you all right?"

"I will be," I said.

I took another cleansing breath and then sat back on my heels to look up at the night sky. A million winking stars stared back. The full moon hung big and bright in the inky blackness, illuminating the snow around us in a blue-white glow. I got to my feet and picked up the duffel, casting a glance toward the entrance for Station 211. It was nothing more than a dark gray square in the center of a snowy mountain.

"I'm ready. Let's get this done," I said.

"I will retrieve you when you're ready," Sariel said. "Good luck and Godspeed."

Natasha and I took off toward the hidden lab. As we crested a hill, she suddenly stopped and peered around, looking confused.

"Where are we?" Her voice sounded almost a panic.

I reached for her, took her gloved hand in mine. "We're heading to Station 211. Remember?"

Her gaze met mine. In the moonlight, I saw the lucid light in her eyes had faded. Something changed. She no longer understood who and where she was.

"I don't."

She pulled her hand out of mine and started to back away. Panic rose within me. I stepped toward her but she put a hand up to stop me.

"Stay away. I don't know who you are."

"Yes, you do. It's me. Anna."

She shook her head and then she turned and bolted into a run back the way we came.

Great.

Now what?

I sighed.

What had changed to make her forget?

And then it hit me.

The moment she saw Sariel standing in the parlor doorway, she had clarity. She had clarity the whole time we were with him. I thought back to all those moments in the past when she had lucid thoughts and then they were gone in a poof. All those times were the same ones when Sariel was present. When he disappeared, she forgot.

"Sariel!"

I shouted his name to the wind and took off at a run after my mother. I needn't have worried. As I crested the hill, they were standing huddled together. His wings spread out behind him reflecting the light of the moon and looking magnificent. She clung to him as if he were her last salvation.

I had no doubt in my mind he was.

He lifted his head and gave me a rueful smile. "It appears my presence is the only thing that keeps her mind clear."

"What do we do now?" I asked.

"I can take you inside but it will have to be one at a time."

I shook my head. "I don't have time to recover from the teleportation sickness. I need all my senses to be on full alert. And we need to do this together."

He took my mother's face in his big hands and pressed his forehead against hers, their faces partially hidden under the voluminous hood of her coat.

"You're going to be fine. You can do this."

She clutched his wrists as if she held him in place while the cold wind whipped. Snow flurries danced in the air around them making the scene appear all the more magical. And something deep inside me melted a little seeing them together, knowing they were my parents.

"I'm afraid..." She whispered the words, her breath white smoke.

"I know but you don't have to be. Because I'll be right here waiting for you."

"I don't want to lose you again."

"You won't." His breath plumed white as he spoke. "I give you my word. And a gift to help you maintain your clarity."

He bent to kiss her, their mouths fusing in a kiss of longing. I understood what he was doing even if she didn't—using his angel magic on her. A gift to maintain her clarity must mean it would help her focus and keep from forgetting. When they broke, she nodded and stepped back but as she turned to me, I saw the fear and uncertainty in her eyes. I moved to her, taking her gloved hand in mine and gave her a squeeze, hoping she felt it through the thick layers.

"Stay with me and we'll be all right," I said, trying to put her mind at ease.

She brushed the back of her free hand across my cheek, the material cold against my exposed skin. Then she took a deep breath, expelled it into the wind in a white fog and said, "I am ready."

She gave one last glance at Sariel. I still gripped her hand in mine as we hurried down the hill toward the bunker hidden in the snowy mountain. As we neared, I made out two guards standing on either side of the door, both of them buried in layers upon layers to keep warm. Even their eyes were protected by clear goggles. Not one inch of skin was visible.

Next to me, Natasha tensed as she approached. No doubt the adrenaline rush punched through her at seeing them. As we moved closer, she released my hand and hurried a few steps ahead of me. I wanted to call out to her, but something stopped me.

She lifted her arms the way she did when she used her powers. She never broke stride as she did so. A moment later, both men fell to the ground in a heap. I hurried to catch up to her but she was already kneeling by one of them, rifling through his pockets. When she didn't find what she was looking for, she unzipped his thick coat and reached in. She gave a swift yank and then held up what appeared to be a badge. Her eyes crinkled with her smile of triumph.

I kneeled next to the other guard, looking for a similar badge. I shoved his scarf aside to yank down the zipper and retrieve it. The material fell away from his face. Blood trickled from his nose and the corners of his mouth. His sightless eyes peered up through the clear goggles, bloody tears streaming from the corners.

She'd killed them.

With a thought.

I tried not to think about that too hard as I yanked the badge from around his neck like she had. She was on her feet and using the other guard's badge to open the thick metal door. It groaned with a horrible noise as it slid open to reveal the long entrance into the station dotted with pale white lights.

No hesitation as she entered and started down the long ramp, her feet leaving snowy footprints behind. She paused, turned to me, and motioned to the bag of explosives in my hand. I knelt, placed it on the ground and unzipped it. Both of us peered inside at the arrangement of weapons there. There were several charges as well as detonators. As she reached inside the bag for one of the charges, we heard footsteps.

She stood straight and turned to face whoever was coming from the depths of the station. Two men rounded the corner. The instant they saw us, they both reached for their guns. But my mother was faster.

She lifted her arms and then made a swooshing motion with them as if to wipe them away. Both of them convulsed and dropped to the ground. I didn't have to look to see the blood in their eyes, nose, and mouth. The metallic twang of blood filled the air.

"We must hurry. Follow me quickly."

She didn't have to tell me twice. We crept through the station. It was much as I remembered from the last time. I was here but I had no idea where we were going. I kept close as I followed her through the twisting corridors.

Whatever Sariel did to put her mind at ease seemed to have worked. She remained completely lucid the entire time we were in the place. She led me right to the lab, the one in which I found her DNA in a vial marked with the name A WALKER. The one I smashed on the tile floor under my boot.

She pushed open the door and led me inside. I spied the cooler right away with the vials of blood inside. Each one had a first initial, last name. She was at the cooler before me, opening it and rifling through the vials of blood. She froze, staring into it and then reached inside. She brought out several vials and rose, turning to me.

I hurried over to her and looked down at them in her gloved hands. Each one of them were marked with A WALKER. My stomach turned as bile rose to my throat.

"Let's blow this motherfucker," I said.

She merely nodded.

I placed charges in each corner of the room.

"Is there a place where they would keep notes about the experiment?" I asked. "A file room or something?"

"Yes. This way."

She was out the door. I snatched the duffel off the floor and hurried after her. She was down the dimly lit corridor, walking at a quick pace. So fast, it was hard for me to keep up with her. My legs burned with the sudden burst of exertion.

Natasha came to a halt. I skittered to a stop, too, to keep from running into the back of her. Three more men headed toward us. A shout rose up in German. She stood perfectly still, raising her arms. I watched in horror as she killed them with nothing more than a thought.

When they were dead, she stripped off her coat and dropped it. Then unwound the scarf around her neck and face. She removed the gloves, leaving all the winter wear in a heap on the floor. She kicked it to the side. The dim light illuminated the beads of sweat on her forehead and running down the side of her face.

"Come."

She took off to the left at a near jog. I rushed after her, struggling to keep up. We wound our way through the depths of the station. Along the way, she killed every guard we ran into in a silent, deadly fashion. Eventually, they were going to be onto us and start hunting down who was doing all the killing. Eventually, our luck would run out.

We made it to the living quarters, where she took me to an office. The office I recalled was Schneider's at one time. The one in which I stole the book of all his scientist's notes, which I still had hidden in my bedroom back at Walker Manor.

A metal desk on one side of the room hosted a pile of messy papers, a laptop, a notepad with more scribbled notes. A filing cabinet stood in one corner. I didn't recall that being in the room the last time I was here, but then, I was in a hurry to get the fuck out.

She motioned around the room. I quicky laid more charges.

"Anywhere else?" I asked.

"The hospital where they do the experiments."

And she was off like a shot.

As we entered the hallway, our luck had run out.

CHAPTER 20

Four men waited for us. I shoved the duffel into Natasha's hands and went into action. I drew down the dagger but quickly realized it was going to be hard to fight them in this thick winter coat. My range of movement was limited and I was fighting against myself to attack them.

One of them came at me. Suddenly, his back arched, a scream ripped from his lungs, and he dropped to the ground. I didn't have to look to know his face was bleeding and he was dead. Natasha killed the other three in a matter of seconds. What I expected to be a long, drawn-out fight, she dispatched them with ease.

I turned back to her. She'd dropped the duffel, her arms stretched at her side. I took the moment to strip out of my coat, hat, gloves, and scarf and discard them in the hallway. I grabbed the duffel and motioned for her to lead the way.

I lost count of how many men she killed but I didn't question it. She had some sort of vendetta against them all and I didn't blame her one bit. They stole part of her. They made an army of super dream walkers like her, and she was getting even.

And so was I.

I followed her through the endless corridors all in the same gunmetal gray and lit with that garish yellow light. I was grateful she came with me because I hadn't a clue where we were going and doubted I would be able to find my way out. We entered the hospital where they had several women waiting for their next experiment. When I was here last, I talked to one of them who was ready and willing to give up her life for that of the Knights of the Holy Lance. I didn't understand it then just as I didn't now.

I hesitated, though. Blowing up the lab was one thing. Taking the lives of these innocent women was something else. The dead men we left in our wake, however, were not so innocent so I had less guilt about their deaths. Natasha gave me a questioning look as I remained rooted in place. I gave her a slow shake of my head.

"I can't."

"Why not?" It sounded like a demand.

"Because..." My words faltered as I motioned toward the women in the beds.

"They are soldiers, Anna," she said. "They will not hesitate to harm others."

"But..."

"If we spare them now, there is a chance they will rise up and continue the work of the Knights," she said.

"But their blood won't be on my hands."

"Then they'll be on mine." She turned toward them and started to raise her arms.

I dropped the duffel and wrapped a hand around her wrist. "No."

Her head snapped to me, her eyes wide with shock. "Anna—"

"No, Mother." It was the first time I called her mother. I admitted it seemed strange.

Her eyes softened. "Then what do you propose we do with them?"

I glanced at the three restrained to the beds. "We release them and give them a choice."

She nodded and headed for the first bed. Behind me, the door burst open and Sofia, the super dream walker I encountered in my first visit to Antarctica, entered brandishing a gun. I dropped the duffel and drew down the dagger in one smooth motion. She turned the gun on me, but I was faster. I lunged, she dodged but the blade grazed her upper arm.

"I remember you, bitch."

"Get away from her," Natasha growled.

Sofia's gaze flickered to my mother. "*You.*"

I was forgotten as she turned the gun on my mother. I launched at her, shoving her backward to the door. I pushed her through it and didn't stop until she banged against the wall. The gun fell from her hand and clattered to the ground. I shoved the dagger against her throat but she laughed.

"You tripped a silent alarm," she said. "In minutes, this place will be overrun with guards."

"Most of them are already dead."

"Oh, I saw your trail of destruction." She kept smiling. "There are many more to replace them."

Then she closed her eyes and a moment later, she was in my mind. Bloody hell, why didn't I have my mental walls up? The pain was excruciating as it exploded behind my eyes and in my head. I stumbled backward away from her. The dagger dangled from my hand until I lost its grip. I heard it hit the floor moments before I fell to my knees. Warm blood seeped from my nose and eyes. I cried out and curled into a ball on the floor.

"I should have killed you the first time," she taunted.

Faintly, the hospital door behind me banged open. Sofia cried out and released me. My mother stepped around my prone position on the floor. I swiped away the blood from my eyes and looked up though my hazy vision. Natasha had a hand wrapped around Sofia's throat as she pushed her against the wall. Sofia's eyes watered, her face turning purple as Natasha crushed her windpipe. When she took her last gasp, my mother released her. The dead girl crumpled to the floor.

"We don't have much time." Natasha stepped around me and snatched up the duffel.

I didn't have time to respond as she entered the hospital while I still tried to recover huddled on the floor. Everything hurt from head to toe. In the distance, shouts rose up as the guards Sofia promised neared. I reclaimed the dagger and reached for the discarded gun and then climbed to my feet. Moments later, the three women who were restrained on the beds ran out of the hospital. My mother followed.

"Come." She motioned for me to follow her away from the guards.

Gunfire rang out behind us. A bullet narrowly missed me and lodged into the nearby wall. My mother shoved the duffel into my hands.

"Keep going. Follow the corridor. Don't stop."

"What about you?"

"I'll be right behind you."

Somehow, I wasn't sure I believed her. I hid the dagger back in the cloud. With the gun in one hand, I took the duffel in the other with the detonators and what few charges were left and headed down the hallway. I stole a glance backward to see my mother plant her feet shoulder-width apart, her arms raised, as she prepared to face the enemy.

I rounded a corner. Heard shouts and screams and gunfire. I stopped and spun back around. Leaving her was a mistake. I hurried back around the corner. She came into view, her back to me, her arms still held out as she killed guard after guard and then she faltered.

One charged her through the sea of dead bodies but she collapsed before he reached her. Fear clawed its way to my throat. I broke into a run and leapt over her, putting myself between her and the guard. I still had the gun in my hand and pointed it at him.

He stared at the gun, then me, then his gaze flickered to my mother unconscious on the floor.

"Don't," I warned.

Though I wasn't sure don't what. Don't try anything? Don't come at me again? I lowered my body to the ground, placed the duffel next to her. I pressed two fingers against her throat. Thankfully, there was a pulse.

One of the guards behind him fired his gun. I saw him too late to react and the bullet lodged into my shoulder. I cried out as I crumpled.

"Take them," the first guard said as a second joined him.

Then a few more arrived and suddenly guards were converging on us. I wasn't going down without a fight. I released the gun and stood. Lightning flickered between my fingers as I held my hands, palms out, by my side. They warily eyed the fiery white bolts dancing there.

"Don't take another step," I said.

There we were. Me and four guards in a standoff. I was unsure of my next move. They were unsure of my next move. On the floor, my mother emitted a weak groan.

"Back away," I said. "All of you."

When they refused to move, I pushed my hands outward toward them. Bolts licked toward them. They backed up in a hurry. One stumbled over a dead guard and fell into the pile of bodies. I tried not to gag at the thought.

"Drop your weapons," I ordered.

When they refused to do as I said, I lifted my lightning hands toward them in warning. They dropped their weapons. Behind me, Natasha groaned again.

I was paralyzed with uncertainty. If I extinguished my hands to see about her, then I risked the guards taking up their weapons again and firing on us. Though I didn't want to kill the men in front of me, I realized with a sickening feeling I may not have a choice.

But perhaps I didn't have to kill. Only neutralize them. I glanced down at the lightning flickering in my fingers and had an idea. I hadn't really learned how to control the power Ronan had given me yet, but today seemed like a good day to start.

I glanced back up at the guards who all stood with their hands in surrender.

"Sorry about this," I muttered.

And then I pushed my hands toward them. Lightning fired from my fingertips, hitting them all in a brilliant flash of white light. They all went down and the lightning fizzled out. I stepped over a dead guard to check the pulse of one. He was dead. So much for trying to control the power.

I turned back to Natasha and helped her to a sitting position. She groaned. Her skin was pale and there were dark circles under her eyes. She used too much power too quickly and paid the price.

"We need to go," I whispered. "Can you walk?"

"You're hurt."

"I'm fine." As I said it, my shoulder throbbed with excruciating pain.

She moaned as I helped her to her feet. I leaned awkwardly to pick up the duffel and then eyed the gun I'd left on the floor. Holding my mother in one arm and the duffel in the other hand, there was no way I'd be able to grab the gun, too. I decided to leave it behind.

We headed down the hallway away from the pile of bodies and into the shadowy corridor.

"I should have remembered the cameras," she said on a whisper. "I'm sorry."

"Don't be. We have enough charges set to light the place up. We need to get out of here now."

I tried to hurry us along but she limped and it was slow going. At the end of the hallway, we turned left—the only way to go—and followed it down deeper into the bunker. Or at least it felt as though we were going deeper and deeper.

"How do we get out of here?"

"There is a door ahead." She nodded with her chin forward. "We're deep inside now. They won't follow us."

"How do you know?"

"Because they don't know there's an exit here."

Sure enough, looming ahead in the shadows was what appeared to be a metal rolling door. At the door, I paused, looking for some way to open it. She pushed out of my grasp and leaned heavily on the wall, expelling a breath.

"I'm tired," she said.

"I know. But you just need to hold on a little longer. How do I open this door?"

She pointed to a small red button on the right side of the door. I pushed it. Seconds later, the metal groaned and squealed as it lifted, exposing the frozen tundra. At that moment, I wished I hadn't left all my cold weather gear behind. We wouldn't last a minute out there without a coat.

I put my arm around her waist and led her outside, the wind whipping through my hair and cutting through my body like an icy knife. I sucked in a sharp breath as we stumbled several steps into the snowy oblivion. There was nothing but snow and ice and cold and wind before us.

She moved from me and turned back to the door, pushing the palm of her hand flat against the side of the mountain. The door rolled shut with a groan of horrible sound.

I knelt in the snow, unzipped the duffel, and pulled out the detonators. Three of them. One for each area we laid charges. I handed one to her and held the other two. She took it, shivering, teeth chattering and her lips turning blue. Our eyes met in that frigid moment.

"On three?" I asked.

She nodded.

"One...two...three..."

We pushed all three buttons at once.

The explosion started slow, as though the great belly of the beast in the mountain developed a terrible case of indigestion. Then the ground rumbled with a horrible sound followed by the *kaboom* of the explosions going off one after the other. Rocks and snow flew upward and it was then I realized we were not in the right place.

I lunged for her, wrapping an arm around her waist. We stumbled in an awkward run but she wasn't at full strength and was unable to move fast.

Then Sariel was there in a flash of light and alabaster wings. He wrapped his arms around both of us. I gritted my teeth as he teleported us away from the bunker. When we came to a halt, I collapsed on the ground, my hands fisting in snow as I dry heaved and coughed. My eyes watered, from the frigid wind or the teleportation sickness or both. My stomach clenched again as another dry heave came. When it was over, I sat back on my heels and looked out toward the bunker. Or what was left of it.

Yellow-orange flame and gray smoke billowed upward toward the starry night sky. It was over. The lab was destroyed. My hope was that we managed to destroy all the research in the process but some niggling sensation at the back of my mind told me we hadn't.

I'd worry about that later.

"It's done," Natasha whispered.

I rose and turned to them. She was huddled against Sariel's form, his wings wrapped around her to ward off the cold, biting wind.

"Let's get the hell out of here," I said.

I stepped into Sariel's arms and we flashed away.

CHAPTER 21

WE WERE BACK IN the tiny hotel room in Punta Arenas. As soon as we arrived, Sariel released me and I collapsed to my knees to wait out the nausea. I curled into a tight ball on the cold floor with my eyes closed until at last it subsided enough for me to move to a sitting position. My mother handed me a thick blanket she dug out of the closet.

Grateful, I took it, got to my feet and wrapped myself in it. Blood from my shoulder smeared on the material.

"You are injured," Sariel said.

I shrugged my good shoulder, trying to ignore the pain in the other. "I'll heal."

Sariel moved to me. "Let me see to it."

As much as I wanted to argue, I didn't. The bullet had to come out. I shoved off the blanket and sat back in the chair. He examined the wound as the blood seeped from it, soaking my dark colored shirt.

"You were shot?" he asked.

I nodded.

"This may hurt."

He placed the palm of his hand over the wound and closed his eyes. A warming sensation went through my shoulder, pulsing into the wound. Then a sharp stinging pain. I sucked in a breath through my nose to keep from crying out. It felt as though the bullet was moving within the tissue of my shoulder. As though it were inching its way out of my body. Another sharp pain. This time, I was unable to contain the cry of pain.

It took everything in me not to shove off his hand. I clenched my fist, my nails digging into the fleshy part of my palm. I pressed hard into the chair, biting my lip, as the bullet was dislodged from my flesh. He opened his eyes, peering at the wound. And then he plucked the bullet out as though it were nothing more than a splinter. It was covered in my blood as were his fingers. He handed the object to my mother.

"Now I will close the wound," he said. "This will be painful."

Not as painful as the wound itself. It pulsated with a deep ache. He placed his palm over it once more, closing his eyes as he went to work. I did my best to ignore the way it felt as though the muscles, tissue and skin were weaving itself back together. I clenched my jaw and focused on a point on the wall on the other side of the room. Until finally, he removed his hand. His palm was smeared with blood.

I glanced down at it but saw nothing but my blood-soaked shirt. I pulled aside the neck of my shirt. The wound was nothing more than a pink patch of skin. There was an odd aching sensation but I suspected that would go away in time.

"Thanks," I muttered.

He sat on the edge of the bed next to my mother, their hands laced together as though they would never let go.

I pulled my knees up to my chest, resting my chin there and closing my eyes as I slowly thawed out. I would not soon forget the sight of the billowing gray smoke or the belches of flames coming from the bunker. How many had died? How many had my mother killed with merely a thought? And what about the women? Did they escape or were they collateral damage? Guilt swept through me as I clutched my legs. Legend said there were numerous artifacts buried there. Had I destroyed them all? Perhaps I should not have allowed my rage to take over my good senses. Perhaps I should not have destroyed Station 211.

"Anna?" Natasha's voice was a quiet plea in the silence.

"I'm fine," I said, my eyes still closed as I answered.

"We did the right thing," she added.

My eyes popped open and I glared at her. "Did I? How many people died today? How many did *you* kill?"

Silence and a deadly stare from her. Then, "Would you rather have died?"

I said nothing. I put my chin back on my knees and closed my eyes.

"What's done is done," Sariel said. "There is no going back."

"I'm glad it's done," I said. "I'm glad the lab is gone but at what cost?"

"The Knights of the Holy Lance don't care who they hurt or why, Anna," my mother said. "They recruit women, brainwash them, and then train them to do what I did. They train them to kill others, to get what they want."

"And what do they want?" I asked, a hiss in my words.

"They want what Hitler wanted," she said, her voice soft and low.

My stomach clenched upon hearing that. I gripped my knees tighter and pressed deeper into the chair, thankful for the warmth of the thick blanket. I pinpointed Sariel with my gaze then.

"And you, Sariel. What do you think about all this?"

He stole a glance at my mother, who looked up at him with an expression I was unable to read, then back at me.

"Your mother is correct and you were right to destroy the lab. But I fear there are others out there like her and you."

My feet dropped to the floor as I sat up straight, fear pounding through me in a flash. "You think there's another lab?"

"I think this is not the end of the Knights of the Holy Lance," he said.

I shoved off the blanket and stood, pacing the small confines of the hotel room. I raked a hand through my hair, or tried to. My fingers caught in all the snarls and tangles.

"Anna, there is something I must tell you," he continued.

I halted and faced him, clutching my elbows and waiting. Was he going to admit, finally, after all this time who he truly was to me? I waited, my heart beating a wild tattoo. He glanced back down at my mother, who gave him a sweet smile and a little nod of encouragement. Then he met my gaze again, discomfort flickering across his face. I wondered if he was scared to tell me the truth.

"What is it?" I demanded, still clutching my elbows.

"The truth about your father," he said.

Irritation clawed through me. "He's dead."

His face blanched. I don't know what made me say it. Maybe some cruel part of me that wanted to get back at them both for abandoning me when I was a baby.

"He is not," he said, slowly, quietly.

"Oh?" The word came out as a breathy question.

"No." He paused, swallowed. "I...am your father."

I stared at him, my pulse racing. My palms broke into a hot-cold sweat and a weird sensation went over me. Even though I already knew, hearing the truth—from him—made me sink back into the chair.

"You," I said.

"Yes."

"How?" I glanced between him and my mother. She blushed to the roots of her hair.

"I think you understand how that works, Anna," she said.

I rolled my eyes. "Yes, *Mother*, I'm not an idiot. I understand the mechanics. What I don't understand is..." I paused, motioning at Sariel and his giant wings spanning behind him and her.

"Ah, that is a very long story."

"We have the room until eleven tomorrow morning," I said and suddenly I fought off a yawn.

"Perhaps now is not the time to—"

"Oh, yes, it is. *Now* is definitely the time. You *abandoned* me to be raised by someone else. You left me in the States alone, defenseless, homeless, with no family to speak of." My breath hitched and suddenly I fought back hot tears springing to my eyes. "You *left* me."

"It was not by choice," Sariel said.

I noted my mother remained silent and pinpointed her with my gaze. "Nothing from you? You who call yourself Natasha now. Your given name is Annabelle Walker. You named me after you. At least that's what my uncle told me."

"He was right. I did." Tears danced in her eyes. She took a deep breath, expelled it. "There are...gaps in my memory. I remember some things, but not all."

I looked back to Sariel. "Now is the time. I want to know the truth. All of it."

He swallowed hard, his throat working, as he nodded. "Very well then. I will tell you the story. Perhaps it will help your mother remember, too."

I waited as he collected his thoughts. He met my mother's gaze who gave him a reassuring smile. Then he kissed the back of her hand.

"We met when you were younger than Anna. Do you remember that?" he asked her.

She nodded. "I do. You came to me in a dream."

"I was so enamored with you, I had to find you."

I cleared my throat, shifting in my chair. Their display of affection somehow made me uncomfortable. He turned his attention back to me, his face a little pink. I had no idea angels blushed.

"I met her in the gardens of Walker Manor wandering through the colorful scented flowers. It is a moment frozen in time for me. She was beauty and grace and everything I had hoped. We loved each other immediately," he said.

"I knew when I met you, I would never be able to live without you." She placed her head on his shoulder and nuzzled his neck.

I tried not to roll my eyes. I wasn't exactly a mushy person, so seeing their outward displays made me even more uncomfortable. "Can you get to the part where I was born and you left?"

"Anna!" My mother's head snapped in my direction, her tone chastising.

"It's all right. We will reminisce later." He gave her a soft smile, then turned back to me. "Edward did not approve of our romance and so we did what we thought was best. We moved to the United States."

"As soon as we arrived, I discovered I was pregnant," she said. "That much I remember clearly. We were in Boston for a time until Edward found us. He urged me to come home, but I refused. After he returned to England, we packed up and moved to Texas. We were happy there."

"We were living as a normal family," Sariel said and I eyed his giant wings. "I used a glamor to hide them from the real world."

"Why Texas?" I asked. "Why Dallas?"

"It seemed like the best place for us to raise a family." She gave Sariel another eyelash-fluttering look. "You were born that winter. On the Solstice."

"Did you know about the prophecy?" I demanded. "The one written in the family history book."

"We all did," she said. "And we all thought it nothing more than a farce. Except for Edward. He believed in it with all his heart. I think that was why he was so determined to return me to England."

"How did I end up in the foster system?"

"Your mother has always been a powerful dream walker. She did not learn to control it like you. The Knights of the Holy Lance took notice."

I almost snorted at that as I recalled Sariel was the one who suppressed my powers after Azriel's attack on me.

"You were about six months old when they attacked," Sariel said. "I tried to fight them off but there were too many of them. They kidnapped her. I didn't know where they had taken her and since I had a child, I was not able to search for her. I was alone and unable to care for you like she had. That's when I realized I had to give you up to someone who would raise you and take good care of you. Someone who wanted a child as much as we did."

"Why didn't you take me home to England? To Edward?"

"Because I knew your mother wouldn't want that. And I feared the Knights would take you, too. I thought you should be hidden from the Walkers. I thought you would be more safe with someone else. Not Edward."

But he was wrong about Edward. My uncle did everything in his power to make sure I was safe from those who would harm me. I stared at him as I thought about everything I knew about my life with Grace.

"You arranged for Grace to foster me, didn't you?"

He glanced to the ground, as though ashamed. "I admit I had some influence on that, yes. But I had to make sure you were safe, happy, and healthy."

"And Edward finding me when I was thirteen. Was that your doing as well?"

He wouldn't meet my gaze and I realized the truth. I clutched the blanket tighter around my frame.

"You did, didn't you?"

"Grace was struggling," he said. "She needed help. When I realized who and what you were, I understood the mistake I made when I gave you up. I should have taken you home to England. To Edward, but we had not parted on the best of terms." There was a twinge of regret in his voice.

I sat in silence as I stared at the two of them.

"I don't remember what happened to me after the Knights of the Holy Lance took me away," my mother said.

"Perhaps you don't need to remember, my love." He kissed her hand again. Then to me, he said, "So, we did not abandon you. We wanted you very much."

"You helped me find the Holy Relics and my mother because you felt guilt about leaving me behind. Is that it?" It was hard to contain the venom in my words.

Sariel, at least, had the decency to look ashamed. "I wanted to make things right."

"And Kincade. He knew all this time and didn't tell me. Did you tell him?"

He shook his head. "I didn't. The Brotherhood of Watchers has always known the One Who Was Promised would claim the Holy Relics and fight Lucifer."

At least that matched up with Kincade's story but I was still angry with him.

"Can you forgive me?" Sariel asked.

I thought about that, wondering if my life would have turned out different had the Knights of the Holy Lance not taken my mother. Wondering if they would have raised me as the Keeper of the Holy Relics, to embrace my destiny. Or would they have tried to keep me from it? My mother said herself they didn't believe in the prophecy.

"I can in time," I said at last. I clutched the blanket. "Now, it's clear you two have some catching up to do so you can have the room."

"What about you?" Natasha asked.

"I'll get my own, thanks. Good night."

Because the last thing I wanted to be was a third wheel in their romantic reunion. I left them alone, closing the door behind me with a soft click, then headed down to the hotel bar to drown my feelings in a bottle of whiskey.

CHAPTER 22

MUCH TO MY DISMAY, the hotel bar was closed. That's when I realized the hour was very late and I was very tired. Shoulders slumped, I trudged through the lobby, thinking of nothing but getting my own room and falling into bed when I halted.

There, seated in one of the plush leather club chairs, was Kincade. He had an ankle propped on his knee and held a glass of amber liquid in one hand. My heart immediately climbed to my throat in a wild, reckless beat. He lifted the glass in an invitational salute. Then lifted his other hand and showed me the almost full bottle.

I straightened my shoulders and sauntered over, trying to pretend like I wasn't bone-deep exhausted from everything I'd just been through. I took the chair next to him as he handed me the glass.

"You sure know the way to a girl's heart." I downed the two-fingers-neat liquid in one gulp, then held out the glass for more. He obliged.

"I know the way to *your* heart." He smirked, just a little.

Despite my anger with him, butterflies erupted in my stomach. Or maybe that was merely the alcohol.

He eyed the blood stain on my shoulder. "You want to explain that?"

"No," I said, matter-of-factly, then changed the subject. "I'm still mad at you. How did you know where to find me?" I rolled the glass between my hands, peering into the amber perfection looking for answers.

"You stole the duffel of explosives. And you and your mother were gone. It didn't take a detective to figure out you both headed to Station 211. Was I wrong?"

I gave him a look through my eyelashes, tilting my head up ever so slightly. "No."

"What did you do?"

"What I said I was going to do."

"You left without me." The almost-hurt under the words hit harder than if he'd shouted.

"I didn't want to be anywhere near you." I met his angry gaze.

For a moment, the regret flashed through his eyes before he managed to contain it. "You know why I didn't tell you."

"Doesn't mean I accept it." I sipped the liquid, letting it sit on my tongue and then the back of my throat, burning and searing its way down to my gut. "I'll forgive you. Eventually."

"That's good to hear," he said, deadpan.

I sat back in the leather chair, the material crinkling with my movement. The lobby was deserted at this time of night. Not even the front desk was manned.

"We destroyed the lab," I said.

"Good."

"My mother used her super dream walker powers and killed guards. A lot of guards." He said nothing to that, so I continued. "I don't know how many died."

"You did what you thought was right."

"Did I?" I gave him a surreptitious glance and sipped again.

"The lab is destroyed. Now the Knights of the Holy Lance can't hurt any more people and create any more super dream walkers." He took a swig from the bottle. "I wish you had waited for me, though."

Guilt swept through me. Yeah, I should have waited for him. But I'm stubborn on a good day. And when I want something done my way, I usually find a way to do it.

"Why are you here?" I asked.

"Why do you think?" He wiggled the bottled, the liquid sloshing against the square glass.

"Oh, so you figured Anna is having another tragedy and needed a drink?"

"Was I wrong?"

"No," I said softly. "Sariel accompanied us. He told me he's my father."

"And how do you feel about that?"

I blew out a breath. "Pissed off mostly."

He refilled my glass, then took another swig from the bottle. I tried not to think about us swapping spit that way.

"Why?" he asked.

"Because he orchestrated my entire life. From placing me with Grace to coercing my uncle to come find me in Dallas to making me the Keeper of the Holy Relics."

"I don't think it was only Sariel who orchestrated your life." He gave me a pointed look, one brow raised.

"Are you suggesting there was a higher power at work?"

"You know I am. Look, Anna, we can spend all night on how pissed you are about your parents...or we can talk about the Ark. That's why I'm here."

I sat up straighter, clutching the glass tighter in my grip. "What about it?"

"While you've been busy blowing up labs and screwing around with your parents—"

"I haven't!"

"Lucifer has been sending an army of archaeologists all over the Middle East digging for the Ark."

I stared at him in shocked silence. "But...how?"

"Think, Anna. He has the power of the high lords on his side. All he has to do is kill a few significant people, steal their souls, and then he maneuvers them into place. Like pieces on a chessboard." Again, that pointed look. "It's your move."

"Fuck." I downed the whiskey and held out the glass for more. "I should have been more focused."

"Should have been, yes. Weren't." He poured more than two fingers neat.

"I had shit to do, okay?" I snapped.

"I get it. I get why you're mad and why you needed to do it. For you, for your mother, it gave you both a sense of justice and closure. But the reality is the Ark is more important than anything else."

"How did you find out about this?" I asked.

"Unlike you, I keep up with the world news. And I still have a few Brotherhood contacts who'll take my calls."

"The outcasts?" I asked.

"Yes. It's time to stop messing around, Anna, and get to work."

I bit my lower lip, nodding. He was right. I hated when he was right. I also hated that he sounded more and more like my uncle every day.

"Where are your parents?"

"They're having a lovely reunion in the hotel room." I sounded bitter even to my own ears. "I came down to get another room but there is no one at the front desk."

He dropped his foot and stretched out his long legs, reaching into his pocket. He brought out a room key and held it up. "I have a room."

"Of course, you do."

"You're exhausted. You have dark circles under your eyes. You need rest."

"You're not the boss of me." I frowned, that stubborn streak rearing its ugly head.

He heaved a sigh and got to his feet, holding a hand down to me. "Come on."

"I'm good here, *thankyouverymuch*."

"No, Anna." He jerked his head toward the lobby elevator.

"Fine." I said it on the most annoyed breath possible.

I also refused his outstretched hand as I got to my feet. He dropped his hand and started for the elevator. In my exhaustion, I stumbled after him. Or maybe that was the effects of the whiskey burning its way through my gut.

One silent elevator ride later and we were in his room which was more spacious than the one I booked. It had a king size bed on one side and a beautiful bathroom on the other. I plopped down on the bed and toed off my boots, still holding the half-filled glass.

"How did you know which hotel I was at?" I asked.

"There aren't that many in this town that you'll stay in. It was a process of elimination."

"How did you get here?" I wasn't sure why that question suddenly needed answering.

"You certainly have a lot of questions. It wasn't easy with the pandemic spreading. They are talking government shutdowns. I took the liberty of contacting your pilot and making arrangements to get here as quickly as possible."

I blinked, staring at him. "You did?"

He gave me a look that said I was ridiculous. "It's a twenty-plus hour flight, Anna. I wasn't going to hitchhike."

I shrugged.

He clenched his jaw as though embarrassed to say, then muttered, "Cashiel."

I almost laughed out loud but managed to hold it in. While I adored my uncle and even more as Cashiel, he wasn't the best at his angelic teleportation skills. However, I kind of loved Kincade managed to talk him into bringing him here, especially since I knew how much he hated that type of travel.

"Well, that was...nice of him."

"Not. One. Word." He gave me a warning glare.

But the smile broke free anyway.

"And, by the way, Ophelia isn't very happy with you."

My smile fell. "I ditched her again."

"You did."

With a heavy sigh I fell back into the thick pillows, placing the glass on my chest as I peered up at the ceiling.

"Stop being so damned impulsive, will you?" he said. "Because one of these days it's going to get you killed."

"It won't." I said it so confidently, I believed it. And then I yawned, my eyelids heavy. "What time is it anyway?"

"Nearly four in the morning."

I groaned. I was no longer able to keep my eyes open. Still holding the whiskey glass, I drifted to sleep.

* * *

I awoke to bright winter sunshine streaming through the one window and slashing across my closed eyes. I no longer held the whiskey glass, so I assumed at some point Kincade pried it from my hand. When my eyes flickered open, I saw it sitting on the nightstand with alcohol still in it.

I laid there a long moment basking in the glory of the soft mattress and the silence in the room. I heard no movement so assumed I was alone. Until a soft snore behind me. My eyes widened. I slowly turned my head, craning my neck to see behind me. Kincade's back was to me. The gentle rise and fall of his breathing indicated he was deep in sleep. And still fully dressed. As was I.

Well, at least he was still a gentleman.

There was something comforting having him sleep next to me. I told myself that was silly and yet a small part of me delighted in the knowledge he was there. I moved from the bed and padded to the bathroom, in need of a shower. I hadn't brought a change of clothes with me, though. Instead, I stood at the sink and splashed warm water over my face. I examined the wound on my shoulder to see the pink flesh was gone and everything looked normal. When I exited the bathroom, he was awake and sitting on the edge of the bed.

"I suppose we should be going," I said.

"We should." He yawned and stretched his arms over his head before he stood.

"Sariel can take us back."

He gave me a thin-lipped expression that told me he wasn't a fan of traveling with an angel.

"I know it's not your favorite," I said, "but since I don't have the plane, it seems like the best option."

With a sigh, he nodded, then waved to the door. "Lead the way."

We left his room behind and headed for the one I'd paid for one floor down. At the door, I hesitated.

"Don't you have a key?" he asked.

"Do you think I really want to barge in on them without a courtesy knock?" I gave him a sidelong glance. "I mean... they've been reunited, after all."

Understanding flickered through his eyes. Without waiting for me to decide, he reached past me and rapped hard and quick on the door. I heard movement and voices on the other side before the door opened.

My mother stood there, her hair disheveled and her eyes bright with something I'd never seen before. I shifted from one foot to the other.

"We, ah, should get going."

She stepped aside. "Come in."

Kincade followed me in. The bed was rumpled and unmade. I tried hard not to look at it, not to think about the possible activities that happened between the sheets. Sariel stood in the center of the room with his giant wings spread behind him.

"We need to get back to Walker Manor," I said.

"It's time for you to begin your search for the Ark," Sariel said with a nod. He waved me toward him. "I'll take you first."

I didn't argue. I cast a glance back to Kincade who stood there with an expressionless face. I stepped into Sariel's arms and a moment later we were back in the manor in the front hall. I dropped to my knees, as I always did after teleporting, and tried hard not to heave. The nausea hit me hard and fast that time as he disappeared and then returned once more with my mother. Kincade was last.

By the time he arrived, I managed to get to my feet. I hadn't a clue what time it was, but I thought I smelled bacon and coffee wafting in from the dining room.

Kincade, though, was all business. "Let's get to the library and get to work."

My stomach growled. "But—"

"No time for that, Anna. Let's go." He stomped up the stairs.

I glanced at Sariel and my mother with a shrug. Reluctantly, I followed him up the stairs with my stomach growling, my bones aching, and my body desperate for a shower.

"Can't this wait another hour or so?" I whined as I followed him into the library.

"You've postponed long enough." But it wasn't Kincade who spoke.

Cashiel sat behind the large desk. The top was littered with papers and what appeared to be maps. I halted, staring at him in wonder. For a moment, he was my uncle, Edward. Not Cashiel, the angel. The only thing that convinced me otherwise was the span of his brilliant white wings threaded with gold behind him. He perched on the edge of the leather executive chair to make room for his wings and then eyed me with those fierce blue eyes that told me everything I needed to know in a flash.

He condemned my act of violence at the lab in Station 211. More guilt.

"Well?" I blurted.

"Well, what?" His expression was stern.

"You don't like what I did."

"I don't."

"Are you going to chastise me for it?"

"No. That's between you and your conscious. Now, can we get to work?"

He shoved a map toward the edge of the desk as I approached. I stared down at the large map of Africa. There were several markings in the middle of the desert in Egypt, one in the Sudan, a few in Ethiopia, and some in South Africa and Zimbabwe.

"What are these markings?" I asked.

"Lucifer's excavations," Kincade answered.

I traced a line from Cairo down to the first marking in Aksum, Ethiopia. He'd told me in the hotel in Punta Arenas that Lucifer had digs going on all over the place. While I believed him, I didn't fully grasp the extent of his reach.

"How?"

"I told you," Kincade said.

"He's been slowly building a way to find the Ark without your help," Cashiel said.

"Stealing souls and controlling them," I said.

"Yes." Cashiel nodded.

"He's excavating in Aksum?" I gave my angel-uncle a questioning look.

"Yes. Some believe Menelik, Sheba's and Solomon's son, visited Jerusalem when he was twenty. He brought the Ark back with him to conquer Ethiopia as well as a number of surrounding territories. Scholars believe he then hid the Ark in a sacred chapel where it is guarded by a monk forbidden to step foot outside the chapel grounds until he dies. He will spend his life guarding the Ark."

"At least until Lucifer or one of his high lords is able to control him." I pointed to one of the markers on Lake Tana. "And here?"

Kincade answered this one. "Some think the Ark rests there. It was believed the Ark was transported there instead of Aksum. The island is guarded by monks who keep it safe from outsiders and who refuse to let anyone inside their island church."

Finally, I pointed to a remote region near the border of South Africa and Zimbabwe. "And here?"

"Another theory," Cashiel said. "In 586 BC, when the Babylonians attacked Jerusalem, some scholars believe a few of the Israelites removed the Ark before they could sack the temple. They carried it away from Jerusalem by the Lemba Tribe and hid it in this region here. They believe it can be found by decoding the cryptic messages on one of the Dead Sea Scrolls."

"Where is this scroll?" I asked.

"An archaeologist has it," Kincade said.

"Let me guess. An archaeologist controlled by Lucifer?"

"Yes," Cashiel said.

I thought of the last postcard Sariel handed me. "The last postcard I received was of Cairo."

"A place to start." Cashiel's feathers ruffled, as if he understood who gave me that postcard and why.

"What will I find there? Not the Ark."

My uncle shook his head. "No. More clues."

"A clue you know about?" I lifted a brow in question as I peered at him.

His face remained impassive as he replied. "There is pertinent information for you in Cairo. A clue that will help you with your quest."

I sighed. "Why can't you just tell me where the Ark is? Why all the mystery?"

"Even I do not know where the Ark is," he said. "But there is someone who can help you in your quest. Seek out the merchant in the Khan el-Khalili bazaar."

I cut a glance at Kincade who remained stoic. "Who is the merchant?"

"A man by the name of Ahmed Kamal. He is the proprietor of a shop of maps."

My brows drew together. "Does he have a map to the Ark, then?"

"No, but information that will help you find it. He knew me as Edward Walker. Mention that when you meet him and that you are the Keeper of the Holy Relics. He'll know you by that."

"All right," I said slowly. Then glanced between the two of them. "How close is Lucifer to finding the Ark?"

"The Ark will not be found by Lucifer," Kincade said, matter-of-factly.

"What does that mean?" I pressed.

"The Ark is exactly where the Most High intends for it to be," Cashiel said. "And that will not be in Lucifer's hands. It will be revealed when He is ready for it to be revealed."

They both gave me a pointed, chilling look. Gooseflesh erupted on my arms.

"Then I'll start in Cairo."

"*We'll* start in Cairo," Kincade corrected.

"Fine. You can come, too." I said it in jest but I didn't miss the dark flicker of annoyance cross his face.

"Good. When do you leave?" Cashiel asked.

I fought off a yawn. "Tomorrow. I need time to rest and make travel arrangements."

"What about the pandemic?" he asked.

I shrugged. "What about it? I have a private plane."

"Yes, but some cities are beginning to go into lockdown."

"Then we'll figure it out when the time comes." My stomach rumbled loudly. "Right now, I need food."

I didn't wait for another response as I headed out of the library.

CHAPTER 23

KINCADE FOLLOWED ME, MUCH to my annoyance. Ever since that one time I nearly died, I don't get far from him. It probably really irked him I went to Antarctica without him.

I said nothing. He said nothing. I entered the dining room, cut through to the kitchen, and went straight for the fridge like a woman on a mission. Food, then existential dread.

Cold air brushed my face as I opened the door and scanned for leftovers. Behind me, I felt Kincade hovering. A quick glance over my shoulder confirmed it—him leaning against the wall, big forearms crossed over his chest like a living "do not attempt" sign.

I spotted a plate of roasted chicken, yanked it out, and peeled back the plastic wrap.

"Well?" I prompted.

"Well, what?"

"Well, why are you standing there staring at me?" I propped my hands on my hips, suddenly irritated just by his presence.

"I'm keeping an eye on you."

I rolled my eyes and grabbed a big piece of white meat, tearing off a bite. Warm, savory, perfect. I was mid-chew when Ophelia banged into the kitchen. She stopped dead.

Surprise. Then instant fury.

"You left without me. Again."

"I know," I said around a mouthful.

"That's all you have to say for yourself?"

"It was something I had to do alone." I popped the rest of the chicken into my mouth.

"But you weren't alone, were you?" Her tone went sharp enough to slice bone. "You took your mother."

And Sariel, but I didn't feel like tossing more gasoline on that fire. I opened my mouth to explain, but she lifted a hand.

"Save it, Anna. I don't want to hear any more excuses."

"How about an apology?" I suggested, trying my best to sound sincere. The last person I wanted to piss off was Ophelia. She was a decent fighter. And I needed her.

She frowned. "Do you know that while you were gone, Killian and Astrid confronted me?"

"Confronted you? About what?" Even though I asked, I was pretty sure I already knew.

"About my sword."

"What about your sword?" Kincade asked.

"He thinks it's the Sword of Light," I said.

The Sword of Light—one of the four sacred Fae treasures Lucifer had stolen. He'd used them to wreck Faery the same way he wanted to use the Holy Relics against mankind. Killian had asked me to inspect Ophelia's sword. I told him I'd talk to her first but never got the chance. It irked me he went around me and talked to her directly.

Not that he needed my permission. Still didn't mean I had to like it.

"Yes, he does. And he demanded I hand it over to him." Her normally pale face flushed pink with fury.

"Did you?"

"No! Because it's not the Sword of Light. Lei Mei gave it to me, same as she gave you the dagger. They both have Alpha and Omega engraved on them. You know that as well as I do."

Lei Mei. Enigmatic, terrifying, Hong Kong demon-killer auntie. She'd given me the dagger and called me demon killer, too. It still gave me chills.

I took a breath. "Killian and Astrid asked to see your sword. I tried to put them off by saying I'd talk to you first. I'm sorry about that."

"I showed him the symbols. Only after that did he decide it wasn't his sword."

"Why would he think Ophelia's sword belongs to the Fae?" Kincade asked.

"Because of the way it shimmers—and because Lucifer stole all four of the Fae treasures," I said.

Something tugged at the back of my mind. All the artifacts and relics locked up in the library vault. I remembered seeing a sword there, but I wasn't sure it was the one Killian wanted. And how would my uncle have gotten his hands on it, anyway?

Then again, my uncle had a talent for collecting dangerous things and tucking them away.

"I'll talk to Killian," I said.

"Don't bother." She sighed. "He understands the sword isn't his."

She stepped past me and snagged a piece of chicken off the plate like she had every right. "So, when are we leaving to find the next relic?"

Excitement lit her pretty face. I darted a glance at Kincade. He just stood there, unreadable. Useless. And while I didn't want to ditch Ophelia again, I also wasn't prepared to have her tagging along.

When I hesitated, she huffed. "You're not going to tell me, are you?"

"I, uh..."

"Because you don't want me to come." She folded her arms, chin lifting.

"It's not that."

"It is that. Do you expect me to sit around here and do nothing all day?" No attempt to hide the anger now.

I understood her restlessness. With Darius gone, she didn't have anyone to spar with, no side missions while I was off chasing doom.

"This is bullshit. I'm leaving." She turned and stomped toward the door.

Panic rose sharp in my chest. "Ophelia, wait. Where are you going?"

She cut me a look over her shoulder that said she was officially Done With My Shit. "Wherever I'm needed."

Then she stormed out, her footsteps fading through the house. I sighed.

"She's just lonely, you know," Kincade said. "And mad."

"I know."

"She'll get over it."

"Will she? Because I'm not so sure." My appetite vanished. I covered the food and shoved the plate back into the fridge.

"She misses Darius. And having a purpose." His voice softened, just a little. "She misses her friend. You."

Kincade followed me out of the kitchen and up the stairs.

"I'm aware of that, too."

I didn't say the rest—that I was quietly praying she'd show up when I needed her most, when this all came down to the final battle. Hard to focus on that when I'd been too busy blowing up Station 211.

"She'll be back after she cools off," he said, like he could hear exactly where my head was.

And he probably did. He was always able to read me. I hoped he was right. He knew Ophelia better than I did.

We split at the landing. I headed for my room. He went to his.

Once alone, I dug the postcard of Cairo out of my desk. I stood in the center of my bedroom and stared at it. The photo showed the city with the Great Pyramids in the background, rising out of haze and history.

If the Ark wasn't there, what was I supposed to find? My uncle had said it was a place to start. But what clue could a merchant in a bazaar possibly hold for me?

I didn't exactly have a gold medallion with a red crystal in the center. Nor did I need to hire the best digger in Egypt. I wasn't Indiana Jones. I was more like...reluctant relic thief with trauma.

Still. The question remained.

What information did Cairo hold?

There was only one way to find out.

* * *

The following day, Kincade and I took the private plane from Heathrow to Cairo. Five hours of almost dead silence. He wasn't chatty and, honestly, neither was I. I was too busy brooding about Ophelia walking out—and how it was totally my fault.

I had a feeling she was somewhere kicking demon ass with that sword of hers. I hoped so, anyway.

We stepped off the plane into the harsh Egyptian sun, each with a duffel in hand. I slid on my black aviators. The warmth wrapped around me, the air dry and bright. The kind of day that made you want a terrace, a drink, and absolutely zero apocalyptic responsibility.

My stomach growled at the thought of roasted meat and whiskey.

I'd booked us a large suite at the Nile Ritz-Carlton—massive floor-to-ceiling windows in both the living area and bedroom overlooking the Nile. There was one small problem.

Just one king-sized bed.

"I'll take the sofa." Kincade said it like it wasn't even a question.

He dropped his duffel by the sofa and moved to the window, staring out over the calm sweep of the river. I drifted into the bedroom, taking in the view and the soft luxury of the space. I set my duffel on the curved sofa by what I thought was a window.

Turned out to be a sliding glass door.

I opened it and stepped out onto the tiny balcony. Expecting river-brine, I got only cool, clear air and a faint city tang. The breeze tugged loose strands of my hair.

Here I was in Cairo, the Great Pyramids not far away, and there was no way for me to enjoy it. No pretending to be a tourist. No carefree vacations. Just a girl on a balcony, wishing for a normal life she was never meant to have.

"Well, let's not waste any time. Let's go see your cartographer," Kincade called from the living room.

He was right. We didn't have time to waste, and I wanted to know what this merchant had that was so important.

We went back down to the lobby and grabbed a taxi to the Khan el-Khalili bazaar in the historic center. A few minutes later, the cab dropped us at the edge of chaos.

"Stick close," he ordered.

Easier said than done. The bazaar was a riot of color and sound, reminding me of the shopping districts in Hong Kong and Marrakesh. Stalls overflowed with silverware, antiques, lanterns, candles, jewelry, pottery, perfume, instruments, incense. Coppersmiths hammered, gold merchants glimmered, spices perfumed the air. The handmade carpets were so soft, it felt like running my fingers through a kitten's fur.

The smell of roasting meat and rich Turkish coffee curled around us like temptation.

Kincade ignored all of it. He moved like a man who already knew his way, and I hurried to keep up.

The mapmaker's shop was a sliver wedged between a lantern stall and a candle stall. Open-fronted like the others, but barely wider than a doorway. Rolled maps filled cubbies along one side—souvenirs by the look of them. The opposite wall held laminated maps: world, Middle East, Egypt, a map of ancient Babylonia.

A man greeted us with a bright smile that reached his deep brown eyes. He wore a red fez, a brown tunic, and a copper bracelet snug on his left wrist.

"Hello! Are you looking for something particular?" he asked, addressing Kincade and practically ignoring me.

Kincade, however, stepped behind me and nudged me forward.

The man's gaze slid to me, his smile dimming a fraction.

"My name is Anna Walker," I said. "Are you Ahmed Kamal?"

His gaze searched my face, then flicked to Kincade towering behind me. "I am."

"I believe you knew my uncle, Edward Walker," I said.

His smile brightened. "Ah, yes. I did. How is Edward?"

My chest tightened. "I'm afraid he passed away."

His smile fell at once. "I'm sorry to hear that. Edward was a good friend of mine. How can I help you?"

"My uncle told me once you would have a map to help me find something. That I should tell you I'm the Keeper of the Holy Relics."

"And what would that be?" he asked.

I stepped closer, lowering my voice. "The Ark of the Covenant."

His eyes widened just slightly. "I have no such map."

"Lie," Kincade said.

There were a few times I really appreciated his built-in lie detector. This was one of them.

Ahmed spread his hands. "I assure you, I don't have anything of the sort."

"Lie again," Kincade said, flat.

Ahmed's gaze bounced between us. "I'm telling the truth."

"It's kind of his superpower," I said. "He's a walking lie detector."

A beat of silence stretched. Ahmed studied me.

"Can you offer proof you are who you say you are?" he asked.

I tipped my head. "You knew my uncle?"

"Yes."

"You met him personally?"

"Yes. Many times."

I glanced at Kincade; he met my look with quiet curiosity. I flipped open the pocket on my cargo pants and pulled out the photo I carried everywhere now. Me and my uncle—both younger. Him in his usual designer three-piece, looking like he was about to give Parliament a dressing down. Me with the most bored, annoyed expression on earth.

A moment in time I barely remembered until I found the photo. Piers had given me a box of Edward's things when he started renovating the main bedroom.

I handed the photo to Ahmed. He studied it for a long moment, then looked at me with a sharp, searching gaze. Finally, he handed it back.

"Wait here."

He moved deeper into the shop and disappeared through a curtain I hadn't noticed. Kincade's thoughts brushed mine. *Stay alert.*

I nodded once.

A few minutes later, Ahmed returned with a small cylindrical canvas bag in his hands.

"I met Edward several years ago when he was in Cairo," he said. "He told me one day someone would come looking for this. Someone he called the Keeper of the Holy Relics."

He cradled the object against his chest, then stepped closer and extended it to me with both hands. "This will aid you in your quest for the Ark of the Covenant."

I took it. Whatever was inside felt like a rolled cardboard tube.

"This is a map?" I asked.

"Ah, not any map, Keeper. A copy of a special scroll that will give you clues to the final resting place of the Ark."

I nodded like that made sense. It didn't. Not yet. "What do I owe you for it?"

"Owe?"

"How much for the copy of the scroll?" I clarified.

"There is no cost. Your uncle asked me to hold it for you until the day you came to retrieve it. I swore an oath I would, and now that oath is fulfilled." His smile returned, faintly relieved, like he'd just offloaded a very heavy secret.

"Thank you," I said. "I appreciate your help."

Kincade and I turned to leave.

"The End of Days is coming, isn't it?" Ahmed asked, voice low, threaded with fear.

A hot prickle ran up my spine. I looked back over my shoulder. "Why do you ask?"

"I have seen the signs."

I swallowed, not quite brave enough to ask what signs. I'd seen enough myself to fuel nightmares for the rest of my life.

"You should prepare yourself," I said quietly. "Farewell."

Understanding flickered across his face. He nodded. "Peace be with you, Keeper."

"And with you," I replied.

We stepped back out into the crush of the bazaar. I paused at a lantern stall, drawn to a blue glass lantern glittering in the sun. The proprietor launched into hard-sell mode. I pretended to ignore him, keeping the canvas bag tucked close like it was nothing more than a rolled-up newspaper.

Kincade haggled with the seller and bought the lantern I'd been eyeing.

"That was interesting," he said, handing it to me.

I took it, the lantern dangling from one hand, the canvas bag clutched tighter in the other. "What signs do you suppose he saw?"

"Likely the same ones we have," he said. "Things we shouldn't speak of."

"Agreed. Let's get back to the hotel. I want to see what this thing is."

He nodded. Together, we walked out of the bazaar, flagged down a cab, and headed back to the hotel in companionable silence.

CHAPTER 24

BACK AT THE HOTEL, I took a seat at the small dining table and tugged open the drawstring on the bag. A cardboard tube slid out and landed on the table with a dull thud. Kincade sat opposite me, watching.

I popped the cap off the tube. Inside was a roll of paper, which I carefully eased out.

The pages had been rolled together for so long they refused to uncurl. We ended up using coasters as makeshift paperweights to pin down the corners of four pages. I stared at the black-and-white images, trying to make sense of what I was looking at.

"What is it?" I finally asked.

Kincade pushed to his feet and moved behind me, leaning over my shoulder for a better look. His sandalwood-and-patchouli scent washed over me and my nerves did a stupid little happy dance.

Damn nerves.

"It's photos of the Copper Scroll," he said.

I blinked, squinting at the strange markings. "You mean the Copper Scroll? Part of the Dead Sea Scrolls?"

"Yes. It was the last one found. In the back of the cave."

The cave. The Dead Sea Scrolls. My brain connected dots on autopilot. From what I knew, the Copper Scroll was in a museum in Amman and supposedly listed sixty-three locations tied to some massive treasure hoard.

Did it contain a clue to the Ark?

Everything inside me tightened with anticipation.

"Look." Kincade pointed to the top left corner of one of the pages.

In faint pencil were the initials: **ECW III**.

Edward Clifton Walker III. My uncle.

"How the bloody hell did he get this? And why leave it with a merchant in a Cairo bazaar?"

"Likely the safest place for it," Kincade said.

My angel-uncle had sent me to that merchant because he knew the scroll copy was waiting. Sariel had sent me to Cairo because he knew there was a clue waiting. I started to wonder if those two were conspiring behind my back.

"I don't understand this language. It looks like Hebrew, but not."

"It's an early form of Mishnaic Hebrew." He pointed to one blurry line. "'In the ruin that is in the valley of Achor...'" He paused, eyes flicking over the page like it was nothing more than a menu. "The structure of each section is a general location, a specific location, and what to find."

A cold shiver skittered through me. "You can read this?"

He nodded. "I used to. I'm a bit out of practice."

I gaped at him, shocked—though I didn't know why. Kincade was far older than he pretended to be. I knew he'd been around during the First Crusades, but this? If he could read this ancient dialect, he was older than even that.

Much older.

I dragged my focus back to the photocopies. "You think the location of the Ark is listed in the Copper Scroll?"

"Wouldn't it have to be? Why else would your uncle leave this for you?"

Why else, indeed? If Edward already knew there was a hint in the Copper Scroll, why all the mystery? I remembered what Kincade said earlier—that Lucifer had control of an archaeologist with one of the Dead Sea Scrolls.

My gut clenched. "Lucifer already has a lead on this."

Kincade went quiet, considering. "The archaeologist he's controlling must have another copy and can translate it."

"Yes, because we know the original Copper Scroll is in a museum." In a flash, I made up my mind. "Then you have to translate it."

He didn't move, but I *felt* the hesitation. "It will take some time."

"I'd like to say we have all the time in the world, but you know we don't." I leaned back in the chair and shot him a faint grin.

His lips flattened into a straight line. "I'll get right on it."

"And I'll order room service because I'm starving. I'll leave you to it."

I hopped up and headed for the bedroom. My stomach rumbled as I grabbed the menu and tried to remember when I'd last eaten. The last few days had been long and brutal. What I really wanted was a shower, food, and about sixteen hours of uninterrupted coma-sleep.

After ordering, I returned to the living area and paced the length of the room as the sun sank in the western sky. Outside the windows, lights began to twinkle along the Nile, turning the river into a ribbon of magic.

"Anna, sit. You're distracting," Kincade said.

I ignored him, biting my thumbnail as I paced and listened to my stomach complain. A thought hit me and I halted, watching him work. He'd found a notepad and pen somewhere and was scribbling his translations in tight, neat lines.

"Aren't you hungry?" I asked.

"Not really."

He didn't look up, just kept writing. I realized I'd hardly ever seen him eat. The last real meal we'd shared was in Poland after recovering the Holy Grail.

"You're left-handed," I blurted.

No reaction. Not even an annoyed glance.

"And you don't eat very much, do you? But you drink a lot of whiskey. How the bloody hell do you survive?"

He lowered the pen, inhaled slowly, and lifted his gaze to mine. Those green-gold eyes sparked with annoyance. His mouth formed a grim, irritated line.

"You sound like your uncle," he said, then picked the pen back up and resumed translating.

A knock sounded on the door. I practically danced toward it, thrilled at the promise of food. I opened it wide as the server pushed the cart inside. I flashed him a big smile and slipped a twenty into his palm. He nodded and left.

"How much food did you order?" Kincade asked, eyeing the cart loaded with covered dishes.

"I was hungry, okay?"

I swept one of the lids off with a flourish—stuffed grape leaves. Another lid revealed falafel. There was shawarma, hummus, baba ghanoush, baklava. I dug in like a starving teenage boy, scooping creamy hummus with warm pita.

Kincade suddenly stopped writing. He sat up straight and dropped the pen. His wide-eyed gaze met mine.

The food in my mouth lost all taste. I swallowed hard.

"You found something?" My voice came out dry and thin.

He glanced down at his notes. "I told you the cadence of each stanza. A general location, a specific location, and what to find."

"Yes." The word slipped out like a breath of ice.

"This follows that same pattern." He tapped his notes, then read aloud from the translation. "In the valley north of the walls of the city. In the Place of the Skull under the cracked slab. At a distance of thirteen cubits underground. A chest made of acacia wood covered in gold."

His gaze lifted to mine. A hot-cold sweat washed over me as we stared at each other in stunned silence. My gut clenched, the food I'd just eaten threatening to revolt.

"A chest made of acacia wood covered in gold," I whispered.

He nodded slowly.

"The Ark?"

"It has to be," he said.

"This feels too easy. If that truly is a clue to the Ark's location, then my uncle knew where it was all along." I shook my head. "He *left* this for me."

Kincade shrugged. "You were led to the other relics, weren't you?"

"Yes, but with Sariel's help."

"And now with Cashiel's," he pointed out, one brow lifting.

I worried my lower lip, turning over just how much of my Holy Relics scavenger hunt had been guided by divine hands. Was that baked into the prophecy too?

"Where is this Place of the Skull?" I asked.

"Golgotha," he said, matter-of-fact. "North of Jerusalem."

I stared at him. "The site of Jesus' crucifixion?"

"It's the only place I can think of that's referred to as the Place of the Skull." His face went grim, like he knew more than he was willing to admit.

"You know something more."

His jaw clenched, the muscles ticking as he held the silence.

"Tell me, Kincade."

"Thirteen cubits is approximately twenty feet underground. Under the cracked slab..." He hesitated. "I don't know exactly what that means. Perhaps it cracked during the earthquake that coincided with the crucifixion."

My mind flipped through everything my uncle ever taught me. "Matthew says there was a great earthquake on the day of the resurrection."

"But the earlier quake came with darkness and the splitting of rock," he said.

"And the opening of graves," I added, not to be outdone by his Bible trivia.

"At any rate, one of those quakes must have caused the stone slab to split."

"The stone slab we assume is under the crucifixion site at the Place of the Skull."

"And possibly covers the Ark," he said. "In Golgotha."

"Also known as Calvary," I added.

"Showoff," he muttered.

I grinned.

"The bottom line is, we have to go to Jerusalem again," I said.

Kincade pushed back from the table and wandered toward the food cart. Fatigue bracketed his mouth and shaded the skin under his eyes. He still hadn't shaved; pale blond stubble shadowed his cheeks and jaw. He tore off a piece of pita and dipped it into the hummus.

"We do," he said at last, then popped the bread into his mouth.

I sucked in a deep breath and let it out slowly. "When do we leave?"

"That's going to be difficult with everything going on in the world."

"Difficult but not impossible. We have a private jet. We made it to Cairo, after all."

"*You* have a private jet," he corrected.

Silence settled between us. My mind went back to Ahmed in the bazaar.

"What do you think he meant when he said he'd seen the signs? What signs?" I asked.

Kincade picked up another piece of pita and dipped it in the hummus. "He must have seen one of the Four Horsemen."

I shivered. We'd seen them too. Conquest in Spain. War in Dublin. And likely worse to come.

"I don't want to think about the last two," I said.

"It's coming for us all, Anna. Whether you like it or not."

I blew out a breath. "Then we better get to that Ark before Lucifer does."

He lifted a lid off another plate, revealing the shawarma. "We can figure that out in the morning. Let's eat and get some rest. We'll need it."

Though I agreed, impatience gnawed at me. Instead of arguing, I said, "All right."

I grabbed a pita stuffed with roasted lamb and sank into a nearby chair. He was right, much as I hated to admit it. We were both wrecked. As I chewed, I couldn't stop thinking about how old he really was.

"What?" he snapped.

Realizing I'd been staring, I jerked my gaze away and looked out at the deepening twilight. "Sorry," I muttered.

"Why were you staring?"

"I wasn't."

"Lie."

I sighed. I hated when he used his lie detector on me. "Just wondering how old you are."

"Why does it matter?" A faint thread of offense colored his tone.

I glanced back at him. He stood by the cart, holding a pita in one hand and a skewer of roasted chicken in the other. Somehow that image—ancient immortal warrior with snack kebab—was weirdly endearing.

"It doesn't," I said.

His shoulders slumped just a fraction. If I hadn't been watching, I would've missed it. "But it's important for you to know."

Another thing I hated—how well he read me. "I suppose," I said.

He took a deep breath, exhaled, then crossed to the chair opposite mine and sat. His gaze—glittering, intense—locked on mine. In those eyes, I saw it: he was about to tell me something he'd never told anyone. A secret he'd carried alone for a very long time.

I sat a little straighter, heart knocking, and waited.

"I was there that day at the crucifixion," he said.

The hairs on my arms stood up. "The crucifixion?"

"Yes." His eyes didn't leave mine.

I was afraid to look away, afraid that if I did, he'd think the revelation—that he was over two thousand years old—would somehow change how I saw him. It didn't. Not really. It just made everything click into sharper focus.

"I have never told anyone," he added. "Only you."

"Thank you for telling me." My voice sounded small in the quiet room.

As I sat there, I understood what that meant. He hadn't just read about it. He'd *been there.* He'd seen it happen. He'd lived through the quakes, the darkness, the graves opening, the world tilting on its axis. He knew, in a way no one else alive did, what that moment meant.

I sensed there was more he wanted to say. He stayed silent.

He leaned back in the chair, still holding the skewer and half-eaten pita. Any other time, I might have laughed. Not now. He swallowed hard, his throat working. Words building.

"I have seen things in this world, through time, that changed me," he said. "I lived through the Crusades when Christians tried to convert those who would not be converted. When there was so much bloodshed over a difference of faith. I've seen religious wars and Popes rise and fall. I've seen kings start wars for no reason but power."

He paused, looking away, his jaw tight as he chose his next words. Then his gaze returned to mine.

"But I have never seen anything like the times now. Lucifer has been planning this for centuries—killing guardians, stealing souls, building his army of high lords and demons. I spent over a millennium trying to save those guardians, trying to hold back the darkness. The End of Days are upon us all, Anna. War is coming. It can't be avoided. I think you know that now."

Another pause. Cold prickled down my neck.

"I've only known one person in all my long years who has the courage to face that darkness," he said quietly. "Only one person willing to fight and die for those who can't fight for themselves. One person who accepts her fate and destiny for what it is, even when she spent so long refusing it. Deep down, she understood who and what she was. She's the strongest woman I know. That's why I'll be there by your side. Fighting the darkness with you until death, if that's what it takes. You have my word."

I tried to swallow, but my mouth had gone bone dry. My throat tightened. Hot tears burned my eyes. I looked away and blinked them back, not wanting him to see how much his words gutted me—in the best possible way.

He believed in me. More than anyone.

It was the most he'd said about anything. I understood then just how deep his faith ran. He was willing to die for the cause—*my* cause—to fight the darkness. He was willing to do whatever it took to keep me alive long enough to get to that last fight.

Deep in my soul, I knew I could never let him go. My hands shook with the realization, with the heavy, beautiful truth of what we were to each other.

He was more than my guardian.

I loved him. I would always love him.

I pushed up from the chair, forcing my rubbery legs to cooperate.

"I, uh, think I need a drink. I'll be back with whiskey."

I had no idea where I was going to get whiskey, but I didn't wait for him to answer. I slipped out of the room and headed for the lobby bar.

As I walked, I remembered what he'd said once—we drink when Anna has a tragedy.

But this wasn't a tragedy.

This was the best day of my life.

And I wanted to celebrate.

CHAPTER 25

I LEFT THE HOTEL room and headed to the rooftop lounge, my mind in a fog as I replayed everything he said to me, the weight of two thousand years in his voice. I didn't really recall how I ended up at one of the tables by the floor to ceiling windows with an incredible view of the river. All I realized was I held a glass of their finest whiskey in my hand as I peered out at the glimmering lights along the rippling water trying to come to terms with my feelings for Kincade.

He had never expressed what he thought or how he felt about me. For a long time, I figured I was mostly a nuisance. That he hung around because my uncle had something to do with it. Later, when he kissed me, I started to change my mind about that. But things were never what they seemed with Kincade. He was an enigma, but perhaps no longer.

Just as he understood who I was, I understood who he was.

I sipped the whiskey slowly, letting it burn down my throat to my gut. The scent of cinnamon wafted over me as an uninvited man took the seat across from me. My gaze flickered in his direction. I scowled.

"Hello, *chérie*." Azriel's familiar dark eyes pierced me.

"What do you want?"

"Is that how you greet an old friend?" He didn't bother to hide the hurt expression on his face.

"It's how I greet you." I took another sip, keeping my gaze focused on him.

Azriel hid his black wings behind a glamor and wore an expensive suit. Other than that, he hadn't changed in the months since we first met. Something to which I wasn't accustomed. He was still devastatingly handsome with that sinful, savage look and that wolfish grin he never bothered to hide. His obsidian eyes glistened with malicious mirth. Since I had discovered how to keep my mind guarded from him, he hadn't bothered me much. He hadn't appeared in my dreams or stalked me when I least expected it. I had gotten used to his absence and I liked it.

He glanced around as though looking for someone. "Where is your *gardien*?"

"Close enough to fuck you up if you mess with me," I said, gripping the highball glass until my fingers ached. If he noticed the tremor in my hand, he didn't comment on it.

He chuckled.

"I'll ask again. What do you want, Azriel?"

He sat back in the chair as the waitress arrived and placed a brandy snifter in front of him. He gave her a nod of thanks, then took the glass in his hand and swirled the amber liquid as though he were a pompous billionaire on a night on the town.

"It's a pity you and I never came together. I still dream of you, you know."

Disgust rolled through me. "I don't dream of you. I'd rather set myself on fire."

"No, I assume you dream of another." He said it with a flippant disgust. "Did Kincade tell you why we are mortal enemies?"

"I know the story of your betrayal of the Brotherhood, yes."

Azriel was once a man named Marcus, part of the Brotherhood of Watchers like Kincade. He gave up his place in the Brotherhood to become a Fallen high lord, to take his place next to Lucifer. He corrupted my ancestor, Ezra, who, at the time, held three of the Holy Relics.

"If you're here to try to recruit me to the dark side, forget it," I said.

He frowned as he took a sip of brandy. "I believe we understand that is not going to happen. Edward prepared you well. Your resolve is higher than we anticipated."

"We?" I lifted a brow in question.

"Come, *chérie*, you understand of whom I speak."

"Yeah. You and your boss man."

"I come with a message," Azriel said, ignoring my quip.

"And what is that?" I gave a half-grin as though he were making a joke.

"The Ark is ours for the taking. We know where it is. And we will recover it. If you try to claim it, then you will die. You and your *gardien*. Slowly." He swirled the liquid once more before sipping.

In my imaginary world, I smashed the snifter against his face. "Is that a threat, then?"

"No, my dear." He smiled that wolfish grin. "A promise. Stay away from Jerusalem. If you know what's good for you."

"You know I can't do that," I said, rising to the challenge.

"I know." Again, that smile. "That is why I look forward to seeing you there. And fighting for the right to claim the Ark. Farewell for now, *chérie*."

He rose from the chair and disappeared into the shadows, weaving his way through the late-night crowd. The waitress reappeared at my table.

"Can I get you something else, miss?"

"Yes." I lifted the glass. "A bottle of this."

"You want the whole bottle?"

"Yes. And charge it to my room."

She cut a glance to the bartender. "The bottle is quite expensive, miss."

"Okay," I said without blinking an eye.

She scurried off. A few minutes later she came back with a full bottle and placed it on the table in front of me. "My manager put the bottle on your room as requested."

"Thanks." I scooped up the bottle and staggered away from the bar. I needed to talk to Kincade.

I hurried back to the hotel room with the whiskey in hand trying to ignore the butterflies in my stomach and the burning in my gut. The burning from the alcohol. The butterflies from facing Kincade after his heartfelt speech. I should have stayed and acknowledged that speech but I wasn't good with emotions. And now I had to face him.

I hesitated a moment at the door, wondering what to expect from him. I took a deep, cleansing breath and swiped the card key. I shoved open the door to the small suite to see him sitting in a chair by the windows brooding at the night. He didn't acknowledge my presence. I didn't blame him.

I grabbed the two cups in the suite that were usually for coffee. I filled one of them, moved to stand next to him and handed it to him. For a few heartbeats, he didn't move. Then he glanced at me, a shadowed expression in his eyes I was unable to read, and took the cup from me. I filled mine and took the chair across from him.

"You're a coward," he said, his gaze still focused on the Nile and the lights twinkling on the calm water.

My gut clenched again. The smell of the whiskey turned my stomach. "You're right."

He said nothing, nor did he move to take a drink from the cup.

"Feelings and I have never gotten along. The ones I have for you are the worst of the lot." It was an admission I never wanted to make and yet there it was. I said it out loud for him to hear. My hands broke into a cold sweat.

He turned his head slowly. His gaze met mine. Understanding was in his eyes. We were not so unlike, he and I.

"Do you think that was easy for me?" he said.

"No," I muttered. "It wasn't easy for me to hear, either."

"Then I guess we have a lot of baggage to overcome, don't we?" His gaze went back to the night.

We, he said. I understood what he meant by baggage. He was over two thousand years old. Was he immortal? I assumed so. How many mortal women did he fall in love with and then watch age and die? He didn't want to get close to me just as I did not want to get close to him. Ben was taken from me too soon in the most horrific manner.

I sensed, though, the powerful emotions pulling us together could not be ignored for much longer.

I sat back in the chair, gripping the bottle in my hand and gazed out at the night as if that held the answer to our damaged hearts. My feelings for Kincade had grown and changed over these last few months. I didn't want to admit how deep they ran because that meant I acknowledged my love for him. I didn't want to love him, but I was unable to change that. Instead of voicing any of that, I changed the subject to something we both related to.

"Azriel paid me a visit in the hotel bar."

He turned to look at me, his face impassive. The only movement was that of one brow raised. "What did he want?"

"He told me to stay away from Jerusalem. He said they knew where the Ark was and if I tried to claim to it, they would kill both of us."

"A blind threat." He lifted the cup and took a sip. "He won't be able to touch it."

"And you think I will?"

"If the Most High wills it, yes."

My mouth turned to ash as I stared at him, clutching the bottle in one hand and the cup in the other. His gaze never left mine.

"And you think He will?" I asked.

"There's only one way to find out." One corner of his mouth lifted in a half smile before he downed the rest of the whiskey. He held out his cup for a refill. I obliged with a shaking hand. "Don't get cold feet now, Anna."

"I'm not."

"Lie."

I huffed. "I don't have cold feet, but I know what we're up against. It's the two of us against Lucifer and his army of high lords."

"That's never scared you before."

"Well, it scares me now."

"Why?"

"Because this is the Ark of the Covenant. The final Holy Relic. Lucifer hasn't been able to pull me into the darkness to use me to find the relics himself. What do you think he'll do to keep me from the Ark?"

Kincade had a stoic expression that reminded me much of my uncle. "I see your point." He leaned forward and dropped his voice. "However, you forget one thing."

"What's that?"

"You are the One Who Was Promised. Lucifer knows that."

"So?" My brows drew together in question.

"He can't touch you. Why do you think you're still alive?"

The worst part was he wasn't reassuring me. He was naming the cage.

I downed the whiskey, remembering something my uncle once said. *Lucifer wants you alive.* And yet, the threat from Azriel was very real. Perhaps he thought once he gained control of the Ark, he wouldn't need me anymore.

"But that's just it. He can't gain control of the Ark without you," Kincade said.

I clenched my jaw. I disliked when he read my thoughts. Mostly because he was right too fast—and I didn't want him in the rooms of my fear.

"Because I'm the One Who Was Promised."

"Right."

"This is a confusing mess."

"It doesn't have to be. Lucifer wants the Ark. You want the Ark. We will likely converge on the place at the same time," he said.

"And then what? We fight to the death?"

He smiled. "It won't be to the death. Likely he'll try to use you in some way to gain control of the Ark."

"Gee, that sounds wonderful." I didn't bother to hide the sarcasm or bitterness in my voice.

"This isn't anything new," he pointed out. "But this is the final relic. Lucifer and his buddies will pull out all the stops. You should be ready for that."

I refilled my cup, drank it in one gulp, and cringed as it burned. "Then I guess it's time to visit the Old City."

He rose from the chair and moved to the dining table where he'd translated the Copper Scroll. He set aside his cup and picked up one of the pieces of paper, flipping it over.

"I've been thinking about that." He reached for his pencil and started to sketch something on the back of the paper. "The Damascus Gate is here. And here is the Garden Tomb. The Place of the Skull should be right about here. However, I believe there is a bus station near there now."

"A bus station? That seems sacrilegious."

Interested in his drawing, I moved from my chair to the table to watch him sketch out a crude map of the city.

"The Church of the Holy Sepulchre was built on the hill on what is thought to be the site of the crucifixion. It also holds Jesus' tomb, so it's considered one of the most holy places. It makes sense, at least to me, the Ark would be nearby."

"If the Ark is in the Place of the Skull under the cracked slab, then where is that today? Surely not the bus station."

"That's a good question. Not the bus station. There are abandoned quarries here outside the city which may be accessible through tunnels. This is where the Place of the Skull is." He marked an X on the paper. "Erosion has taken away most of the face. I think the cracked slab must be somewhere in those caves under or near the church."

"What makes you think that?"

"A story I heard once from a man who claimed to have found the Ark. I never believed him. Not entirely. But I also never forgot it. When Jesus was crucified, his blood flowed down and trickled under a crack in the earth where the cross was embedded. There, his blood landed on the mercy seat of the Ark."

"And you think the Ark is under the crucifixion site?"

"I do."

I peered at his crude drawing, the first jitters of fear and excitement trickling through me. "How do we access those caves?"

"I'm not sure. Years ago, that same man who claimed to have found the Ark sealed the caves to keep others from going in and trying to recover it. He said it would be found when it was time to be found."

We exchanged a glance. Gooseflesh broke out along my arms. "Who was this man?"

"Just a religious mortal who was known for scouring the earth looking for holy relics. I remembered it after you stomped off to the hotel bar."

I frowned. "I didn't stomp."

"You did. At any rate, Lucifer will be expecting us to go in through the caves in the abandoned quarry."

I folded my arms across my chest. "Then how do you propose we get there?"

He gave me a rare smile. "There are other tunnels nearby."

"And you have a plan for that?" I asked.

"I do."

"And I should trust you regarding said plan?"

"You should."

I chewed on my lower lip, more questions swimming in my mind. What was his plan? Why wasn't he sharing it with me? How was I going to get us to the Old City from Cairo?

"It's late," he said. "We can plan the trip in the morning."

"But—"

"I see the questions in that head of yours," he interrupted. "We can discuss tomorrow." He gave a nod toward the bedroom.

I cut a glance to the sofa which didn't look nearly long enough for his six-foot-plus frame. "What about you?"

"Me? I'll be fine."

He picked up the whiskey bottle I had abandoned on the table. I stood rooted in place as he sank once more into the chair beside the windows and turned to face the night. After several quiet moments, I finally forced my feet to move. In the bedroom, I closed the door behind me and leaned against it. I had a hard time shaking the thought that I'd somehow hurt him. And I hated that.

As I lumbered to the bed, I kicked off my shoes then sank into the soft mattress. He'd vowed to fight the darkness at my side until death, and I'd run away to a bar. I owed him more than whiskey and apologies. I didn't know how yet—but I vowed to find some way to make it up to him.

CHAPTER 26

I SLEPT AND DREAMED of a place I had never seen. A place of darkness with nothing more than cold stone surrounding me. Somewhere nearby was the trickle of water. I pressed my hand against the stone wall. A deep chill settled into my bones.

I was not alone.

And though I was unable to see someone in the chamber with me, I sensed the presence standing next to me trying to give me comfort and urging me onward.

Ahead, there appeared to be a stone slab. I moved toward it, trying to force my eyes to adjust to the darkness. I reached out a hand as I approached and touched the cool stone. My fingers grazed a jagged crack down the center.

I leaned over the slab and looked into the crack. Inside, I saw a hint of a golden wing. A gasp escaped.

Then the dream ended.

I woke, bolting upright on the bed. Sweat dampened the back of my neck. I shivered, clutching my elbows against my chest, and looked out at the Nile beyond my room. It was nearing dawn. I understood what the dream meant—it was showing me the Ark under the cracked slab.

I shoved off the bed and moved to stand at the windows, watching as the night sky lightened as the sun rose in the east behind us. Traffic increased on the waters and, beyond, the streets were jammed with cars and buses.

My head throbbed with a fierce pain. Too much stress, anxiety, and fear pressed against me. I wondered when I would be free of it all, though I doubted I ever would.

I turned from the windows, my steps heavy as I trudged to the bedroom door and opened it. Kincade sat at the small dining table with papers scattered around him. He looked as though he hadn't slept. His hair was disheveled. He had dark circles under his eyes and the bristling of beard on his cheeks and chin thickened.

"I ordered room service," he said without looking up. He waved toward a rolling cart with a couple of covered dishes.

Despite my growling stomach, I ignored the food. Still clutching my elbows, I stepped toward the table and peered at the mess of papers scattered around him. He'd drawn on the back of all of the photocopies of the Copper Scroll and put them together like an elaborate puzzle.

"What is this?"

"A map."

He tapped his pencil on top of one of them. One that was the beginnings of his crude map he'd drawn before he'd ordered me to bed.

"And a way in." His gaze met mine then. "There are tunnels at the Western Wall. Tunnels we can access. If my memory is right, there is an elaborate labyrinth of them under the Old City. They're all connected."

I stared at the drawings as though they were made by an expert mapmaker. "It looks like your memory is pretty damn good."

"Some is from memory. Some is my best guess."

"Your best guess?"

"Based on what I know of the Old City, I pieced together where I thought the tunnels were connected, though we won't truly know until we're there. But we start here." He stabbed the paper with Western Wall scrawled in his handwriting. "There should be tunnels that lead under the city to here." He slid his finger across the paper in a diagonal and paused where he'd written Church of the Holy Sepulchre.

"And if the tunnels don't lead us to the Ark?"

"Then we keep trying."

I questioned this plan. It wasn't nearly concrete enough for me but I didn't argue. "All right. I'll call for the plane."

I turned to go back to the bedroom to find my cell phone buried in the bottom of my carry-on. I never carried it unless I absolutely had to.

"Anna," he called.

I looked back at him over my shoulder, waiting.

"I know this is part of your destiny, but... if the Ark is there..." he paused, clenched his jaw as though looking for the right words. Something troubled him. "I'm not sure we should disturb it."

I faced him, confusion flickering through me. "Why do you say that?"

"Some things are meant to be found. Not all of them are meant to be moved. It's a powerful relic. I have my doubts that even the Keeper of the Holy Relics is allowed to move it."

He was worried. About me. Hell, I was worried about me. I didn't know what I would face when I arrived back in the Old City. We had been there once before when we stole the Staff of Moses. I doubted Israeli police would want me to return. Not only that but I also had Lucifer and Azriel on my tail. None of this was looking great for me.

Plus, I hadn't really considered how I was going to get it out of the cave in the first place. It would take both of us to move it.

"Then what do you suggest?" I asked.

"We look for it. See if it's where we think it is and then…" His words trailed off. He looked away. His gaze focused on the wall of windows.

"And then?" I prompted.

His gaze returned to mine. He gave me a rueful grin. "And then we see what happens."

Fear slipped through me. It wasn't often Kincade sounded doubtful but he did now. And that troubled me. I merely nodded, though, taking his word for it as I headed back into the bedroom. I closed the door behind me, leaning against it with my heart racing and my gut clenching into a tight knot.

I had a feeling this would be the most dangerous trip I'd ever make.

I called the pilot and told him to meet us at the airport. Then I made arrangements for the car service to pick us up. When I finished, I packed up the rest of my belongings, grabbed my bag and stepped out of the bedroom.

Kincade had tidied up the area by stacking the papers together. He rolled them up and put them back in the tube in which they came and handed it to me.

"You might want that."

I took it from him, nodding. "I might." I stashed them in my duffel.

Neither of us had slept much or even taken a shower since we returned from the merchant in the bazaar. It had been a short trip to Cairo. We left the hotel and headed to the airport for our next leg of the trip, apprehension rolling through me with such a force I wanted to turn back and tell him never mind. I had the sudden urge to return to England, crawl under the covers of my bed and never come out.

But that wasn't an option.

Instead, we boarded the plane for the hour and a half flight. Kincade took the seat across the aisle from me and settled in for his usual nap. On the way, I checked the news channels on my phone and was disturbed to see all the headlines. A volcano had erupted in Iceland. An earthquake in Japan followed by a tsunami. War had broken out in the eastern European countries. Unrest in Northern Ireland. Riots in Colombia, South America. Drought in African nations causing disease and death. And then, of course, the spread of the latest virus hitting all the major cities in the UK and the US.

"What's wrong?" Kincade asked.

I closed the screen and pocketed the phone. "Nothing."

"Lie." When I didn't respond, he said, "You were looking at the headlines, weren't you?"

"I skimmed them, yes."

"There's nothing you can do about what's happening in the world."

"And yet the world is going to shit," I said. I dropped the back of my head against the leather headrest. "I thought what I was doing mattered."

"It does matter," he said. "Everything you've done since Hong Kong has mattered."

"It doesn't feel like it."

"Don't get discouraged now. We've come too far."

"And we have even farther to go. Finding the Ark is just the beginning."

Because once I found the Ark, then the inevitable was going to happen.

War with Lucifer.

* * *

We landed at Ben Gurion International Airport, about thirty miles from Jerusalem. Truthfully, it was closer to Tel Aviv than Jerusalem but we didn't have much choice in the matter. We had to land where we were allowed.

We took a taxi into the city. The last time we were here, we stayed at the King David Hotel. Since our departure had been less than friendly, I decided to choose something close to the Western Wall and a little less high profile. It was a vacation apartment in the Old City Jewish Quarter that was a five-minute walk to the Western Wall. The entire apartment was less than four-hundred-square-feet but had all the amenities we needed. The only problem was there was only one bedroom with a queen size bed.

As we entered the apartment, exhaustion hit me hard and fast. I dropped my duffel on the floor by the tiny kitchen table. The views from the apartment were actually quite stunning.

"How did you find this place?" Kincade stood in the middle of the small living room which had nothing more than a sofa and a tiny flat screen TV and peered out the windows.

"I researched. It was lucky the place was available."

I joined him at the windows in front of the couch. We said nothing. Merely stood in amicable silence, the weight of what we were there to do pressing on both of us.

"I suggest you get some rest," he said. "We'll go under the cover of darkness."

Much like when we acquired the Staff of Moses, we went at night. It seemed to be his preferred method.

"When?" I asked.

"Midnight tonight," he said.

As I headed for the bedroom, he headed for the apartment door.

"Where are you going?" I asked.

"Recon," he said without turning around.

"Don't you want to rest?" I called as he opened the door.

"I napped on the plane."

And then he was gone. I sighed. Something had shifted between us since Cairo. I had to find a way to mend that rift though I didn't know how yet. I wasn't ready to admit my feelings for him, even though I was fairly certain he knew how I felt already. He was intuitive and he had the ability to tap into my thoughts and feelings anytime he wanted. I both loved and hated that.

I paced the confines of the small apartment, restless, clenching and unclenching my fists. I had a sort of nervous energy that had taken up residence deep inside me. The last time I experienced this was in Istanbul. I'd left the hotel room spoiling for a fight and that's when I met Ophelia.

I halted in the middle of the tiny living room, missing her and regretting our last interaction.

Without really thinking, I walked to the apartment door and slipped out. I wasn't sure what I was looking for or intending, but I wasn't tired and I needed to blow off some steam.

I didn't intentionally go looking for trouble. Trouble usually found me.

Outside, I headed down the steps. The apartment was in a densely packed residential area with nothing more than a walkway that felt like an alley. I walked through a shady courtyard where children played as if there was nothing wrong in the world, as if there was no outside influence. I wished I had their innocence.

I wandered through the streets, winding my way through the buildings, lost in my own thoughts, when I found myself at the Western Wall Plaza. It was crowded with those standing at the wall, praying. While others milled about the plaza itself. In the crowd, a familiar figure walked with an unmistakable gait toward one of the buildings. I would know Kincade anywhere. He was taller than most and strode in a way that told the world he wouldn't take shit off anyone. I remained in place as I watched him move past the crowd at the wall, not acknowledging anyone, and then disappear under an archway.

It was wrong to follow him but I was unable to stop myself. With my heart in my throat, I hurried across the plaza making for the same arched entrance in which Kincade had disappeared. I joined a tour-guided crowd flowing through a series of rooms moving eastward down through the tunnels along the Western Wall trying to keep my eye on Kincade's head bobbing above the rest.

The tour stopped along one point to discuss Temple Mount and how it was built by Herod and then later destroyed by the Romans. I didn't linger to listen. My mind was on Kincade and where he was headed. I stepped my way through the crowd, trying to be as inconspicuous as possible. He disappeared down the length of the tunnel. When I broke free of the group, I stepped up my pace.

At one point he paused, and turned to look behind him. I pressed against a wall, hoping he didn't see me. He remained still, his eyes searching, until he finally turned and headed back down the tunnel and around a corner.

I started again and found myself at a narrow steep staircase going down. I held the handrails as I took the steps one at a time. They ended at a large ancient cistern. I gaped at the sheer massive size of it, imaging how it was used thousands of years ago.

"What are you doing here?"

I yelped at the sound of his voice, my heart throbbing madly as I turned to face him. I pressed a hand against my chest. "You scared me!"

"Why are you following me?" He stepped closer to me, his eyes narrowed. He looked every bit peeved as I expected him to be. In the shadowy light, the bristle on his cheeks and chin glistened.

"I-I don't know. I was...bored." I spread my hands in surrender and gave him my best innocent look, unsure if he bought it. Kincade, though, would know if I was lying.

He sighed, his shoulders dropping. "I told you to stay put."

I nodded. "You did."

"You never listen."

I shook my head. "I don't." I glanced around the cistern. Voices echoed behind us. Likely the tour group catching up. "What are you doing down here?"

He heard them, too, and took me by the upper arm. "Come on."

I stumbled after him as he practically dragged me several feet past the cistern. There was a weak barricade consisting of nothing more than a wooden rampart to deter tourists. A notice in both Arabic and English read Authorized Personnel Only. He completely ignored the warning sign and stepped around the barricade like he owned the place.

Kinda loved that about him.

As we did, he released me and we were plunged in a deep shadowy darkness.

"Stick close," he warned.

"You're the boss."

"If only." He said it with a deep annoyance that ricocheted through my bones.

Sticking close meant I was practically stepping on his heels. It was so dark it was hard to see anything other than the back of his head. Even my breathing was loud in the deafening silence. He felt his way along the wall, which I assumed was still part of the Western Wall. Here, the tunnel took a sharp left turn.

"Where is this place?" I whispered.

"We're under Temple Mount," he said, his voice quiet. "Heading northwest."

I recalled his hand drawn map and realized we were heading through the underground tunnels toward the Church of the Holy Sepulchre. My pulse pounded hard as I realized where he was headed.

"How did you know about these tunnels?" I asked.

"I know a lot of things."

Another mysterious thing he didn't want to share. Fine, then. I didn't press for more information.

He halted with his hands outstretched in front of him. He rested them on what appeared to be a dead end.

"Now what?" I asked.

"Shh."

We had been in a similar situation before when we were searching for the Staff of Moses. Or was it the Holy Grail? The chamber we were in had a secret entrance. Either designed by the Jews or the Templars, there was always a secret entrance.

His left hand moved across the wall toward the corner where his fingertips dug in. He yanked. There was a faint scraping of stone against stone. He glanced back at me with a grin, then used both hands in the corner of the wall. He pulled but the wall only budged a little.

"Help me."

He reached up higher as I moved to stand next to him. To get my fingers in the corner crack, I pressed against him which wasn't all that unpleasant. His body was rock solid.

"On three, we pull at the same time." His chest rumbled with the words against the back of my head. I nodded. "One. Two...three."

We pulled harder. My hands and arm muscles strained against the weight of the stone. Kincade did most of the heavy lifting, though. He grunted as we both pushed the stone enough for us to squeeze through the opening.

It was even darker on the other side.

He didn't hesitate as he stepped through, the shadows swallowing up his entire form. I stood rooted in place, my hands throbbing and my heart hammering.

"Are you coming?" he called. When I didn't answer right away, he poked his head through the opening. "Well?"

"It's dark in there."

"Scared of the dark, are you?" He cocked a grin.

"No," I shot back with a frown.

"Then quit stalling and come on."

He disappeared again. Taking a deep breath, I stepped in and ran right into him. He grunted his displeasure. His hand fumbled against mine until he found it and grabbed it. He pressed his other hand on the wall to his left and started walking.

"How can you even see where you're going?" I asked.

"I can't."

"Then how do you know—"

"I just know."

I pressed my lips together to keep from asking more senseless questions. As we descended, the air around us grew cold. I walked closer to him if only to absorb some of his body heat.

He halted again. Another dead end. He released me and pressed both hands against the stone wall. The swish of his hands over the wall was the only sound. Then he dropped his hands.

"Dead end. I was afraid of that."

"Now what?" I asked.

"Now we backtrack." He took my hand again and headed back the way we'd come.

"And then what?"

"And then I find another way," he said.

I stuck so close to him, my shoulder brushed against his upper arm. "Is there another way?"

"That's why I was doing recon."

I imagined him giving me his best annoyed side eye. "Perhaps there are other tunnels off the Western Wall."

"That's what I have to find."

"You mean what we have to find," I corrected.

He halted and turned to me. His face was unreadable in the inky black. He gripped both of my upper arms, his fingers pressing into my muscles.

"I want you to stay put while I search."

"Why?"

"Because it could be dangerous."

"I thought we were in this together," I said.

"We are but I don't need you getting hurt or dead while I find the passageway."

I was touched but it still didn't change my mind. "I don't like being left behind."

He sighed again, the warmth of his breath whispering over my face. "You're stubborn."

"That's not news."

He squeezed my arms one last time before releasing me, then started walking again. Silence descended between us, which was never a good thing because it gave me all kinds of time to think about things I didn't need to think about. Like what he said to me in Cairo, how I reacted by running away from those feelings and not facing them. So much regret and guilt flooded me.

"Kincade, about what you said in Cairo..."

"Forget it." There was a deep bitterness in his voice.

"I can't and won't." I made sure he heard the determination in mine. "I suppose I have some...residual trauma from losing Ben and Edward. I don't want to lose you, too."

He stiffened next to me. "You won't." His tone was soft but emphatic.

"I mean it."

"I know," he said.

"The thing is," I continued, feeling the words bubbling up inside me. Words I was unable to stop. "I loved Ben. He wanted to get married. He asked me more than once but I never could commit. My excuse was we hadn't known each other long enough." My hands shook, a cold sweat breaking out in my palms.

"And why are you telling me this?"

My mouth went dry. I swallowed hard, thankful for the dark so he didn't see the blush rising up through and burning my cheeks. It was time to tell him the truth. "Because I—"

A loud boom shook the ground above us. The tunnels shuddered with the vibration. Dust trickled down from the ceiling above our heads. I fell into him, as though he were a shield.

"What the hell was that?" I asked.

"I don't know. We should get out of here quickly."

He grabbed my hand and practically dragged me from the tunnel through the dark. More than once I bumped into him or stepped on the back of his heels in our haste. We were back at the opening a few seconds later, slipping through and then winding our way back up and through the tunnels.

Another boom. The earth rocked above our heads. We both halted. I glared up at the ceiling, willing it to stay put. We exchanged a glance. He didn't bother to hide the concern in his eyes which was not comforting at all. Still holding my hand, we started again. Past the barricade at the cistern.

By now, the shouts and screams of others in the tunnel echoed off the walls. My heart rammed hard in my chest as I clutched his hand. He didn't falter, though, as we headed through the tunnels and ended up at the back of the tour group in a panic to get out.

They pushed and shoved their way toward the opening. Kincade held me back. We waited until most of them had cleared out, still screaming, and shouting their terror. I had a suspicion of what it might be.

Finally, we were out of the tunnel and into the late afternoon. The rest of the tour group spilled out onto the plaza ahead of us running in every direction. Mass hysteria seemed to be rippling through the crowds as they dispersed through the plaza. Something was on fire and there was a gaping hole in the center.

We both halted outside the tunnel as we took in the scene.

"Time to get those weapons out," Kincade said.

I wasted no time. I drew down first the dagger, then my uncle's sword. I handed him the dagger. I didn't know what danger we were facing yet but it didn't bode well. My answer came in the form of a giant demon with curved horns around its head, a fiery hole for its nose, and two bright red eyes. It had oily leather skin, long arms and legs ending in taloned hands and feet. It opened its mouth to roar, showing off the bright red and orange embers deep in its throat. Four black leathery wings flapped behind it as it stepped toward the two of us and flicked his fire whip.

"What the fuck is that?" I whisper-shouted.

"Demon of the dark."

Kincade looked at me. It did not inspire confidence to see the fear flickering in his eyes.

Then he said, "Run."

CHAPTER 27

HE TOOK OFF LIKE a shot through the plaza, dodging the fire-breathing demon of the dark, clutching the jade-handle dagger. I stood frozen in place, my feet refusing to move. The demon started to follow him until I decided to do something incredibly stupid and lit my uncle's sword with one swipe of my hand. That caught the demon's attention. It halted and turned back to face me, its giant clawed feet pounding the stones beneath it.

I clutched the sword in both hands, holding it aloft as the thing roared at me, sans fire.

"Anna!" Kincade shouted. "What the hell are you doing?"

Doing what I do best. Kicking some ass, I said, throwing the thought at him.

His response was a growl deep in my head. He was displeased.

Despite the horror slashing through me, I stood my ground and refused to back down from the thing. I shut off my mind to Kincade so he wouldn't interfere with my focus.

The demon took one step, two. The closer it got the more I realized how huge the thing was. It towered over the Western Wall

243

which was just over sixty feet tall. I gazed up at it as it crouched down toward me, its bright red eyes boring into me, as though it saw right into my very soul. Terror sliced through me as we stared each other down. Then it opened its mouth. Fire bubbled up deep from its throat, making it glow a bright hot red.

I didn't run. I held up the flaming sword above my head as it belched fire. Fear lanced through me as I prepared to be burned to a crisp. Instead, my uncle's flaming sword protected me. When the demon was unsuccessful, it reared back and roared frustration toward the sky. Then barked a cry of pain.

I moved the sword from in front of my face to see Kincade had dug the dagger into the back of its leg. The dagger hissed as he jerked it out, black blood smeared on the shiny blade. The demon swung its long, gangly arm with it claws outstretched. Kincade ducked and the thing got nothing but air. It barked its frustration again.

I took the moment of distraction to charge and swing my sword. The tip of the flaming blade connected with the back of its leg. It cried out in pain as its skin sizzled. Black blood bubbled from the wound. The thing stumbled sideways, nearly toppling into the Western Wall. I couldn't bear the thought of it crashing though that ancient fortification. Before I was able to move, it took a swipe at me with its giant claws. It narrowly missed me. I hustled through the thing's legs and stabbed it at the base of its foot.

Another wail of pain but at least it stumbled away from the wall. And toward Kincade.

I didn't really think that one through.

He shouted something I didn't hear over the wailing of the beast. He ran through the plaza, zig zagging away as it finally lost its footing and toppled. I took advantage of its moment of confusion and attacked. I swung my sword trying to connect with anything when it reared back up and took a swipe at me. Its long talons connected with me, ripping through cloth and flesh with a wet tear and sending me flying across the plaza. I sucked in a sharp breath as I crashed against the stone and slid, every bone in my body rattled. I dropped the sword in flight. The flame snuffed out as it clattered to the ground.

I rolled to my side, trying to catch my breath. I pushed to all fours and glanced up in time to see the thing get back to its feet. Since it didn't really have facial expressions, it was hard to tell how furious it was. Perhaps the fire whip it produced in its left hand was evidence enough.

It snapped the whip at Kincade as he ran across the plaza toward me, his face a furious mask of rage and worry. The demon was so big, though, it was having a hard time finding Kincade, who appeared to be nothing more than an ant in comparison.

After several agonizing moments, I shook off the pain. The sword had landed near my feet. I wrapped a shaking, sweaty hand around the pommel and got to my feet just as the demon cracked the fire whip.

Kincade must have sensed it coming because he fell on his left hip, ducked, rolled and then got back to his feet in one smooth choreographed movement.

Back on my feet, I relit the sword with the swipe of my hand as he made it to my side.

"Are you insane?" he barked. "I told you to run."

"And let this thing kill innocent people?" I shook my head. "I don't think so."

The whip sizzled through the stone plaza next to us, punctuating my words.

"Then let's finish it," he said, turning back to the demon.

I didn't get to reply as the demon backhanded me. I crashed against Kincade and we both went flying again. The sword snuffed out. I landed with a crash sure I broke something that time. Burning pain shot through my shoulder and down my left side.

Kincade seemed to fare better. He landed and popped right back up as if he was some kind of invincible superhero. He spied the sword on the ground and dove for it. Just as his hand wrapped around the pommel, the beast cried out as if in pain. I rolled to my good side, lifting my head enough to see an arrow sticking out of the thing's side.

Kincade took that moment to run toward the demon, sliding between its massive legs with the sword in one hand and the dagger in the other. When the blades sliced through the inner legs of the demon, there was an audible hiss. Steam rose from the two wounds, black blood gurgled out. Another arrow embedded in its other side.

Confused, I tried to get up. Cradling my left arm against my side. The demon staggered again. In one horrible moment, I realized it was going to fall right on top of me. Somehow, I found the strength to shove to my feet, pain lancing through me as I limped to get out of the way. I gave it a glimpse over my shoulder to see how much distance I had managed to put between me and it when suddenly an arrow pierced one of its eyes. It barked with its pain as it continued its slow descent with me still in its path.

Suddenly, Kincade was there swooping me into his arms. He moved across the plaza away from it in seconds with his lightning speed. The ground reverberated with the force of the demon falling to it. Kincade put me on my feet, but I leaned heavily against him. His around slipped around my waist to steady me.

"You idiot," he muttered.

"I am," I agreed. "Where are the weapons?"

"That's what you're concerned with?"

"Well...yes." I winced in pain.

He gave me a thin-lipped look of disgust. "They're safe." He nodded to the ground.

He must have dropped them before he came to my rescue. I reached for the dagger and put it back into the cloud, then did the same with the sword.

"Happy now?" he asked. His words held a hint of annoyance and humor.

"Yes, thanks."

We examined the carnage before us. The demon's eye with the arrow oozed black blood and hissed, steam rising out of the wound. The other eye, once red, was now snuffed out.

"Is it...dead?" I asked.

"Aye, it is, thanks to me."

A woman with a lilting Irish accent stepped into our line of vision. She was tall, thin, and muscular, with fierce blue eyes and a riot of fiery red curls framing her round face. She carried a bow and wore a quiver of arrows on her back. She wore a blue tunic that matched her eyes, dark blue jeans and black knee-high lace-up suede boots that had seen better days.

She looked the dead demon over, then nocked an arrow and released it. The shiny tip embedded between the thing's eyes. It belched one final puff of smoke.

"For good measure. Should be dead now." She slung the bow over a shoulder as she approached.

I sagged against Kincade, relieved. She turned her bright blue gaze on me then.

"It was a brave thing you did, lass, if a bit daft," she said. "Still, I can't say I've ever seen anyone take on a demon of that size alone before."

Two things of note. She called me daft and she had seen big demons before, which made me wonder who she was.

"I was daft, I suppose. I'm Anna. This is Kincade."

"I know who you are, Anna Walker."

She said my name with such vehemence, I stared at her, trying to recall her face. "I'm afraid you have me at a disadvantage."

"Kiara FitzGerald." She bowed with a flourish, then paused, waiting for my reaction.

Her name sounded vaguely familiar but I couldn't place it. I gave her a shrug.

"One of the clans in the Order of the Holy Relics," Kincade said.

Recognition slammed me, then. I read about the Order not too long ago in the family history book. There were four clans who came together to form the Order of the Holy Relics and assist me, the Keeper, whenever I had a need. My uncle had been a leader of one of those clans. Colum FitzGerald was another.

A shot of guilt and sorrow pounded me. Ronan, who gave me his lightning powers and died saving me, was in love with Colum's daughter.

Kiara.

Her hot blue gaze flickered to Kincade. "Aye, I am." Then she fixed her heated gaze back on me. "And secretly engaged to Ronan Harred."

I swore under my breath. Ronan, son of Alexander Harred and the man I was betrothed to, told me about the girl he was in love with, though at the time he said they hadn't spoken of marriage. Perhaps he lied to make me feel less guilty about our marriage contract. He also said she had fiery red hair and a temper to match. This definitely sounded like his Kiara.

You know her? Kincade asked in my head.

Not personally, but yes, I know who she is.

"I don't know why I saved your life. I should have let the demon kill you." There was so much venom in her words, I wanted to duck.

"That's uncalled for." My words were not nearly as hostile as I wanted them to be. "Ronan died for—"

"I know what he died for," she snapped. She looked me up and down as though I were a piece of filth.

"I told you to wait for me!" A woman's voice called across the plaza.

She ran toward us, her strawberry blonde hair bouncing behind her and her face flushed with exertion. She carried a sword in one hand, the steel stained black with demon blood. Her brilliant green eyes glanced from Kiara to me and back again.

"Who's this?" she asked, out of breath.

"Anna Walker," Kiara said.

Her eyes widened, then her pretty face broke into a wide grin. "Keeper of the Holy Relics! I'm Bridget MacKeller."

I glanced between the two of them. Bridget must be the daughter of Malcolm MacKeller, the other clan leader in the Order.

"Great," I muttered. Then for them to hear, I said, "Nice meeting you both, but I'm in a bit of pain so..."

Kincade, as least, understood that was his cue to leave. He started walking across the plaza, his arm around my waist as he helped me maintain my balance. My labored breathing sounded deafening to my ears. The women fell in step behind us, much to my displeasure.

"Dinna think we are done here," Kiara said.

"Oh, we are so done here." I groaned as the pain lanced through me.

Bridget sheathed her sword in the scabbard at her waist. "Kiara, I told you to leave it. Nothing good will come of it."

"She killed my love." There was no denying the accusation in her tone.

I pulled Kincade to a stop and turned to face her, wishing I had the capacity to fling myself around and confront her with all the anger pumping through me.

"Listen here—" I started, but Kincade interrupted.

"She didn't kill him. He sacrificed himself to save her."

Her lethal gaze turned on him, disbelief in her eyes. "And who are ye, then?"

"Her guardian."

"And a former member of the Brotherhood of Watchers," I added.

He groaned. *Not necessary information, Anna.*

But I wanted her to know who she was dealing with.

She stood rock still. Next to her, Bridget cut a glance between the two of us. "The Keeper and her guardian," she said with a sort of reverence.

"I'd love to stand here and chit chat all day, but I'm in a bit of pain." I turned back to Kincade, stepping closer. I wrapped my arm around his waist. "It hurts to walk."

Without another word, he scooped me up into his arms. My heart did a stupid flip, which I immediately blamed on demon poison and not on him. Absolutely not on him.

I had hoped the two women would get the hint and stay behind. Alas, they didn't. They continued to follow as we headed back to the apartment in the residential district.

Behind us, Bridget and Kiara whispered to each other, their words indecipherable. I didn't care what they were saying as long as they didn't end up following us all the way to the back. When the demon took a swipe at me, his claws dug in and left behind demon poison. I'd had dark demon magic poisoning my blood before, so I was familiar with how it felt. My head was throbbing. Sooner or later, I was going to have to send Kincade to find a healer who could remove the poison.

"I can help you," Bridget said.

I grunted my displeasure.

"She doesn't need a healer," Kincade said.

"She was scratched by the demon's claws," Kiara said. "She has demon poison. If she doesn't have it removed soon, it will kill her."

"Not the first time," I muttered, recalling my own run in with the stuff.

"Bridget has...certain abilities," Kiara said, making her case. "She's a healer."

Kincade halted, turned to face them both. We stood in the middle of one of the walkways between buildings. People passed by us not giving us so much as a wayward glance as if nothing was amiss in the Western Wall Plaza. As if there wasn't a giant dead demon littering the ground.

It's up to you, he said in my head.

I sighed. "Fine. Come on then."

He resumed walking. I hoped I didn't regret my decision.

We returned to the small apartment. Kincade eased me down onto the bed in the tiny bedroom, then stepped aside as Bridget entered behind him. She craned her neck to look at him towering over her. He must have a foot in height over her.

"I'll need room to work."

"I'm not leaving," he said.

She frowned. "I can't heal her with you in the way."

"You'll have to work around me." He practically snarled the words.

I almost laughed. Kincade was no pushover, that's for sure. And the ridiculous part? Some traitorous part of me liked that he refused to leave. Kiara squeezed into the tiny room, then.

"What do you need?" she asked.

"A couple of towels and a bowl full of warm soapy water." She cut a glance at Kincade, who folded his thick forearms over his chest and remained planted in place. "And, uh, maybe some rubbing alcohol if you can find it."

Kiara disappeared out of the room. In the kitchen, she banged around looking for the required items.

"Can I see the wound?" Bridget asked.

"Sure, why not."

I rolled away from her, facing the opposite wall. With a gentle touch, she tugged my torn shirt out of the way. She sucked in a sharp breath.

"Looks bad," Kincade said.

"How bad?" Even though I didn't want to know, I needed to know.

"The skin is already turning black. Hopefully I can save it," she replied.

Kiara bustled into the room, then. "Here are the towels and water. I didn't find any rubbing alcohol, but I found some antiseptic cream."

"I'll make do with this." She paused, took a deep breath. "To cleanse the wound, it would be helpful if you could remove your shirt."

"Sure, no problem."

Despite the pain, I managed to push to a sitting position. Bridget helped me pull the ripped shirt off over my head. I stole a glance over my shoulder to see Kincade standing in the doorway wearing his best glare with his arms still crossed. He was perfection—and that was becoming a real problem.

Bridget dipped the edge of one of the towels into the warm soapy water. With a gentle touch, she dabbed along the claw marks one at a time. Every time the towel hit the wound a stinging sensation went through me. I clenched my jaw and did my best to keep from crying out with the pain.

"I've cleaned them as best as I can," she said. "Now, please hold very still." She placed one hand on my shoulder.

"What are you doing?" I asked.

"I will attempt to draw out the poison."

The last person who did that was Darius and it poisoned him. It took the Staff of Moses to heal him.

"Wait," I said. "How do you do it? Will it hurt you?"

"No. I have a way of removing the poison without harming myself. Please try not to move."

"I'll try."

She flattened her other hand on the claw marks. The pain was almost unbearable. I had no idea what she was doing because I was unable to see. She removed her hand from my back. When she did, a black puff of smoke filled the air, then disappeared. She placed her hand on the next slash. Removed it. Puff of smoke. And so on until she had touched each one. With every movement and every release, the pain dissipated slightly. Then she dabbed the antiseptic cream along the claw marks.

"There," she said. "You should heal in a few days. I have successfully removed all the demon poison."

"Thanks. Now if you don't mind, I'd like to put on a shirt."

"Sure. Nice tattoo, by the way."

I blushed to the roots of my hair as she left the room. Great. Exactly what I needed—someone admiring the magic tattoo that used to be Azriel's mark on me before Kincade rewrote it. Basically branded by one fallen angel and then overwritten by the infuriating man currently guarding my doorway. Totally normal. Not emotionally significant at all. Nope.

I shoved those thoughts away and reached for my duffel. I pulled out a clean Henley. As I tugged it on, Kincade remained firmly planted in the doorway of the bedroom.

"You didn't have to stand guard, you know." I kept my voice low so only he heard.

"I did." His face remained impassive as he moved aside to allow me to exit the room.

I tried—really tried—to ignore the warm fuzzies curling through me as I brushed by him. And I also tried not to think about the confession I'd almost made in the tunnels. The demon attack had killed that moment, and while part of me was relieved, another part of me regretted it more than I wanted to admit.

Because the truth was there, clawing at me—I wanted to tell Kincade I loved him.

And that terrified me.

Too many people in my life had been ripped away. Too many I'd cared about had died. And despite his ancient age, I knew Kincade wasn't immortal. He could die like the rest of us.

And I wasn't sure I could survive losing someone again.

Kiara and Bridget had made themselves at home on the sofa in the tiny living area. Kiara placed her quiver and bow against one of the walls. Bridget was busy cleaning the black demon blood off her sword. When I emerged from the bedroom Kiara jumped to her feet.

"Now about Ronan—"

"Kiara!" Bridget scolded. She hastily put her sword on top of the small table in front of the sofa.

"Quiet, Bridget." She shushed her with a slash of her hand.

"What about him?" I went to the fridge and pulled it open, looking for something that wasn't there. Trying to stall.

"You were betrothed to him," she said.

"I was." I closed the fridge and turned to her. "But neither of us wanted to go through with it."

"Then why did he go with you?" Her carefully crafted anger was beginning to crack. Her voice wobbled. Sudden tears filled her eyes. "Why did he have to die?"

Bridget wrapped an arm around her shoulders and led her back to the sofa. I turned to Kincade, who stood like a sentry behind me.

"I think we're going to need some provisions."

"I'm not leaving you here with them." He jerked his chin toward the two women.

I placed a reassuring hand on his arm. "I'll be fine."

He cut a glance back to them, then gave me a quick nod. "I'll be back."

With that, he left.

The door clicked shut, and for a heartbeat longer than I liked, I wished he hadn't.

CHAPTER 28

KIARA HID HER FACE in her hands as she silently sobbed. Bridget did her best to console her. She looked up at me, her apologetic gaze meeting mine.

"I'm sorry about Ronan," I said. "I liked him very much. He was honorable and trustworthy and decent."

Kiara sniffed. She wiped away the tears with her sleeve. "I know all that."

"But what you don't know is he gave me a gift."

I lifted my hands, letting the lightning dance between my fingers. She shot to her feet with her hands balled into fists at her sides. There was no mistaking the anger creasing her brow.

"You whore! How do I know you didn't steal it from him when you killed him?"

I quickly snuffed out the lightning, ready to fight her if I had to. A familiar rage snapped through me—not the smart-mouthed kind, but the deep, bone-level fury that came when someone tried to cheapen the people I'd lost.

"Kiara, sit down. That's unfair of you to say to her. She didn't kill Ronan." Bridget slowly got to her feet. She put a hand on her friend's shoulder and tried to push her back to her seat. But Kiara was having none of it.

"Do shut up, Bridget. You're only saying that because you're a fan."

"Kiara, please—"

"I've had enough of you." She shoved her friend away, then brushed by me and stomped out the door, slamming it behind her.

I sighed.

Bridget gave me a sheepish grin. "It's true. Since we learned of your return to England, I've been dying to meet you. I was trying to wait until you called upon the clans, but..." She spread her hands and shrugged.

"Well, I do appreciate your healing skills," I said.

"Kiara took Ronan's death very hard. When she heard, she immediately wanted to confront you. I talked her out of it as we navigated his funeral. His father did not make things any easier," she said.

I nodded. "Yes, I can understand that. He's not exactly my biggest fan."

"Kiara is a tracker. It's one of her dream walker skills and she's very good at it," Bridget said. "She tracked you here to confront you."

I had been so wrapped up in my own thoughts and feelings, I hadn't picked up on the fact that someone was following us. I wondered if Kincade knew. But if he had, I was certain he would have said something.

"I see your confusion," she said. "She's not a traditional tracker."

My brows drew together with concern and question. "What does that mean?"

"She can track people through their dreams without them knowing. She's done it to me. She did it to Ronan when you were in Spain. The only thing that kept her from following him then was her father."

I pulled out a chair from the small dining table and sank into it. Having a power like that was beyond my comprehension. My uncle once told me I was one of the most powerful dream walkers. I believed him. I also believed Kiara ranked up there with me.

"Her father," Bridget continued, "insisted she stay in Dublin where she belonged. But she picked up your trail and then wouldn't let it go. I believe you were in Dublin recently?"

Hot pricks of light danced behind my eyes. "Yes, we were in Dublin."

"There was a riot near Temple Bar," she continued. "Kiara was there that day, too. She said she fought against the demons. She said she fought against one of the Four Horseman."

I nodded as my hands shook. "War," I whispered.

"We waited for you to call for aid from the Order of the Holy Relics, but you never did. We would have helped."

"I only recently found out about the Order," I said. "My uncle wasn't exactly the best at sharing information."

"Edward Walker was a strong-willed man." She smiled.

"Don't I know it."

We shared a laugh.

"Kiara will come around. And she wants to know how he died. She just has a funny way of asking you to share those details. It's easier for her to blame you than to accept the truth, I think."

"Then I'll tell her when she's ready to hear the story."

"Good." She sat back in the sofa and propped her feet on the small table. "Where did Kincade go?"

"I sent him for food and whiskey."

She lifted a brow. "Whiskey?"

"We made a pact once. When there's a tragedy in my life, we drink whiskey together."

She laughed. "I like that pact."

"You're welcome to join in when he returns."

"I never was much of a whiskey drinker, but I might give it a try."

We lapsed into silence and waited. It seemed like an eternity stretched on and I was forced to make small talk with Bridget. Not that I minded. She seemed enamored with who I was, though I didn't understand why.

At last, the apartment door opened. Kiara, her face tear-stained, entered followed by Kincade. He carried a large bag of what I hoped was filled with booze and food.

What took so long? I asked.

Found her outside. We had a little chat. Go easy on her, eh?

Kincade moved into the small kitchen as though nothing was amiss and started unloading boxes of takeout that smelled delicious. He handed me a bottle of lovely whiskey.

"I believe Kiara has something she wants to ask you." Kincade handed me one of the takeout boxes.

I gave her a questioning look as she stood in the middle of the room, shifting from one foot to the other. Bridget joined her. Kincade passed them their own takeout box.

"First, I want to apologize," she said. "I was wrong to accuse you of killing Ronan."

"I understand why you did." I placed the whiskey bottle on the nearby table, wishing I had a glass to fill.

"Second..." She paused, cut a glance at Kincade who gave her a nod to continue. "Kincade and I spoke outside. He said you would tell me what happened to him and how it happened."

Though I expected it, I still cringed. I nodded. With my free hand, I waved to the small living area adjacent to the dining area. "Have a seat and I'll tell you about Ronan."

They sat and I told them about the quest for the Holy Grail. I told her Ronan had a vision of my death and that he was insisted on going with us to help protect me. Our trip led us through Spain from Valenica to the King of Spain's birthday gala in Madrid. At that gala, I was nearly killed by a dark high lord named Hadrian. My friends and I narrowly escaped with our lives. We ended up in the hidden Fae Forest with Killian and Astrid, but Lucifer and his high lords found us there.

I told her of the battle we fought against him, Azriel, Hadrian and the demons who attacked the forest. Hadrian had used his demon magic on Ronan, but Ronan turned his lightning hands on the high lord, harnessing the power of the sky to fight back against him. I remembered how he seemed to pull down the lightning from the sky. He injured Hadrian, but it wasn't enough to stop him.

Hadrian was determined to kill me. He used his power dark magic, sending a final blow toward me to take me out. Ronan, though, dove in front of me, saving my life. He took the blast square in the chest, falling to the ground.

"I fell to my knees beside him. I told him he was a stupid fool." I shook my head, remembering the horror of it all. "I will never forget how his face looked. Like a map of black and white veins. He gripped my shirt, then. His hand was cracked and bloody. There was light flickering between his long, slender fingers. He flattened his hand on my chest over my heart..."

I paused, clenched my jaw tight. Bridget and Kiara waited for me to continue. Their faces were blanched of color.

"He said, 'It's all you now.' And then the power came into me. Like a pulse of energy that pounded through me with a force I had never experienced before. He gave me his lightning." I lifted a hand, let the light dance between my fingers.

Kiara pressed her hand against her mouth. She inhaled and released a long, shuddering breath.

"Thank you for telling me." Her voice was barely a whisper.

Bridget patted her arm to console her.

"You're welcome."

I opened the takeout box. My food had gone cold. Kincade had remained in the kitchen, listening, and not moving. The microwave was only a few steps into the kitchen. I popped open the door and put my container inside.

"You did a good thing," he said, his voice low.

"Did I?"

"She wanted to know. Now she knows."

I punched the keypad on the microwave unnecessarily hard. "What did you tell her outside?"

"That she was wrong about you. That she should listen to you."

I watched the numbers count down, my stomach grumbling with both hunger and nerves. "And she listened to you."

"Most people do. You should listen to me more often."

I would have rolled my eyes if my chest wasn't so tight. I lifted my head and met his gaze, one brow arched. "Should I?"

"Yes." He reached over my head and opened a cabinet door, then pulled out a glass.

"Kincade, I—" I halted, unsure what I wanted to say. Instead, I said simply, "Thanks."

I wasn't sure what I was thanking him for. The food, the whiskey, saving my ass again, or what.

"It's what I do," he said and poured the whiskey. Two fingers, neat. Just like I liked it. "Here's to the Ark."

"The Ark?" Bridget said. Despite our hushed voices, she clearly heard that one. "I'll take one of those."

"Yes, the Ark," I said.

"Do you mean the Ark of the Covenant?" she asked.

Kincade poured her a drink. We exchanged a glance. Should and could we trust them? They were part of the Order of the Holy Relics, after all.

"Yes," I said at last. "We have reason to believe it's here."

"We can help," Bridget said.

I almost laughed. "I don't think so. You should return to your homes."

"No." Kiara put her food on the table. She joined us in the kitchen. "We're coming with you."

"I don't think that's a good idea," I said.

"Why not?" she demanded. "I helped you kill that demon."

"Yes, and I can't figure out where it came from," I said.

"Someone unleashed it," Bridget said.

"Only one person has that kind of power," Kincade said.

"I think we know who," I replied.

"I tracked that demon to you," Kiara said.

"You tracked it?" I stole a questioning glance at Bridget who remained mute.

Kiara shifted from one foot to the other. "Aye, I...was tracking you."

"You were?"

Her face registered discomfort. "I was and then I saw...we...saw the demon. It suddenly appeared in the middle of the plaza as though it had been conjured."

"It likely was," Kincade said. "Lucifer doesn't want us here."

"He warned us he'd kill us if we went after the Ark," I added. "He knows it's here, too, and intends to retrieve it."

"Well, he can try," Bridget said with a smirk. "He'll never be able to touch it."

"And you know this how?" I asked.

"Only angels are allowed to touch it," Kiara said. "It's a known fact."

Well, maybe to most but not to me. Clearly, I needed to brush up on my Ark facts.

"Let us help you," Kiara urged. "I can track whoever you want me to track. And Bridget is a skilled healer, as you know. She may be needed again."

"Your reputation precedes you," Kincade said.

"You're hilarious," I snipped. I turned my attention back to Kiara. "Lucifer is controlling an archeologist. I suspect that's how he knows where the Ark is. Can you find him? Track him?"

"I could if I knew more about him," she said. "Like his name. What he looks like. That sort of thing."

I gave Kincade a questioning glance.

"I'm on it." He didn't even hesitate as he headed for the door.

The instinct to follow him rose sharp and stupid in my chest. "Wait, I want to come with you."

He turned on me, his face inches from mine. "You will stay here and behave. Like a good girl. Got it?"

I pouted and puffed out a breath of annoyance. "Fine."

"I'll be back as soon as I can."

And then he was gone, leaving me alone once again with Kiara and Bridget.

"Can you trust him?" Kiara asked.

"Yes. With my life." I turned to face her. "And yours."

CHAPTER 29

KINCADE WAS GONE FOR hours. In those hours, as I paced, there were two things I realized. One was the tiny one-bedroom apartment was not nearly big enough for the three of us, soon to be the four of us. The second was I was determined to tell Kincade how I felt about him. Just as soon as the time was right.

Problem was the time was never right to tell someone you were in love with them.

And I posed numerous questions in my mind. I guessed he was over two thousand years old since he mentioned he was at the crucifixion. But how old was he really? And since he clearly had longevity, what did that mean for the two of us? That is, if he didn't reject me. Judging by our previous kisses, though, he wouldn't reject me.

My uncle told me once dream walkers had unnaturally long life. I didn't take that to mean we were immortal, but rather we lived longer than most normal people. If that were the case, then perhaps there was a chance for the two of us. I finally made myself stop pacing and settled into one of the chairs at the small dining table.

At last, the apartment door opened and Kincade returned. I jumped to my feet, relieved and elated to see him. Kiara and Bridget also got to their feet with expectant looks on their faces. He glanced between the three of us, his brows drawn together.

"Bored, are we?"

"Just waiting for your return," I said.

"Anna nearly paced a hole in the carpet while you were gone," Kiara teased.

"I did not," I said, offended.

Kincade ignored our banter. "It took some time, but I found Lucifer's camp. He's just outside the city. Azriel is with him."

I frowned.

"Who's Azriel?" Bridget asked.

"My archenemy," I said. "He's one of Lucifer's high lords in the Fallen. Did you find out who his archaeologist is?"

"Yes," Kincade said with a nod. "His name is Arthur Carter."

My frown deepened. "You're kidding, right?"

"I am not."

"You know him?" Kiara asked.

"He's one of the foremost leading British archaeologists on Christian antiquities. He's a professor at Oxford. The one the students hope they don't get," I said.

"How do you know?" Bridget asked. "I've never heard of him."

"If he heard you say that, it would deeply wound his ego. I know because everyone who lives in England has heard of Arthur Carter. He led teams all over Israel and Jordan looking for holy relics and Templar artifacts."

"It was rumored he came close to finding one of the Templar treasures," Kincade said.

"But he never did?" Kiara asked.

"No. Call it divine intervention," Kincade said.

I didn't have to ask for clarification to know what he meant. I assumed the Brotherhood of Watchers had something to do with that intervention.

"How would Lucifer get close to him to control him?" I asked.

"Simple. He had one his high lords steal his soul. They're using it to force him to do what they want. He also has a copy of the Copper Scroll and transcribed it like I did."

"You have a copy of the Copper Scroll?" Kiara asked, shocked.

"Yeah. It's a long story." I waved away her follow up questions. "If he transcribed it, then he surely knows where the Ark is like we do."

"He does," Kincade nodded. "They plan to move out tomorrow to Zedekiah's Cave. That's where he believes it is."

I stared at him. Did Kincade also believe that was where the Ark was? I suspected he wanted to be the one to find it first and then led me to it.

"Where is this cave?"

"Just inside the city walls near the Damascus Gate."

"Then we follow them there." I turned to Kiara. "What other information do you need to track him?"

"A description," she said. "As close as you can get."

Kincade said, "He's tall and slender. Smokes a pipe. He has short brown hair and a beard. He wears glasses."

"I can do one better," I said.

I sprinted to the bedroom where I retrieved my smartphone from the bottom of the duffel. A quick search brought up a picture of Arthur Carter. I showed it to Kiara.

She nodded. "I will get to work."

She headed back to the sofa in the small living area and sat, crossing her legs under her. She placed her hands on her knees, closed her eyes, and began her tracking.

Kincade took me by the arm and pulled me into the small bedroom, closing the door behind him. My heart immediately leapt into action, though I suspected he didn't have romance on his mind. Not when he turned to me, and gripped me by the arms.

"I don't want them with us," he said, keeping his voice low.

"Why not? You don't trust them?"

"I have a bad feeling about this, Anna. This Kiara...she tracked you here. She intended to kill you. She wants revenge for Ronan's death. I heard her thoughts," he said.

There were so many things about what he just said that struck me. The first being that he'd read her thoughts. Jealousy hit me harder than I expected at the thought that he would read another woman's mind—see her fears, her secrets, the way he'd been seeing mine for months. Then I shoved that aside because he would be able to read that in my mind.

"She wanted to know how he died. She blamed me for his death."

"I heard your story," he said. "She hung on every word. I watched her face, her expressions, her reactions as she listened. I'm not convinced she hasn't changed her mind."

"Well, we're just going to have to trust that she has."

"Anna—"

"She's part of the Order, Kincade. I have to trust her until she gives me a reason not to. They're going with us."

He released me, stepped back, and raked a hand through his short-cropped hair making it stand on end.

"Fine. But we're doing this my way tomorrow."

"Okay."

"I mean it."

"I said okay."

He gave me a look that said he didn't believe me.

I held up my hands in surrender. "I'll do what you tell me. Swear."

"You'd better."

He sat on the edge of the bed. I remained where I was, afraid to sit next to him. Now would be a great time to tell him what I'd wanted to tell him since the tunnel. But he looked deep in thought and I didn't want to break into those thoughts.

"There's a tunnel that leads to that cave," he said. "I'm almost sure of it. I thought the tunnels under the Western Wall would lead us there, but I had it all wrong. I think we need to start with the church. It's not far from the cave."

"Lucifer will be expecting us to show up in the same place as him anyway."

"He will. That's why we have to go about it at another angle. That's why we have to start at the church."

I nodded agreement. Then said, "I thought you said the Ark was under the church. Is that where the cave is?"

"No, it's not. But if a renowned archaeologist thinks it's there, then we should at least look."

I nodded agreement again.

His gaze lifted to mine then, which caused a riot of butterflies to erupt in my stomach.

"In the tunnel," he said, "you were trying to tell me something."

"Oh…" I smiled, waved it away as though it were nothing. "That. It was nothing important."

The lie tasted like ash, but cowardice had always been my favorite armor.

Kincade, though, read me like a book and would know I lied. He would also know I did everything in my power to conceal my true feelings. I perched on the edge of the bed next to him, putting a respectable distance between us. Thankfully, he didn't call me out on it. This time.

"You should get some rest." He got to his feet. "Tomorrow will be a busy day."

"Where are you going?"

"To stand guard."

I didn't argue as he opened the door, slipped out, and closed it behind him. I kicked off my shoes and laid back on the bed. It wasn't long before the exhaustion hit me and I was out.

* * *

It seemed only a few minutes had passed when Kincade was shaking me awake. It took me several minutes to remember where I was.

"Time to go," he said.

And then he was gone again.

I sat up on the bed, ran a hand through my long, tangled hair and wondered where I put my shoes. They were still on the floor where I'd kicked them off. I shoved my feet into the pink combat boots and trudged outside the bedroom. Kiara and Bridget were waiting there with Kincade, all with expectant looks on their faces. Kiara, I noticed, looked as though she'd had the worst day of her life.

"Did I miss the staff meeting?" I asked.

"I have the location of Arthur Carter," Kiara announced.

"Great. Where is he?"

"He's dead."

The blood drained from my head. I pinched the bridge of my nose with my thumb and forefinger. Of course Lucifer would break his toy the instant it stopped being useful.

"He killed him," I said.

"Yes," Kincade said. "Which means he's now one of them."

"Fuck."

"What does that mean? He's one of them?" Bridget asked.

"It means when Lucifer takes a soul and crushes it, that person then belongs to his dark army," I explained. "And that means he's already found the Ark."

"Not necessarily," Kincade said. "It could mean he simply knows where it is."

I took a deep breath, expelled it. "Then we better get going."

Kiara picked up her bow and quiver of arrows. Bridget placed her sword back into the scabbard at her waist. I eyed both of them and imagined them walking through the Old City carrying their weapons. It probably wasn't a good idea.

"You should leave your weapons," I said.

"What if we run into trouble?" Kiara asked.

"I have mine." I pulled down the dagger and the sword to show her.

"How did you do that?" Bridget was complete dumbfounded at the ability to hide the weapons in the cloud.

"I'll show you when we return." I replaced the weapons in the cloud. "It comes in handy."

"Maybe you should hide their weapons in the cloud," Kincade suggested. "Just in case."

It wasn't a bad idea. I didn't exactly know how all that worked, if there was limited space or what, but I was willing to give it a try.

"Is it safe?" Kiara asked, sounding suspicious.

"It's perfectly safe."

They handed over their weapons and I hid them along with my sword and dagger. We left the apartment without another word, following Kincade through the streets of the residential area, heading northwest. The church was a five-minute walk from the apartment.

As we approached the church, my stomach churned with all the anticipation that had led to this from the first moment I decided to accept my fate as Keeper of the Holy Relics.

The first thing we saw as we entered was the Stone of Anointing. We didn't linger there. Kincade immediately turned left and led us past the Chapel of the Three Marys into the rotunda, where the tomb of Jesus was located. But we didn't stop to go through the tomb. Instead, Kincade kept moving beyond it, deeper into the church into the Syrian Chapel, past all the crowds. No one seemed to notice the four of us making our way through the church.

Here, there was an entrance to the tomb of Joseph of Arimathea. We entered the tomb in total darkness.

"Stick close," he said.

He didn't have to tell me twice. I reached for him, hooking a finger in one of his belt loops to keep him within reach. He didn't seem to mind. Good. Because the dark down here terrified me more than I cared to admit, and he was the only anchor I had.

Behind me, Kiara and Bridget kept close enough to bump into me every other step. We passed two burial chambers and moved deeper into the tomb. He halted.

"This is it." His voice was quiet in the darkness.

He knelt. Though I was unable to see his movements, I heard the scraping of metal against stone. Then he stood and turned to me.

"Wait here until I tell you."

He lowered himself to the ground. As he did, I saw the yawning black hole he stepped in. I grabbed his sleeve.

"Where are you going?"

"Just wait here."

He disappeared into the abyss. Kiara and Bridget flanked me. All of us stared down into the pit of darkness. I squinted, as if that would make the shadows miraculously disappear. Suddenly, a burst of light and then Kincade appeared below, gazing up holding a flickering torch. He gave me a wave.

"Come on."

The hole wasn't as deep as I thought. Only about two feet. I jumped down. Kiara and Bridget followed.

"You might want to get those weapons handy," he said.

I drew down Bridget's sword first, then Kiara's bow and arrows, then my dagger, which I handed to Kincade, and finally my uncle's sword. It remained unlit as we made our way through a tunnel with him in the lead.

Still, I stuck close.

It was cold and damp as we made our way down under the church. A shiver skittered up my spine. I didn't question where he was going or how he knew the way. He led. I followed. It seemed like the best course of action. Even Kiara and Bridget behind me didn't speak. I did note they both had their weapons at the ready. Kincade carried the dagger in one hand, the torch in the other, as he made his way through the winding tunnels.

I lost all sense of direction. It seemed as though it went on forever. Ahead, we heard voices echoing back to us. Kincade gave a motion to halt. We stopped. My breath pooled in my throat as we listened.

Definitely voices.

"Who?" I asked.

He gave a shrug of one shoulder. "One guess. Let's go."

We resumed walking. The tunnel opened into a large cavern as we neared the voices. I clutched the sword tight in my sweating hands. A glance behind me and the two women were both at the ready. Kiara had an arrow nocked. Bridget clutched the sword with both hands.

Kincade waved us to the side of the cave as we neared a corner. He put the torch on the ground and snuffed it out, plunging us into total darkness again. It took several moments for my eyes to adjust. Ahead, there was a faint white light like a flashlight.

I pressed against the cold stone wall as he peered around the corner. Then he turned back to us.

"It looks like some of Lucifer's men," he whispered. "They're in Zedekiah's Cave."

"This leads us there?" He nodded. "Can we get closer?" I asked.

"Not without being seen."

"I'm willing to risk it," I said, clutching the sword and putting on a false bravado.

Truth was, I was scared out of my wits. Which was unusual for me. Throughout all the quests I'd been on, I had never been this nervous or fearful.

"You sure about that?"

"I am."

He cut a gaze to the two women behind me. "What about you two?"

"We're in," Kiara said.

He took a deep breath. "All right. Into the fire we go, then."

My fingers tightened on the hilt. Into the fire we go, then. And this time, there was no coming back without the Ark.

CHAPTER 30

As we approached, a distinctive voice echoed through the cavern. "I'm telling you the Ark is not here."

"I don't believe you," Lucifer replied. He punctuated that with a hiss of annoyance.

The group came into view. Lucifer, Azriel, a few lesser demons and the man I assumed was the archeologist, Arther Carter. Lucifer spotted us immediately.

"Well, well. Look who we have here. I see my demon failed to kill you both. Pity." He eyed Kiara and Bridget behind us.

"I'd say I was sorry you failed, but I'm not," I said.

"I did warn you not to come here," he said.

"And yet here we are." I gave him my best winning smile.

"It seems it's all for naught," Lucifer said. "The Ark is not here."

I glanced around and spied what appeared to be a stone slab in the middle of the cave. The top had a four-inch crack snaking down the center, reminding me of my dream. In the half light, I was certain there was a glint of gold beneath that crack.

Do you see it? I mindspoke to Kincade and glanced up at him.

His gaze searched the cave. I see nothing.

Lucifer noticed I stared at the crack. He snapped his fingers and made a gesture for Azriel and one of the demons to approach the slab.

"See what's there," he ordered.

Azriel gave him his famous wolf grin, which I ignored, as he and the demon approached the slab. He ran his fingers down the open crack.

"Nothing," Azriel said.

"I told you it wasn't here," Carter snapped.

Lucifer moved to stand next to Azriel, then shoved him out of the way. He put his hand in the crack, then pulled it away a moment later. He glared at me.

"What are you looking at?"

I smiled sweetly. "I thought I saw something but I was wrong."

"She is never wrong, my lord," Azriel said. "She's lying."

You are lying. What do you see? Kincade asked in my head.

The Ark is here, I think.

"Smash the stone slab and open this tomb," Lucifer ordered.

Lucifer's band of dark demons went to work smashing the slab and removing the stone pieces. I watched in fascinated horror as they revealed the Ark of the Covenant. I did my best Oscar performance and kept my face passive so as not to reveal my inner freak out.

Azriel pushed aside his demon friends and stared at the Ark. How did he not see it?

"Nothing, my lord. The archaeologist was right. It's not here."

But it was. It was right there and looked exactly as I imagined with the mercy seat on top.

Lucifer turned away from the destroyed stone slab, his dark eyes landing on me. The malice he exuded shuddered through me. I stood my ground, holding the sword in my sweating palm.

"What did you do to conceal it?" He took a threatening step toward me.

Kincade moved to block his path, putting me behind him.

"Your men are right," I said. "There is nothing here."

I forced myself not to glance at the Ark. I kept my gaze on Lucifer's. He took another step toward me, but Kincade barred the way.

"Don't," he said, in his most threatening tone.

Lucifer laughed, showing his pointed teeth. "This is not over yet, girl." Then to his band of demons, "Come."

Tension eased out of my shoulders as they walked away and left the cave. I blew out a heated breath.

"I can't believe he left without a fight," I said.

"He's saving that battle for another day," Kincade said. "He thinks you know where the Ark is. He'll be back for you."

I waited a long, silent moment. My heart had picked up speed. Kincade turned to me, question creasing his brow.

"You lied, though," he said.

"I did." I nodded.

"Is it here?" He turned to look at the destroyed slab. "I see nothing."

"I don't see anything either," Kiara said.

"Neither do I," Bridget said.

"I don't understand." I hid the sword in the cloud and took a step toward the Ark. "Why can't you see it? I can. It's right here." I pointed to it.

When I turned to face the three of them, they appeared frozen in time. My breath hitched as I glanced around the cave. An ancient pressure filled the air—like the cave itself bowed beneath her presence. A woman dressed in a white robe with enormous white wings appeared. Her face had delicate features, with high cheekbones, a pointed chin, bright eyes fringed in dark lashes.

"They cannot see it," she said. "Only the most divine can."

"They fight for me. With me. Why can they not see it?"

"They are not the One Who Was Promised." She gave me a faint smile.

"Lucifer was unable to see it, too."

She nodded. "Because he is darkness. He is Fallen."

Of course. I reached out a hand to touch it, to confirm it was truly the Ark of the Covenant. Every instinct screamed to reach for it—like it was calling me by name. Upon touching it, it would reveal its long history. She swatted my hand away with surprising force.

"You must not touch it."

"Why?"

"You may be divine, but you are still human. Those who touch the Ark will be struck down."

I peered at the Ark, confused. "How am I to retrieve it, then?"

"You aren't."

I tipped my head to one side, my brows knit. "But I thought that was my quest. To find and retrieve the Ark."

"The Ark cannot be revealed to anyone but you." Her tone softened. "When the time is right, only the Most High will reveal the Ark and its true purpose to the world."

I looked from her to the Ark and back again. "So, I'm to leave it?"

"You are."

"Until when?"

"You will know." Her smile was patient, ancient. "Tell no one what you saw. Do you understand?"

I nodded.

She waved her hand over the broken pieces of stone. The slab returned to the state it was in before with nothing more than a crack down the center. She gave me a farewell nod and left the cave. Kincade, Kiara, and Bridget returned to normal. They glanced around the cave as though searching.

In my best confused voice, I said, "The Ark isn't here."

"Are you certain?" Kincade asked. "The Copper Scroll said it would be under the cracked slab."

I shrugged. "I guess it was wrong."

"Now what?" Bridget asked.

"We keep looking," Kincade said, sounding determined. "We will find it."

I nodded. "We will. For now, I think we should return to the apartment. It's late and I'm tired."

As Kincade led us out of the cave the same way Lucifer and the angel went, guilt swarmed through me. With his internal lie detection, I had no doubt he knew I was lying. I also had no doubt he intended to question me about it when we were alone.

* * *

We made it back to the apartment without incident. Kiara and Bridget took up residence on the small sofa which, to my surprise, turned out to be a pull-out. They set about making up the bed as if it were just okay for them to be there sharing the apartment with me and Kincade. They hadn't asked and I hadn't the heart to kick them out.

I stood in the center of the small kitchen, poured a glass of whiskey for myself and one for him. I handed it to him. He eyed me with one raised brow in question.

"So..." I began and glanced at the bedroom with the one queen bed.

"Don't worry, sweetheart. I don't snore."

He took his glass, picked up the bottle, and headed to the bedroom. He sat on the edge of the bed, his back to me, and pulled off his shoes as if it were the most normal thing for him to do. I took a deep breath and downed the whiskey to give me liquid courage.

"Good night, then," I said to the two women, then followed him into the bedroom, closing the door with a soft snick behind me.

The air shifted—charged, intimate. I hated how it flustered me.

I leaned against the door. Night pressed against the one window, the curtains were still parted and open showing the twinkling lights of the city beyond. When we returned and walked through the Western Wall Plaza, the dead demon was gone and everything had been righted as if nothing was amiss. I wondered if the Brotherhood of Watchers had anything to do with that. Despite their difficulties, I assumed they still had a job to do—cleaning up dead demons so humans didn't know of their existence.

"The demon was gone from the plaza," I said.

"Yes." He didn't elaborate.

"The work of the Brotherhood?"

"Likely," he grunted.

"What do you think is going on with them?" I was stalling.

He gave me the side eye and ignored my question. "Are you going to tell me the truth about what happened in that cave?"

My pulse spiked. Kincade never asked anything he didn't already know the answer to.

He slid back on the bed and propped his back on the fluffy pillows, then stretched his legs out on the mattress. He held the bottle against a thigh. The amber liquid sloshed in the bottle.

"What do you mean?" I kicked off my shoes and did my best to play dumb.

"Please." He poured another drink, then held the bottle out to me. "You know exactly what I mean."

I perched on the other side of the bed, took the bottle, and refilled. If I lied, he would know so it was best to tell him the truth and get it over with.

"I saw it."

The words came out a whisper as I gripped the glass so tight my hand cramped. I turned to look at him. I felt exposed—stripped bare under his gaze. He remained so still I wasn't sure he still breathed.

"It wasn't there," he said at last.

"It was," I insisted.

He downed his drink and then held out his glass for more. I obliged.

"Explain," he said.

"It was there in that cave. Just as the Copper Scroll described. Under the cracked slab."

His eyes narrowed. "Are you sure?"

"Yes, Kincade. I'm sure. It was there. I saw it. Lucifer was unable to see it. You were unable to see it. Kiara and Bridget were unable to see it."

"But...you did. How?"

I was unsure how to explain it to him. "An angel came."

"No." He shook his head, emphatic. "I would have seen."

"You didn't see, though. She froze time by using some kind of angel magic to hide you and the others from seeing her. Only I saw her."

His jaw clenched. His hand tightened on the glass. He downed the drink but didn't hold it out for more.

"She told me the Ark cannot be revealed to anyone but me because I am the One Who Was Promised. She said only the Most High will reveal the Ark and its true purpose until such time as it's needed."

He was silent as he took in my words. Something fractured across his expression—fear? Wonder? I couldn't tell. His hand still clenched the glass so tight, his nailbeds turned white. He said nothing. He didn't even meet my gaze.

"That internal lie detector of yours will tell you I'm not lying," I said.

"You aren't," he finally said. "But you did lie when we were in the cave when you said it wasn't there."

His gaze met mine. For the first time, I caught a glimpse of a little alarm there. I tried to ignore that and not let it bother me.

"Yes, because I didn't want the others to know." I nodded toward our new roommates.

"Why?"

"Because the angel told me not to tell anyone."

"You told me," he pointed out.

"You're different." I cut a glance to the living area. "Besides, you may be right about Kiara. Not sure I can fully trust her yet even though she's part of the Order."

"What changed your mind?"

"I thought about what you said. I never met them until they showed up in the plaza killing that demon," I pointed out. "I never met any of them except the Harreds and we both know how that turned out."

"Valid point. What else did this angel tell you?"

"She also said I was not to retrieve it. Or touch it." I searched his face for some answer, some glimmer of wisdom. But nothing came. "What do we do now?"

He leaned his head back against the headboard with a quiet thump. "I suppose we go home."

"And leave it here?"

"You said yourself you were not to retrieve it."

"Yes, but—"

"The Ark serves a higher purpose, Anna. And somehow you are a part of that."

I didn't like the sound of that. Not one bit. I refilled my glass, downed the liquor, refilled it again. Kincade held out his glass. I splashed whiskey in it, watched him down the liquid, then hold it out for another refill.

"What do we tell the others?" I asked, nodding toward the living room where the women had bedded down for the night.

"Nothing. There's no need to tell anyone anything."

"That's it, then? We just...go home?"

"For now."

"And then what?"

"And then we wait."

"For what?" I demanded.

His green-gold eyes met mine. And somewhere deep in that gaze was distress. "The End of Days, Anna."

CHAPTER 31

AFTER OUR LITTLE CHAT, Kincade placed his glass on the nightstand, rolled over, and promptly went to sleep. He was right—he didn't snore. But he did have that lovely deep sleep breathing I so envied since I wasn't sleeping.

For one reckless heartbeat, I wanted to roll over, press my face into his shoulder, and steal some of that peace for myself. Instead, I lay rigid on my side like a corpse with a pulse and tried not to think about how safe his back looked.

How I longed to fall asleep as quickly as he did, without a care in the world, without a worry pressing upon the soul. I laid on the bed staring at the ceiling trying to figure out what to do next. We return to England and then what? Sit around and wait for the war to come to us? That seemed like the cowardly way out. And I wasn't a coward.

Even though I wanted to be. Oh, how I wanted to be. I wanted to shirk my duties as the Keeper of the Holy Relics or the One Who Was Promised or whatever fun title someone decided to give me that day. I wanted to run away from my duties and responsibilities and say to hell with it.

But I was in too deep now. My uncle, Kincade, and Sariel all convinced me I would win this war against Lucifer. But what if I didn't? What if I couldn't? Then would all mankind die or become enslaved to Lucifer and the Fallen?

I didn't sleep at all. Dawn came far too quickly. As the sun rose in the east and lightened the sky from indigo to a yellow-orange glow, I realized if I was going to tell Kincade how I felt about him, I should do it soon. Next to me, he stirred. He rolled to his back, his eyes blinking open, and then he looked at me.

"How long have you been awake?"

"All night," I said and gave a little laugh. "Fun, huh?"

He pushed off the bed, running a hand through his short-cropped hair as he came to a sitting position. "You need sleep."

"I need sleep, food, a life that doesn't involve interaction with demons," I snapped.

He leaned over to tie his boots. "Don't be cranky."

"How can I not be cranky, Kincade? The weight of the world is on my shoulders. Since this whole thing started, I was told I was responsible for saving all of mankind. How can one person—me—a total fuck up—save all of mankind?"

The words bounced around the tiny room, too big for these thin walls, too big for my thin skin. I'd seen the bodies, the broken cities, the way people looked at me like I was some kind of answer. I didn't even feel like a complete person most days, much less a savior.

It was something I pondered all night long. Something that gnawed at my very existence as I laid on the bed and stared at the ceiling wishing for sleep that never came.

"You are not a total fuck up. And it's not just up to you." He stood and rounded the bed, standing in front of me, towering over me with his formidable size. "Don't you get it?"

"What am I supposed to get, exactly?"

He grabbed my shoulders, gave me a little shake. "You are not alone. You never were."

Something in my chest gave a painful little crack, like old ice shifting on a river. I wanted to believe him so badly it hurt—but wanting and trusting were two very different things, and I'd buried trust with Ben and Edward.

"Well, that's news to me."

I shrugged off his hands and pushed up from the bed, shoving past him and then immediately wondered where I was going to go. I opted for the tiny en suite bathroom. I slammed the door harder than I intended and instantly regretted it. In the room, there was no movement. Nothing but silence.

I turned on the water, splashed cold water on my face, then looked at myself in the mirror. A haunted face stared back at me. Dark circles were under both eyes. The two streaks of white on either side of my head seemed to be whiter, if that was possible. Exhaustion lined my hollow face.

I was tired. So tired of it all. For so long, I yearned for a normal life and a normal family. I understood, of course, that wasn't possible due to my lineage. My mother was a powerful dream walker. My father was an angel. My uncle understood this better than anyone and tried to prepare me for my destiny. A destiny I ran from every chance I got. And now, here I was, standing in a tiny bathroom in the middle of the Old City, wondering what the fuck I was going to do next.

"Anna, I think you better come see this." Kincade's muffled voice called through the bedroom.

I huffed out an annoyed breath as I yanked open the door and stomped through the bedroom. In the tiny living room, Kiara and Bridget sat on the disheveled bed, their faces drained of color. Kiara pressed a hand against her mouth. They were focused on the one television in the apartment.

"What is it?"

He pointed to the TV. I turned to see a news report of a major earthquake in California that went from Los Angeles up the coast all the way to San Francisco. An over three-hundred-mile quake that devastated the state. Homes destroyed, businesses flattened, highways demolished, people injured or killed.

As the news reports went on about the tragedy in the United States, a ticker scrolled along the bottom in Hebrew. My brain translated it to read about the horrors of war happening in Eastern Europe. Governments failing. Riots. Famine. A volcanic eruption in Iceland. More news about the pandemic spreading throughout the world. The sickness didn't care of you were young or old, poor or wealthy, black or white. Hospitals were overrun. Nurses were exhausted. People were dying.

My chest hurt. I sank into the nearest chair as I watched the horror play out on the small screen. Kincade was right. We should leave this place and return to England. His words echoed in my head.

The End of Days.

It wasn't just prophecy anymore. It was headlines and body counts and bright red tickers crawling across the bottom of a cheap television screen in a cramped rental flat in Jerusalem.

I understood what was happening in the world. Three of the Four Horsemen were unleashed. Conquest, War, Famine. It was only a matter of time before Death showed up. White-hot goosebumps exploded on my exposed skin. I clutched my elbows, warding off the shiver.

"We have to get home," I said.

"What about the Ark?" Kiara said. "I thought we were going to keep looking for it."

I shook my head before she even finished. "The Ark will have to wait. I need to get home and so do you. We have families to see to."

"But the Ark—" Kiara began.

"Forget it," I snapped, my nerves fraying. "And for god's sake turn off that damn television."

Bridget turned the TV off with the remote, then dropped it on the nearby table with a clatter.

I had no intention of telling either of them what I told Kincade last night. I wanted to keep the information close and besides, he was the only person I trusted.

"Pack your bags. I'm calling the pilot and we're getting the hell out of here."

I returned to the bedroom to gather my things. I packed light, so it didn't take long for me to get it together. Kincade stood in the doorway, leaning on the jamb eyeing me.

"What?" I barked.

He stepped in the room and closed the door. He approached me.

"What about those two?" He nodded toward Kiara and Bridget, his voice low so they wouldn't overhear. "You taking them, too?"

"I should don't you think?"

"It's up to you but you said you didn't know if you could trust them."

I chewed my lower lip and stared at the wall where they were on the other side. "I don't but it feels like the right thing to do." I glanced up at him, meeting his gaze. "What do you think?"

"I think the decision is yours to make."

I frowned. "You're no help. Fine. They can come, too."

He stepped around me and picked up his bag. He waved for me to go first. I opened the door and stepped out of the bedroom. Kiara and Bridget were both ready to go.

"We have to check out of our hotel," Kiara said.

"I don't think there's time for that."

I had a sudden urgency to get the hell out of the Old City and back to England. I wanted to run up the stairs to my room, jump into bed and hide under the covers forever.

"But our clothes and things—"

"Replaceable," Kincade snapped.

I sensed the same urgency from him which scared the hell out of me.

"You have your weapons," I said. "That's all you need. I have a car coming to pick us up to take us to the airport."

"But—" Kiara began.

"Look," I huffed. "This is a limited time offer. You can stay here and take your chances with the commercial airlines and the pandemic or you can get your ass on the private plane with us."

They exchanged a glance. Kiara took a deep breath, expelled it. "We're coming with you."

"Then let's go."

I turned toward the apartment door and flung it open. Kincade, Kiara, and Bridget were right behind me. We made our way through the residential district heading for the Western Wall Plaza and the main thoroughfare that would take us out of here and to the airport. My nerves were on edge. My heart was in my throat. As if I expected to run into some kind of trouble. Maybe I sensed it. Maybe because Lucifer left the cave and gave up too easy. He wasn't the type to give up like that and the worry gnawed at me.

As we exited the residential neighborhood and stepped into the plaza, the dark magic veil I associated with demons and high lords and Fallen descended. Before us was Lucifer and a dozen of his high lords and demons.

My hand automatically twitched toward the invisible weight of my sword in the cloud, muscles remembering battle long before my brain caught up.

"Well, fuck," I said.

"You didn't think we were going to escape that easy, did you?" Kincade asked.

He glanced down at me. I met his gaze. And that's when I saw the corner of his mouth lift in a quirk of a smile. He expected it just as I sensed it.

"No, I didn't."

"What's going on?" Kiara moved to stand to my right.

"Lucifer," I said.

"I did warn you, girl," Lucifer said. "If you came to the Old City, I'd kill you and your guardian."

"You did," I said with a nod.

I drew down the dagger and handed it to Kincade. Then drew down the sword and lit it.

Lucifer gave a long, low laugh. "Oh, you are delightful." His gaze lingered on Kiara and Bridget. "Looks like I get bonus kills."

"We're getting out of this city," I said. "Even if that means we have to go through you and your high lords and demons."

His eyes narrowed into dark slits. "And me."

And then he morphed from the man into the dark angel he truly was. His skin changed to leathery onyx skin covered in scales. Six giant back wings unfurled from his back. His hands changed from fingers into long claws ending in yellow talons. Red eyes stared out of a dragon-shaped head. Gray smoke curled from his snout.

I saw him in the form one other time and that was during a dream walk.

It was worse in daylight. Dreams had a softness to them, a blur at the edges. Here, every scale, every burning coal of an eye was brutally real. The monster under the bed had climbed out and stepped into my morning.

"What the holy hell...?" Kiara's voice was a breathy whisper.

"Ladies, get those weapons ready," I said. "It's go time."

Lucifer stood back in his dragon form while he sent his demons to attack us. He had Azriel and a few others hang back likely to see what carnage they'd cause. Possibly hoping they wouldn't have to deal with us.

Cowards.

We were outnumbered. That much was for certain. But that didn't seem to intimidate Kiara or Bridget. Fighting demons and dark lords was somewhat normal for Kincade and me. He stuck the dagger in his belt, then drew his gun. I eyed it with surprise. I didn't realize he'd brought it.

He wasted no time aiming and firing. The gun did that high-pitched whine followed by the white flash. He killed several of the lesser demons.

Kiara nocked an arrow and fired off several rapid shots with amazing skill. The demons went down one right after another like bowling pins in a strike. Bridget emitted a war scream and charged. I liked the way she operated.

While Kincade fired round after round, I followed Bridget into battle, screaming my own war cry and holding my flaming sword aloft. My gaze was firmly planted on Azriel. I wanted him dead and though he hadn't turned up in my dreams lately, I had many bones to pick with him for all the things he had done to me for years.

I cut down demon after demon, slicing them in half with the flaming sword moving closer and closer to my prey. Even Bridget was a fierce warrior woman with her sword as she cut down demons. She was fearless in her pursuit to sever heads.

I no longer heard the high-pitched whine of Kincade's gun and assumed he was out of ammo. A moment later, he was next to me with his lightning speed, wielding the jade-handled dagger and killing all those who stood in his way. It seemed he understood where I was headed without me having to tell him. We'd fought together enough to know each other's moves. Like a well-choreographed dance.

I slashed. He stabbed.

I hadn't really taken notice of what Lucifer was doing until the ground rumbled with his footsteps. He dropped his head and roared right us as if he thought to scare us away. None of us were.

"Watch out!" Kincade shouted.

He shoved me out of the way as Lucifer's tail landed between us. The ground shook beneath my feet as I stumbled. I turned, swinging my sword in an arc but missing the damn beast altogether.

Kincade had his gun back in his hand and fired off several more rounds hitting the giant dragon in the side of his leather hide. It did nothing to stop him. All it did was infuriate him. He roared at Kincade. I took the moment of distraction to slash one of his hind legs. It left a searing wound behind. The dragon wobbled, turning his very large head toward me.

I glanced at Kincade who had put away his gun and now held the dagger. Our eyes met and suddenly I understood what he wanted to do. I nodded.

Together we ran toward Lucifer. Before the beast realized what was happening, we were under him. Kincade slashed one leg with the dagger. I slashed the other with the sword. The dragon let out a roar of pain as he crumbled to the ground falling right for us.

Kincade wrapped a hand around my upper arm and dragged me out of the way with a jerking force and his quick speed. I lost my balance and fell right into him. He wrapped an arm around me as we tumbled to the ground together. His large body cushioned my fall. The sword snuffed out. I landed on top of him with a thud and an audible oof.

For half a second, all I could register was the solid heat of him beneath me and the ridiculous, traitorous thought that this would be a great position under literally any other circumstance.

He rolled to his side, deposited me on the ground and then was on his feet again in an instant. His gun was in his hand. He charged toward the downed dragon and aimed.

Azriel stepped in his path, his face a mask of anger and determination. I rolled to my feet, snatching up the sword.

"We meet again, *gardien*."

Kincade said nothing as he aimed and fired. I sucked in a sharp breath as I saw the high lord jerk backward. He'd been hit in the shoulder. Kincade rarely missed. I suspected that was a warning shot.

And while I wanted to see the end of Azriel, I really wanted it to be me who handed him his death blow. I lit the sword, gripping it, focused on Azriel and how to get to him before Kincade. I bolted into a run.

Black blood oozed from Azriel's shoulder. His eyes widened when he saw me charging him. He had no weapon, so I assumed this would be a great time to cut him down.

I assumed wrong.

"Anna, look out!"

Kiara's warning shout got to me as someone barreled into me as though tackling a wide receiver. The sword flew from my hand, the fire going out once again. Whoever it was, pushed me to the ground, landing on top of me and shoving my head into the stone. White hot pain exploded behind my eyes and throughout my entire body. I cried out with the pain.

My attacker grabbed my hair and jerked my head back so hard I had no choice but to get to my feet. A knife went to my throat. Before me, Azriel smirked with that wolffish grin I hated so much.

"Put down your weapon, *gardien*, or she dies," Azriel said.

"You know as well as I do you won't kill her," Kincade said.

"We have no more use for her," Azriel said.

"You haven't found the Ark, though," he said.

Azriel lifted his uninjured shoulder in a half shrug. "It matters not. The Four Horseman have been unleashed. We will have what we want soon enough."

The high lord walked slowly toward me, pausing inches from me. His face softened but that feral smile remained as his dark, lethal gaze met mine.

"I told you once your god will fall. Do you remember?"

I remembered, all right. It was the day I met him in his underground crypt. The day he told me I was going to help them get what they wanted—redemption. The day Man would worship his leader instead. The End of Days was a threat looming over me since this whole ordeal began.

Spit gathered in the back of my throat. I released it, hitting him on the cheek. He laughed.

"You do, don't you?"

"Let her go, Azriel," Kincade said. His voice sounded strained.

His gaze left mine and flickered to Kincade behind me. "You are in no position to make demands." That smile returned to his face as he looked at me once again. "You friends are brave fighters. I'm impressed, really." He circled me. Like a predator circling his prey. "But they made mistakes. Too many. And now they will pay with their lives. And then I'll slit your throat like I did your lover's."

Ben's face flashed through my mind—his laugh, the way his hand felt wrapped around mine, the way his body went slack when the life left him. Fury rose up inside me so violent, I jerked. The knife at my throat pricked my skin. Blood oozed.

"You son of a bitch. I will kill you." The words came out a roughened whisper.

"Not if you're already dead and your soul is mine."

The hand around my hair tightened, the knife at my throat pressed deeper. Azriel reached for me, placing his hand on my chest. He intended to take my soul, pull it from me and turn me into one of their mindless demon followers.

Something ignited deep inside me, burning and warring against his dark power. I closed my eyes, envisioning the white light within me. The Godlight surged forward. For a heartbeat I felt Ronan's lightning twined with it, echoing through my veins like a remembered storm. Azriel shrieked. My eyes opened. He stumbled backward, holding his wrist, and clutching his singed fingers.

The lightning came alive within my hands. I reached up a hand and wrapped it around the wrist holding the knife to my throat. I gave a swift jerk. A scream and then I was released. I spun to see a high lord back stepping away from me. His eyes were wide with terror. His wrist had a burned place where I touched him.

Other high lords held Kincade, Kiara, and Bridget captive. I wiggled my fingers, closed my eyes, and directed the light at the one holding Kincade. When I opened my eyes, the high lord was dead on the ground behind him. Fried to a crisp. His corpse smoked from the death blow I handed him.

A wave of dizziness punched through me so hard my knees nearly buckled. The Godlight always took something from me—strength, breath, sanity—but this time it felt like it ripped straight through my bones. Kincade reached out instinctively, steadying me with a hand at my elbow before I could face-plant. The contact grounded me—like my body recognized him as safe before my mind could argue.

I turned to the others, the lightning dancing between my fingers.

"Release them or you die, too."

Behind me, I felt him—ready. Watching my edges for cracks.

They did immediately.

Dead demons littered the plaza. However, I noted the dragon was gone.

"This isn't over, *chérie*," Azriel warned.

I smiled. "I certainly hope not."

And with that, they all disappeared and the veil was lifted.

The plaza snapped back into ordinary sunlight and stone and distant traffic noise, like someone had changed the channel. My hands were still crackling with leftover lightning, and every nerve in my body screamed that nothing about this was ordinary ever again.

CHAPTER 32

KINCADE PICKED UP MY uncle's sword and handed it to me. His gaze flickered from my face to my throat. He reached for me, swiped his thumb across the line where the knife pricked me. It sent a little thrill through me when he touched me. His skin came away smeared with blood. He wiped it off on his thigh.

A little stupid flutter went through me at the sight of Kincade casually wearing my blood like it meant something.

"You should let me clean that," he said.

I shrugged off his concern. "I'm fine. It's a shallow wound."

His expression told me he was annoyed by that remark, yet he didn't argue. "You could have warned me, you know."

"Warned you about what?"

"That you were going to flambé the high lord holding me captive."

A tiny part of me preened at the fact he thought I needed warning labels.

"I didn't miss." I gave him my best cocky grin.

His lips thinned in annoyance. "One day, you *will* miss. I hope I'm not in the line of fire when you do."

"I'd never intentionally hurt you," I said, and meant it.

He didn't get a chance to retort as Kiara and Bridget joined us. Bridget's eyes were wide and full of wonder. Sadness creased Kiara's face.

"You used the lightning," she said. "Ronan's lightning."

I nodded.

The weight of it settled over me again—Ronan's legacy still flickering in my veins.

"And something else," Bridget added. "A brilliant bright light came out of you when he tried to steal your soul."

"The Godlight," I said.

Bridget sucked in a sharp breath.

"You have the Godlight," Kiara whispered.

"Yes."

She swallowed hard. "You really are the one, aren't you?"

I took a deep breath, expelled it. "That's what people keep telling me."

And every time someone said it, a little part of me wanted to run screaming into the sea.

"Are we going to stand here all day and chat about Anna and her powers, or are we going to get the hell out of here?" Kincade's snappish voice brought us all back to the present.

"Right. We have a car waiting for us. Let's go."

I put all the weapons in the cloud so we wouldn't garner any more unnecessary attention. Kincade and I took the lead. I noticed he walked exceptionally close to me.

Too close. Close enough that my stupid heart tried to mistake protection for affection. Again.

"You could have been killed," he said.

"I knew what I was doing."

"By taking on Lucifer in dragon form?" He shook his head. "That was reckless."

"Reckless maybe, but you had my back." I gave him a playful nudge with my elbow.

"*This* time. Do you realize why Azriel couldn't steal your soul?"

"I have an assumption," I said.

"The Godlight inside you won't allow him to steal it," Kincade said. "Because of who and what you are, he will never be able to steal it."

I contemplated this for a long moment as we hurried toward the waiting car. "Then why did he try?"

Kincade opened the back door, holding it open as Kiara and Bridget crammed inside.

"Because he didn't know you had it."

He waved me inside the car. I slid into the back. He slammed the door after me, then got in the passenger side. The car felt too small suddenly, packed with nerves and Kincade's barely contained adrenaline.

He barked an order to the driver and moments later we were headed to the airport. I'd allow the relief to swarm over me as soon as we were airborne, until then, I gnawed on my lower lip.

We arrived at Ben Gurion International Airport, disembarked from the car, and bid the driver farewell. The plane waited on the tarmac, ready to depart as soon as we were on board. I sensed some awe from both Kiara and Bridget as we took the stairs and entered the plane. Kincade took his usual seat. I took mine directly across from him. Kiara and Bridget sat together several rows behind us.

I buckled my seatbelt. Kincade leaned his head back, crossed his arms over his chest and was out minutes later. I gripped the arms of the seat, gritting my teeth as we taxied down the runway. There was some unexplainable sense of foreboding niggling at me.

The tension went out of me, and I relaxed as we took flight, heading back to England. In just over six hours, I'd be home. I couldn't wait. I leaned my head back and allowed sleep to over-come me.

Sleep felt like the enemy, but my body didn't give me a choice.

* * *

When we arrived back at Walker Manor, I was bone weary, even though I managed to nap throughout the flight. Kincade had to wake me from a sound sleep to get me off the plane. Then I dozed off and on during the car ride from London to Somerset. Much to my surprise, Kiara and Bridget tagged along. I thought they'd be hitching a ride back to wherever their homes were, but nope.

Piers greeted us at the door with his stoic British expression I came to know and love. He gave me once over. Though his expression gave away nothing, I sensed his disdain at my disheveled appearance.

"Welcome home, my lady." His deadpan expression cast toward the two newcomers.

"Hi, Piers. This is Kiara FitzGerald and Bridget MacKeller. They're, ah, staying with us."

Grace bounded down the stairs with a bright smile plastered on her face. She enveloped me in a tight embrace, hugging me hard.

"You're home! I'm so glad." She pulled back, gave me a good once over. "You look exhausted."

I was pretty sure I'd reached a new plane of existence—skele-ton-with-eyeliner tired.

I gave her a weak smile. "I am."

"That's why she's going straight to bed." Kincade placed a hand on my shoulder and steered me toward the stairs.

Before I followed orders, I turned back to the old butler. "Piers, will you make sure Kiara and Bridget have rooms?"

"I'm afraid we have one vacant room, my lady. They'll have to share."

I gave them a questioning glance.

"Fine with us," Kiara said. "We travel together a lot."

I cocked my head to the side. "You do?"

"We like to kick demon butt together," Bridget said with a laugh.

A pang of guilt went through me as I thought of Ophelia. She and I had kicked demon butt together. I missed her and wondered where she was, if she was okay, if she was killing high lords with her shimmering broadsword. But I quickly shoved aside those thoughts.

I couldn't afford grief right now—it clung to me like wet sand, dragging me under if I gave it an inch.

"That reminds me..." I drew down their weapons. I handed Kiara her silver bow and quiver of arrows, then Bridget her sword.

"Thanks for holding them for us. I need to learn that trick," Kiara said.

"Later," Kincade grunted. He gave me push toward the stairs.

"I'll make more introductions later," I called to them around a wide yawn.

Fatigue slammed into me hard as I took the stairs with slow, methodical steps. Kincade remained by my side as he pushed open my bedroom door. The master suite was still under construction. He stood in the doorway and let me pass. I perched on the edge of my bed, pulling off my shoes.

"Are you going to stand there and watch me sleep?" I snapped.

"If I have to, yes."

I yawned again. "You don't."

He hesitated a long moment in the doorway. I sensed the conflict warring within him if he should go to stay.

A tiny reckless part of me wanted him to stay. Which meant he absolutely shouldn't.

"I'll be fine."

He grabbed the knob. "Get some rest."

As he closed the door behind him, I shoved down the blankets, slipped inside the cool sheets and curled around my pillow. It was familiar and gave me a sense of comfort. I closed my eyes and was asleep in an instant.

The dream started almost immediately. I flung my arms in the air out of sheer frustration. When I was at my most tired, there always seemed to be some intruder who wanted to invade my dreams and chat me up. Perhaps it was because I had been thinking of Ophelia and worrying about her well-being that she came to me in a dream. Or maybe I was so exhausted, my subconscious dream walked her.

"Anna, is that you?"

Darkness pressed around her and me. Strange shadows flickered along the walls behind her. Her face was partially hidden from me, but it was clear she had been beaten. She had a black eye, a split lip, and dirt smudged along her jawbone.

"Ophelia? Are you all right?"

She whimpered. "No. Anna…"

Her feet shuffled as though she tried to come closer. I heard the distinct clink of a chain. Hot fear pumped through me, tingling the back of my neck.

"Where are you?"

"I was in Lisbon. I'd heard there was a group of high lords in the city killing guardians and stealing souls. I found them." Her voice hitched for a moment as she stopped to collect her thoughts. Her eyes filled with tears. "They were there, Anna. And…" She paused again. "The Brotherhood was helping them."

I sucked in a sharp breath. "What do you mean the Brotherhood was helping them? The Brotherhood of Watchers?"

She nodded. "Yes."

"Are you sure?"

It was a senseless question, I realized. When we met in Istanbul, she worked with the Brotherhood and Kincade tracking down the high lords to kill them before they killed human's guardians. She understood them and how they operated. Likely, she used her former contacts to find them again.

"I wouldn't lie to you!"

"Where the hell are you, Ophelia?"

"I killed a few of them," she said, ignoring my question. "The high lords, I mean. But the Brotherhood...they were led by Decker. He's gone mad or something. I don't understand it."

Decker. Kincade's brother. The one person Kincade still mourned and hated in equal measure. It was like she had sucker punched me.

"*Ophelia.* Where are you?"

There was a long pause. She glanced around, as if seeing if someone overheard. "I was captured by one of the high lords. I'm in some underground prison."

"I'm coming after you."

"How? You don't even know where I am. Hell, *I* don't even know where I am!"

"I will find you," I said, and meant it. Somehow, some way I'd find her.

"Okay," she said, sounding relieved. And then, "Please hurry."

I bolted upright, my heart pounding a wild beat. The room spun for a second—too much Godlight, too little rest, too much fear threading through my bones. I glanced at the clock. I was only asleep an hour. One fucking hour. I rubbed the back of my neck, trying to stop the tension headache from forming.

There was only one person who might have the answer.

Ophelia was right. I didn't know where she was and I hadn't a clue how to find her. I hoped Kincade would be able to help, especially if Decker was somehow involved. I didn't understand how he was, but there had to be some explanation. Of all the things I thought about Decker, being a traitor to the Brotherhood wasn't one of them.

I slid off the bed, flung open the door, and stopped short. Kincade stood in the hallway, across from my room, leaning on the wall with his arms crossed as if everything was situation normal. Like some sentry on guard. He scowled the second he saw me.

Trust him to be furious and protective in the same breath.

"Why are you up? I thought I told you to get some rest." He must have read the panic in my face, because he straightened and said, "What happened?"

"I dream walked Ophelia. I don't know why. Maybe because I've been worried about her and thinking about her a lot. She's been captured."

Worry creased his features. "Where is she?"

"The only information I have is that she was in Lisbon fighting and killing high lords and one of them got her. She said she was in some sort of underground prison. She also said somehow the Brotherhood was involved and..." I halted, unable to tell him the truth about his brother. I hoped he wouldn't be able to sense my lie by omission. "They were somehow leading them."

His brows drew together. "What does that mean?"

"It means they were helping the high lords."

He shook his head. "No. I don't believe the Brotherhood would help them. That goes against everything they stand for."

"I don't think she'd lie."

He ran his hand over his scruffy chin. "She wouldn't," he agreed.

"How am I going to find her?"

"You mean, how are *we* going to find her. You said she was in an underground prison?"

I nodded.

"I doubt it's an underground prison. If a high lord grabbed her, then they likely took her to a specific place. Especially if they're keeping her alive."

That hot fear tingled the back of my neck again. "Is that place what I think it is?"

"It has to be."

I clenched my jaw until my back teeth ached. It was the last place I wanted to go.

We were going back to Hell.

Of course we were. Because apparently the universe had decided sleep, peace, and sanity were all luxuries I no longer deserved.

CHAPTER 33

IT WASN'T THE FIRST time I visited the treacherous, malevolent underworld. The first time was to retrieve the Horn of Gabriel, which was now in the hands of the archangel himself. The second time was to save Kincade from Azriel's clutches when he captured him to force me to hand over the Spear of Destiny.

It wasn't exactly my favorite place to visit. Kincade and I knew where to enter—through a cave in Dante's Forest. But the question was how we were going to get to the forest.

"Okay, then let's go get her. We need a way to get there as quickly as possible," I said.

He gave me a look of disdain.

"Don't give me that look," I said. "We either ask Sariel or Killian to take us."

"Anna, did it occur to you this could be a trap?"

"Well...no..."

It actually hadn't but now that he'd said it, I shifted from one foot to the other. Perhaps he was right and it was a way to lure me to them since they were unable to capture me, force me to do their bidding, and numerous other heinous things.

A cold little pebble of dread dropped into my stomach, but I refused to let him see it.

"If they have Ophelia *and* are keeping her alive, it's for one reason only." He lifted a brow as if I was supposed to read what he meant.

I waved away his concern. "It doesn't matter. I'm going after her. I can handle myself."

"Can you?"

The worst part was, I heard the doubt in his voice and knew some traitorous part of me shared it.

I narrowed my gaze at him. "You know I can."

"Fine," he grumbled. "Ask Sariel."

I didn't have a preference but I found it curious Kincade did.

"You'll have to dream walk her again to try to find out what circle she's in."

I frowned at the thought of that.

"You didn't think we were going to be able to search every level without being detected, did you?" he asked.

He had a point. I hated when he was right about stuff. "I suppose not."

"Dream walking her is the quickest way."

"Why don't you do it?" Although we didn't speak about it much, we both knew Kincade had the ability, too. He had appeared in my dreams more than once. "Besides, you're more familiar with the place than I am, aren't you?"

He gave me a deadpan stare—the kind that said he was two seconds from putting in for guardian retirement.

"Funny girl. I'll do it while you talk to Sariel." He stalked down the hallway to his bedroom and closed the door with a snap behind him.

Bossy, infuriating man. I had no idea how to function without him snapping orders at me anymore. I smiled as I trotted down the hallway to my parents shared room.

And halted outside the door.

I had no idea what I was going to say to Sariel or even how to ask him. *Hi, Dad. Can you take me to Dante's Forest so I can save my friend from the depths of Hell?*

Wonder how that'd go.

The word Dad still felt strange and sharp in my head, like a new pair of boots that hadn't been broken in yet.

I raised my hand to knock. The door opened before I had the chance. My mother stood on the other side with a surprised look on her face.

"Oh, Anna." She pressed a hand against her chest. "You scared me."

"Sorry. I need to speak to Sariel."

She opened the door wider and stepped through the threshold. "Sure. I was on my way to the kitchen. Do you want anything?"

"No, thanks." Despite my refusal, my stomach growled with a fierce roar. I gave her a faint smile.

"Are you sure?"

I nodded. I watched her head off down the hallway to the top of the stairs and then disappear down them. As I stood there gaping after her, I thought how remarkable it was she seemed like she was back to normal. Well, I didn't exactly know what normal was for her but she didn't seem like the killer dream walker Natasha anymore.

I wasn't sure if that made me relieved or more afraid, knowing what still lived under her skin.

"Hi, Anna."

Sariel stood in the doorway and motioned me inside the room. He seemed to take up most of the space with the expanse of his white wings threaded with gold. Their room was one of the larger ones in the manor on the opposite end of the hallway as mine. The bed was made and everything seemed to be in its proper place.

"She seems...better," I said, referring to my mother.

"She grows stronger and remembers more every day," he said.

As much as I hated to admit it, Sariel's constant presence with her made a difference. She *did* remember things more than she had in the past. Her mind had a clarity it hadn't had since the moment we met in Istanbul.

"I have a favor to ask," I said, cutting to the chase.

"Anything." He gave me a congenial smile that said he was willing to do whatever I needed.

I took a deep breath. He wasn't going to like what I asked of him. "I need you to take me and Kincade to Dante's Forest."

His smile faded as he stared at me in utter disbelief. "Why?"

"My friend, Ophelia, is in trouble. I'm going to find her."

"Anna, you realize where that place leads?"

I was nodding before he finished. "I've been there before. I know exactly where it leads and I intend to go there and find her."

"Are you...certain?"

"I can't leave her there. She's been taken by a high lord."

"How do you know this?"

"She told me in a dream walk."

He paced the confines of the room, his wings ruffling in agitation. "It could be a trap."

I tried not to roll my eyes. "I'm aware."

"And yet you want to go anyway?" he asked.

"I don't have a choice." I stepped in front of him, forcing him to halt. "She's my friend."

His gaze searched my face, worry lines creasing his features. "You have your mother's eyes."

"I've been told," I said, irritated. "Are you going to take us or not?"

As if I needed another reminder that half of me was chaos wrapped in pretty packaging.

He was silent a long moment as he contemplated, then at last he nodded. "I will. But it is against my better judgement."

Such a dad thing to say. "Thanks."

"When do you wish to go?"

"As soon as possible." I stomped toward the bedroom door, realizing I was still in my socks. "Meet us downstairs in ten minutes."

I headed back to my bedroom. I didn't remember the last time I had on clean clothes, so I did a quick change. Tank top under black Henley, black cargo pants, black socks, pink combat boots. Combat-chic disaster. At least if I died in Hell, I'd be on-brand.

In the bathroom, I splashed cold water on my face then ran a hairbrush through my tangled hair. I swept up the long locks into a high pony tail and grimaced at the two white streaks on either side of my head. I tried to pretend the dark circles under my eyes weren't there. Or the lines of fatigue on my face. I double-checked to make sure the weapons were in the cloud. Satisfied, I headed back to Kincade's room.

I pressed my ear against the door. Silence. I turned the knob and pushed it open to peer inside. He sat on the edge of his bed with his back ramrod straight, his eyes closed, his hands resting on his knees. His face was impassive and wiped of all emotion. His breathing was slow and steady. I never witnessed someone else doing a dream walk, not even my uncle, so this was fascinating. He looked older then—ancient, almost—like the weight of every century he'd lived finally showed.

Finally, he opened his eyes, that green-gold gaze focusing on me.

"She's in the Second Circle." He sounded grim.

My stomach dropped. Of course it was that circle. Hell apparently liked its greatest hits.

When Kincade was in Hell, he was in the Second Circle. He had been chained up in a cell while Azriel tortured him.

"Super. I can't wait to go back. Sariel is waiting for us downstairs."

"Good. He agreed."

He rose from the edge of the bed, disappeared into his bathroom. Water splashed followed by the rustle of clothing which made me blush and inch toward the door. The last thing I wanted was for him to come out of the bathroom shirtless. I wasn't ready to see him like that again. He re-emerged wearing a fresh shirt and the gun holster on his waist. He checked the gun. Satisfied, he put it back in the holster.

There was something obscenely comforting about how methodical he was—violence as a practiced ritual.

"Let's go."

He followed me out of the room and down the stairs. Sariel, true to his word, waited for us there. Along with my mother and Grace. Both of the women had stern looks on their faces which told me I was about to get chastised for my upcoming trip. I decided to head them off at the pass.

"You can't talk me out of it," I announced to them all.

"Anna, honey, are you sure?" Grace asked. She fingered the tiny gold cross at her neck. "It sounds dangerous."

"It is," I said, not willing to sugar coat it. "But it isn't the first time I've been there."

She looked aghast. I placed a hand on her shoulder to reassure her. "I'm not going alone. Kincade is going with me."

I said it like it was a plan. My heart heard it like a confession.

She glanced at his hulking form behind me. He stood so close, his body heat radiated over me and that sandalwood scent tickled my fancy. It was not unpleasant.

"You'll keep her safe, you hear me?" she asked.

"I always do." He paused, then leaned a little closer to my ear. "Or try. She's a loose cannon sometimes."

"Only when I have to be," I retorted, ignoring the thrilling sensation of his warm breath on my ear. It shouldn't have made me want to lean back into him. It did anyway.

I was unable to escape the worried look in my mother's eyes, though. "I'll be fine. I promise."

"Sariel will wait for you at the edge of the cave," she said. "He promised me to bring you back in one piece." She cut a glance to Kincade. "All of you."

"He will," I said, sounding more confident than I felt.

"Anna, I want you to take this." Grace slipped off the tiny gold cross necklace from around her neck and handed it to me.

"No, Grace. That's yours." She'd worn that cross for as long as I remembered.

She took my hand in hers and dropped the cross and gold chain in my palm. "I insist."

She didn't say it, but she wanted me to have it for luck or protection or something. I nodded and put the necklace on. The gold chain was so delicate, I was afraid it would break before I returned. I tucked the cross under the neckline of my shirt, letting it nestle there with the angel pendant Kincade had given me as a belated birthday present.

Faith and angel steel, both pressed over my heart. If that didn't help, nothing would.

"If you're done with your goodbyes, can we go now?" Even though he sounded annoyed, he wasn't. I knew him better than that.

I looked up at him, gave him a nod. "Let's get this over with."

"You go first," Kincade said.

Sariel wrapped his arm around my waist. I took a deep breath, steeling myself against the coming nausea that would no doubt follow. A second later we were flashing away from the manor to the forest. The floor fell away from beneath our feet. Time and space spun around us in a flash of brilliant color. And moments later we were at our destination.

As soon as my feet landed in the bracken, my knees buckled. No matter how many times I traveled angel express, my body still hadn't gotten the memo we weren't actually dying.

I crumpled to the ground, my stomach clenching as I dry heaved. I was thankful I hadn't had anything to eat or drink that day, so the result was unproductive.

"You all right?"

I waved his concern away and gave him a nod, trying to reassure him I was fine. I remained on my hands and knees while I waited for the dizziness to pass.

"I'll be back."

Some childish part of me wanted to grab his sleeve and make him swear it twice.

And then he was gone.

I took several deep, cleansing breaths, then sat on my butt. I drew up my knees, encircling them with my arms and waited. The forest was strangely quiet, as it was the last time I was here. Not even a bird chirping or a cricket singing. Overhead, the canopy of trees blocked out most of the afternoon sunlight. Only a few beams managed to break through to the ground below.

I glanced toward the opening of the cave which was still about a hundred yards away. It was nothing but a black yawning chasm awaiting our arrival.

My skin remembered the last time before my mind did—every lash of heat, every scream echoing off stone.

Sariel returned with Kincade, who looked less than amused at that mode of transportation. He wasn't a fan of traveling with an angel, but he did it for me because he knew it was the fastest way to get here. He had a backpack slung over one shoulder, which he didn't have before we left. Smart man. He must have quickly gathered some provisions. Trust Kincade to think of snacks and survival gear while I was busy fixating on Hell and worst-case scenarios.

I shoved up to my feet, my knees wobbling a little but I managed to maintain my balance.

"I will wait here," Sariel said. "Good luck."

"Thanks," I said.

I looked to Kincade who gave me the go-ahead nod. Together, we started for the opening of the cave. Our boots crunched on the leaves and dead limbs as we made our way closer to the cave of Hell. As we neared, I smelled the familiar peculiar metallic twang. That same sulfuric odor as when I scented demons. That same yawning abyss with the demonic face staring back. Kincade reached into the backpack and brought out two flashlights. He handed one to me.

"Glad you thought of that," I said.

"Someone had to. You didn't."

It wasn't anything but the truth. He was right. I was so distracted with getting to Ophelia, I didn't think of anything that might be useful on this little trek down to the underworld. I clicked the flashlight on, then drew down my uncle's sword. I left it unlit. The weight of it made me feel better having it in my hand.

Kincade clicked on his light. He pulled his gun and held it in his other. He, like me, was ready. Together, we stepped through the opening of the cave.

The temperature dropped, and with it, any illusion that this was going to be a simple rescue mission.

CHAPTER 34

THE AIR AROUND US grew humid and hot. It was how I remembered from the last time I visited. That time, Edward came with me. And while Edward was a capable fighter, there was no one I would rather have at my side than Kincade.

As we descended the long dark tunnel, the air shifted from hot and humid and cold and damp. A chill ran through me, igniting the gooseflesh on my arms under my sleeves. I ignored it and pressed on. The only sound was that of our boots and my shallow breathing.

"The First Circle is ahead."

I recalled that from the last jaunt down here. I also recalled the ferocious minions guarding the stream of lava. A brightly lit opening was ahead and the temperature rose to an oppressive heat the further we traveled. Death, decay, and rot wafted to my nose. Cries of pain echoed through the cavern ahead. My stomach twisted into a tight knot.

As we entered the cavern, I clicked off the flashlight and handed it back to Kincade. He returned it and the other one to the backpack, sticking them in the side pockets for easy access in case we needed them again.

Ahead, skeletal figures writhed in pain along the edge of the lava. Some with skin barely hanging onto their bones. Others with skin beginning to melt away, then return, and start all over again. Our boots crunched on remnants of bones as we made our way through it. And then the sound I dreaded—the scratching sound of claws on stone.

I lit the sword. Kincade cocked his gun.

"We need to get across the lava," he said. "Kill as many as you have to."

The last time I did this with Edward, we killed enough to form a dead minion bridge. It was disgusting then. It was disgusting now.

Kincade aimed and fired. But instead of the usual whine then flash, his handgun emitted a steady stream of fire. He took out a several dozen before they even made it to the other side of the lava. I was so shocked, I halted and gaped.

"Anna, come on!"

He charged ahead. I slashed my way through the minions he missed and followed.

"Did you get an upgrade?" I asked, panting to keep up with him.

"You could say that." He fired another round of flames.

The heat washed over my face, and for a split second, I forgot we were in Hell—because apparently my boyfriend-I-wasn't-confessing-about-yet had a flamethrower now.

The lava filled up quickly with the disintegrating bodies. He stepped across them like skipping across stones on a river.

"Hurry up," he barked.

Hesitating would get me killed so I took a deep breath and ran. I bounced off body after body, the lava licking the bottoms of my boots, until I made it to the other side. A misstep sent my ankle wobbling—a jolt of panic spiking through me—but momentum carried me forward. I leapt onto solid ground, stumbled, and fell into Kincade. He caught me and set me back on my feet, giving me his best scowl. But for a moment, a thrill danced through me when I was in his arms.

I really needed to stop reacting like a middle-schooler with her first crush every time he touched me.

"Stop fooling around."

The minions gave way to a group of beasts. The same ones Edward and I faced. I slashed and killed them as we made our way through them. Kincade's fire gun was out of juice. He stuck it in the backpack and pulled out another. I realized this was his usual handgun, the one with the high-pitched whine and flash.

"Give me the dagger," he said.

I paused long enough to draw it down and then hand it off. He held the dagger in one hand, the gun in the other. He hacked and slashed his way through the demons and the beasts. When he was unable to kill a beast with the dagger, he shot them. All the while I marveled at the way he moved with the fluidity of a big cat. Feral yet graceful.

It was deeply unfair how lethal he looked in demon light.

I realized how much I depended on him and how much of a badass he really was.

We battled our way through the beasts, killing the last of them. I snuffed out the sword as we arrived at the black gate. The entrance to the First Circle was guarded by a horned demon with red eyes and hooves for hands and feet. The first time when I had arrived with my uncle, I negotiated with the demon guard to let us pass. Kincade, though, was clearly not in the mood to negotiate.

He shot the demon in the head without so much as blinking.

"Well, that was easy," I said. "Negotiations are a lost art with you."

He only shrugged, which somehow made it worse.

He stepped over the dead demon oozing black blood from his forehead and shoved open the black gates. He said nothing as he entered the First Circle. He stuck the gun back in the holster, then handed me the dagger.

"I might need that later," he said.

I nodded and returned it to the cloud.

We traveled in silence as he made his way through the cavernous abyss, winding our way deeper and deeper. Those demons or beasts we encountered ignored us which was fine by me. I was exhausted from all the fighting. Sweat poured down my back and dampened the nape of my neck. And yet Kincade looked as though he hadn't even broken a sweat.

We rounded a corner and were greeted with a stone staircase winding down into a dark cavern. He halted, pulled out the flashlight and handed one to me.

"This leads to the Second Circle." He clicked on his flashlight. "You'll want to stick close."

"Don't I always?"

As we descended into the shadows, it reminded me somewhat of the cavern tunnels we traveled to find the Ark. But this would not lead us to the Ark.

The garish white light bounced off the damp stone walls as we made our descent. Here the smell of death and decay was overwhelming. I tried not to gag from the putrid odors.

What I remembered of the Second Circle was nothing like this. But I didn't trek my way in. Instead, I hitched a ride with Azriel when he returned to taunt Kincade. And even then, I only saw the inside of the cell in which he was held.

Kincade seemed to have a wealth of knowledge about all the things. From the depths of Hell to the Templar secret tunnels under churches to even the Holy Relics. I admired that about him. When one walked the earth for more than two thousand years, one acquired a lot of experience. What I *didn't* understand was how he knew so much about the circles of Hell.

"You think too loud." He broke the silence around us.

"You're awfully nosey," I said. "Do you always listen in on my inner monologue?"

He paused, gave me a half grin. "Not always."

The way that grin hooked at one corner—small, dangerous—sent a low pulse straight through me. Ridiculous, given we were literally in Hell, but my body didn't seem to care.

As he continued on his merry way, I flushed hot to the roots of my hair. Maybe it was the heat. Maybe it was him.

Probably him.

"I find your streaming consciousness fascinating," he added. "Mostly, though, your face gives away everything you're thinking."

Again, I flushed hot. I decided that was the effects of being in the cave in the pit of Hell rather that my embarrassment for all the things I thought about Kincade. He was definitely right about one thing. I was never one to hide my emotions. My expressions were often out loud.

"It's not fair you can hear my thoughts but I can't hear yours."

I tried to detract him from thinking about my ridiculous stream of consciousness. No one needed that in their life. Especially Kincade.

"Maybe you shouldn't think so loud then."

He moved past me down the tunnel, close enough that his shoulder grazed mine—barely a touch, but it lit up every nerve like a struck match.

"You sound cranky. I think this heat is getting to you."

He rounded on me, the beam of the flashlight wiggling around me. His eyes held a deep worry that I hadn't seen before. For a moment, I was completely taken aback. Something tugged at me—something raw and unguarded that made my breath falter. If he said one more soft thing, I wasn't sure my heart would survive it.

His gaze searched mine. He started to say something, then stopped and pressed his lips together.

I was as transparent as plastic wrap to Kincade, but he was far from that for me. I often tried to read him, but failed. And God help me, I wanted to. I wanted to know what he felt—if he felt anything close to this maddening, magnetic pull twisting in my chest every time he looked at me.

It really sucked he detected every lie I ever tried to tell him. It also really sucked he read my thoughts.

Finally, he said, "Someday, I'll answer all your questions. Today, we have other, more important business."

Then he turned and started down the tunnel once again, the flashlight bouncing in rhythm with his steps. I was shocked. He had never been so open with me before.

"I'll try to keep the loud thoughts down," I said as I followed.

"It's fine." He sounded exhausted.

His jaw flexed, the muscle ticking once—his tell when I'd worn down the last ounce of his patience. But beneath the annoyance, I caught the faintest flicker of something else... something like affection wrapped in misery.

"I can't help it, you know. You're as much as an enigma to me as my uncle was. Maybe that's why we get along. You like to keep information from me like he did."

"He did it to you protect you."

"Is that why you do it, too?" It was hard to keep the bite of annoyance from my voice.

"Yes. Now, shh, and let me concentrate."

Oh, so that was it. He was *concentrating*.

"The prison is ahead," he said.

"I'm surprised we've made it this far without being detected by Azriel or Lucifer or any number of his high lords," I said.

"Oh, we've been detected," he said, crashing all my hopes and dreams.

"Groovy." I sighed. "How do you know?"

"They haven't come after us yet, but they will." His tone was full of confidence.

He turned a corner. Ahead, a faint yellow light illuminated the hallway. This looked vaguely familiar, like the hallway we were in when we rescued Kincade. We being me, Edward, Darius, and Ophelia. That seemed eons ago but in truth was only a few months ago.

As we approached and entered the splash of light, I clicked off the flashlight. I still gripped it in my hand. In the other, I held the flameless sword. Kincade, ahead of me, also turned off his flashlight. He stuck it in the backpack, then took his gun in hand. He paused there, peering down the hallway and waiting. For what, I had no idea.

"Do you hear that?" he asked.

I strained my ears and squinted into the deep shadows on the other end of the hall, as if that would help me hear whatever he heard. I held my breath for ten seconds and listened harder.

"No," I whispered.

The roar shook the walls and scared the shit out of me. I shuddered, goosebumps erupting all over my arms and legs. And then it went silent again. I lit the sword with a swoosh of my hand.

"What the fuck was that?" I asked.

"A message," he said.

I wanted to ask how he knew, then I reminded myself he spent quite a bit of time here in the Second Circle while I was off trying to find the Spear of Destiny and save his soul.

"Let's find Ophelia and get out of here," I said.

"Agreed."

He stared down the hallway again. I followed. Stone wall was to the right of us. To the left, prison cells that looked exactly like the one he had been in when he was Azriel's prisoner. Hopefully, that meant we were headed in the right direction to finding Ophelia.

My palms broke into a hot sweat. I wasn't sure if that was because of the sweltering heat or the nerves plaguing me. Either way, I gripped the sword with both hands as I followed him. He held his weapon at the ready like an FBI agent ready to gun down his suspect.

I peered into each cell as we passed by and was disgusted and horrified by what I saw. Decaying corpses. Skeletal remains. In one cell, a woman huddled against the back wall, her wrists and ankles in shackles. She gave us a fearful look as we passed by. Something inside me wanted to stop and break her out.

"No, Anna. We have to keep going."

He sensed my hesitation or maybe he read the pity in my mind for the woman.

"But—"

"We can't release anyone else."

I swallowed hard. He was right. Logic didn't make it feel any less awful.

"Why not?"

"It's bad enough we're breaking Ophelia out. What do you think will happen if we break out the entire prison?" He cut me a glance over his shoulder. "Do you *really* want all the demons and high lords to come after us?"

"Good point."

We passed another cell. As we did, the maniac on the other side of the bars charged with a howl that nearly broke my ears. Thankfully, he was chained up, too, and unable able get close to the bars. *Don't look, don't look, don't look.*

But I looked. And what I saw horrified me.

After all the demon killing, the high lord killing, I should have grown accustomed to seeing disgusting, rotting creatures. But not. This one was unlike any I had ever seen. Balding and rotten teeth. He had a missing eye—there was nothing but a black socket there. His hands were long, slender, bony ending in yellow, pointy nails.

His clothes hung off his decaying, emaciated body. Feral wide eyes never left me as we passed.

I shuddered. Every instinct I had screamed *get out,* but I forced my legs to keep moving.

"Not the worst one you'll see," Kincade said.

"That's comforting."

"Stop looking then."

He wasn't wrong, damn him. From that moment on, I kept my gaze forward and out of the prison cells. Kincade halted then and peered into one.

"Ophelia," he said, softly.

I paused next to him. There she was, shackled to the wall like the others with iron manacles around her wrists and ankles. She looked awful. Her hair was matted with blood on one side of her head. She had a black eye. Her lip was split. She had dark circles under her eyes.

"God," I whispered.

Rage and guilt stung the back of my eyes, but I shoved the emotions down. This wasn't the place to fall apart.

She saw us then. She stood straight as hope and relief erupted on her face. She was about to exclaim her joy when Kincade put a finger to his lips to keep her quiet. She gave a nod of understanding. Then he turned to me.

"As soon as I open this cell door, they'll be alerted to our presence. We're not going to get out of here without a fight." He kept his voice low.

In the next cell, the disgusting man started moaning as though he were dying. After each moan, he jangled his chains. It sounded like he hit them against the wall to make as much noise as possible.

"What's our move, then?" I asked.

"Know how to pick a lock?" he asked.

I shook my head. "Not really."

He shoved the backpack at me, which made me drop the flashlight with a crash. It shattered and broke.

"Awesome," I hissed. "Let's alert Hell we're here."

He grimaced at the noise as he holstered his gun. As I held the bag, he unzipped the front pocket and pulled out two small metal instruments.

"I'll do it then."

He set about picking the lock on the cell door. Seconds later, it swung open. Then he was inside, picking the locks on her wrists and ankles. She gave him a weak smile of thanks. But when she took that first step, she faltered. I sucked in a sharp breath as she started to fall.

He caught her, held her up, wrapped an arm around her waist. He said something to her I was unable to hear. She nodded. Then took slow steps out of the cell and into the hallway. The second her weight sagged, my heart shot to my throat.

And that's when the invisible beast roared again.

CHAPTER 35

"Time to go," he said.

But Ophelia was having a hard time walking. He scooped her up and draped her over his shoulder as if she weighed nothing. I slung the backpack over my shoulder, still gripping the flaming sword. Kincade moved past me as the shadow at the other end of the hallway exploded into the shape of a very large beast pounding its way down the hall on all fours toward us.

"Run!" I shouted.

And then we were off.

The beast crashed into the wall, slamming it with all its body weight making the walls and ceiling shudder with the impact. Several loose stones trickled down around us. This wasn't looking good. I stole a glance over my shoulder to see the thing snarling, showing off sharp yellow teeth and a bright pink tongue and a whole lot of drool.

I halted and turned to fight.

"What the *hell* are you doing?" he demanded.

"Get her out of here," I said, gripping the flaming sword tight. "I'll buy you some time."

For a heartbeat, raw animal terror clawed at my throat—then it crystallized into something colder, sharper. If somebody was getting eaten today, it wasn't going to be them.

"I'm not leaving you here," he snapped.

"Put me down," Ophelia said. "I can fight. I'm not dead. Just weak."

Kincade set her to her feet. He palmed his gun.

"Where's your sword?" I asked.

"Azriel took it," she said. "I don't know where it is."

Naturally, he would want to take her high lord killing sword and keep it for himself.

The beast was closer now, but the hallway was too narrow for us to stand three-wide and attack all at once. I put my feet shoulder-width apart and prepared to do battle.

But when the beast was only a few feet away, it stopped and reared its head with a roar. I held my ground. Then it lowered its head. It was only then I saw the passenger. A passenger who slipped down the thing's body and landed with a thud next to it.

Azriel.

The expanse of his glorious black wings extended behind him. He peered at me with those dark, mirthless eyes that frightened me right to my core. Even in the depths of Hell, he still smelled distinctly like cinnamon.

"Ah, *chérie*, you are so brave coming here to save your friend. I admire your loyalty. True friendship." He reached up and petted the beast's head as though it were a favorite pet.

I said nothing as I stood there holding the flaming sword aloft. He glanced at it. Then his gaze went beyond me to Kincade and Ophelia.

"I am glad you came," he said.

"Are you? Why?"

"Because you and I have unfinished business," he said.

I clenched my jaw, knowing he taunted me. Knowing he was trying to get me to react. I stood my ground, refusing to move, refusing to answer. He waved his hand. A whoosh of air went over me and snuffed out the sword.

"Do you remember when you were young? How you begged for my touch?" He gave me his famous wolf grin.

I hated him with everything inside me.

"How you allowed me to tattoo you." His gaze raked over my body.

That tattoo was full of his dark magic and a way for him to track me. Kincade remade it into something else, rendering it useless to Azriel.

Heat crawled up my neck. For years that mark had been my secret shame—proof of how young and stupid and desperate I'd been. Now, with Kincade at my back and Azriel throwing it in my face, it felt like being stripped bare in front of them both.

"That tattoo is gone now," I said, without thinking.

"I know. Such a pity." He clicked his tongue as he took a step closer.

Behind me, Kincade moved closer. I sensed his powerful, hulking body inches from mine. Azriel cut him a glance then back to me.

"Your *gardien* is useless here. You're in my domain now, *chérie*. Do you realize what that means?"

"You're going to kill me now?" I asked.

He smiled. "Killing you outright would be too easy. No, I'm not going to kill you. I have a proposal for you."

Kincade's voice boomed in my head. *Don't, Anna.*

"And what is that?" I asked, sounding as casual as possible.

"We duel." He paused for dramatic effect, which he was very good at. "To the death. With your friends as witnesses."

Ophelia sucked in a sharp breath. Kincade growled low in his throat. And I realized then this was what Azriel wanted all along. Everyone was right. It *was* a trap and I fell for it.

For a split second, guilt tried to choke me—over Ophelia, over Kincade, over dragging us all into this. Then I shoved it down. I didn't have room for self-loathing and survival at the same time.

"You took her because you knew I would come for her," I said.

"I had hoped. I'm glad I was right." He smiled. His black wings ruffled with smug satisfaction. He produced Ophelia's shimmering broadsword from the cloud. Apparently, this was a thing. "Do you accept my proposal?"

I pondered this a moment. "So, we duel. If I die, you win and get, what, Kincade and Ophelia?"

He grinned. "Their souls forever. Yes, of course."

I nodded. "Of course. However, if I win, that means *you* die and we walk free. Is that right?"

Anna...no... Kincade again in my head.

"That sounds like acceptable terms to me." He gripped the sword in both hands. "But this is not the best location for our duel."

"And where do you suggest we go then?"

"I thought you'd never ask."

He whisked us all from the prison to Lucifer's lair where he sat on his onyx throne presiding over the festivities like some pompous king watching a jousting match. His two red-eyed dogs were on either side of him. A cheering crowd of minions, demons, and high lords looked on. Kincade and Ophelia were disarmed and in chains next to Lucifer. The backpack that was on my shoulder was gone.

Seeing him bound there knocked the air out of me more than any blade could. Kincade was supposed to be unshakable—my unmovable mountain. Shackles didn't suit him. They made something feral and ugly uncurl in my chest.

Azriel raised his hand to silence the crowd. He turned toward Lucifer. "My lord, I have done as you've asked and brought the intruders to you."

Bastard.

Lucifer's face was impassive. "You have done well."

"She has agreed to a duel to the death," he said.

One dark brow rose in amusement. "Has she? What do we get if you win, Azriel?"

"All three of their souls."

"Wait a second," I said. "That wasn't part of the agreement."

Azriel gave me a wicked grin. "Oh, did you not think your soul was at stake too, *chérie*?" He clucked his tongue.

I wanted to rip it out.

One of the high lords next to Lucifer said, "Why not just take their souls now and be done with them?"

I eyed the bastard who spoke. He was tall, good looking, with an expanse of black wings interspersed with gray and white and a shimmering thread of silver running through them. He glared right back at me. I lifted my chin in defiance.

"What fun would that be?" Lucifer said. He rose from his throne in a slow, languorous movement. "Long have I watched this one. She refused to give me what I want. Even after everything I've done to make her see things my way. You will die today, girl, and your soul will be mine."

"Do you think so? Perhaps I should remind you I killed Prince Mammon, Abaddon, and Hadrian."

He waved it away. "Luck no doubt." He sauntered back to the throne and sat. "Proceed, Lord Azriel."

This is a really bad idea, Kincade said in my head.

I tended to agree with him, but I was in this now with no way out. If all else failed, I still had the Godlight and the lightning at my disposal. I remembered the tiny cross at my throat and reached up, running my finger over it even though it was nestled under my shirt. That and the angel pendant Kincade had given me weighed heavily against my chest. Whatever happened, faith resided inside me. Faith that I would not be defeated.

Trust me, I said.

Azriel and I had a long history. I'd been wanting to get my pound of flesh for a long while, now, and I finally had the chance. I wasn't about to give it up, even if that meant the possibility of dying in Hell and losing my soul for all eternity.

I readied my uncle's flaming sword while Azriel circled me like he was prepared to pounce. I had never been in a sword battle before. What were the odds of surviving? What were my odds of being able to kick his ass with this thing? I was used to swinging and killing and nothing more than a light-weight dagger. But this...this heavy steel sword was easily two-handed. It felt like trying to fight a hurricane with a church bell.

Azriel took the first swing. My sword met his with an audible clang. The second the flaming sword met the shimmering broadsword, the flames snuffed out. Poof. Gone.

Super.

He grinned.

"Your flames will not work against the shimmering broadsword," he said.

"I see that."

I swung again, aiming for his head. He blocked with his sword. When the blades met, it was so violent the bones in my arms rattled all the way to the back of my teeth. I wasn't going to win this easily. I understood that now. But that was fine. I was still going to fight with everything I had.

Clang. Clang. Clang. Our swords met up, down, sideways. I met his thrusts with everything I had in me but the oppressive heat was starting to get to me. Sweat rolled down the side of my face and my back. My arms were starting to weaken and my legs ached from the exertion. Azriel, meanwhile, hadn't even broken a sweat.

Of course, he would have the advantage here since this was his domain.

I lost my focus for only a moment. But that was long enough for him to swing the sword. The tip of it grazed my upper arm, slicing through the material of my shirt. Blood oozed through the material. It wasn't a deep cut, but enough to impede. Cheers erupted from the crowd that he'd drawn first blood.

Holding the sword with both hands, I swung and connected once again with his blade. He retaliated with a quick slash through the air that nearly got me across my ribs. I sucked in sharp breath and scuttled backward.

Stop exposing your side, Kincade said. *He knows that's your weakness.*

Well, fuck. How was I supposed to do that?

A bead of sweat dripped in my eye. I refused to wipe it away to give him more of an advantage than he already had. I cringed as the salt stung.

I had a sudden sharp pain in my left side. A raucous cheer went up from the onlookers. I didn't understand it until I spun around to see a fucking minion with a Hell blade in his hand. He'd stabbed me.

Heat flooded out from the wound, like someone had poured liquid fire straight into my veins. My knees wobbled. The world tilted.

"Cheater!" I shouted.

Holding the sword in one hand, I immediately drew down the dagger, spun, and stabbed the damn minion. He turned to dust. There was an audible gasp in the crowd followed by a few cheers. I dropped the heavy sword. It was doing me no favors and only serving to turn my arms into wet noodles. I was much better with my old friend, the dagger, anyway.

My time was limited now that I'd been stabbed with a Hell blade. The poison would be coursing through my body quickly and begin to impair my vision, my judgement, everything.

Kincade was strangely silent in my head. Like he was holding himself back by sheer force of will so he wouldn't distract me at the worst possible moment. I stole a glance at him, saw him standing at the edge of the fighting arena with an impassive look on his face. Like he wasn't worried or concerned or anything. Ophelia, however, looked as though she were about to crawl out of her skin with the fear and worry.

Azriel, meanwhile, was exceptionally proud of himself.

"You didn't specify the rules of the fight, *chérie*."

"Fuck you!" Even though it did nothing to wound him, it made me feel better to shout it at him.

I staggered to the left, trying to maintain my footing. I clutched the blade in my sweating palm and then decided to hell with all this. I wasn't going to let him win.

He held the shimmering broadsword with two hands and circled me, an evil glint in his black eyes. He swung the blade. I ducked. He missed me by inches.

In my peripheral, another minion moved to attack. I was able to dispose of it before it stabbed me again.

All of this reminded me of the fight my uncle had to the death with the Prince of Greed. Mammon killed my uncle. His minions stabbed him multiple times to give the prince an advantage. As if this was all orchestrated for me as a reminder of what I'd done and what it cost me.

And that really fucking pissed me off.

Azriel still held the weapon with two hands, not giving me much to work with. He was one of the most powerful high lords and he knew it. But I had killed my fair share of lethal demons and high lords. I slashed Mammon's throat and watched him bleed out. I fried Abaddon with my Godlight, turning him to nothing more than ash. I shot the high lord, Hadrian, with Kincade's demon-killing gun.

Azriel was nothing compared to them. And I was not afraid of him.

My vision blurred as I moved a step toward him. He gave me that wolf grin.

"Not feeling so well, *chérie*?"

"I feel fine." With my free hand, I swiped the sweat from my brow.

"The poison is slowly killing you," he said. "You will lose your strength first. You will not be able to stand. Then you will fall to the ground. Then I will take your soul. Then you will belong to the darkness at last."

"Oh, you think so?"

"I know so."

He didn't make a move to attack me again. My knees threatened to buckle. I charged toward him, swinging the dagger. He easily stepped out of the way.

"But you cheated to win," I said.

"No one said the fight had to be fair."

I hated him with every ounce of my soul. Hated him with so much vehemence that it coursed through me right alongside the poison.

And then I recalled the Godlight residing deep inside me. I didn't need a dagger to kill him. I only needed the Godlight and my lightning fingers. I dropped my free hand to my side and allowed the lightning to come, flickering in my palm.

Another minion. I yawned, as if bored, as I fried the fucker where he stood. Then I turned my lightning fingers on Azriel.

"You thought you could defeat me by cheating," I said. "But I have more power than you realize."

I flung my hand out toward him. He blocked the flash of light with the shimmering broadsword, blinding me. I cried out as I fell to the ground, my eyes temporarily blinded by the flash of light. The clink of the sword landed nearby and then suddenly Azriel was on me in an instant.

The dagger fell from my hand as he wrapped a hand around my throat. I gasped for air when he squeezed so hard, I saw stars. He flattened his hand against my chest, ready to pull out my soul.

"I wanted to love you," he said, his face inches from mine.

Once, the girl I used to be might have believed that. Might have twisted it into some kind of dark, tragic romance. Now, with his hand on my throat and Kincade chained in the corner, it was just what it always had been—obsession, control, and rot.

"I wanted you to be mine forever. I wanted *you*."

I gasped, wishing I could spit in his face or tell him off. Instead, I fought for air into my lungs. The shouts of the crowd were deafening as they cheered him on. He'd tried to steal my soul before, but then I was not in his domain.

I called the Godlight, willing it to come forward. But it was strangely silent deep in my breast.

Panic scraped its nails down my spine. The one thing that had never failed me suddenly felt distant, muffled—like trying to pray through glass.

"I want your soul, Annabelle Marie Walker. And I will have it."

Dammit, Anna, fight him! Get the dagger. Stab him. Something! Kincade's angry voice burst through my mind.

He slowly pulled his hand away, bringing with it a bright white light. It felt as though it were being dragged through me, pulling away from my body. My vision blurred. I gasped, clawing at the hand around my neck with one hand, while reaching for the dagger with the other. Where was that bloody Godlight, anyway?

"Your power is beautiful and something to behold," Azriel said. "Once I have it, I will crush it and you."

Still, he pulled the light away from me. My hand swished on the hot ground. Where was that dagger?

Reach. You almost have it.

And then my fingers grazed the cool jade-handled dagger. I bent my fingers to scoot it closer and then I had it in my palm. I jerked it forward, stabbing Azriel in the ribs as hard as I could.

He cried out, released my throat, and stumbled backward. The light he'd pulled from me immediately sucked back inside with a blistering power momentarily incapacitating me. The hot pain seared through my chest all the way down to my toes as I rolled to my knees, trying to get my bearings.

Get up. Get the sword. Kill him now.

Having Kincade's voice in my head was both annoying and inspiring. I searched for the damn sword as sweat blurred my eyes. Or maybe that was the demon poison. I stuck the dagger in my belt, then stumbled after Azriel who held a hand against his side. Black blood streamed through his fingers. Lucifer stood now with his hands clenched at his side as he watched. As least, that's what I thought I saw through my hazy eyes.

The scrape of a blade on the ground indicated Azriel picked up the shimmering broadsword. I scanned the ground, frantic to find my uncle's blade. *There.* I dove for it just as Azriel dove for me. He missed me as I landed on the ground, skidded past the sword, and came to a halt near the edge of the crowd. Minions clawed me, ripping through my hair and tearing the skin on my face. I shoved backward from them and crawled my way back to the sword in time to grab it and block a blow from Azriel.

Get UP, dammit.

I was trying but I was so tired. All I wanted to do was lay down on the ground and sleep for the next ten hours.

That's the poison talking. Get on your feet now.

For a second, that sounded like my uncle. I scanned the faces of the crowd but didn't see him. I did see Kincade's angry face, however. He glared right at me with such a ferocity I flinched.

I had the dagger in one hand and the sword in the other. And not nearly enough energy to fight Azriel anymore.

"You are weak, aren't you?" Azriel taunted. "Give up, *chérie*. Let me have you."

"Never." The word whispered out of me.

He circled me, ready to pounce. I called up the Godlight, trying to use it against the high lord, but it was only a flicker. Azriel's attempt to steal my soul was an attempt to eradicate the Godlight inside me.

I need a distraction, I said to Kincade. *Anything. I don't care what you have to do.*

Silence. I stole a glance, met his gaze, and he nodded. I wasn't sure what he would be able to accomplish with his hands shackled, but he was Kincade, after all. He'd figure something out.

Suddenly, he barked an order in a language I had never heard. The two red-eyed dogs at Lucifer's side leapt into action. They charged into the arena. One was faster than the other and latched onto Azriel's leg with his mouth full of sharp teeth. Azriel screamed with the pain. The other barked and snapped at the crowd, as if holding them back.

I didn't question how or why Kincade knew whatever attack phrase that was but I appreciated it. If Azriel could cheat, then so could I.

Lucifer had a look of complete and utter fury on his face. His fists were clenched at his side. He shouted a counter-command just as Azriel kicked the beast in the face. It released him with a whine.

I took that moment to strike. I dropped the dagger and held the sword with two hands. Gripping it with all I had, I charged Azriel, swung the sword with every strength I had left in me and sliced his head from his shoulders.

It landed on the ground, bounced, rolled, and stopped at Lucifer's feet. Black blood spurted everywhere. The crowd had gone eerily silent. Even the dogs had stopped growling. My arms went slack the second the blade finished its arc. The sword suddenly felt three times heavier, my legs like soaked sand. The only thing keeping me upright was pure, stubborn spite.

Azriel, my archenemy, was dead.

CHAPTER 36

I DROPPED THE SWORD to my side, my strength obliterated. My arm muscles trembled. My knees still threatened to buckle. Somehow, I managed to have the forethought to pick up the shimmering broadsword. I placed it along with the flaming sword into the cloud for safekeeping.

I focused my gaze on Lucifer's terrible face, standing my ground, even though I was ready to pass out. He snapped his fingers at the dogs. They returned to his side. I still wondered how Kincade knew the command to make the dogs attack.

"It's over," I said. "Let us go."

"You think this war between us is *over*?" He laughed. "On the contrary, girl. It's only the beginning."

I hated when he called me girl. I stole a glance at Kincade. His face remained impassive. Ophelia didn't bother to hide her fear as she glanced between me and the devil.

"Azriel convinced me we needed you and the relics. He promised me your soul would be easy to take. That once he did you would lead us to the Ark of the Covenant. But now..." He paused, looking thoughtful. He tapped his long-nailed forefinger against his chin. "I don't think I need the Ark after all. Or any of the relics. They have been nothing but a distraction."

I wasn't sure where he was going with this diatribe, so I remained silent and let him continue. All the while, I fought the nausea pounding through me.

"And while I've been distracted, you've become stronger, more powerful. You are now a formidable opponent. I underestimated you." He stole a glance at Kincade. "As is your guardian."

"Release us," I said again, ignoring his monologue. "That was the rules."

He scoffed. "Rules? My dear, I make the rules here."

"You agreed to let us go," I snapped. Dizziness swept through me. I wobbled on my feet, trying hard to remain standing.

"Azriel agreed. Azriel is dead." He waved his hand toward the headless corpse.

Fury pounded through me.

"However," Lucifer paused as his gaze swept over me. "I think I should like to defeat you and your kind once and for all."

Warning bells went off in my head. "What does that mean?"

"There is a valley in northern Israel. The Jezreel Valley near Megiddo. Do you know it?"

I shook my head.

Somewhere in the back of my mind, dusty Sunday school lessons and my uncle's notes tried to line up—Megiddo, Armageddon, battlefields soaked in prophecy. My mouth went dry.

"Ah, well, you will soon enough, I imagine. We will meet there this time on the battlefield. My army against your army. And this time, my dear, you will have to defeat *me* to save yourself and mankind."

Words from the family history book haunted me.

She will be the one to save Man from the evil that walks the Earth.

I swallowed hard but my throat was desert dry.

"In one week. That should give you enough time to recover from the poisonous Hell blade."

He turned away, walking slow, methodical steps back toward his onyx throne. With a wave of his hand, the shackles fell off Kincade's and Ophelia's wrists. Most of the crowd had scattered, leaving only a few lingering behind.

"Until the day of your defeat comes," Lucifer said as he turned to sit on his throne, "be gone from my sight."

He clapped his hands. Thunder pounded through the underworld and a moment later, the three of us were whisked back to the entrance of Dante's Cave. I crashed against the ground, jarring my shoulder. The sudden cool air of the forest slapped my overheated skin, but it did nothing to clear the spinning in my head. I was so dizzy I was unable to lift my head.

"She's been poisoned by a Hell blade," Kincade said.

Then strong arms picked me up off the ground. I peered up through hazy eyes into the face of Sariel and then a moment later, we were traveling through space and time. The world whirled around us in a blinding flash of brilliant light. We were back at Walker Manor. Sariel placed me on the bed.

"Stay with me, Anna," he said.

His hand gripped mine. It was the last thing I remembered before I passed out.

* * *

I slept and did not dream. When I awoke, my eyelids were still heavy and refused to open. As if they had been glued shut. My body hurt everywhere. As if there was lead in my blood. As I regained consciousness, I took stock of my surroundings. Familiar sounds and scents surrounded me. I was in my own bed with heavy blankets on top of me. Somewhere in the room was Kincade. His familiar sandalwood scent wafted to me.

At last, I opened my eyes. Kincade sat in the chair across the room with a book in his lap. One of my tattered, well-read volumes though I was unable to make out the title. The spine was already cracked to hell; he'd probably been stuck on the same page for hours. He closed the book with a snap. His gaze focused on me with an expression I was unable to read.

His grip lingered on the cover a second too long before he let it go.

"Welcome back," he said at last. His voice was steady. Too steady.

The last thing I remembered was defeating Azriel, pissing off Lucifer, and then...

"The poison?" I asked. My voice croaked like I hadn't had anything to drink in days.

"Sariel removed it. The wound wasn't deep. You had just enough of the toxin to incapacitate you."

His voice was even tempered. It was hard to read him. Everything from his tone of voice to his body language to the way he looked at me with that glittering gaze.

"What you did..." He began, then stopped.

"It was stupid."

"You almost died. He almost won and took your soul."

"But he didn't win," I said.

"For fuck's sake, Anna."

He scrubbed a hand over his face, breath dragging in his chest like he hadn't realized he was holding it.

The words landed harder than any blow Azriel had thrown—sharp, clean, deserved.

When his hand fell away, I really looked at him. He had dark circles under his eyes and more growth on his chin and cheeks than normal. Deep lines of fatigue and worry creased his face. Guilt swamped me. I'd done that to him. Because I was blinded by my own hatred. My own need to win and defeat Azriel who had thwarted me for most of my life.

"Azriel didn't win, no," he said, his tone gruff.

Silence descended between us. I nudged at his mind but it was strangely silent. That was nothing new. I was never able to get into his thoughts unless he allowed it. He, however, was always able to read mine.

"How did you know the dogs would attack Azriel?"

He didn't answer right away and for a moment, I thought he wasn't going to at all.

"I didn't. I gambled they were dumb beasts. You needed a distraction. I gave you one. It could just as easily have gone wrong. You *have to stop* taking chances like that, Anna."

"It doesn't matter now, does it?" I asked. "The war is upon us."

He clenched his jaw, the muscles flexing there. "Yes, and since you were out for two days, we only have five to prepare."

"Two?"

Time dropped out from under me. Two days gone—wiped away in a haze of poison and angelic intervention.

No wonder I sounded like I'd been in a bar all night drinking whiskey and smoking cigarettes. I wanted to sit up, but my exhausted body refused to move. I rolled to my back and stared at the ceiling. It was the only movement I managed to accomplish. My stomach rumbled with a ferocity I had never felt before.

"Yes, two. Perhaps when you're done convalescing, we can figure out what the fuck we're going to do about it."

His jaw tightened as he said it, like every other response had been locked down by sheer force of will.

"We're not going to *do* anything about it," I said, still staring at the ceiling.

"You mean you plan to go through with it? You plan to meet him on the battlefield?" He didn't bother to hide his surprise.

"Yes," I said.

I had my own army, after all. The Order of the Holy Relics were willing and waiting. And the Fae. They would likely help me. I'd talk to Sariel about having Darius and his warrior angels join in, too. Maybe an archangel or two. I was no military tactician, but I figured the more bodies we had to fight against Lucifer, the better. Plus, I had three of the five Holy Relics, not that I really understood what to do with them during the battle. Gabriel had his Horn back, but I had the Spear of Destiny, the Staff of Moses, and the Holy Grail. The Ark was a wild card.

Kincade rose from the chair and dropped the book into it, then headed for the door.

"You have a fan club waiting to see you."

The light, throwaway words didn't match the tight line of his shoulders as he walked away. Whatever we were, whatever we could be, was buried under anger and fear—for now.

Before he made it to the door, I said, "You don't approve."

He paused, turned to me. "It doesn't matter if I approve or not." He reached for the door.

"It *is* my destiny, Kincade. It always has been."

He halted mid-reach, clenched his hand into a fist and closed his eyes. He took a deep breath, expelled it. As though he were coming to terms with what he knew all along. That protecting me meant watching me walk toward the end of the world. What we all knew. He gave me one last glance.

"I know."

Then he opened the door. Ophelia rushed inside, relief on her face.

"Oh, thank God!" She perched on the edge of the bed, taking my hand in hers. "We thought you were done for."

Her black eye had faded. Her split lip healed. The stress and fatigue lines were gone from her face.

"Anna, I'm so sorry I left. I—"

"Don't," I snapped. "Don't apologize to me."

Though I spoke to her, I watched Kincade slip out of the room. Emotions warred within me. I wanted him to stay. There were things left unsaid between us. Things that needed to be said before we went to war with Lucifer and his Fallen.

"But it was because of me you have a war to fight."

"No, not because of you."

I thought of the family history book once again. The words echoed through my mind.

The one to save mankind from Hell.

"As corny as this sounds, it's my destiny to fight him."

She clutched my hand harder. Confusion drew her brows together. "I don't understand."

I expelled a deep sigh. "It's a long story. One that goes back hundreds of years. I'll tell you all about it someday."

"Thank you for getting my sword back," she whispered, keeping her eyes downcast.

Ah, yes. Her broadsword. "I'll return it to you as soon as I have the strength."

A knock sounded on the open door. I glanced up to see Grace enter. She carried a steaming mug of what smelled like Earl Grey. I struggled to sit up. Ophelia helped me, then fluffed the pillows behind me. I leaned against them as Grace handed me the hot tea.

"We've been worried about you," she said. "All of us."

"Kincade refused to leave your side," Ophelia added with a knowing grin.

"He barely slept," Grace said. "Every time you stirred, he was on his feet."

And yet, where was he now? Likely brooding away his anger in his own room. I understood his anger. He was right. I shouldn't have taken on Azriel. I let him taunt me and anger me and pull me into the duel to the death and almost lost my friend's soul in the process. If I had died, Lucifer would have won.

"He kept a watchful eye on you the whole time," Grace added.

I said nothing as I sipped my tea. She shifted from one foot to the other. The tea burned my tongue, but I didn't care.

"And the others? Are they still here?" I asked.

"Yes," Grace said. "Your mother, Sariel, Killian, and Astrid have all visited. Even Piers."

"What about Kiara and Bridget?"

"They've been asking about you," Ophelia said.

Good. Then they would be able to help me activate the Order of the Holy Relics. What was it the family history book said? Something about the Keeper calling upon the order to come to arms for the battle of all mankind.

"I'll want to speak to them eventually but I'm still too tired to think," I said.

"We should let you rest." Grace waved Ophelia toward the door.

Rest was the last thing I wanted, but my energy hadn't returned. "Grace, wait."

Ophelia left the room while Grace moved to my bedside. She perched on the edge, worry in her eyes. Worry and fear and everything else. Holding the mug in one hand, I dug the small cross necklace out from under my shirt. I realized then, with some interest, I was in clean clothes.

"This belongs to you. Help me take it off."

"No." She shook her head. "I want you to keep it."

"But—"

"I insist. Keep it. A small part of me likes to think it helped you when you were...away." She smiled, but the worry was still in her eyes. She patted my hand and rose.

"Everyone was right. It was a trap."

She halted and turned back to me. "Ophelia told us what happened. About the duel and the coming war."

"Kincade didn't?"

"He's been somewhat silent on the matter," she said.

"He's angry with me."

"Because you almost died," she said. "He's in love with you, you know."

Hearing the words was like an arrow to my heart. It pounded hard in my chest as I gripped the mug tighter in my hands. The warmth burned through the ceramic into my palms. It was both everything I wanted and yet I was terrified to admit the truth to myself. Terrified that if we told each other how we felt, it would somehow change our relationship. Terrified I would lose him in the coming war. I'd already lost so much. The idea of losing him—*after* finally saying the words—felt like a cruelty even Hell wouldn't dream up.

"Tell him, Anna. Before it's too late."

Grace slipped out and softly closed the door behind her.

CHAPTER 37

I SAT IN THE bed still holding the mug and wondering what the fuck to do next. My brain was ready to figure out the next steps in this horrible nightmare but my body refused to move from the bed. Grace was right. I had to tell Kincade the truth about how I felt. But then what? The thought of seeing him die on the battlefield was unfathomable. In fact, it made me sick to my stomach.

A knock sounded on the door.

"Come in."

My mother and Sariel entered. My emotional reaction to seeing them enter the room wasn't one of elation. It was disappointment. Disappointment Kincade hadn't returned. My fingers tightened around the mug until the heat bit my skin.

"How are you feeling?" she asked.

I'd been thinking about the two of them and the prophecy or destiny that I was the One Who Was Promised. What I came to realize was that Sariel knew this prophecy long before he even knew my mother. He knew who Ezra was, that he was a dream walker.

He knew that someone of the Walker line would become the One Who Was Promised and Keeper of the Holy Relics, which caused me to look at him in a different light.

"Fine." I sipped my tea, then realized I was being rude. "Thank you, Sariel."

"I was glad to help," he said.

"We wanted to check on you," my mother said.

"I'm exhausted." I leaned my head back on the fluffy pillows, the cooling mug still in my hands. "What happened when we returned?"

"You appeared outside the cave," Sariel said. "Quite suddenly. I brought you back here to remove the poison. Your mother tended your stab wound and the cut on your arm."

I was aware of the bandage on my ribs and the itchy wound.

"After that?" I asked.

"You were unconscious the whole time," she said. "Grace helped me change you into clean clothes and then we tucked you into bed."

I nodded.

"Anna, this war with Lucifer. Are you certain?" Sariel asked.

I cut him a glance. Even he had the worry creasing in his face. Everyone around me was worried. So why wasn't I? And why the worry. He was the one who helped make me who I was.

"Sariel, you and my mother know better than anyone the circumstances of my birth. I'm fulfilling the prophecy as not only the Keeper of the Holy Relics, but the One Who Was Promised."

He stared at me with a wide-eyed shocked expression. "The One Who Was Promised? Who told you that?"

"Kincade and I met someone from the Brotherhood of Watchers. They've been expecting me for a long time, haven't they?" When he didn't answer, I continued. "They believe it was foretold the One Who Was Promised would bring balance between the Darkness and the Light. You knew this, didn't you?"

It was a shot in the dark. But since Silas and Kincade both told me this, I'd pondered its meaning. Someone aside from the two of them had to know the truth. Otherwise, why would my great-grandfather write it all down in the family history book? Michael, the archangel definitely knew because he told my ancestor James Edward Walker.

"The dream walkers were chosen by Michael as guardian of the Holy Relics," I said. "Am I wrong?"

Slowly, he shook his head. "You are not."

"And as guardians, it was prophesized that someday the Keeper would have to defeat the ultimate evil," I said.

He said nothing.

"I've been thinking about this a long time," I continued. A strange calm settled over me—cold, precise. "And I think you knew very well what you were doing when you seduced my mother."

"Anna!" She said my name on a gasp.

I ignored her. "You understood what was at stake. And you understood there had to be someone from the Walker line that would be the one to bring balance between Darkness and Light."

"*Anna*, stop," my mother said with abject horror.

But I continued on with my wild theory. A theory that had suddenly come to fruition in my mind.

"You *hoped* it would be your offspring. Me. What you didn't foresee was that a powerful faction like the Knights of the Holy Lance would want my mother for their own nefarious deeds. Because she was more powerful than even you anticipated."

Sariel was strangely silent. My mother clutched her hands together as she glanced from me to Sariel and back again. Again, guilt swamped me. It was evident by the look on Sariel's face everything I said was right. Sariel had orchestrated my birth with the knowledge I would be the one to stand in the face of evil.

The prophecy in the family history book seemed to think I would defeat it. I, however, had my doubts.

"You are wrong about this, Anna," my mother said.

She had never sounded more lucid and yet more confused.

"Am I?" I gave her a pointed look, then turned that look on Sariel. "Tell me, Sariel. Am I wrong?"

"Please understand, Anna, I did what I had to do."

"*You...*" My mother said the word on a strained whisper.

"I only figured this out because of the way Azriel tried so hard to seduce me for years. He was desperate to have me as his own. Because he knew what was at stake. He knew who and what I was," I said.

It was hard to ignore the devastation on my mother's face and the terrible, terrible remorse on my father's. She had no idea and yet she had loved him with all her heart and soul. I almost felt sorry for her.

"Everything has been a lie, then," she spat.

Something twisted low in my chest—but I didn't reach for it.

"No." He turned to her, gripped her arms, and held her. "Our love is not a lie. It never was."

"Then why...how—"

"It *is* true I was sent here to protect you as your guardian. You were supposed to marry Alexander. I never intended to fall in love with you."

She shrugged off his hands and stepped back. Tears filled her purple eyes, threatening to spill. "I don't believe you."

"Annabelle, please—"

"Do *not* call me that. My name is Natasha."

Well, fuck. That wasn't what I intended.

She stormed out of the room leaving Sariel behind. Super.

"I believe you had the best of intentions," I said, my voice hollow. "However, you never should have lied to her. She and I are a lot alike. We hate to be lied to."

"Anna—"

"Save it. I don't want your fake apologies now. I accept you are truly my father. I do not accept how you orchestrated every facet of my life. Get out."

He looked absolutely destroyed. He exited the room, his white wings drooping in despair behind him. The door closed far more softly than it should have.

I didn't call him back.

And suddenly I was the worst person on the planet. A home wrecker. A destroyer of love and happiness.

The mug in my hand had gone cold. I placed it on the nightstand by the bed. Then burrowed under the blankets and allowed myself to drift into sleep.

* * *

I awoke in the middle of the night. I opened my eyes to the darkness of my room. I was alone. When was the last time I was alone? I didn't recall.

My stomach grumbled letting me know how empty it was. I shoved off the blankets and swung my feet to the floor. I seemed to have more energy than previously. My bladder, though, insisted on taking care of that first. Afterward, I made my way out of my room and down the stairs to the kitchen.

The house was quiet except for the tick of the grandfather clock.

In the kitchen, I pulled open the fridge and rummaged through looking for something to eat. I found a large container of what appeared to be chicken soup. Feeling like I hit the jackpot, I set about heating it in the microwave.

When I had it heated in a bowl, I stood in the kitchen and ate it as though someone might take it away from me. As though the world might decide I hadn't earned it. Two more bowlfuls later, my stomach was happy with me once again. After cleaning up, I left the kitchen and ran right into Cashiel. I squealed my surprise as he caught me.

"Damn, you scared me!"

"Apologies." He flashed a faint grin.

Relief at seeing him swept through me. Before I knew what I was doing, I hugged him. He patted my back.

"Where the hell have you been?" I asked when I released him.

"I've been detained." He didn't elaborate.

"Doing angel stuff, huh?" I waved him toward the parlor. He fell in step next to me. "I suppose you know what's going on."

He nodded. "I do. I came to talk to you about it."

"Not talk me out of it?" I asked, giving him a sideways glance.

When we entered the parlor, I pulled the door closed. I clicked on a lamp, then took the wing-back chair. He remained standing, the expanse of his wings shimmering in the pale light.

"No." He stood at the fireplace, examining the photos I had there. One of him and one of the two of us when I was a child.

"Good. Because I don't have that fight in me."

He drew his finger down the silver frame holding the two of us. "My hope is that I've prepared you for this."

"As much as you could, I suppose."

He turned to face me. "You know what you must do, don't you?"

My brows drew together. "A bit of a broad statement there, uncle. Care to clarify?"

"Call upon the clans. The Order of the Holy Relics will come to your aid."

"And the others?" I asked, recalling what I'd read in the family history books.

It stated the Order would call upon the Brotherhood of Watchers to come to arms and that the Brotherhood would call upon the Seraphim. I wasn't sure if the Brotherhood would be interested in helping me since my little escapade at their secret hideout.

"The Brotherhood has been compromised."

"How?"

A trickle of fear skittered through me. I recalled what Ophelia told me—that they were helping the high lords steal souls. My question to Cashiel was in the hopes he'd have more information.

"I don't know. I only know there is a growing danger within the organization."

"I've heard that, too."

"I doubt we can count on them to come to your aid."

"That's fine." Even though I suspected the answer, disappointment still swept through me. "The Seraphim?"

"Leave them to me," he said. "I have some influence over Michael and the others."

"What about Darius?" I asked.

"What about me?"

Suddenly, he was there in the room with us. His voice startled me. I jumped to my feet and launched myself at him, hugging him hard. He was somewhat taken aback by that and remained statute still.

"I'm glad to see you. Ophelia will be, too."

Darius hadn't changed a bit since the last time I saw him. He still had the snowy wings, the strong physique, and was still drop dead gorgeous.

"News of your...adventure in the underworld has spread to us," he said.

I cut a glance to Cashiel who nodded affirmative.

"I have come to offer you my assistance as well as the assistance of my fellow warriors."

A broad smile broke out. Relief sputtered through me. For the first time since Hell, my chest loosened. "You understand what we're up against, I hope."

"We are prepared to fight Lucifer and his demons," he said with a nod. "When the time comes, we will join you in the valley."

"Thank you, Darius." I wanted to hug him again, but managed to refrain. "You better find Ophelia. She's been missing you."

He nodded, then slipped out of the parlor on silent feet.

"I will speak to Michael," Cashiel said. "But, Anna, I should warn you. Lucifer has been building this army of his for a while now. His numbers could be in the tens of thousands."

"I'm aware."

I didn't like it, but I understood that was the case and we were outnumbered. How I was going to defeat him, I had no idea.

"Uncle, the relics. How am I to use them in the fight?"

He looked thoughtful for a long moment. "I'm unsure. Bring them with you to the battlefield."

"And the Ark? What of it? I was unable to retrieve it."

He gave me a knowing smile. "I believe the Ark has a will of its own."

And with that, he disappeared leaving me with more questions than answers.

CHAPTER 38

I RAMBLED AROUND THE house until dawn. When the sun began peeking over the horizon, I opened the front door and stood on the stoop to watch the sky lighten from deep indigo to brilliant blue. For the first time in a long while, the sky was cloudless yet there was still a bite to the wind. I clutched my elbows and shivered.

In the distance, the Fae camp was just coming to life. I thought of Killian and Astrid and wondered how their new forest building was going. A quick glance to the wooded area told me nothing. The trees were still thick and silent.

I thought of the sword in the vault, then. I wasn't sure why it popped into my head. It wasn't a thought so much as a pull. And I wondered how or where my uncle had acquired it. If I had thought about it earlier, I'd have asked him.

Killian was the last remaining Fae King. Lucifer destroyed their world, stolen their four Fae Treasures and killed all the royals except Killian. I didn't know much about the Fae Treasures other than Killian was searching for the Sword of Light. On impulse, I spun and headed back inside the manor. My bare feet pounded up the

353

stairs to the library where I hurried inside and closed the door with a snap.

The vault was behind a bookcase. I slipped the book out of its spot and waited as the shelf hissed and clicked and then slid open. I entered the code to the vault and pulled open the heavy steel door. Once inside, I paused, scanning the contents.

My uncle was a collector of fine things. Everything from first edition books to priceless paintings to his own collection of holy relics. The Spear of Destiny, Staff of Moses and Holy Grail resided here now. Carefully placed upon the shelves of the vault awaiting their own destiny.

For the first time, I noticed the gold jeweled box on the self. A fine layer of dust covered it. My hands shook as I reached for it and opened the lid. Nestled on a piece of garnet material was a small wooden cross.

I was unable to resist and reached for it, touching it. The history of the small cross pounded through my mind in a flicker of movement. My knees nearly gave out, and I had to brace a hand on the shelf. From the moment the dogwood tree was cut down to the moment Jesus died on the cross. Even to when a small piece of it was carved into this tiny crucifix.

It changed hands numerous times until it landed with the man who brought it to a woman who touched it. It returned to a man in a Templar robe and from there it was stolen and ended up in a tent with other artifacts. In the tent, a man removed the box and pocketed it.

From there it resided in a secret location until it appeared to have been passed down from generation to generation to my uncle, who carefully placed it in the vault. The vault that didn't hold all the relics and antiques it did now.

I stepped back from the box, staring it down as my heart pounded a wild beat. Who was the man who took it from the tent?

I shook free of the vision and closed the box with a snap. Then returned to the true purpose for being in the vault. The sword leaned against the wall in an aged leather scabbard that had seen better days. As if it had been forgotten. My heart pumped wildly as I reached for the scabbard and picked it up. I examined the hilt. The handle was wrapped in old, tattered leather. The pommel had the shape of a Celtic triskelion.

I sucked in a sharp breath.

Why hadn't I noticed this before?

Because I hadn't been ready to.

Because every time I was in the vault it was to deposit one of the Holy Relics or, in the last case, retrieve one.

With a shaking hand, I gripped the hilt and slowly pulled it from the scabbard with a soft *shing*. The blade itself took my breath away. It was not like Ophelia's shimmering broadsword but something different. A breathtaking rainbow of colors danced along the steel edges. I gently returned it to the scabbard.

I had no doubt in my mind this was, in fact, Killian's Sword of Light.

It was time to pay Killian a visit.

I closed the vault and left the library. As I rounded the corner, Kincade emerged from his bedroom. As soon as he saw me, he went on high alert. Like he'd been waiting for the sound of my footsteps. I ignored him, though, and pounded down the stairs.

He pounded down the stairs right after me.

"Where do you think you're going?" he asked.

"I need to see Killian."

"Right now?"

"Yes," I said. "It's urgent."

"In your pajamas? You don't even have shoes."

"It doesn't matter."

His gaze flicked over me again—bare legs, bare feet—before his jaw tightened. "Then I'm coming with you."

"I expected you would," I replied.

Out the front door, I headed across the wet lawn. I did my best to ignore the chill running up my legs and dancing along my spine. I did a quick glance at my attire and almost turned around and went back inside to my room to change. Kincade was right—I was still in pajamas which consisted of sleep shorts and a long-sleeved cotton shirt. But I was too far now. It would have to wait and Killian would have to understand my urgency.

I wound my way through the Fae encampment looking for the King of the Fae. A few of the fair folk were just starting to emerge from their slumber with tangled hair and sleep still in their eyes. They didn't hide their shock and surprise at seeing me charge through their camp, barefoot and bare legged holding a sword with Kincade trailing after me.

At last, I came to the final tent in the row. Astrid appeared with a yawn and then immediately stood straight as soon as she saw me, her bright blue eyes wide with curiosity. Her usually plaited hair hung free in thick waves around her face. Her gray-white wings ruffled behind her in a magnificent display.

"Anna?" She eyed the sword in my hand then glanced at Kincade behind me.

I halted in front of her, my legs aching from the pain of walking so far and so fast. My breath came in heavy see-saws as I tried to catch it.

"Hi," I said on a pant. "Killian around?"

"He's in the forest." She nodded toward it with her square jaw.

"I need to see him."

She looked me up and down, pausing on my legs and feet. "Right now?"

I huffed. "Yes. It's urgent."

"Would you...like some shoes first? I wouldn't recommend walking barefoot in the forest."

"There's no time for that," I said, waving away her concern.

She grinned. "I can take care of that for you."

Astrid was more powerful than I gave her credit. With a wave of her hand, she created a pair of sneakers on my bare feet. I glanced down, wiggling my toes. The shoes certainly felt real enough. She waved for me to follow her.

I fell in step beside her. Kincade continued to trail behind us.

"What's this about anyway?" She once again eyed the sword in my hands.

"It's about something important," I said.

Astrid halted, putting a hand on my arm. Hope bloomed in her pretty face. The kind of hope she'd learned not to trust. "Did you find it?" She nodded to the sword.

"I need to see Killian," I insisted.

She paused a brief moment before resuming her walk, picking up speed a little. Perhaps sensing the urgency in my voice or perhaps guessing correctly that I had, in fact, found the Sword of Light.

We entered the edge of the forest. Deep shadows pressed all around. Here, the temperature was cooler than outside. Faint shafts of light slashed through the treetops but it was still fairly dark beneath the canopy.

Astrid fashioned a lantern out of air and led us down the makeshift path. It had been some time since I had visited the forest. The Fae had made excellent progress with building their new homes in the trees. Already, there were footbridges and ropes leading up to the tops. One tree had a magnificent staircase carved into the trunk winding around and up higher and higher until it disappeared inside what appeared to be a small house. Not unlike the Fae forest they lived in before Lucifer destroyed it.

I was impressed.

"There he is." Astrid pointed ahead.

Killian was working with a few other Fae chopping wood. Sweat dampened his tunic. As we neared, he looked as though he hadn't slept in weeks. His brow was damp and his hair was plastered against his head making it obvious he had been working a while. The others were also tired and sweaty.

When he caught sight of us approaching, he halted working. Those mesmerizing eyes of his lit up upon seeing Astrid and then turned to curiosity when he saw me and Kincade. He said something to the others then walked away and met us.

"Anna, what a surprise."

"Killian, wow. You've done an amazing job here." I indicated the progress above us in the forest.

His gaze narrowed as he eyed my odd attire and the sword in my hands. "Yes, we've been working day and night to get something habitable. To what do I owe the pleasure?"

I took a deep breath, expelled it. "I have something for you."

I took a step closer to him and extended the sword. He stared at it a long, silent moment before reaching for it.

"What is this?"

"I want to say the obvious—a sword—but then that seems a little sarcastic," I said.

He held the scabbard up into the light and his eyes instantly went wide. His breath caught, sharp and disbelieving. He stared at it for a long moment, then his kaleidoscope gaze met mine full of wonder, excitement, and confusion. He wrapped his hand around the hilt, then gently pulled it from the scabbard. The light exploded all around us in that rainbow of color, much brighter than what I experienced in the vault. Astrid gasped. The others approached us, pausing behind Killian.

"I...I cannot believe it." He tore his gaze away from the brilliance and looked at me. "Where? How?"

"I wish I could take credit for finding it, but I can't. My uncle did. I don't know when or how or where. It was in his vault. Under my nose all this time," I said.

"How did you know it was there?" Astrid asked. She gazed in wonder at the sword.

"I didn't," I said. "But I saw it when I was in the vault weeks ago. I'm not sure what made me look at it closer this morning. It was almost as if I had an epiphany."

"You have returned Prince Nuada's sword to me, the ancient sword of my people. The Sword of Light." He returned it to the scabbard. "I do not know how to thank you for this."

"Well, I have an idea, if you're interested." I flashed a smile.

"Name it," he said.

"In a few days, I'll face Lucifer on the battlefield. His army against mine," I began. "I don't have much of an army yet and I have no idea how many Lucifer has. I suspect his numbers will be greater than mine. I understand if you don't want any part of it. Especially after all the horrendous things Lucifer did to you and your people."

"We will join you in this fight. I will lead the Fae as their king," he said without hesitation. Not a trace of fear—only resolve. He patted the sword and gave me a rare smile.

I was hopeful he'd accept but stunned all the same. "Are you sure?"

"It would be my honor to fight alongside you," he said.

"And me, too," Astrid added.

And that reminded me. I should probably tell her I offed her half-brother but now didn't seem like the right time.

"Thank you, both. It means a lot to me that you'll fight with me."

"How could I say no after all you've done for me and my people?" he said. "All I need to know is where and when this will take place."

I shifted from one foot to the other. I slept for so long, I'd lost track of the days.

"In four days," Kincade said. "I'm leading the war council. We'll meet this evening in the library."

Stunned, I looked up at Kincade. He'd already stepped into the role I was still learning how to wear. But he refused to meet my gaze. Which somehow felt worse than anger.

"Astrid and I will be there," Killian said.

"Good. See you then," Kincade said.

Kincade headed back the way we'd come, leaving me looking awkward and dumb. I flashed a smile.

"Okay, see you then. Bye!"

I trotted after him, a little out of breath as I caught up to his long strides. "You could have warned me, you know."

"It's clear you need help. And you need someone to help make these decisions," he said, his eyes forward. He refused to look at me.

"So, you appointed yourself in charge of my war council. I've never had a war council before."

"I've never led a war council before." One corner of his mouth lifted in a half-grin.

"I appreciate it," I said and meant it.

He shifted his eyes down to me. "I understand there's trouble in paradise with your parents."

I flushed, heat burning my cheeks. "Yeah. That's my fault."

"What'd you do now?"

I flashed him a heated look, but he was smiling. I relaxed. "Nothing."

"Lie. Now spill your guts."

I didn't want to tell him the ugly truth I'd exposed between my parents, but who else was I going to tell? Kincade was the only person on the planet I trusted fully and completely.

"I might have exposed Sariel's true intentions."

His brows drew together in question. "What does that mean?"

"I suspected he showed up in my mother's life for a very specific reason. Me." I thumbed at my chest. "He knew the prophecy of the Keeper of Holy Relics and the One Who Was Promised and he exploited it."

"You think he—"

"Yes. Like Azriel tried with me," I said. A sick feeling crept into my stomach. "The worst part is he didn't deny it."

That hurt more than any excuse would have.

"Fuck, Anna. I'm sorry."

"Meh." I waved away his sympathy and shrugged it off, as though it were all situation normal. "It's fine. It made me who I am. I've accepted that and my destiny."

I should tell him now. Tell him exactly how I felt about him while I was in a sharing mood. But somehow, I was unable to form the words. I didn't know *how* to tell him. Anything mushy I managed to say would sound insincere. I wasn't mushy. Neither was he. I wanted it to come from the heart and *not* be mushy. I wanted him to know I meant it.

And that scared me more than any battlefield.

So, instead, I said, "Four days, huh?"

"You slept away most of the allotted week."

We exited the forest and headed across the lawn. The cool breeze tickled my exposed arms and legs. "Sorry. I was tired. Who's on this war council anyway?"

"You, me, Killian, Astrid, Cashiel, your parents."

"Super. This should be a fun time tonight, then."

"I can't wait," he said, deadpan.

Yeah. Me, too.

CHAPTER 39

As we approached the manor, Piers waited at the door for us, impatience on his face. He adjusted his cuffs—sharp, precise, irritated. Whenever I saw Piers with that look, it was a sign something was about to go down. It was also a sign someone was waiting for me in the parlor. I heaved a sigh.

"What's wrong?" Kincade asked.

"There's someone in the parlor waiting to see me."

"How do you know?"

"Because Piers." I nodded in his direction.

Kincade's mouth twitched like he approved of my logic. He stepped behind me allowing me to go first. Such a gentleman. His hand hovered near my back—not touching, just there.

"My lady," he greeted with a bow of his head.

"What's up, Piers?" My repeated attempts to get him to stop calling me *my lady* fell on deaf ears.

"You have visitors in the parlor."

I cut Kincade a glance. "Told ya." Then to Piers, I said, "Who is it this time?"

"I believe he said his name was Alaric Dawson."

"Oh, good. Another cousin." I headed for the parlor but Piers cleared his throat loudly. I gave him a questioning look. "What?"

"Perhaps your attire..." He waved his hand up and down at my pajamas and funky shoes Astrid created for me.

Heat crawled up my neck. Damn it.

"Oh, right. Maybe I should get dressed."

Piers nodded. "I will let him know you'll be delayed."

I headed for the stairs, but Kincade remained behind. "You're not following me?"

"I'll be right here." He pointed to the floor.

Which was his version of, *I'm not leaving you alone with a stranger who shares your blood.* I didn't seem to have good luck with cousins.

In my room, I kicked off the shoes. I decided I didn't have time for a shower and prayed I didn't smell. I pulled on clean clothes. My signature Henley, cargo pants, and pink combat boots. I managed to run a brush through my tangled hair and pulled it into a high ponytail. I splashed cold water on my face and then examined it in the mirror.

I still had the deep circles under my eyes and basically looked a fright. But I would have to do, and this Alaric person would have to take me as I was. I hurried back down the stairs. True to his word, Kincade was where I left him. He followed me into the parlor.

Kincade didn't touch me. He didn't have to. His presence was its own kind of contact.

Alaric Dawson was tall with a slender but muscular frame and classic features like all the rest of the Walker family. Hazel eyes peered at me with interest as I entered the room, then examined the hulking bear of a man behind me. If I recalled my family tree correctly, Alaric was Isobel's brother and Matilda's son.

"Hello, Anna. Alaric Dawson," he greeted, extending his hand. His accent was that of a perfect and proper Brit.

"Nice to meet you. This is Kincade."

Alaric shook his hand to be polite but I noticed neither of them enjoyed that little courtesy. Their grips were polite. Their eyes were not.

"The tents on your lawn—"

"Temporary guests," I interrupted. I was unwilling to elaborate. "What can I do for you?"

Before he had the chance to answer, Piers wheeled in the cart. Instead of tea and lemon cakes, he had an offering of coffee and toast with a side of bacon. God bless Piers. My stomach rumbled at the sight of the food.

Piers poured a cup of coffee, added cream, stirred, and handed me the cup. He turned to Alaric.

"Coffee, sir?"

"No, thank you."

"Anything else?" Piers asked me.

I wondered why he was lingering in the parlor. Piers didn't hover. He supervised. Usually, he wheeled in the cart and then disappeared.

"We're good. Thanks."

He gave a nod and exited, closing the doors behind him.

"I believe it's rather what I can do for you," Alaric said when he was gone.

I sipped the coffee. "And what is that?"

I waved him to a nearby chair. I swiped a piece of bacon and took the chair opposite him. Kincade continued to stand near the door with his arms crossed over his chest looking like a bouncer. I really loved that man.

"First, might I ask you if you've heard of me?"

That was a weird question. "Only through the family tree."

"I teach theology at Lancashire University."

He said it with such pride it was clear he expected some sort of reaction from me. When I offered none, his gaze flickered from me to Kincade and back again.

"Doesn't that mean anything to you?" he asked.

"Should it?" I retorted.

War didn't care about tenure. I hadn't intended for it to come out so bitchy, but there it was.

He looked taken aback as only a Brit could do. "You are the Keeper of the Holy Relics, aren't you?"

I pressed my lips together in a straight line. "I am. And?"

"I've come to help you search for the Holy Relics."

I stared at him, trying to comprehend what he was saying. Did he think being a professor of theology was going to help me in my quest for the relics? Also, did he think I would have allowed him to help me with the quest for the relics? I had trust issues.

I turned to look at Kincade who had an equally perplexed look on his normally stoic face. Even he looked like he didn't know whether to laugh or shoot him.

I rose and went back to the cart where I took a piece of wheat toast. I munched while I considered my next words.

"I'm afraid you're late to the party, pal," I said.

His brows drew together. "But you've only just returned to England to fulfill the prophecy in the family history book."

I almost laughed out loud but managed to maintain it. I took another sip of coffee and returned to my seat.

"Chief, not sure where you've been. I guess Lancashire is a bit sheltered or something, but I've been back in England for months. I've searched for and acquired several of the Holy Relics. In fact, I'm a bit busy at the moment planning a war so I don't really have time for this conversation. It's a bit of a waste of time." I got to my feet and turned for the door. "Piers will see you out."

He rose to his feet, too, looking exasperated and puzzled. "What do you mean, planning a war?"

I heaved a sigh and turned back to him. "Exactly what I mean. And quite frankly, I'm tired of all you cousins popping up at the most inopportune moments."

He still hadn't wiped the quizzical look off his face. "The others have been here?"

"First, Lexi. She betrayed me and left me for dead on a rooftop in Hong Kong. Then, Isobel. Your sister, if I'm not mistaken. She blamed me for the death of her husband which was not my fault. Then William and Victoria showed up here a few weeks ago demanding I tell them where *their* sister was. Lexi in case you're keeping score. Incidentally, she's dead. So is Isobel. Pretty sure you're the last remaining cousin and, quite frankly, I'm not interested in connecting with you or the others on any level. Now, if you'll excuse me."

"I had no idea," he said softly.

The anger that kept me upright faltered for half a second. Then I shoved it back in place. I almost felt sorry for him. Almost.

"No idea about what?"

"I had no idea Isobel was dead."

Oops. I probably should have softened that blow had I known he wasn't aware of her death.

"Nice going," Kincade muttered.

"How did she die?" he asked.

"We were attacked by demons," I said. "A high lord named Azriel killed her."

I spared him the gory details of Isobel's fiery death from the car bomb. That was the day Azriel kidnapped Kincade. The day everything shifted and my feelings for him took a dramatic turn.

"Where is this Azriel now?" He clenched his fists, no doubt wanting his own revenge.

"Dead," I said. "I killed him."

His throat bobbed as if he'd swallowed a prayer. He nodded.

"I'm sorry about Isobel," I said.

"How did Lexi betray you?" he asked.

My shoulders drooped a little. "That's a *very* long story."

He nodded again, though he clearly didn't understand.

"I'm sorry, Alaric, but I don't see how you could be of any help to me or us," I said. "I *am* quite busy. Kincade and I have a meeting later and I really need to get cleaned up for that."

He was silent a moment as he ruminated over my words. "To plan your war?"

Sheesh, this guy just didn't give up, did he? "Yes."

"Your war against...?"

I stopped myself from rolling my eyes in annoyance.

Are you sure this guy is a cousin? He seems out of it, Kincade said.

I bit the inside of my cheek to keep from smiling.

I was sure. I recognized him from the few photographs I found when he was younger. He was one of my few blood relatives. I figured I had nothing to lose and maybe I'd scare him off if I told him the truth.

"A war against Lucifer."

He stared at me for a long moment, his face impassive. "I see."

"Do you? I'm not sure you do. Listen, I'm not trying to be rude, but I don't really want to stand here all day and discuss...whatever it is we're discussing. Piers will see you out," I said.

Again, I started to leave.

"How many do you have to fight your war?"

I peered up at Kincade who didn't bother to hide his own annoyance. I took a deep breath, trying to maintain my cool.

"Enough."

"Are you sure?"

This guy was starting to get on my nerves. I gulped down the rest of the coffee. "What do you want?"

"I want to help you. I think I can. I, like you, am a dream walker. I have connections across the world with the other dream walker sects."

My uncle had mentioned that once. When we were in Rio de Janeiro, we used the apartment of a fellow dream walker. I was aware of there were others like me.

Should I trust him? I asked Kincade.

Hear him out, he said.

"Allow me to stay and help."

I glanced up at Kincade. "What do you think?"

His face never gave away his thoughts, unlike me. He stepped around me and halted in front of Alaric. The man practically towered over the poor guy. Alaric had to crane his neck to look up at him.

"Call the other sects," Kincade said. "Have them meet us in four days in the Jazeel Valley near Megiddo. And." He paused, leaning down close to his face. "If you betray her, I will hunt you down and kill you myself."

Kincade smiled. It didn't reach his eyes.

Alaric swallowed hard, his throat working. He nodded. "I believe you."

Kincade straightened and then stalked out of the parlor, leaving the door open. I flashed an apologetic grin.

I should've been horrified. Instead, something warm and reckless unfurled in my chest.

"He means it, doesn't he?"

I nodded. "He does."

"Very well, then. I think I'll see myself out. I'll see you in four days."

He passed by me without as much as a goodbye or fare thee well. I watched him depart the parlor and wondered if he would make good on his promise to bring the other sects of the dream walkers. I had my doubts.

But if he lied, Kincade would know. And so would I.

Before leaving the parlor, I refilled my coffee and snagged more bacon. Then headed to the dining room where I hoped I'd find a full breakfast. Much to my happiness, there was. Scrambled eggs, pancakes, more bacon, toast, hashbrowns. The smell alone made my knees go soft. I grabbed a plate from the server and started filling it, my stomach still rumbling with hunger.

Grace entered the dining room from the kitchen.

"I helped Piers make all your favorites. I thought you might be hungry."

"Grace, you're the best."

I sat at the table and tried hard not to shovel food into my mouth. Despite my midnight snack of soup, I was hungry again. Sleeping for several days straight, though, had depleted all my energy and resources. Plus, I was trying to heal from the Hell blade.

My mother entered, then, her gaze landing on me. In her left hand, she held a suitcase. The wheels made the quietest scrape on the floor—loud as a gunshot. I stopped eating and gaped.

"I'm leaving," she announced.

I shot up from the table so fast, my chair scraped backward on the wood floor. "What do you mean you're leaving?"

"I don't belong here. And he won't leave, so I am."

"Wait." I hurried around the table. "You *do* belong here. This is your home. It's always been your home. And will continue to be your home."

"Anna..." She said my name on a sigh. "I wish I could stay but I can't. I have to leave."

"I don't understand. Why?"

Unhappiness creased her face. "My whole life has been a lie."

I reached for her, took her free hand, held it, and met her gaze. "I understand, probably more than anyone, how that feels."

Understanding came into her eyes. "I suppose you do. But it doesn't mean I have to stay here with him."

"Then I'll send him away." I dropped her hand and started for the door.

"But he's your father and—"

I spun aback around to face her. "So? You're my mother—a *Walker*. You belong here with me. If you don't want to see him anymore, I'll banish him from this house."

Somewhere in the hall, a floorboard creaked. Like the manor itself had opinions.

"May I say something?" Her voice didn't shake. But her hands did, slightly.

We'd both forgotten Grace was still in the room.

"Yes, of course," my mother said.

"I'm not sure what happened between the two of you or even the three of you. Quite frankly, it's none of my business. What I do know, though, is Sariel loves you both very much. He would do anything for Anna. Even leave if that's what she wished." Grace walked around the end of the table and halted in front of my mother. "I don't understand a lot of what's going on. But I do understand how he looks at you, Natasha. There is a deep love there. And I may not know all the heavenly rules, but I know love when it's sitting right in front of me."

Grace said no more as she exited the room.

"She's right," I said. "I never should have said anything."

"Everything he did with me—with you—was to get us to this point," she said.

"Yes, and now I have to face it."

She dropped her suitcase. "Then I can't leave you to face it alone."

I wanted to point out I wouldn't be alone. I had Kincade, Ophelia, and several others willing to fight and stand with me. I gripped her hands. Plus, her super dream walker powers might come in handy during the battle.

"I want you to stay."

"I'll stay, then." She picked up her suitcase and turned to leave.

I made a mental note to have a discussion with Sariel. I returned to my seat at the table. But it was Sariel who made an appearance then. With a frown, I put down my fork.

"I suppose you want to leave," I said.

"Under the circumstances, I think I should."

"Why didn't you deny it?" I asked.

"Because it was the truth." He ran a hand over his face. "I was assigned as her guardian, the one to keep her safe from those who would harm her. Azriel was one of them."

So, even then that Fallen bastard was after my family.

"I had no intention of falling in love with her. I had no intention of taking her from her family. But then she was pregnant. And suddenly I understood what I'd done without really thinking about it. I created the one person who would be able to defeat Lucifer. You."

"I think she also had something to do with it," I pointed out.

"You were right. In a way, I helped orchestrate every facet of her life and yours. I suppose that's why I was compelled to help you find the Holy Relics."

"Guilt is a powerful emotion," I said.

"Indeed." He gave me a nod of farewell and then he was gone.

The air felt colder where he'd stood.

CHAPTER 40

AFTER I FINISHED EATING, I headed upstairs to shower. I still had the bandage on my side from where I was stabbed with the Hell blade. With a gentle hand, I peeled it off and was shocked to see it was completely healed. New pink skin remained. It was still tender to the touch, but I was glad to see I didn't need to cover it with a bandage again. That meant Sariel's magic didn't just burn the poison out of me—he'd knit me back together.

Standing under the hot shower was heaven. I scrubbed my scalp and skin and stepped out with dewy, rosy skin. For the first time in months, I didn't have to worry Azriel would pop in on me while I was trying to dress.

It made me happy to think Azriel was dead and gone.

For the first time in months, the bathroom door was just a door. No shadows. No cinnamon. No wolf grin.

I dressed in my usual attire and then went in search of Kiara and Bridget. After searching the entire manor, I headed outside and found Kiara doing target practice with her bow and arrows.

Bridget stood beside her cheering her on. Kiara nocked an arrow, then released it. She hit the bullseye with ease.

"You're getting better!"

Bridget laughed when Kiara gave her a narrowed look of disdain.

"I can hit the bullseye with my eyes closed," Kiara said.

"Oh, yeah? Let's see you do it then."

I paused, waiting, and watching. Kiara nocked another arrow, pulled it back, closed her eyes, and fired. The arrow landed nestled against the other one in the center of the bullseye.

"Told you," Kiara said.

"Show off." Bridget caught sight of me, then, and waved me over. "Hi, Anna!"

I headed over. "Nice shooting."

"Trying to keep my skills up," she said with a smile.

Bridget trotted out to the archery stand and retrieved the silver arrows. She jogged back and handed them to Kiara.

"I wanted to talk to you both about—"

"The Order," Bridget said with a nod. "We know."

"Oh." I snapped my mouth shut.

"I already talked to my father," Kiara said. "The clans are willing and ready to back you."

I was dumfounded as a new and unexpected warmth surged through me. "How did you know?"

"Ophelia told us everything," Bridget said. "That you killed a high lord. That must have been something to see."

"I suppose..." I gaped at them, speechless.

"I talked to my father, too," Bridget said. "The MacKeller clans are ready to fight with you."

"I...don't know what to say."

Kiara turned back to the archery stand. She nocked an arrow. "Not much to say, really. We're doing what we need to do." She let the arrow fly. It landed in the center. "Help you save mankind. Right?"

I was touched. It was true I hadn't trusted these two at first. Kiara wanted to murder me, after all, but I was thankful they both called their clans and decided to fight alongside me.

"Thank you."

"They'll meet us there in the valley," Kiara said as she nocked yet another arrow.

"You're going to make your fingers bleed if you keep at it," Bridget chastised.

"I need all the practice I can get if we're going to face the devil and his army." She released the arrow. Again, it hit its mark.

"Come to the war council tonight," I blurted.

That got both of their attentions.

"War council?" Bridget tucked a wayward lock of hair behind her ear.

"Kincade's idea." I gave them a weak smile. "In the library. After dinner."

"We'll be there," Kiara said with a nod. "By the way, we heard about the thing you did for the Fae king."

News in this joint traveled fast. "You did?"

"Bridget's nosey."

Bridget flushed, her cheeks turning bright red. "I'm not."

"You are. Don't deny it."

I admired the way they ribbed each other as if they were more than friends. Almost as if they were sisters. And maybe in a way they were. We all had a common enemy and a common purpose. They knew, as I did, it would come to war with Lucifer.

"*Anyway*, it was pretty awesome. Heard they're going to fight with us," Kiara said.

"They are."

She nocked another arrow and released it. I was fascinated by the way she hit the target every single time with an effortless ease.

"Cool. Never fought with the Fae before."

"I don't think anyone has," I pointed out. "See you this evening."

I started to go when Kiara said, "Oh, hey, Anna. About me wanting to kill you before. You know, for Ronan."

I paused, tipped my head to the side in question. "Yeah?"

"Sorry about that. I was just mad and hurt and was looking for someone to take it out on. No hard feelings, eh?"

I grinned. "No hard feelings. You're still alive. So I'd say we're good."

"Good. Glad we cleared the air." She let another arrow fly.

I was, too. I gave them a wave and headed back inside.

* * *

That evening, after dinner, we gathered in the library for this war council Kincade insisted on having. I was the first to arrive, then Kincade. Minutes later, my mother. It was hard not to notice how sad she looked.

Kincade poured two glasses of whiskey and handed one to me. His fingers brushed mine on the pass—barely there. Enough to feel. "Where's Sariel?"

I sipped. "He left."

Surprise flickered over his face. His jaw tightened, like he'd swallowed whatever he wanted to say. "Left?"

"It was either him or my mother and she belongs here." The words tasted like ash, but they were true.

He downed his drink, then refilled. He didn't ask follow-up questions. He was smart enough to figure out the dynamics without me having to tell him.

Astrid and Killian arrived next, followed quickly by Bridget and Kiara. Kincade shot me a questioning look.

I asked them to come, I said.

Ophelia and Darius arrived Ophelia beaming her happiness that Darius was back in the manor house. The last to arrive was Cashiel in typical angel fashion.

Chairs scraped. Wings rustled. The library filled the way storms do—slow, then all at once.

"Let's get started," Kincade said. "Cashiel, what do you know about the Jezreel Valley?"

"A broad fertile plain in northern Israel," Cashiel said. "The Valley of Megiddo—Jezreel. Farms, grazing land, Mount Gilboa on the east, Megiddo National Park on the northwest." His gaze lifted. "And yes…tradition calls it the place where good and evil settle their accounts."

Silence descended in the room. I understood this was why Lucifer picked this location. He was fulfilling his end of the prophecy. Cashiel walked to one of the bookcases and pulled out a large book. He placed it on the desk, flipped it open and paused at a two-page spread with a map.

We leaned in like the paper could tell us how to live.

"Megiddo National Park is here," he pointed to the map, then glanced up. He waved everyone closer. "And here is Mount Gilboa. This is the valley." He swiped his finger across the page from one end to the other.

"Lucifer wants to use the mountains as cover, perhaps?" Kincade asked.

"Perhaps," Cashiel said with a nod. "My suggestion is we form up here in the national park."

"And meet him in the middle?" I asked.

"Yes," Cashiel said.

"Like ancient warfare," Killian said. "What are we fighting with? Swords?"

"And bow and arrows," Kiara said.

"And the Holy Relics, though I'm not sure what good the Holy Grail will do," I added.

"We bring them all," Cashiel said.

"Gabriel has the horn," I said.

All eyes landed on me. Kincade's, specifically, glared. The glass in his hand creaked—too much pressure, not enough patience.

"What do you mean, Gabriel has the horn?"

"Joachim came to me and demanded it," I said. "I gave it to him for information about where the Brotherhood was holding you."

"If Joachim retrieved the horn and returned it to Gabriel..." Cashiel's voice trailed off.

"The End of Days," Natasha said, her voice quiet. Her worried gaze pierced me.

The words landed and didn't bounce.

"Yes," I agreed. "That's why we have to be ready."

"But we don't know what Lucifer's numbers are," Kincade pointed out.

"We don't know what *our* number are, either," I said. I turned to Kiara. "How many in your clans?"

"Several thousand willing to fight," Kiara said. She gave Bridget a questioning glance who nodded agreement.

"Your best guess," I said.

"Three thousand between us," she said.

"What about Alexander Harred?" I asked Cashiel. "We didn't exactly part on good terms."

Before he could answer, Kiara said, "He has to answer the call. He swore an oath to the Order of the Holy Relics."

"So did the Brotherhood of Watchers but I have my doubts they'll show up," I said.

"Let me handle that," Kincade said.

The way he said it made my skin prickle. Like he already knew who to call. Perhaps he intended to contact Silas to try and recruit those who were on the outs with the Brotherhood.

Cashiel said, "Anna is right. Alexander swore an oath but that doesn't mean he'll honor it. He's not exactly a fan of us these days."

"You've seen our numbers. There are not many who can fight. The women and children will remain here," he said.

"Yes, of course."

"But I would estimate close to a thousand."

Four thousand. I didn't think that would be enough to defeat Lucifer and his demon army.

"What about the warrior angels?" I asked Darius.

"You have our swords, Keeper," Darius said. "At least three thousand."

Seven thousand. My mind ticked the numbers like prayer beads. Still not enough.

"And the Seraphim?"

"They will fight," Cashiel said. "But I have no way to know what their strength is."

"Then I guess we hope for the best, don't we? What's our plan? Aside from standing in the middle of the valley trying to kill each other."

"The Holy Relics will be an integral part," Cashiel said. "At least, that's what my gut tells me."

He sounded like Cashiel. Like my uncle. Like a man who'd already decided we'd survive. Especially with the expanse of white wings behind him. Even as an angel, he was still taking charge and making it look easy.

"But we don't know how to use them," I pointed out.

"Not yet," Kincade said.

I looked at Kincade. "You were there when you took down Ezra. How did he use them?"

"He used the Spear of Destiny to kill and control," he said.

I thought of the Ark still hiding in that cave under the Old City. How, exactly, did the Ark play into all of this? I hadn't a clue.

"I need to do more research on the location," Cashiel said. "Perhaps we should reconvene tomorrow after luncheon."

I yawned. "That works for me."

"Nothing has been planned," Kincade said, his irritation evident.

"It will be impossible to plan anything against an opponent like Lucifer," Cashiel said. "But I have some ideas."

"Good. Then we start again tomorrow," I said.

We dispersed as a group from the library, leaving Cashiel behind. Exhaustion hit me. I wasn't fully recovered from the Hell blade. I bid everyone goodnight and headed to my room. I didn't see Kincade follow me. But I felt him, somewhere in the hall—like a guard who refused to clock out.

Closing the door behind me, I kicked off my shoes, fell into bed and was immediately asleep.

CHAPTER 41

THREE DAYS OF PLANNING later, we called it "ready." I wasn't sure anything could prepare me for what waited in that valley. In reality, I wasn't sure anything fully prepared me for the war that was to come. I communicated with the clans of the Order of Holy Relics our plans. Kiara and Bridget also relayed the information to their fathers. We were as ready as we would ever be.

The day before we were to meet Lucifer on the battlefield, we planned to transport to the battlefield. There, Astrid agreed to set up a camp with her powers now that she was back to full strength. The Fae and the angels would transport us to the site a few at a time. The rest planned to travel and meet us there.

Late in the day, I sat on the edge of my bed and took a long look around, memorizing the place the way my childhood bedroom looked. Piers insisted I move into the newly renovated and now completed master suite, but I put him off. I told him I would when I returned. I didn't expect to return.

He and Grace were the only ones we were leaving behind. I hated the thought of it, but I needed someone here to manage the manor.

In my hands, I held the paper I'd written expressing my wishes should I not return. The ink had smeared where my fingers kept sweating through the words. And though I was ready, I wasn't. Who would be willing and ready to face death?

A knock on my door.

"Come in."

Kincade stepped inside. "It's time. All the others are there. You and I are the last to go."

I took a deep breath, released it. "I want to see Grace before I leave."

"I assumed. She's waiting for you downstairs."

He left, closing the door behind him.

I lingered a moment, closed my eyes and whispered a little prayer.

Hey, God. I don't know what I'm doing. I don't know how I'm supposed to beat him. If you're listening... I could really use a sign. And please—please—keep my family safe.

I paused and thought about that for a moment. My family. All my life, all I wanted was a family, a sense of belonging. As I sat there on the edge of the bed, the realization came to me in a flash.

The people living in this manor—my mother, Grace, Piers, Ophelia, Darius, and even Kincade—had become my family. They had given me that sense of belonging. They'd given me the family I'd longed for. Even my uncle in his angelic form was part of that. And, yes, Sariel, too, I supposed. Despite his error in judgement, he truly meant no harm. But I was still angry with him.

I was never any good at prayer or speaking to the Most High. I rarely did it. And I doubted he heard me.

I stood, clutching the paper in one hand. I picked up my one duffel in the other. I'd hidden the Staff of Moses, the Spear of Destiny, and the Holy Grail in the cloud for safekeeping. One last glance around at the bookshelves stuffed with books from my childhood and the wardrobe housing my drab attire and an extra pair of pink combat boots.

It was time to go.

I headed down the stairs where Grace waited inside the parlor. Kincade stood at the bottom of the stairs with his usual impassive expression. I handed off my duffel as I passed by him and entered the parlor. She rose when she saw me, that worried look in her eyes.

I hated she looked at me like that. She hugged me, hard, squeezing me tight. When she pulled back, she gave me a weak smile.

"I'd say be careful, but..." Her words trailed off.

"I will." Even though it was a lie, I tried to reassure her. "In the event I don't return—"

"You hush up," she said with such intensity, I blinked. "Don't go borrowing trouble."

I pressed the paper into her hands. "In the event I don't return, this paper outlines exactly what's to be done with the estate."

"Your will?" She glared down at the paper as if she were offended.

"Sort of. Not an official will. I don't know why I didn't think of it sooner. I should have. But hopefully this will help you figure out what to do."

"Me?"

"You're the only one I trust to handle it," I said. "You're my executor."

She sniffed, fighting back tears. "When you return, I plan to rip this to shreds."

I kissed her on the cheek. "Good. I'll see you then."

I flashed her a smile and joined Kincade in the foyer. I read the look on his face. He'd overheard our conversation and knew I liked to put Grace at ease. Something flickered in his eyes—gone before I could name it.

"Killian is waiting for us outside," he said.

"Oh, we're sifting with the Fae king?"

"Would you rather go with Darius?" One brow ticked up. Jealousy—thinly disguised as sarcasm.

"I'd rather not be sick on the eve of battle," I said.

"That's what I thought."

We exited the manor. Killian was on the other side of the drive waiting. I retrieved my duffel from Kincade as we joined him.

"Who goes first?" he asked.

Before I answered, Kincade said, "Anna."

Killian wasted no time as he wrapped an arm around my waist and away we went. Moments later, we were at the edge of the national park. The tree line was behind us. Ahead of us a sea of colorful tents. He disappeared a second later and then returned with Kincade.

"The clan leaders want a meeting," Kincade said.

He sounded so in control and in charge. I kinda loved it. I followed him through the tent city. The Fae and humans were intermingled. Though tomorrow we would be facing Hell, they all seemed to be in good spirits. They were grilling meats, drinking, talking, laughing, playing card games, dice games. As if everything was situation normal. Like laughter could keep Hell from finding us. It was weirdly comforting.

In the heart of tent city was an oversized tent that reminded me of something available as a rental for weddings. It was huge with white sidewalls flapping in the evening breeze. Inside, globe lights went around the perimeter to give it a warm, yellow glow. Near the center, a long wooden table with benches on either side. Several men sat at the table with the map of the valley spread out in front of them. Among them Killian, and my angelic uncle, Cashiel, who seemed to be in charge of the discussion. When he saw us, he waved us over.

"Gentlemen, the Keeper of the Holy Relics," he announced as if I were someone important.

I tried not to roll my eyes. There were several men I didn't know. One I recognized immediately and was shocked to see him—Alexander Harred. He had that look of pinched disgust on his face. Clearly, still angry with me after the death of his son, Ronan. Another was Alaric, which gave me hope he brought more dream walkers with him.

I gave Alaric a nod of greeting. He returned it with a faint smile.

"Anna, this is Colum FitzGerald and Malcolm MacKeller." Kiara's and Bridget's fathers. "I think you know Alexander Harred."

"I do." I gave him a nod of hello. He merely glared at me.

"When we heard the Keeper had arrived in England, we weren't sure it was true or not," Colum said. "Glad to see it is."

"You have the relics?" Malcolm asked.

"I have the Spear of Destiny, the Holy Grail, and the Staff of Moses," I said. "Unfortunately, I had to return the Horn of Gabriel."

"Return the horn to who?" Colum asked.

"To Gabriel," I said, matter-of-factly.

"What about the Ark?" Alexander asked.

"I found it, but it was...unattainable."

Disdain crossed his face as he scoffed. "She was unable to attain it," he said to the others as if I didn't exist. "Who's to say she truly has the other relics?"

"Show some respect," Kincade snapped.

The heat in his voice made my head snap to him. He had genuine anger on his face.

"Show him, Anna, since he doesn't believe you," he said.

I said nothing as I drew down the Spear of Destiny, which was still wrapped in the protective cloth. I placed it on the table in front of me. Next, the Staff of Moses. I handed that off to Kincade. Finally, the Holy Grail, which I placed on the table next to the spear. Alexander stared at the three relics, his face still pinched with anger and annoyance. He folded his arms over his chest and remained silent.

Kincade waved his hand over the relics on the table. "Proof."

Cashiel cleared his throat. "If we may continue now that the curiosity has been satisfied."

Thanks, I said to Kincade.

I'm sick of his shit, he replied.

And I smiled to myself as we all took our seats around the table.

Cashiel marked the map with what looked like chess pieces. "We will convene here, just outside the national park. Lucifer and his forces have been gathering here, as we suspected." He placed a black pawn at the other end near Mount Gilboa. "I understand his army numbers well over a hundred thousand."

No one spoke. Even the lantern light seemed to pause.

My stomach dropped to my shoes. My mouth went bone dry. A sense of hopelessness swept through me. "A hundred thousand? We don't have close to that."

"Alaric, how many dream walkers do you have?" Kincade asked.

"Two thousand," he said.

"We have no cavalry," Cashiel said. "Neither does Lucifer for that matter."

"So, it's to be a war fought entirely on foot," Colum said.

I did a quick mental math of how many we had against Lucifer. It wasn't nearly enough. My stomach churned acid while they continued to talk and plan a war that was impossible to win. I clenched my hand into a fist, holding it in my lap.

Even with the Fae, Astrid and her powers, the clans, the dream walkers, and the warrior angels, I didn't see how we'd win. As I listened to them talk about the plan of attack, all I thought about was how many would die because of me. Faces I could already picture. Names I already knew. How many would fall fighting for me? Did they believe in the cause? Did they believe in me?

"Anna, are you all right?" Cashiel asked.

"Yes," I said but my voice was weak.

It seemed senseless to me to try to plan something that was impossible to plan. Someone continued to talk—my uncle I think—but I wasn't listening.

The words crawled up my throat like bile. "How many will die tomorrow?" I asked, my voice cutting through the others.

Silence fell as they all looked at me, question in their eyes. Even Kincade gave me a sidelong look.

"Unfortunately, we will have casualties," Cashiel said.

"But how many? How can we sit here and plan something that is beyond our control?" Before anyone responded, I rushed on. "We all know what Lucifer and his army is capable of. He wields dark magic. He commands the biggest, most deadly demons and beasts. He can transform into a giant dragon. Our army is no match for theirs."

"You're saying we're doomed to die before we even step foot on the battlefield," Malcolm said.

"Yes, that's exactly what I'm saying," I said. "Because his army far outnumbers ours. We don't even know how many warrior angels will come to help. Or Seraphim for that matter." I gave Cashiel a pointed look. "Do we?"

He shook his head.

"What do you propose then, Anna?" Colum asked.

I thought about that a long, quiet moment as I chewed the inside of my cheek. Kincade's mind poked against mine but I pushed him away because I didn't want him to hear what I was thinking before I said it out loud.

"Lucifer wants me," I said. "He wants to defeat me. To kill me. So, I'll offer myself up as a sacrifice for the greater good."

Kincade went still. The air around him tightened.

"Absolutely *not*," Kincade said. "You'll be ending the war before any of us have a chance to fight."

"And die," I said with a nod. "That's right."

Mostly I was thinking I didn't want my friends to die. Kincade, Ophelia, Astrid, Killian, all of them. Cashiel looked thoughtful instead of outraged like Kincade.

"You are correct, Anna, that his numbers far outweigh ours," Cashiel said. "However, I propose a different plan."

"What is that?" Kincade demanded.

"Perhaps Lucifer will not be expecting Anna to do something so bold."

He pulled out more pawns. White ones this time. Then he placed the white queen in the center of the field between the national park and Gilboa. The map suddenly looked less like a place and more like a graveyard with lanes.

"Anna stands here. Meanwhile, we split our forces. Half stand here behind her, the other half move behind Lucifer."

He split the white pawns and placed them as markers on the map. Four white pawns behind the black ones. He placed the black king opposite the white queen.

"We move this half under cover of darkness," Cashiel said pointing to the ones behind his representation of Lucifer's forces.

"And then what? Anna and Lucifer fight each other in the middle of the field?" Kincade asked. "To what end?"

"Perhaps not fight. Perhaps a distraction. If it comes to it, then I'll fight him one-on-one." My heart quickened. "His high lords, demons and minions will be distracted enough it may give us an advantage. They won't attack without his signal."

"How do you know that?" Malcolm asked.

"I don't. But Lucifer commands them. They do nothing without his orders," I said. "We'd need some sort of signal to attack. Something like..." My voice trailed off as I thought of something suitable.

"Something like perhaps a fiery arrow?" Colum said.

I gave him a lopsided smile. "Or a fiery sword."

My pulse kicked. That was something I understood.

"What if we had Astrid create something flammable near their ranks," Killian said, speaking for the first time. "I have several Fae who are excellent marksmen."

"So is Kiara FitzGerald," I said. Her father's face beamed pride. "Do you think Astrid can produce something like that?"

"She produced explosives for you to destroy Azriel's underground crypt, didn't she?" he said.

"Good point. Make it so, then."

He gave me a nod. Meanwhile, Cashiel was busy drawing a line in pencil on the map. "Then we place that line here. Anna will distract Lucifer and his forces."

"Then we light it up," Kincade added.

We made a few other tweaks to the plan and then dispersed. Kincade followed me out of the tent. I stood in the walkway glancing up and down the area.

"Your tent is over here." He pointed to a large green and white one, then started walking toward it.

I followed him.

"I don't agree with you making yourself a sacrificial lamb." His voice was clipped—too controlled. He wouldn't look at me.

"Isn't that what I am?"

"No, dammit, Anna." The words came out harsher than he probably meant.

"I think we both know what's going to happen tomorrow."

He halted and spun toward me so fast I took a step back. Whatever he'd been holding in finally cracked.

"But you're practically giving yourself to Lucifer on a platter."

"And that's what he wants."

"You're giving up." His jaw flexed, like he was biting back everything else he wanted to say.

"How am I supposed to defeat him? How are *we* supposed to defeat an army ten times our size?"

He raked a hand through his hair. "What do you want me to say, Anna? That the odds are against us? That I know you're going to die no matter what? Don't you think I realize that?"

He gripped my arms, pulling me closer to him. His hands were warm—too real for a man who pretended not to feel. There was fire deep in his eyes. Fire I had never seen before. He lowered his voice to a near whisper.

"I've dreaded this day since the moment we met."

The world narrowed to his voice.

My heart skipped a beat. My breath caught in my throat. I wanted to ask him why, but I knew the answer. I wanted to make him confess his deepest feelings. Hell, I wanted to tell him I was in love with him, that I couldn't imagine life without him. But then, Kincade and I didn't have that type of relationship. We weren't touchy-feely people. It wasn't fair to spill my guts to him on the eve of battle when I was surely going to die.

If I said it now, it would become a goodbye.

"So have I," I said, my voice low.

His gaze searched mine. "Then don't give up so easily."

"I'm not. I'm giving us our best chance."

His hands hovered at my arms, as if he'd forgotten how to let go. For a breath, I thought he might pull me back—might finally say the thing we were both circling.

He didn't.

He dropped his hands. "You should get some rest then." He started to walk away.

"Where are you going?"

"To make sure Astrid can deliver what Killian promised."

I watched the distance expand between us. His shoulders were tight at first, squared like he was bracing for impact—then they sagged, just a fraction, as if the fight had gone out of him.

As if he, too, understood what we were up against. As if he couldn't bear to tell me the truth about his feelings when he also understood what we faced. What I faced.

He and I were so much alike in that respect.

How would I survive the coming war? I didn't see a way for me to. But then, I didn't see a way for me to find the Holy Relics, either.

I stepped inside my tent. There was a low cot on the ground with a sleeping bag and a camp pillow. That was it. I dropped my duffel, then kicked off my shoes. I perched on the edge of the cot, took a deep breath, and then laid down.

Outside, someone laughed. Someone else sang. Like tomorrow didn't exist.

I lay back and stared at the canvas ceiling. Tomorrow, the sky would be wider. And I might never see this one again.

CHAPTER 42

I DIDN'T SLEEP. I stared at the canvas roof over my head for what seemed like hours. Finally, I got up, put my boots on, and stepped out into the night.

The camp was quiet. Only a few low voices drifted to me. Somewhere in the distance, someone was singing. Several campfires were still going as evidenced by the gray-white smoke curling upward into the night sky. I walked through the tents, clutching my elbows as if that would help keep the evening chill at bay. A slight breeze blew, ruffling my long hair.

A few Fae were still awake, sitting outside their tents, smoking pipes, and drinking out of wooden tankards. The sight of it made me think for a moment I had stepped into an alternate dimension or perhaps even back in time. They gave me a nod of greeting and a smile as I passed.

I had no idea where I was headed. Only that sleep refused me—and I refused it right back. I was counting on the adrenaline rush of battle to keep me going. I'd been in enough of battles to expect it. Just not one this big. At the edge of the make-shift tent city, I paused to peer into the darkness and shadows, squinting as if that would help me see more clearly. I saw nothing more than dark shapes of trees and the flat plane of the valley with its patches of agriculture. Somewhere in the distance, a cow mooed. I wondered if Astrid and Killian managed to set the trap behind enemy lines we'd discussed.

Something more than fear gnawed at me. There was a cold knot in the pit of my stomach, tight enough to steal my breath, as I stood there contemplating sending all these people to their deaths. But wasn't it for the greater good? Wasn't it to stop Lucifer and his band of Fallen from killing more guardian angels and stealing human souls? Wasn't it worth it to keep him from ruling all of mankind?

"Couldn't sleep?" Ophelia's voice next to me startled me and I jumped.

I pressed a hand against my racing heart, trying to calm it. "Call your shots."

"Sorry. I didn't mean to scare you."

"I'll recover."

"I've heard what the plan is for tomorrow," she said. "That you're going to face Lucifer alone."

"Yes."

She inhaled a shaky deep breath and then exhaled. "Are you sure about that?"

"Yes," I said again.

"Nothing can change your mind?"

"Not even Kincade."

Her mouth pressed into a thin line. She nodded once.

We stood together there in the darkness, looking out at everything and nothing, in silence. She must have understood the deep conviction I had for what I intended to do, especially if Kincade was unable to change my mind.

Finally, she said, "I understand you're sending half the forces to attack from behind."

"I am."

"Darius said he and his warrior angels volunteered. I'm going with him," she said.

I nodded.

"You're my best friend." Her voice was quiet in the still of the night.

I was touched. A sudden lump formed in my throat. I tried hard to swallow it, but couldn't. "I've never had a best friend before."

"Now you do." She granted me a smile. "You better not die."

I grinned. "I'll do my best not to."

She launched herself at me, hugging me so hard my ribs protested. Hot tears sprang to my eyes. I blinked to keep them at bay, not wanting her to see the emotion there. She pulled back, holding me a moment at arm's length. She had tears in her eyes. Then she spun on her heel and hurried away.

I remained where I was, standing there until the indigo sky began to lighten with the coming dawn. As the sun rose over the horizon, a dark smudge appeared in the sky in the distance. I stood a little straighter as I realized angels headed toward me. A lot of them, too. They landed on the valley led by Sariel, Michael, and Gabriel.

Cashiel appeared beside me in true angel fashion. He looked well pleased as he watched them approach.

"The Seraphim?" I asked.

"Yes, and the archangels. They answered the call."

"I didn't think they'd come."

"You didn't think Sariel would come," he corrected.

I nodded. "That, too."

They halted in front of us. Sariel did his best to avoid my gaze.

I had only seen Michael once and that was in what I perceived as a dream walk. He, like the others, had enormous alabaster wings with gold threaded through them. He'd told me the truth about my ancestor, Ezra, who'd used the Holy Relics as weapons.

Gabriel had dark hair and eyes, a dimpled chin, and a smooth ageless face. I noted he held the silver horn in one hand. The first Holy Relic I had retrieved from Hong Kong. That didn't really seem to bode well.

"Michael," Cashiel said with a nod of greeting.

"We have answered the call for the Keeper of the Holy Relics," he said. His stormy blue gaze landed on me, then. "Did you bring the other relics?"

"I did."

"Let me see them."

I drew down the Spear of Destiny first. I handed it off to Michael. He unwrapped it, discarding the cloth. As if the relic didn't affect him at all, he held it in his hand. Then the Staff of Moses. Sariel took this from me. Finally, the Holy Grail. Cashiel retrieved this one.

That familiar thin veil appeared, surrounding the valley—the air thickening, charged, as if the world itself were holding its breath—the national park, and the mountains. I scented the faint rotten stench on the wind and knew what and who was coming.

"You have fulfilled the prophecy, Keeper of the Holy Relics. Now, it's time to face your final destiny," Michael said.

He pointed to the east where the high lords, demons, and minions gathered. Led by Lucifer dressed all in black. They had appeared as suddenly as the Seraphim.

Kincade joined us then, standing to my left. We exchanged a look but said nothing. His said so much to me in that one glance.

My mother, Natasha, arrived next. Then Killian and Astrid. Darius and Ophelia. A familiar warrior angel was with Darius. Zakiel gave me a nod of hello. I grinned, happy to see he had joined the ranks with the others.

Kiara, Bridget, their fathers, Alexander Harred, and all the clans of the Order. The Fae. I noted the Brotherhood didn't make an appearance. I didn't expect them to.

My cousin, Alaric, and his band of dream walkers he managed to recruit. And, very much to my surprise, my other cousins, William and Victoria. I watched them walk up with the band of dream walkers behind them.

Victoria wore what appeared to be a couture combat fatigues, looking ridiculous and standing out like a sore thumb. War, apparently, was still an aesthetic choice for her. Her hair was in perfect order. Her nails were long, painted pink, and looked as though she'd just had a fresh manicure. I fought the urge to roll my eyes. We eyed each other with faint disdain.

"I brought as many as I could," Alaric said.

"He means *we*," William added, cutting him a glance.

Annoyance flashed over Alaric's face. "*We* brought as many as *we* could. William and Victoria both helped convince the others to fight, though I'm afraid the numbers aren't what we hoped."

"It will be enough," I said, trying to reassure him.

Even though it wasn't, I didn't want to scare them off.

Kincade cleared his throat. "Shouldn't you say something?"

"What do you mean?"

"I believe he means something inspirational, dearie," Cashiel said. "To rally the troops. *Your troops*."

A speech? I was so not good at speeches. I took several steps forward, then turned to face them all. Kincade gave me a nod of encouragement. I met everyone's gaze one by one, thinking of all they had sacrificed to be here. To fight for me. For mankind.

I cleared my throat.

"All of you have come here today as warriors to fight against the darkness. You fight for the right to live in peace. I am here among you to fight with you. Resolved to live or die with you. To fight for all those who cannot fight for themselves. For all that matters *most* in this world."

My hands trembled—not with fear, but with the weight of it. In a dramatic fashion, I drew down the flaming sword, then held it aloft.

"Let's give these hellions a hell of their own."

Cheers went up. Kincade smirked. Cashiel looked pleased. I hurried to Darius and Ophelia.

"Take your forces to the other side," I said. "With as much stealth as you can."

"Most of them are already there, Keeper," Darius said. "Awaiting your signal to attack."

My heart flew to my throat as I nodded. "Good."

"It is time, Keeper," Michael said.

Then Gabriel put the horn to his lips and blew.

The deep timber of the horn echoed across the flat land of the valley. I drew down the dagger and handed it off to Kincade as I passed by him. He grabbed my arm, turned me to face him—and for a heartbeat, he hesitated.

Our eyes met and my heart pounded with a sudden intensity. We stared at each for six heartbeats—I counted—and then he kissed me. Hard and fast. His lips damp and soft. His sandalwood smell wafting over me, giving me comfort and courage. It stole my breath and left me wanting more when he pulled away, leaving my mouth burning with fire. And then he gave me that lopsided grin I loved so much.

"Don't die. That's an order."

I grinned. "Yes, sir."

He released me. I started walking toward the middle of the field. Lucifer stood his ground in front of his horde of darkness. When he realized I was alone, he walked toward me. I noticed then he wore a long black trench coat. It flapped in the wind behind him making him look dramatic and terrifying. Only I wasn't terrified of him. Not anymore.

We met in the center of the valley, pausing a few feet from each other. Lucifer had dangerous good looks. His black wavy hair brushed his shoulders. His bright blue eyes peered at me with something akin to amusement.

"Hello, girl," he said mildly—like we were meeting for drinks, not war. "I assume you wanted to speak to me directly?"

"I have a proposition for you," I said. I was proud my voice didn't waver one bit.

"And what is that?"

"It's me you want, isn't it? I'm the only one standing in your way of getting what you want."

His gaze cut to the army of warriors behind me, then returned to me. "More or less."

"Then fight me." I clutched the flaming sword in two hands. "Fight me one on one."

He stood there a long moment staring at me as if I'd lost my mind. Perhaps I had. I was trying to buy time until I signaled the flaming arrows. Kiara and the Fae archers were waiting for that.

Then he laughed. "Fight you one on one? Whyever would I do that, girl?"

"Because you want me dead."

His expression turned dark. "You don't know what I want."

"Azriel told me once you wanted redemption."

His smile turned deadly. "It's the beginning. Once you're dead and I have the relics, then all I need is the Ark to conquer all that remains."

"Good luck with that."

Joke was on him. He was unable to see the Ark which likely meant he was unable to retrieve it.

In the distance behind me, Gabriel blew his horn again. This time three blasts in succession. Once the sound of the horn faded, movement to the west caught my eye. A rider on a pale horse came into view. The ground seemed to recoil beneath him. He held a menacing scythe. Behind him, a demon horde and beasts I had never seen before.

Death. The last of the Four Horseman.

I was ready to give the attack signal—lighting the sword. Then they would know to release their fiery arrows. But something in the sky caught my eye. A slash of light beaming down as though it were a sunbeam through clouds. Only there were no clouds. I stared at it so hard, Lucifer finally turned to see what had my attention.

The two of us watched as the light descended and then formed into four angels carrying an object between them.

It was the Ark of the Covenant.

They placed it on a hill to the south of us. The four angels stood as though guardians at each corner. I recognized one of them—the one from the cave who told me not to touch it.

Lucifer spun back to me with fury pinched on his face. "You *lied* about finding the Ark. You *bitch*."

"I lied."

With a smug smile, I lit the sword.

CHAPTER 43

I HELD THE SWORD aloft. Lucifer charged me. I immediately called up the Godlight. It burned through my chest, searing, familiar, already asking for more than I wanted to give. It punched into him, sending him flying back several feet. He hit the ground, slid, and came to a halt. When he got back to his feet, fury pinched his face.

Overhead, an arc of flaming arrows sailed across the sky. Even Lucifer paused to look up at them, watching in horror as they landed on the ground. Fire exploded in a spectacular display, torching not only the ground, but most of his forces. He howled with his frustration.

"Attack!" he shouted.

The fighters behind me surged forward, running past me to engage the dark army. Ahead, Darius and his warrior angels plowed through what was left of the forces behind him. More demons and minions appeared from the west, charging in to defend their lord master.

Lucifer produced a black blade in one hand. I was ready for him, though. Our weapons clashed, my flaming sword against his. With his free hand, he reached for me, fisting the collar of my shirt. He dragged me toward him, his face inches from mine. His breath was hot, sulfur-tainted.

"I will enjoy killing you."

But he'd forgotten I had lightning in my fingers. I called it up, then pressed my flickering hand against his chest. He screamed and stumbled backward. His shirt smoked. He tripped over his fancy overcoat. Angry, he ripped it off, throwing it to the ground.

Then he shouted, "Kill them all! Leave no survivors!"

More and more minions and demons and high lords converged in the valley. We were far outnumbered, even with taking out a significant chunk of his men. I charged toward Lucifer. We fought, blade to blade, until my arms ached. Much like when I fought Azriel. Only this time, I wasn't stabbed with a Hell blade.

I sensed a presence behind me and spun in time to see a demon charging toward me. Before I had a chance to take it out, it fell dead. I had Natasha to thank for that. She used her super dream walking powers to destroy the demon.

I'd lost sight of Lucifer. Scanning the battlefield, I found him scampering toward the Ark on the hill. I snuffed the blade and ran after him but he'd put a lot of distance between us while I was distracted by the demon.

Another demon tackled me, shoving me to the ground. The sword fell from my hand. I lifted my head in time to see a familiar face—one I'd hoped never to see again. Ben, the man I once loved, the man whose soul Azriel stole when he murdered him. Now he was a demon with one hand—courtesy of my uncle when he chopped it off.

"Ben, stop!"

I dove for the sword as he came at me again, nothing but hate creasing his face.

"Ben!" I pointed the sword at him, inches from his face.

He stopped. We stared at each other. I realized he was not the same Ben I remembered, not the same Ben I loved. That seemed forever ago. He still had the same depthless blue eyes, the same dark wavy hair, the same menacing scar across his throat.

"You know who I am," I said.

"I do not!"

He charged again. I swung the sword, connecting with his upper torso. I slashed through his shirt, making him bleed black blood. Then Kincade was there, stabbing him in the side and turning him to ash.

I stared long and hard at what was left of him before he fluttered away on the wind. Ben was truly gone. And there was no relief in that. Only finality.

Kincade was in my face, saying something but I ignored him. Finally, he grabbed me by the shoulders and gave me a little shake.

"Anna! Lucifer is heading to the Ark."

"Fuck. I have to stop him!"

I shook free of Kincade's grasp and broke into a run. He was beside me the entire time, keeping pace and fighting and killing demons along the way. Gun in one hand. Dagger in the other. One demon charged me. He fired his high-pitched demon gun just as the thing was within inches of me. It exploded, covering me in demon guts. I gave him a sidelong glare. This was not the first time this had happened to me. Kincade was great at killing demons close enough to cover me in their filth. I smelled like a sewer now. Again. Kincade's signature move—heroic rescue with a side of demon guts.

"Just like old times," I panted.

"Couldn't be helped," he said.

Lucifer scurried up the hill, getting closer to the Ark. Suddenly, he lost his footing and tumbled to the ground. His face was contorted in terrible pain. I halted to scan the battlefield. There was my mother, using her dream walker powers on him. But it was short-lived—her concentration shattered as a minion attacked, stabbing her in the side. She cried out, spun, and backhanded the thing, sending it flying.

"My mother!"

"I'll take care of it."

Kincade darted toward her to help her. Meanwhile, Lucifer started up the mountain again. This time, an arrow found its way into his shoulder. Again, he cried out, halted his progress, and looked back.

Kiara was in the middle of the melee firing arrows as fast as she could nock them in her bow. Bridget was killing demons alongside her friend. Killian wielded his Sword of Light as he cut down demon and high lord alike. I was unable to locate Astrid in the constant motion of the battle.

In his furor, Lucifer leapt from the side of the hill. As he flew through the air, he transformed from human to dragon. The same dragon I'd see before. He was huge, with his giant leathery black wings expanding the distance around him.

Get to the Ark. We'll take care of him. Kincade's voice boomed in my head, spurring me into action.

I snuffed out the sword and started to run. But the sword was so heavy, it weighed me down. My arms and legs burned from the exertion. At the same time, I was afraid to put the sword away as I hacked my way through demons and minions, black blood spurting all over me with every death. I choked on the rancid smell of death and rot as it permeated the air around me.

When I made it to the base of the hill, I put away the sword and started to climb. My breath see-sawed in and out of me. The sound of my own panting wasn't enough to drown out the horrible sounds of war and killing behind me. A roar reverberated the ground. I didn't have to see Lucifer to know it was him.

I clawed my way up the side of the hill breaking every nail I had left and wedging dirt under them. As I took a step, though, something grabbed my ankle. Below me, a minion with his clawed hand wrapped around my ankle. He showed off a mouthful of wicked teeth. I kicked at him with my free foot, trying to dislodge him but he held fast. I didn't have the dagger at my side and the sword would be too unwieldy to draw down from the cloud.

The minion bowed back and screeched. An arrow poked out of its back. It fell to the ground. I glanced to see Kiara lower the bow. I gave her a nod of thanks, then continued to scramble up the side of the hill.

Lucifer flew so low over me, the breeze from his wings ruffled my unbound hair. I glanced up in time to see him bank, turn and head for the Ark. The four angels protecting it suddenly lit up as if they were a beacon. The light between them converged and covered the Ark, almost as if they raised some sort of shield to keep him from grabbing the Ark in his massive claws.

He wasn't interested in the Ark yet. First, he wanted to destroy the angels. He swiped one with his massive back claw, kicking her off the mountain. She tumbled away, likely to her death, breaking the connection with the other three. The light dimmed. Then he went after another one.

I cursed under my breath and climbed to my feet. I drew down the sword and lit it, but trying to make my way up the hill with the weapon was nearly impossible. I looked for Kincade. He was in his own battle against a high lord. I tried to fight my way up the hill again. Then Sariel was at my side, holding the Staff of Moses. He was covered in red and black blood from head to toe. Even his wings.

"Let me help you," he said.

"Get me to the top so I can protect the Ark."

He handed me the staff, then wrapped his arms around my waist and lifted into the sky with his giant wings flapping against the wind. I sucked in a sharp breath as we rose higher and higher.

One of the angels produced a sword and tried to fight back against Lucifer, but he managed to kick her off the mountain with ease on his second pass. Sariel dropped me near the top as Lucifer made another pass. We both ducked as he flew overhead. The two remaining angels did, too.

"Godspeed, Anna." He took the staff from me and then he was off to fight someone else.

I was a few feet below the Ark. Holding the sword aloft, I climbed the rest of the way, my legs burning with the exertion. My arms on fire from holding the sword and swinging it. Lucifer banked and headed for us again. The two angels stood their ground, still guarding the Ark even though their light was faltering.

At the top, I put my feet shoulder width apart, gripped the sword, and prepared to do battle. Lucifer's giant wings beat against the wind with an incredible, deafening sound. I put myself between him and the angels even though I had no idea what I was going to do when he got closer.

Before he made it to us, he faltered. The air around him warped, like reality itself was trying to twist him away. I followed the line of power down to Michael, the Spear of Destiny leveled at the dragon. Beside him, Sariel pointed the Staff of Moses. Lucifer shot straight up, a dark blot against the blue sky.

I spun toward the Ark. The two angels remained, standing perfectly still as if they were determined to continue to guard the Ark. I recognized the angel from the cave.

"He'll be back," I said. "You should take the Ark and go."

"We cannot," she said. "Our duty is here."

"I don't understand. Why?"

I heard the giant wings before I saw them. The angel looked skyward. I did, too, in time to see Lucifer plummet towards me. I didn't have time to react when he swiped me with one of his great claws. I tumbled backward, landed on the slope of the mountain, and slid head over heels back down to the bottom. I'd lost the sword along the way.

When I came to a halt, the breath was knocked out of me. Everything hurt. Breathing hurt most of all. I had sticks and dirt in my hair. I remained still while I regained my strength and my bearings. Kincade stood over me, appearing in my line of vision. He reached for my hand, helped me to a sitting position.

"Fuck, Anna."

He had such a way with words. He helped me to my feet. Lucifer was heading back toward the Ark and the two angels, determined to get the relic.

"We have to take out that dragon."

As I stared at the relic, it appeared to be glowing. The lightning flickered between my fingers. As I stood rooted in place, I called up the Godlight deep within me. I closed my eyes, concentrated on it. The way it felt. The heat of it. The power of it. In the distance was the *whump whump* of Lucifer's wings.

I opened my eyes, pinpointed the great dragon, and released the Godlight with everything I had. It shot out my chest in a bright beam of white light. It was so powerful, a scream ripped from my lungs as it pounded into Lucifer. It knocked him from the sky. As he fell, he transformed from the dragon back into the man and landed with a *boom*. The ground cracked around him.

But he rose.

Bloody. Ragged. Furious.

"Fuck," I said.

All around us, the fighting continued. The dead littered the valley. The minions, the demons, the high lords, all fighting against man and Fae and angel. And losing. The horde just kept coming and coming and coming. Lucifer staggered toward me with a look on his face that said he was done fucking around with me, with the Ark, with everything.

Lightning still flickered between my fingers. I glanced up at the Ark where the two angels remained standing guard.

I knew what I had to do. I spun to face Kincade, my mind racing. His gaze met mine. Understanding seemed to dawn there.

"Anna, don't."

"I have to."

Because if I hesitated for one second, I'd choose him over the world—and I couldn't let love turn into selfishness.

He shook his head, stepping toward me—but I backed away.

"Kincade, I love you." The words tore out of me. "I should have told you the second I knew."

But saying it meant making it real. And real things could be taken.

He started to reach for me but I jerked back. "And I know what I have to do to save us."

I ran.

Ran as hard as my body would allow. Ran until everything burned inside me. Tears burned hot on my cheeks. Behind me, Kincade shouted my name, but I couldn't look back. If I saw his face—if I saw that green-gold gaze—I would falter.

I couldn't falter.

I tore my way up the side once more, this time using the power of my feet to propel myself upward. The skin on my palms and fingertips was shredded as I struggled my way up, up, up. I crested the top and pitched forward, my hands on my knees as I tried desperately to catch my breath. Sweat poured down the side of my face and my back. My hair was stuck to the back of my neck. I looked up at the angel from the cave.

"You know what you have to do," she said.

"Yes."

The two of them stepped back away from the Ark. I called the Godlight again. Let it build. Let it burn. Let hope—small and desperate—kindle in me.

I looked back one last time. Kincade's face swam in my vision. Terror carved deep into him. The others realized what I meant to do and chaos erupted below.

My hands crackled with light as I pressed them to the Ark—and the world answered.

The Godlight surged.

It blasted through me—through my fingers—into the relic. Lightning became conduit, channeling the power into the Ark.

The glow erupted—brighter than creation. A blistering wind roared outward, sweeping across the valley. Darkness screamed. Demons dissolved. Minions disintegrated. High lords burned to ash. Even the monsters Death had summoned were erased.

The dead were swept clean from the earth.

And then the pain hit. Fire. White-hot. Consuming.

I tore my hands from the Ark. They were charred, ruined, unrecognizable.

My knees buckled.

My vision collapsed to a pinpoint—Kincade on the ground, reaching for me, horror etched into every line of him.

He was the last thing I saw when I tumbled to the ground.

Dead.

CHAPTER 44

I knew this place. I'd seen it before in a dream walk—the streets paved in gold cobblestones, lampposts glowing every ten feet like stars anchored to the earth. Peace lived here, a peace so profound it felt alive. No fear. No hate. No demons. Only the soft embrace of unconditional love.

I looked down at my hands.

Whole. Unburned. Smooth.

No pain anywhere—not even the ghost of it.

I walked forward, cobblestones warm beneath my bare feet. Somewhere, faint and serene, a harp played a melody that wrapped around me like a lullaby. Ahead stood a massive double gate made of shimmering pearl, radiant but not blinding.

Beside it waited a tall man with silver hair, a thick beard, warm brown eyes. His robe, trimmed in red and gold, stirred faintly in a breeze I didn't feel. The smile he gave me was gentle enough to break my heart.

"Hello, Anna. I've been waiting for you."

My throat tightened. "Who are you?"

"You know," he said, amusement softening his eyes.

I swallowed. "Peter?"

He nodded.

The words left me before I could stop them. "I'm dead."

Another nod.

"I don't believe you."

"It's true."

I pressed shaking fingers to my mouth. "No. No, no, no. I'm not finished yet."

"I'm afraid it's the truth."

"What about my friends? My family?" My voice rose in panic.

"They survived," he said softly. "You saved them all. You destroyed evil."

The words landed like stones. Prophecy fulfilled. Destiny complete. But my heart rebelled. There *had* to be more—more life, more purpose, more *living* than rising and dying on a battlefield.

"What of Lucifer?" I asked.

A flicker of discomfort crossed his face. "He was banished. Returned to the underworld where he cannot escape."

I should have felt triumph. I didn't. I wanted him dead. As dead as Azriel. But maybe if Lucifer were truly gone, the scales of creation would tilt too far. Humans needed the idea of darkness as much as they needed the idea of light.

"I want to see my friends," I whispered.

"I cannot—"

"Please." My voice broke. "*Please.*"

His smile faded. He nodded once and lifted a hand.

A window opened in the air beside us—clear as glass, sharp as memory. Through it I saw the valley.

My body lay motionless on the ground—small, broken, utterly empty of me.

Ophelia paced nearby, sobbing. Kincade kept up relentless chest compressions as if refusing to accept a universe where I was gone. Cashiel pressed breath into my unresponsive lungs. Astrid and Killian stood together—her pale with shock, him stone-faced and grim, his Sword of Light dripping in his hand. Even Alaric, William, and Victoria hovered close, wearing identical stricken expressions.

"They're trying to save me."

"They will not succeed," Peter said quietly.

My stomach plummeted. "Why not?"

"You have served your purpose." Not unkindly. Not triumphantly. Simply as fact.

I shook my head so hard my vision blurred. "No. No, I haven't. There's more. There has to be more."

I pressed my lips together, but the regret slipped out anyway.

"I should have told Kincade I loved him sooner," I whispered.

"He loves you, too," Peter said. "That is why he's trying so hard to save you."

Tears spilled over. "I...I'm not ready yet."

"What more is there for you to do?" he asked gently.

"Live," I breathed. It felt like a prayer and a plea all at once. "He needs me."

Peter turned back to the scene in the window. Kincade's determination—to the point of desperation—radiated from every motion of his hands. His refusal to give up only made my heart ache more fiercely.

"And..." I added, voice raw, "I need him."

Movement caught Peter's attention. A woman approached from the other side of the gate and beckoned him closer. He stepped away and spoke with her quietly. She glanced at me, nodded, spoke again. Peter nodded back, then returned to my side with a look I couldn't decipher.

"It appears you are correct," he said. "You do have more to do. Another threat rises."

Hope fluttered painfully in my chest.

"What sort of threat?" I asked.

"I cannot say."

I wasn't sure if he didn't know—or simply wouldn't tell me.

"You are correct," he continued. "He needs you. More than he realizes. And your work is not yet done."

A trembling thrill rushed through me. "What are you saying?"

"I'm saying, Annabelle Marie Walker..." His smile warmed like sunrise. "Your time is not yet up."

Before I could speak, darkness swept over me. The world dropped out from under my feet.

Cold crashed into me.

Then—air. Pain. A ragged gasp tore from my throat. My chest seized as agony lanced through my ribs, my skull pounding like it might burst.

Someone cried out in joy. Someone else sobbed harder.

Cashiel rocked back on his heels, exhaling a shaky breath. Kincade hauled me upright, crushing me into his arms. His grip stole what little breath I had left, but I clung to him regardless.

He pulled back, his face wrecked with relief.

"God, Anna," he whispered. "I thought we lost you."

I swallowed, breath trembling. When the moment was right, I'd tell him the truth—that he had. That I'd chosen to come back.

I inhaled deeply, let it out slow, and croaked, "Can we go home now?"

And then the pain overwhelmed me, dragging me back under as I fainted.

CHAPTER 45

I DON'T KNOW HOW we got back to Walker Manor. Frankly, I didn't care. The only thing I knew was I woke up in my own bed with bandages around my hands, parched lips, a sore throat, and a massive headache. I grunted my displeasure at being awake. Movement on the other side of the room drew my attention. Then Cashiel popped into my line of vision.

"Awake, at last."

Grace joined him. She looked overcome with joy and relief. "We were worried sick."

"Kincade?" My voice was scratchy from non-use.

"I shooed him away," she said. "He'd been here for days and he looked exhausted."

"Days?"

"You were out for two days," Cashiel said.

And I was still tired. I wondered if I'd ever have energy again.

"I'll wake Kincade." Grace started to go.

"No," I croaked.

"He'll want to see you," she said.

I shook my head. "Let him rest."

He'd earned it. Because he'd brought me back with his bare hands.

"I've been waiting for you to wake up so I can tend to your hands."

He gave a nod to Grace, who helped me to a sitting position, then bustled out of the room. He paused by the bed and reached for my right hand, picking it up between his. With a gentle touch, he began to unwind the miles of gauze that wrapped my fingers and the palm of my hand up to my wrist. As soon as I saw the wreckage of my hands, bile rose to my throat. Hot tears prickled my eyes.

The immediate pain at seeing the charred flesh punched through me as I recalled touching the lid of the Ark, the lightning flickering between my fingers, and the Godlight flooding through them into the relic.

"My hands..."

"They'll be fine. Keep your hand up."

"But how?"

As I said it, Grace returned to the room holding the Holy Grail. There was a sort of reverence on her face as she handed the cup to Cashiel. She stepped away from the bed, then returned with a large bowl and a thick towel. She placed the towel on my lap and the bowl under my hand. I watched with a strange fascination as Cashiel poured the water from the Holy Grail over my hand.

First, a sizzle. I sucked in a sharp breath as the holy water cascaded over my hand and fingers, dripping into the bowl. He splashed more water over my hand. It bubbled and fizzed. The pain wasn't pain exactly—more like heat being pulled out of me. My skin knitted back together as though it had never happened. He poured the rest of the water over my hand, clearing away the charred remains. The skin was pink and soft and perfectly healed.

Grace removed the bowl, then took the towel and gingerly patted the dampness from my new skin. I gaped at Cashiel.

"How does it feel?" he asked.

"Almost like new."

More tears were in my eyes but not from pain. From the joy of seeing my hand repaired back to normal. Burns like what I had would not heal without skin grafts and months of recovery.

"Shall I do the other one?" he asked with a smile.

I nodded.

He handed Grace the Grail. She hurried away with it and the bowl and returned moments later with a full cup and an empty bowl. Cashiel repeated the process with my left hand. Grace took away the damp towel and the bowl but didn't return. I held up both hands, turning them over, amazed at the healing process with the Holy Grail.

"I'm afraid the Grail can't repair your hair," he said, a hint of dry humor in his eyes.

I gave him a horrified look, then immediately reached for my scalp. I expected it to be devoid of all hair, but my long locks were still there. He reached for my hair and pulled a strand away from my face. My hair, which was once black, was now the color of freshly fallen snow.

I gasped. "How?"

He shrugged. "The Ark. All that power pulsing through you." He reached for my hand, taking it in his. "Healing is what the Grail was meant for. That's why you had to find it."

A lump formed in my throat. "Did you know that?"

He shook his head. "No. Not until I understood how you were to use the Ark."

"What about the Staff of Moses and the Spear of Destiny?" I asked.

"They were reclaimed by Michael. The Grail will be returned as well."

My brow furrowed. "I thought I was the Keeper."

"You are. But the relics aren't yours to keep—they're yours to *bear* when the world requires it. Lucifer has been returned to his place in the underworld. The balance has been restored," Cashiel said.

I assumed the angels returned the Ark to its hiding place deep beneath Jerusalem, awaiting the day it would be needed again.

"The Four Horsemen? What about them? They were wreaking havoc across the world. Death was there."

"Were, yes," Cashiel said. "They, too, have been banished back to where they belong. The world has some healing to do. Now that the war is over, it can begin." He gave a small smile. "Thanks to you."

I leaned my head back into the pillows. "So, my work is truly done."

"For now." He gave my hand a gentle pat, then released it.

I sighed and nodded. I believed him. This war was over. But what was to come? Peter hinted that my work wasn't done, that I had more to do. I suspected that had something to do with Kincade and the Brotherhood.

"What about the dagger and the sword?" I asked, suddenly realizing I didn't remember the last time I saw them.

"They're safe." He smiled and waved to the dresser where both of them rested.

I blew out a breath of relief, glad someone had the forethought to retrieve them for me. "Good."

"What do you remember?" Cashiel asked.

I inhaled a deep breath and released it. "Almost everything."

"Do you remember dying on that hill?" He perched on the edge of the bed next to me.

I nodded. That and talking to Saint Peter at the gates of Heaven and begging to live again. Because I couldn't bear the thought of being without Kincade.

"How long was I..." I paused, swallowed, "dead?"

"Minutes, really," Cashiel said. "I thought for sure you were gone, but Kincade...he refused to give up. Just as he refused to leave your side while you were unconscious."

"I spoke to Peter," I said, my voice hollow and thin.

Cashiel stared at me a long, silent moment. "As did I when I passed on."

"He said there was another threat brewing."

"As I said, evil never truly rests. But you should." He rose from the bed and started for the door. As he walked away from me, I admired the expanse of his snowy white wings threaded with gold.

"Cashiel, thank you."

He paused, gave me a questioning look. "For what?"

"For always believing in me."

He smiled, nodded, and left.

I needed to see Kincade. I wanted to see Kincade.

I shoved off the blankets and stumbled to the bathroom, my legs wobbling. In the bathroom, I clutched the edge of the vanity and peered at an unfamiliar reflection in the mirror. I still had deep fatigue lining my face and the dark circles under my eyes. The hollow cheeks. I looked like shit. And what made it even more strange was seeing my hair had turned completely white. I wound the soft strands around my finger, letting it fall back into place. It was odd.

I examined my hands again. The new flesh was slightly pink. I wiggled my fingers, trying to call up the lightning, but it wasn't there. Then I concentrated on the Godlight that burned deep within me. Normally, I was able to call it up in an instant. Nothing. The silence inside me was the loudest thing I'd ever heard. As if my powers had abandoned me. Or, perhaps, I'd burned them out with the massive amount of power I used pumping into the Ark.

I splashed cold water on my face. I brushed my hair, my teeth. I put on clean clothes. I felt almost human again even if I was still tired. I stumbled out of the bathroom on weak legs, like a newborn foal trying to walk for the first time. I paused, took a deep breath, stood straight, and forced one foot in front of the other.

I opened the door to my room and was startled to see Piers on the other side preparing to knock. He froze, momentarily stunned.

"Ah, my lady. I heard you were awake. I wanted to see how you were."

"Better." I gave him a weak smile.

"Do you perhaps have a moment?"

"Uh…" I glanced down the hall toward Kincade's room, impatience bubbling through me.

"It will only take a moment."

I followed him at a slow pace to the master suite at the end of the hall. The door was closed. This was where my uncle resided when he was alive. Piers reached for the door and pushed it open.

"I do hope you approve."

When I stepped into the room, my jaw dropped. It smelled of fresh paint and new carpet. The walls were a pale blue. The queen size bed had an upholstered headboard in a lovely shade of cream. A thick down comforter in a white duvet covered the bed with big fluffy pillows giving it a wonderfully inviting look that beckoned me to dive in and never get out. I'd almost died. I suddenly understood the holiness of clean sheets.

Two bedside tables in a pale oak, new lamps, a bureau to match. The heavy velvet curtains had been removed and in their place were lacy sheers to filter the light behind panels on either side. Even the bathroom had been renovated with a full soaking tub, a separate shower, double sinks.

"Piers, it's amazing." I turned in the room, taking it all in until I stopped to look at him. "Thank you."

He smiled, looking well pleased. "You're welcome, my lady."

Then he bowed and stepped out of the room. I heard his receding footsteps down the hall and then the stairs, no doubt leaving me to enjoy the new room.

As much as I wanted to close myself into the room and never get out of that bed, I had another mission in mind. I made it down the hallway to Kincade's room. The door was closed. I knocked. A minute later the door opened to a sleepy-eyed Kincade who immediately came wide awake when he saw me. We stared at each other a long moment.

His hand stayed braced on the door like he needed something solid to hold onto. I'd seen him covered in blood and unshaken. This looked worse.

Exhaustion lined his face. He had the glistening bristle of stubble on his cheeks and chin, still, and I wondered when he shaved last. His hair stood up in spikes around his head. His clothes were rumpled as if he'd slept in them. They appeared to be clean and not the dirty, bloody clothes he'd fought in.

"I was nowhere near the neighborhood," I said, hoping to start with a joke.

His eyes flicked over me—fast, clinical—like he was counting what I'd lost. His face remained impassive. He didn't even crack a smile. I tried again.

"Hi." I gave a jaunty wave.

The corner of his mouth twitched like it wanted to obey, then died.

His eyes landed on my healed hands. He caught one in his, turned it over, studying it with wonder. He ran a thumb over the renewed skin of my knuckles. His thumb lingered too long. Like if he let go, I'd disappear again. Even that small touch sent a thrill through me.

"Your hands?"

"Cashiel healed them with the Holy Grail."

He nodded once—sharp. Not gratitude. A verdict. He released my hand, then looked me over with a critical eye. "Your hair is white."

"Yes, it is."

He reached for it, picking up several strands, letting them fall through his fingers. "You scared the hell out of me. Us." His voice roughened on *us*. Like it cost him to include anyone but himself.

"I'm sorry. I didn't mean to." I shifted from one foot to the other. "Can I come in?"

For a second, he didn't move. Then he stepped aside like it was an order he could actually follow.

He stood aside, held the door open, and watched as I walked across the threshold. Then he closed the door behind me. The latch clicked. Final. Private.

"Maybe we need whiskey," I said, trying again to lighten the mood.

"You died." He glowered, ignoring my attempt at humor. His throat worked once, hard, like the words had splintered on the way out. His hands flexed at his sides, opening and closing like he wanted to grab me and didn't trust himself to.

"I did what I was supposed to do."

"But you died." He said it almost as though he was angry with me. "And you never gave me a chance to tell you—"

His words broke off. He turned his head a fraction, jaw jumping once, like the rest of the sentence burned too hot to say. My gut clenched into a hard knot. I was hoping to avoid talking about anything related to feelings. But wasn't that why I was standing in his bedroom? To talk about those feelings? To finally get everything out in the open?

"Tell me what?" I glanced up at him through my lashes, which was probably the coyest thing I'd ever done.

It was a mistake. His gaze went feral for half a heartbeat—then he locked it down.

His jaw clenched. "Dammit, Anna."

It was time to face those feelings, to stop being a coward. "I meant what I said before I went up that hill."

His gaze pierced me, but he said nothing. I forged on.

"I'm not good with this touchy-feely stuff, you know. I don't like getting close to people because they usually disappoint me. But you…you never did. I can't explain why I was compelled to find you when Azriel took you, but I think it was because, deep down, I knew you were mine." Something moved in his face—so quick I might've imagined it. Like relief trying to become real. "You always have my back. Even when I do stupid things. Like dying."

Still, he said nothing. His face remained impassive.

"Yes, I died. I did it to save you and everyone else. But mostly you. Yours was the last face I saw. When I stood at the gates, I asked to live because I don't want to be parted from you."

Kincade had the best poker face. He masked his feelings and buried them so deep it was hard to read him.

"You once asked me how old I was," he said at last.

He said it like a weapon. Like facts were the only thing he could safely hand me.

"I figured you'd tell me when you were ready."

His jaw tightened. "I didn't forget."

I decided this was as close as I was getting to him saying those three little words, so I waited while he collected his thoughts and decided how to begin. He ran his hand over his chin, his skin bristling against the stubble there. He paced the small confines of his sparse room. Once. Twice. Like a caged thing. Then he stopped—because if he kept moving, he'd say the wrong truth. Then he waved me to the bed while he pulled up a chair and sat. He leaned his elbows on his knees, looking at me as he decided where and how to begin.

"I was born in Jericho. Thirty-five years before Christ was born."

The words landed heavy. Ancient.

"Herod was king. My parents were farmers. We lived in a mud-brick house."

Ha paused, then continued, voice flat, precise.

"When I was sixteen, I left for Jerusalem. I wanted something different. Thought it'd be better." His mouth twisted. "It wasn't."

His gaze lifted to mine, then away again.

"I became a slave. Worked on the expansion of Temple Mount. The Second Temple."

I swallowed. Didn't interrupt.

"Three years later, the Brotherhood of Watchers recruited me. We were assigned to watch the people Herod feared."

Feared. Not *monsters*. Not *evil*.

"That was the purpose they gave us."

Something unspoken lingered in the air after that sentence.

"I was there when word spread of a child in Bethlehem," he went on. "When Herod ordered the deaths of every boy under two."

His hands clenched.

"We saved some," he said. "Not enough."

The room felt smaller.

"I saw Christ," he said quietly. "His teachings. His followers. His death."

He swallowed.

"The Brotherhood couldn't protect him either."

Silence stretched between us before he spoke again.

"After that, the oath changed. We swore to protect the ones who couldn't protect themselves."

He didn't say whether he still believed in that oath.

"I followed orders for a long time," he continued. "Wandered. Fought. Guarded relics. Did what I was told."

His gaze lifted then, locking onto mine.

"Until I didn't."

The words hummed with meaning he refused to explain.

"We knew there would be one person," he said after a moment. "Someone who could change everything."

My heart stuttered.

"I broke every oath I pledged the moment I chose you."

He didn't look away. Like the consequences were already accounted for.

He fell silent again, his face drawn, as if even this much had cost him.

"Only one other person knows this," he said at last. "He is no longer the man I remember."

"Decker?" I asked.

He nodded. "Not my brother by blood. My brother in arms. I've known him longer than anyone on this earth."

I thought of the last time I spoke to Decker in a dream walk. How he told me to get lost. How it cut deeper than I wanted to admit. How Kincade had refused to return to break him out of that prison in Turkey.

"Perhaps, like you, Decker is looking for a new purpose."

"What do you mean?"

I swallowed hard. It wasn't going to be easy to tell him. "Ophelia saw him and the Brotherhood helping the high lords kill guardians and steal souls."

Rage flickered across his face before he buried it. The control was worse—tight, practiced, familiar. Brotherhood control.

"I'm sorry," I said.

"Then he betrayed me," he said. "And the Brotherhood."

He went still, processing, weighing what this meant. His eyes lifted to mine, heat burning there—sharp, piercing, alive.

"When you reached for the Ark," he said, voice low, "when your hands lit up with the Godlight...I knew you'd die on that mountain."

My breath caught.

"I knew you'd burn yourself out to save us," he continued. "And I was angry."

His jaw flexed.

"Angry that you chose it."

"To save you," I whispered.

"I know," he said.

The words were rough. Uneven.

"I waited more than a lifetime for you."

He exhaled sharply, like he hadn't meant to say that part aloud.

"And I wasn't ready to watch you die."

My chest ached.

I rose from the bed, my heart pounding as I stepped into his space. His hands came to my waist automatically, his head tipping back to look up at me. Desire and something far more dangerous burned in his gaze.

I braced one hand on the back of the chair and cupped his rough cheek with the other.

"I promise not to die again," I said, giving him a playful grin.

He frowned. "Not funny, Anna. You're a mortal and I—"

I shut him up with a kiss, my mouth landing on his. Our lips fit together in perfect, maddening harmony, confirming what I'd known all along—this was inevitable. His fingers tightened on my waist as he took over, his kiss deepening, demanding. There was a mastery in the way he kissed me, a promise that he had no intention of ever letting me go.

Heat surged through me, hot and wild. A shiver raced over my skin, pebbling my arms. He stole my breath with every stroke of his mouth. One of his hands slid up, cupping my cheek, his thumb stroking just under my eye as if I were something precious.

We broke apart on a shared, ragged breath. He looked at me like I was the only thing in his universe—gaze sharp, focused, burning straight through me. My knees went weak.

His hands shifted back to my waist. He lifted me off his lap, not to push me away, but as if he wanted more room. More of me.

He backed me toward the bed, step by unsteady step. His eyes never left mine. They burned right into my soul, setting it aflame. My breath hitched when the backs of my legs bumped the edge of the mattress.

His hands came up, framing my face. All I wanted was to be pulled into him and never let go. From that first moment I saw him in the hallway in blue pajama pants and a blanket, something fragile and bright had sparked between us. A thread I hadn't understood.

Now, I did.

He had unlocked my heart and soul.

His breath brushed my lips, but instead of kissing me, he lowered his head and found the spot just beneath my ear. The first touch of his mouth there shattered my thoughts. A rough breath escaped me as he trailed searing kisses down my neck.

I fisted my hands in his shirt and tugged it upward. He didn't resist. He yanked it over his head and tossed it aside. There he was—warm, solid, scarred, mine. A jolt went through me as he helped me out of my shirt, then the rest of my clothes, until there was nothing between us but skin and heat and the steady drum of his heart.

My skin tingled everywhere we touched. Warm. Soft. Sandalwood wrapped around me as I fell back on the bed and he came with me, caging me in with his arms.

His mouth covered mine again, gentler this time, then wandered lower, whispering his devotion over every inch of me, leaving a trail of fire in his wake. One hand braced beside my head, the other splayed over my hip, holding me like I might vanish.

When he finally entered me, it was like something inside me clicked back into place. We moved together in a rhythm that felt as inevitable as breathing, as fighting, as falling.

I clung to him—his shoulders, the old scar down his chest, the strength that had held me together more times than I could count—as pleasure built, coiling tighter and tighter until it broke us both open. We came apart together, my cry muffled against his shoulder as his arms locked around me.

He pulled me close, crushing me to him like he had no intention of ever letting me go.

And I never wanted him to.

Hours later, the shadows deepened in the room, cascading over us in a dreamy haze of bliss. I lay draped over his thick torso, basking in the contented afterglow, drenched in sweat and exhausted beyond any sort of reason. When we finished one round, we started all over again. Until it was enough.

It would never be enough.

I was drunk on this newfound feeling of contentment. At last, the weight of the world had lifted, giving me a sort of freedom I never had before.

I came to understand that the love I once felt for Ben—calm, sweet, gentle—was nothing like the love I felt for Kincade. His was wild and consuming, passionate and utterly unfettered. He let me be exactly who I was—without question, without apology, without conditions. For the first time in my life, I felt wholly at ease in my own skin.

His hand slid through the now-white strands of my hair. With my head on his chest, I listened to the steady rise and fall of his breath, the perfect rhythm of his heart. I traced the length of the scar that crossed his chest, gliding my fingertips over the warm skin and the dark dusting of hair there, grounding myself in the solid reality of him.

That was the terrifying, exhilarating truth—I wasn't just in love with him. I was all in. No halfway. No escape hatch. We were meant for each other and he had waited more than a millennium for me. But loving him was not enough. I was consumed with him. Drowning in him. Never wanting to be parted from him in a way that was both alarming and electrifying. I sighed a deep sigh of contentment.

"What happens now?" I asked, my voice a roughened whisper in the silence of the room.

"Now?" His chest rumbled under my ear. "What do you mean?"

"I have no relics to hunt. No archenemy. No wars to fight. I'm going to have a lot of time on my hands."

He chuckled, a delightful sound I would never tire of. "We live. Until we need to fight again."

"As long as you've got my back."

"Until I take my last breath."

His promise wrapped around me as surely as his arms did. Whatever darkness was left in the world, we'd face it together. I wasn't afraid of the shadows anymore.

Not when I'd found my light in him.

What's next in the Dream Walker Universe

Finished the *Dream Walker* series and looking for your next adventure? A new series is coming! Set in the world of *Dream Walker* paranormal romance series, the **War of the Brotherhood** chronicles the reckoning that follows centuries of manipulation, control, and buried power by the elusive and vicious Brotherhood of Watchers. These are stories of devotion forged in darkness. Of men who were never meant to survive their own humanity. Of love that becomes defiance—and a war that will decide the future of every realm it touches.

The war has begun. And no one walks away unchanged.

Book 1 – Dark Night of the Soul releasing September 15, 2026.
Book 2 – Fall of the Forsaken releasing October 13, 2026.
Book 3 – Immortal Everlasting releasing November 10, 2026.

Catch Up on the Dream Walker Series

Book 1: Call of the Dark
Anna Walker's ability to step into dreams thrusts her into a deadly battle between a fallen angel and a heavenly messenger, each demanding she locate a powerful Holy Relic. As secrets of her destiny unravel, Anna must decide whether to embrace her role as the Keeper of the Relics or risk the destruction of mankind in the ultimate clash between Heaven and Hell.

Book 2: Blood and Bone
With the fate of the world hanging by a thread, will Anna risk everything—including Kincade's soul—for a chance to stop Lucifer? The Spear of Destiny holds the key, but time is running out.

Book 3: Flame and Fury
Her soul is on the line, her heart is in turmoil, and the forces of darkness are closing in. Can Anna resist the pull of dark magic, outsmart an angel of destruction, and escape the clutches of the Prince of Greed?

Book 4: Smoke and Ashes
Eternal life comes at a deadly cost. With the Holy Grail in her sights, Anna must face Lucifer's wrath, fend off zealots thirsty

for blood, and trust Kincade—and an unexpected ally—to save her soul. Can she outrun the darkness, or will the grail be her undoing?

Book 5: Light of the World
The Four Horsemen ride, chaos reigns, and the ultimate war between Heaven and Hell has begun. With the Ark of the Covenant as her last hope, Anna faces impossible odds, devastating sacrifices, and a showdown that will decide the fate of all creation. Can she defy Lucifer one last time, or will the darkness claim everything?

BONUS CHAPTER
WATCHER'S VOW

I wasn't sleeping so much as losing the fight to stay upright. The last moments on that hill still played in my mind's eye. The scent of smoke and sanctified ash still filled by nose—of battle, of the Ark, of the Godlight that had seared the night when she died on that hill and I knew I'd lost her forever.

Then came the knock.

I opened the door ready to snarl and words vanished.

Anna. Alive. Whole. Changed.

Her hair—white as moonlit snowfall—glowed under the hallway light like a halo. Her hands were unmarked, skin new and luminous where agony had lived. The sight hit harder than any sword.

"I was nowhere near the neighborhood."

She tried a joke. I didn't have one left.

My fingers found her healed hands. The knuckles were miracle-smooth beneath my thumb and something ancient and stubborn inside me finally surrendered.

"Cashiel healed them with the Holy Grail," she said.

"Your hair is white."

"Yes, it is."

I touched the white strands falling between my fingers and remembered the instant I knew she'd burn herself to save us. Anger
had been living in my bones since.

"You scared the hell out of me. Us."

I tried to correct the slip, but she noticed anyway with one thin
arched brow. Color tinged her cheeks, but her eyes never left mine.

"I'm sorry. I didn't mean to. Can I come in?"

A casual question. She didn't really need permission. It was her
house, after all. *But if I let her in...*

The thought lingered for a moment wondering how that would
feel to have her all to myself for one peaceful moment. Peace never
lasted.

I stood aside, watched as she walked into the room. I never took
my eyes off her as the door closed behind her.

She suggested whiskey, but I didn't want it dulling my senses.

"You died," I said, because the truth burned like fire and brimstone. It sounded like an accusation.

Her face went impassive, still, closed. "I did what I was supposed
to do."

"But you *died*." It came out too sharp. I looked her over. Whole.
Breathing. *Mine.* "And you never gave me a chance to tell you—"

I stopped. A thousand years and I still balked at a simple truth.

"I meant what I said before I went up that hill." The truth of it
still glinted in her eyes.

Her words came back in a flood.

I will always love you.

Words that forever burned within me. Words I could not—but
wanted—to say. Unlike her, my fierce girl, I lacked the courage.
When you live a thousand years, you learn to guard your heart. You
learn heartbreak and loss are worse than any sword in the gut.

She stepped into the silence and filled it with courage.

"Tell me what?" She looked up at me through her lashes in a coy,
sly way that was not her.

My jaw clenched. The woman was maddening on the best day. She knew what she was doing. She was trying to get under my skin. She was trying to make me say the words that were lodged deep in my throat. She wanted to hear them. She wanted to know I felt them, too.

"Dammit, Anna."

She took a deep breath, steeled herself, and looked me right in the eye. "I meant what I said before I went up that hill."

And then she spoke of walls and disappointments, of the compulsion to find me when Azriel took me, of certainty that we were meant, of choosing life at the gate because she refused to be parted from me.

No battlefield had ever made me feel this exposed.

And then, "Yours was the last face I saw."

And hers was the last image burned into my mind when she put her hands on the Ark and turned into a weapon of God. When she destroyed evil and pushed it back into the underworld. When I spent precious moments trying to save her from certain death. When I refused to give up, to let her go.

And now she stood there looking at me with those violet eyes telling me she didn't want to be parted from me.

"You once asked how old I was," I said, and when she told me she'd waited for me to be ready, something unclenched that had been locked since Jericho.

I took a seat and told her who I was. A boy under Herod's rule; a slave on Temple Mount; a Watcher forged by vows and necessity; a witness to Christ's rising and dying; a sword between the helpless and the dark. I told her about the promise we guarded—the one who would keep the Relics, the one who would save mankind when night tried to consume the world—and admitted the heresy that had lived quiet in my chest since the day we met.

"Until I met you."

I had never told anyone who and what I was. Not like this. I spoke of Decker, brother in arms, and swallowed the fury when she told me what he'd become. Later, I promised myself. That reckoning would come later. Betrayal from an enemy was one thing. From someone you trusted cut deeper than any knife twisted in the gut.

"When you reached for the Ark with your hands lit up and the Godlight making you glow," I said, finally letting her see the man under the armor, "that you would burn using the power of the Ark to save us. And I was *angry*. Angry you sacrificed yourself."

Her next words nearly unraveled me. "To save *you*."

She crossed to me from the bed where I sat. My hands found her waist like they'd been waiting there all along. Her palm on my cheek steadied the ground under my feet.

"I promise not to die again," she teased.

"Not funny," I tried, "you're mortal and I—"

She ended the argument with a kiss.

It wasn't the first, but it was the one that changed the axis of my world. We fit like the end of a long pilgrimage fits the pilgrim—inevitable, relieving, holy. My fingers tightened, her breath caught, and the centuries stopped screaming in my head.

When I pulled her to her feet, guiding her back until her knees touched the bed, it felt less like surrender than like coming home. I pressed my mouth to the pulse beneath her ear; her shiver uncoiled what was left of my restraint. She tugged at my shirt with impatient hands and I helped her—God, I helped her—because for the first time since dust clung to a boy's ankles in Jericho, I wanted something that wasn't war.

Cloth left my shoulders. Cold air met hot skin. She traced the old scar that ran long and silver down my left side, the map of a life survived. She touched me, not the marks.

When the last barriers fell, the room became a sanctuary. No archangels. No Brotherhood. No fallen traitor gnawing at the edge of memory. Just breath and skin and the fierce grace of being chosen by the one I swore to protect. I moved with reverence; she answered with trust, with heat, with unguarded joy that felt like the first sunrise after a winter that lasted too long.

If the world had ended beyond those walls, I would have let it.

Later, when quiet settled and the storm of us eased to something steady, she rested her head on my chest. The white of her hair lay bright against my arm; the healed hands were warm over my heart. Outside, night kept its counsel. Inside, I knew peace—real, ordinary, miraculous peace.

I have been a Watcher, a blade, a shield. Tonight, I was a man. Hers.

And if prophecy still demanded its due—if shadow gathered and old enemies sharpened their blades—let them come. The one who was promised lay beside me, not as a burden, but as the woman who chose life when the gate stood open.

And I chose her.

Also by Michelle Miles

Age of Wizards (Epic Fantasy)
In the Tower of the Wizard King
On the Hunt for the Wizard King

Dragon Protectors (Paranormal Shifter Romance)
Desiring the Dragon Lord
Seducing the Dragon Knight
Tempting Her Dragon Bodyguard

Dream Walker (Paranormal Romance)
Call of the Dark
Blood and Bone
Flame and Fury
Smoke and Ashes
Light of the World

Dream Walker Related Novels
Guardian of the Soul (Coming Soon)

War of the Brotherhood (Dark Paranormal Romance)
Set in the Dream Walker Universe
Dark Night of the Soul
Fall of the Forsaken
Immortal Everlasting

Enchanted Realms (YA Fantasy Romance)
Once Upon a Midnight Clear (Cinderella)
Once Upon True Love's Kiss (Snow White)
Once Upon an Enchanted Kiss (Sleeping Beauty)
Once Upon an Enchanted Castle (Beauty and the Beast)
Once Upon a Midnight Dreary (Poe's The Raven)

Enchanted Realms Related Novellas
Once Upon an Ancient Curse (Red Riding Hood)
Once Upon a Silver Strand (Rapunzel)
Once Upon a Woven Wish (Rumpelstiltskin)

Enchanted Realms: Crossroads (Cozy Fantasy)
A Spin-off Series of the Enchanted Realms
Petals and Portals

Five Towers (YA Fantasy Romance)
The Sorcerer's Daughter

Highland Destiny (Paranormal Romance)
Desiring the Highland Laird
Loving the Highland Warrior
Captivating the Highland Rogue

Legends of the Five Crowns (Romantasy)
with Misty Evans
The Lost Kingdom
The Flame and the Dragon
Tide of Stolen Thrones

Realm of Honor (Fantasy Romance)
One Knight Only
Only for a Knight
A Knight to Remember
A Knight Like No Other
Shadows of the Knight

Watch for more at MichelleMiles.net

About the Author

Michelle Miles is an empress with a war map in one hand and a romance vow in the other—writing fantasy, paranormal, and young adult adventures where magic crackles, danger prowls, and love refuses to back down. From fairy-tale retellings to angels and demons to Fae, elves, and time travelers, she builds big-hearted worlds full of quests, curses, kisses, and chaos—often in that order. When she's not plotting her next emotional ambush, Michelle narrates audiobooks and hosts Miles Beyond the Page, a podcast spotlighting writers' real journeys. A proud Texan, she's usually reading, hiking, rewatching favorite movies, or savoring a glass of wine while sharpening the blade for the next adventure.

Quests, Curses, Kisses, and Chaos!

Read more at MichelleMiles.net